POLAR VORTEX

Polar Vortex

Dedicated to the memory
of my father, David Alan Mather,
who passed away while I was writing this novel.

This story is a testament to the love
of a father for their child.

He was, and will always be,
my greatest hero.

Acknowledgements

I'd like to thank Monte Dunard, a pilot for American Airlines who flies Boeing 777s over the North Pole, for his invaluable insights and help in writing this novel. I'd also like to thank Bill Stafford, Station Manager for the Alert base in Nunavut—the most northerly inhabited place on planet Earth.

Finally, I'd like to thank my dedicated fans who helped with early readings. Without you, none of this would be possible, so thank you.

PROLOGUE

I s this heaven?" Lilly held out one tiny hand.
A haze of gold and red shimmered around my daughter and me.
The colors shifted to violet and then pink, enveloping us in a humid
blanket. I held my hand out next to hers—our arms fading into the
mist—outstretched my fingers and then wrapped them around hers.

"It's beautiful," she said.

And it was.

The iridescence pulsed and surrounded us like a living thing.

"Are we dead?" She whispered so low I could barely hear her.

"Of course not."

"How would you know?"

"Mommy is waiting for us. We're going back to her."

"Are you sure?"

"I'm sure."

The light dimmed and flickered.

"I'm frightened," she said.

Me too, I thought, but I held her tighter and said, "Everything is
going to be okay."

TRANSCRIPT AUDIO 1

National Transportation Safety Board.
Mid-Flight Disappearance of Allied 695,
Boeing 777, NTSB/AIR.
Washington, DC

October 18th

No physical evidence, no transponder signals." Richard Marks cleared his throat and spoke louder for the audio recording. "No emergency locator transmitters…"

How did a modern airliner literally vanish in one of the most heavily monitored places on Earth? Like it was swallowed by a black hole.

"Don't want to take a break?" his newly appointed partner, Peter Hystad, asked. "Three days with no sleep. You sure you want to be lead investigator on this?"

"I'm fine," Richard said. "And I'm sure."

Something had happened out there, a bizarre event beyond simply an accident. Even secured back at their offices in Washington, he felt the eyes of the world on them in here. Twelve stories down and through the concrete walls, he sensed the swarming media and grieving families massed outside.

There were only the two of them in the twenty-foot long, wood-paneled conference room. A fresh pot of coffee on a stand in the corner. The door locked.

Peter said, "So, a Boeing 777 with three hundred seventy-eight souls disappears over the North Pole, and all we have is that?"

Richard held up a beaten leather-bound notebook, three inches wide and six long.

"That's it so far."

"Is it real? I mean, given where it was found, it's hard to understand—"

"Seems to be his handwriting from the samples we received."

"I could hand that over to some FBI friends for analysis."

"I'm not giving this to anyone."

A pause. "Matthews was a passenger? That's confirmed?"

"I checked the Chek Lap Kok camera logs myself."

"Hong Kong airport systems are back up?"

Richard opened the notebook. "His entries start two weeks ago. I'm going to read aloud for the record. This is the journal of Mitch Matthews..."

CHAPTER 1
October 4th

"Mitch, could you get some of those?" my wife, Emma, said. "Are they the piggy ones?"

"Let me check," I replied.

Lilly shrieked and ran past me, chased by two of her chubby-cheeked cousins. The trio almost ran straight into a cart stacked high with wooden dim sum baskets. The elderly Chinese woman behind it stoically pushed forward without missing a beat, calling out, "*Char siu bao!*"

I held up a hand to the cart pusher, who with practiced deftness whisked a basket in front of me, paused an instant to see if I wanted more, then continued on without saying a word.

Three pillow-soft-looking white buns adorned with little ears and eyes stared up at me.

"Yeah, they're the piggy ones."

A lunchtime crush of hungry patrons mobbed the entrance of the Lin Heung Kui restaurant. Emma's father had wanted to do lunch at the Four Seasons, but the rest of her family wanted something a little more *yit lao*—lively—so we ended up here, in one of Hong Kong's oldest dim sum parlors.

We had just arrived, disembarked from a bright yellow double-decker trolley that had inched its way through the skyscraper canyons. Crowds of people jammed every intersection. It was the middle of the Golden Week, the holiday after National Day, the Chinese equivalent of the Fourth of July and Thanksgiving all rolled into one.

My first time to Hong Kong. Nearly my first time outside of America.

I wrote a few notes into my journal trying to capture the mood of the place. The leather-bound pad was a gift from my wife. She said it would help stimulate me, get the creative juices flowing.

Emma's family was arranged around a large circular table almost spilling over with wooden baskets. Her grandmother and grandfather were across from us, her British father next to me, her Chinese mother two seats to my right past Emma, and then her cousins. I did my best, but I was terrible at remembering names even in English—never mind Cantonese.

"Lillypad, come on, sit down and eat." I put one arm out to intercept her on her next pass around the table. She squealed but let me wrap her up and pull onto my lap.

I held Lilly's five-year-old body tight, felt her tiny ribs beneath her sweater. She was small for five; had always been small. Wisps of her fly-away blond hair tickled my chin, her head tucked under mine.

My Lillypad.

"Look," I said. "Pigs. Try one."

I picked one up in demonstration and bit into it, tasted oozy salted egg beyond the soft dough. My daughter crinkled her nose. A fussy eater. Like her mother. It was a constant battle to get her to eat, as opposed to me, where the battle went the opposite way.

She leaned into me, and with one of her little index fingers she traced a pattern into the palm of my left hand. It was a secret game we played, a way to talk without talking. It started when I was teaching her letters, and she made up her own "skin signs" as she called them.

This one was easy. She traced an "N" into my hand. No. She wasn't hungry.

I was about to admonish her, tell her she had to at least get something into her stomach when I noticed the wheezing.

I listened closer.

She was panting, struggling to suck air into her lungs.

I reached into the backpack by my feet and rummaged around for her inhaler, shook it and lifted it up to her mouth. I pressed down and she took a breath.

The air in Hong Kong was terrible, the pollution so dense sometimes it was like a hazy fog, and acidic enough to make the eyes water. I shouldn't have let her ride on the open deck of the trolley.

Lilly poked one of the piggy buns, picked it up and took a bite. I was going to put the inhaler back, but on reflection, left it on the table top. She would probably need it again.

"Are you sure it's safe to fly over the North Pole?" Emma asked.

My wife held my gaze with her doe-like brown eyes. She knew she was doing it—worrying—but she couldn't help it, and needed me to play along.

I said, "Do you think it's safer flying across the Pacific?"

"Isn't flying over water safer?"

"Not for me."

She shook her head. "Your daughter is going to learn to—"

"Anyway"—I changed the topic—"it *is* mostly water. I don't think there's much ice left up there." It was a joke, but only half of one.

"It's not that."

Under cover of the table, she showed me an article on her phone's screen. With my free hand I took it and looked closer. *Russian bombers intercepted by American fighter jets over the Arctic,* read the headline.

I handed the phone back. "You have to stop looking up articles like this. It happens all the time. You notice it now—"

"—my husband and daughter are flying over the North Pole?"

"Come on. Your brother is piloting the plane. How many people can say that?"

Josh flew for Allied Airlines, one of the biggest commercial carriers. We hadn't seen him in two years and he had called unexpectedly, said he was flying back to the States on a new assignment. Said he had heard we were in Hong Kong seeing the family.

I had jumped at the chance to fly back a bit early, but my wife needed to stay.

"Maybe I should come," she said.

"You should stay, but Lilly…I mean, do you want us to stay?"

She shook her head. "And he's my half-brother."

Josh was from her father's first wife. From what I had gathered, a tumultuous affair that had ended with the woman retreating back to England. Josh and Emma were almost twenty years apart in age. He was off to college by the time she was born. They had only met a few times, but as her sole sibling, she had tried to stay in touch—at least with what was going on in his life.

She added, "I wouldn't be surprised if that side of the family wanted one of us dumped into the ocean."

"I know I would." I laughed. I could laugh, because it didn't involve me.

It was an old dispute from her father's side of the family over ownership of a house in England. Something about wills and rights, but nothing that affected us.

Family arguments were something I could relate to, and I cringed to think of how things could have spiraled out of control if my own family had any real money to speak of. My father had died twenty years ago. Left us nothing but debt.

Emma's face softened. "Can you talk to Josh? Try and have a conversation with him? He's supposed to meet you at the airport."

Josh was getting divorced. A nasty split. She had learned about it through her aunt, who said he was having a hard time.

"Ask him to come and stay a night when you're back in New York," Emma said. "Make sure you talk to him before you get on the flight."

"I'll try. I mean, he's working." Honestly, it was the last thing I wanted to do.

Her face changed again, her eyes narrowing. "You *know* what I mean."

Her brother had a reputation as a heavy drinker. Never when he flew, of course. I hoped.

"Didn't he say he was going to make New York a regular stop? You can talk to him yourself, when you get back."

Her gaze lowered, her beautiful dark hair falling around her shoulders. She closed her eyes. "I wish I was coming with you."

I whispered, "Stay here as long as you need. I'll take care of Lilly."

We weren't here just for the family reunion. Emma gave me a tight smile and exhaled before turning to her right.

"How are you feeling?" she asked her mother in a way that was more than casual.

Her mother—Nian Zhen was her full name, although we called her Nanni—had been diagnosed with cancer. Seventy-two years old and her mother still had the same graceful beauty as my wife, but Nanni had lost a step since the last time I'd seen her, five years ago on their visit to New York when Lilly was born.

Back then she'd been a whirlwind of energy, and had stayed with us for three months before Emma finally shooed her back to Hong Kong. Now she seemed shrunken and quiet.

"Mom, we're going to see the doctor tomorrow," Emma said.

"But I've already seen my doctor," I heard Nanni reply.

"I mean, a real doctor. You can't ignore this."

"I'm not ignoring it."

"Dad." Emma turned to her father. "Can you tell her? Tomorrow. The doctor with Mom."

"Yes, yes, tomorrow," Alasdair replied.

The old guy was busy picking out a pork dumpling, and it was obvious he didn't really know what his daughter was talking about. He had a habit of agreeing with whatever anyone said. Or thought they said. Hard of hearing. More like deaf. He wasn't much help, but not that he didn't want to be. The codger was eighty-five-years old, thirteen years senior to Emma's mother.

He needed help almost as much as she did.

Alasdair sat on my immediate left. Seeing I'd finished talking with Emma he leaned over and poked Lilly's ribs. Lilly giggled and picked up another piggy bun, even though she had skin-signed she wasn't hungry. She liked the buns. I made a mental note.

"So when are you bringing us another one of these little monsters?" Alasdair asked me.

"We're working on it," I replied. "As a matter—"

Emma interrupted, "—of fact, we're working very hard on it." She smiled at her father, then gave me a stern look.

Her father winked. "Well, you keep working on it." The old man laughed throatily.

Emma and her dad lived halfway around the world from each other, yet somehow remained tight. It was something I envied. I had never felt close with my own father.

Alasdair said to me, "Have you been reading about the Hong Kong independence movement? Bloody well should separate from China. That's what I think."

Emma shook her head. "Dad, I told you to stop talking about that. You certainly didn't think Hong Kong should separate when it was attached to England."

"That was different."

"Different how?" Emma held up one hand to stop him responding. "I don't want to hear it. Can you please stop talking about it? It's not your place to have opinions on this anymore."

"I've lived here almost all of my life."

"Which you should be grateful for."

"But—"

"Stop. Please."

Her father's wispy white eyebrows furrowed but he shrugged and with his chopsticks retrieved another pork dumpling with expert precision. "Did I ever tell you I played polo with the Shah of Iran?" he said to me.

He had. Every time I'd met him, but I said he hadn't and he began to tell his tale again. My wife's father was a relic from a different time. A leftover piece of an empire.

He had stubbornly stayed in place after the handover of Hong Kong to China in 1997. He'd been in import and export, at least that was the story. British Foreign Service, or something. He'd fought the Chinese in North Korea during the war in that peninsula, yet now lived happily with the same people he'd been trying to kill fifty years ago.

Guess that pretty much summed up humanity, and maybe families as well. All of humankind was one big family, come to think of it. At war with each other one minute, then happy together the next. I took out my journal and scribbled that down.

Yeah, that sounded like family to me.

CHAPTER 2

Emma knelt in front of Lilly at the edge of the sidewalk and held our daughter's two small hands in hers. A tour bus growled into gear and belched a cloud of exhaust and pulled away. Blue letters on glass walls straight in front of us announced Hong Kong International Airport in English with Chinese characters over the top.

In front of our taxi, a gaggle of young schoolgirls all in matching white-and-baby-blue tracksuit jackets and pants had disembarked. The girls squealed and chased each other around a pile of suitcases. Jumping out from a divider between the lanes, a woman wound through the departures traffic and barked a command in Cantonese. The girls came to attention and lined up in two rows.

At least I thought the woman spoke in Cantonese. Maybe Mandarin?

Lilly watched the girls with fascination. She'd started Kindergarten and loved it. It was the main reason to go, plus I really needed to get back to work—or try to. My efforts at writing had hit a wall. The frustration was mounting.

Sweat dripped down my back not even ten seconds after getting out of the car—the air stifling hot, thick with humidity and fumes I tasted in the back of my throat.

Early October and the fall season would be in full swing back in New York. I couldn't wait to feel the cool outdoor air. A little morning frost out on Long Island would be welcome.

"Mitch, I can't believe you left her inhaler at the restaurant," Emma said. She inspected our daughter.

"I'm fine, Momma, don't worry," Lilly said.

"We still have one." I took a blue plastic puffer from my hip pocket and held it up. I opened the trunk of the taxi with my other hand.

A passing car's side mirror whipped by so fast and close I felt the wind suck forward the hairs on my left arm. I almost gave the driver the finger before realizing Lilly was looking at me.

"That one is almost empty," Emma said. "You're always so distracted."

"Me?" I hauled my suitcase from the trunk. Why the hell wasn't the driver coming back to help? "I wanted to be here for eight-thirty and it's almost ten. Our flight leaves in barely more than an hour. If we don't get our bags on soon, we won't be boarding. And who knows how long the lineup is."

I hated being late.

Whenever I had to get somewhere, my mind automatically counted backward from the departure point to destination. Five minutes to get out of the car and to the counter. Ten to park. Seven minutes to walk downstairs. Eighteen for the drive. A carefully calculated tally of when and where with estimates and error limits.

My mind was forever adding up and counting. Estimating. I couldn't stop it.

This morning was supposed to be twenty-four minutes on the Airport Express to HKIA, ten minutes downstairs to the taxi, five to the station, five from the station to ticket counter. Fifty minutes travel time—with maximum error—so if we'd left at 7:40 a.m., Lilly and I would have been here for eight-thirty and have more than enough time for bag drop and security.

But no.

My wife decided she needed to come with us. To see us off. Last minute.

Emma was many things, but on time wasn't one of them. When I said we had to leave at seven-forty, for her that meant when she needed to get her makeup on. Why did she need makeup to go to the airport? She fussed around the hotel room for another half hour, and then decided it might be faster to take a taxi all the way there instead of using the airport train.

We got stuck in traffic behind a Golden Week parade down Nathan Road.

It was a Friday morning at the end of a national week off, and where she had figured the roads would be empty, the highway past Kowloon was jammed, even the entrance to the airport slowed to a crawl. I'd watched the misty green hills of Lantau Island creep past our taxi window inch by inch, and decided it wasn't fog but pollution shrouding the peaks.

Chek Lap Kok, Hong Kong's airport, was the busiest freight terminal on the planet and Terminal One was once the largest in the world. All of it built on an artificial island from dredged-up dirt reclaimed from the sea floor.

I'd been looking forward to wandering around it a bit. Usually this stuff fascinated the wannabe-engineer in me. Not today.

"Can you maybe help me?" I had three bags slung around my neck and was trying to maneuver Lilly's suitcase from the back of the taxi.

By the time Emma got to her feet, I'd already gotten everything to the curb. I didn't really need help. I was being snippy.

The taxi pulled away. "Hey, hey!" I hadn't even paid him yet. Was this guy an idiot?

"It's an Uber, remember?" Emma put a hand on my arm. She knew what I was thinking before I did. "Calm down. It's already paid."

I watched the taxi pull into the stream of traffic.

"Calm down," my wife repeated. She took Lilly's hand and with her other hand extended the handle on my wheelie suitcase. "And it's nine-thirty-five. Not ten. We have half an hour for bag drop."

We wound our way a hundred feet down the cement walkway to the indigo entrance posts marked, Allied Airways, in block yellow letters.

Halfway there, a woman sprinted ten feet from the curb to grab a bubble-wrapped cylinder from the hands of a red-capped porter. "No, no, *ne touchez pas*—don't touch that."

The woman took the package and inspected it. She stood straight in front of us and blocked our way forward. Blue surgical scrubs under a white lab coat, her nose freckled under a mound of cascading red hair that obscured her face.

"Sorry," she said as she got out of our way. She smiled at Lilly and then at me.

"That lady was *loud*." Lilly giggled.

Air-conditioned coolness swept over us as the terminal doors opened, the relief palpable as the chill stung my sweat-soaked neck. Cathedral ceilings arched high overhead in triangular white metal sheets, held aloft by forty-foot pylons at hundred foot intervals. Each second row of ceiling tiles was skylights, with sunlight streaming down. Low forests of divider-taped stanchions sectioned off the polished marble floor. Digital displays with block yellow characters gave directions.

Mercifully, everything was in Chinese *and* English. When traveling I felt like speaking English as a mother tongue was cheating, since we didn't need to understand anyone else's language to get around. If not cheating, then lazy.

"This way."

I pointed at the display indicating Allied Airways and hurried us along, but Emma had been right. Still twenty minutes to ten. Plenty of time before the cut off, and rounding a corner I saw that there were only a dozen or so people at the Allied counter.

"It'll be fine," I said to Emma as I slowed my pace.

"She's wheezing again," Emma whispered back.

"It's sixteen hours. If this one runs out, I'll get another inhaler in

New York when we land. At Walgreens on the corner. We'll get there this afternoon. Amazing."

And it *was* amazing.

We took off at 11 a.m. from Hong Kong and landed at 3 p.m. the same day in New York, literally halfway around the world. Not a four-hour flight, but sixteen hours with a twelve-hour time difference folded in.

Kowloon and Brooklyn traded day for night exactly, so while it was ten in the morning here, it was ten at night the previous day in Manhattan.

The flight took us straight north, up over China into Russia, past the North Pole to drop down over Canada and home. Santa's shortcut, they called it.

An adventure.

My wife wanted to go on holiday adventures, like hiking some mountain, but I wasn't an intrepid traveler. Here, however, was an exploit I could enjoy from the comfort of a padded chair with a glass of Chardonnay in hand.

Emma's phone beeped. She took it from her pocket. "Josh says he'll meet you on the plane. Some kind of emergency. I texted him to say I wasn't coming with you."

"Not *too* much of an emergency? He's flying today?"

She nodded. "Said he left us a gift at the counter."

"Gift?"

"That's what he said."

"Uncle Josh is coming to take us onto the ahh-plane?" Lilly asked. She hadn't quite mastered vowels, or maybe had inherited some of my Long Island accent.

"We're going to meet him on the plane. Later."

"Oh, okay." Lilly went back to counting tiles in the floor as we walked.

I had to admit, I was excited.

It wasn't every day that you got to fly over the top of the world. I started a book about Robert Peary's expedition to conquer the North

Pole over a hundred years back. So far I had only made it through the first two chapters, but planned to finish it on the flight as I crossed the same frozen landscape he and his men had toiled across.

At the entrance to the ticket counter, a barrel-chested man in a Gucci-looking business suit argued with a younger man in a frayed khaki army jacket. The older man had a manicured beard as close-cropped as the hair on his head.

The younger one's beard was bushy and wild, the sides of his head shaved but with a long mop of hair on top pulled back into a ponytail. Homeless Viking came to mind.

The younger man's face was blushed red.

We stopped behind a stocky man in a denim jacket, with a nice blue knit tie and white shirt buttoned up. I noticed his tortoise shell eyeglass frames. Those looked expensive. My mind kept categorizing and calculating things about people around me.

Beside him, in the First Class line, was a father and son, the man a six-and-a-half foot, three-hundred-pound-plus flat-faced Chinese man. His son—I assumed it was his son—was a small chubby-faced boy with tan-colored skin and bright brown eyes.

The boy saw Lilly and smiled. My daughter smiled a shy grin back and hid behind her mother's skirt.

Emma pulled at my arm. "Look at this." She had her phone out and held it up.

UK Must Boost Arctic Defenses, ran the BBC article headline. *MP's warn against increasing threat in the far north and the disproportionate military expansion by Russia and its aggressive and revisionist behavior.*

A linked article described Russian bombers flying over disputed Alaskan territory.

My wife whispered in my ear. "I've got a bad feeling."

"About what?"

"This flight."

"You don't want us to go?"

She remained silent.

"Are you serious?"

"I don't know."

"You always get nervous in airports."

"I know. But still…"

"Seriously. I'm sure we could rebook and stay. Talk to Lilly's school and tell them."

My wife shook her head. "It'll be easier if it's just me here with my mom and dad."

"You're sure?" I asked, but I could see she wasn't. She was doing her thing again, trying to rationalize away irrational thinking.

To change the topic I said, "Are you going to tell them?"

"Not until the end of the first trimester."

"Tell them what?" Lilly asked, her face upturned to us both.

"That you have a little brother or sister coming."

My wife shushed me but then rolled her eyes realizing the cat in the hat had escaped the bag.

Lilly's eyes went wide. "Weally?"

"But it's a secret," I said, putting a finger to my lips. "Shhhh…"

"Shhhh…" Lilly mimed.

"Excuse me, *m'hgòi*, excuse me," someone growled in a thick Russian accent.

It was the barrel-chested businessman with the almost-shaved head. His cuff links flashed as he muscled past us, an oil slick of expensive-smelling cologne seeping into the air in his wake.

"Hey, buddy—" I started to say, but Emma held my arm.

Calm down, her grip implored.

The man glanced at me but didn't reply as he pushed through the rest of the people. Seeing the counters full he detoured straight to the First Class sign. What an asshole.

A few minutes later and there was one guy left in front of us in line.

"I have to go to the bathroom," Lilly said in a small voice. She crossed her legs.

"You're going to have to wait," I said. "A few minutes, sweetie."

"You can go ahead of me." The man in the tortoise shell eyeglasses had turned and held out one hand to offer to let us past. "I'm not in a hurry. Please, go ahead."

"Thank you." I admired his knit tie and jean jacket. Cool look for a middle-aged guy.

I advanced to an open counter while Emma brought up Lilly and the bags, and was about to hand over our passports when the fresh-faced woman with a red kerchief around her neck said, "Ah, you must be Mr. Matthews."

"Ah, yeah, um, that's right. Mitch Matthews." Perplexed at how she knew my name, I held out the passports.

"The Captain was down earlier and showed us a picture of you and your lovely daughter," the woman explained, recognizing my confusion. "And I'm very happy to tell you that you've both been upgraded to First Class."

"First Class?"

"That's right."

"Like with the lie-flat beds?"

"And a nice selection of wines from our sommelier." The woman began tapping on her computer.

I turned to Emma. "First Class."

The prospect of sixteen hours in cramped seats had suddenly changed into a pleasure cruise.

Emma wasn't as impressed. "You make sure Lilly stays strapped in."

"Of course."

"I love you, Mitch."

"I love you, too."

"You take care of Lilly. You hear me?"

"I hear you."

"No matter what, you take care of our little girl."

CHAPTER 3

We entered the First Class Lounge past a bonsai garden by the frosted glass-wall entrance and a gauntlet of smiling gatekeepers. Straight away we went to see the food.

A team of busy chefs worked preparing plates for a buzzing hive of waiters. We picked some seats and deposited our jackets beside a woman in a crisp business suit who sat in a deep brown leather chair with a view onto the green hills of Lantau Island in the distance.

"Can I eat any of them?" Lilly asked.

She pointed at a selection of fine pastries on a refrigerated tray. A white-smocked-and-hatted dessert chef worked on what looked like… rum babas? Small brown cakes oozing stickiness, each topped with a puff of whipped cream.

"Take one for now," I said. "Pick whichever looks nicest."

So this was how the other half lived. Or the other one percent. Or one-hundredth of one percent. I made a mental note of details to write in my journal.

I eyed the wide horseshoe-shaped bar behind us but decided alcohol wasn't a good idea, at least until we got onto the plane. *Take care of her.* I heard my wife's words from a few minutes ago when we'd said our goodbyes. Trust me, I'd said.

"Come on, sweetheart," I said to Lilly. "Let's sit down. We've got a half hour."

▼▲▼

"Authorities are now working with local police to protect the city," the newscaster on the TV said.

He had a British accent, and looked the part with a stylishly unkempt mess of hair and breast pocket handkerchief in his suit. I'd tuned the lounge's TV into the only English-language news broadcast, VuiTVsix.

They were talking about the recent protest marches for Hong Kong independence. Of course, they were portraying the protesters as a danger. This was state-controlled media. Then again, I had little more faith in our sensationalized news channels back home.

What was the difference?

"Hey, Mitch, how's it going?"

My wife's half-brother stood grinning over me. A full head of perfectly casually coiffed hair, salt-and-pepper gray, with a protruding square jaw. A poster child for pilots if there ever was one. He had on his Allied uniform—a deep navy blue jacket and trousers and polished black shoes, with the obligatory brass wings over his left breast.

I stood to shake his hand. "Hey," I said around a half-mouthful of prosciutto. "Thanks for the upgrade."

"Call it luck, I guess. My boss asked me if I wanted this flight last minute."

In the eight years I'd been married to Emma, I'd only met Josh three times before. Once at our wedding when he came alone, and two other times when he'd stopped in on legs through New York. He and his family lived on the West Coast—or had lived. I wasn't sure what his situation was now.

I watched his eyes. Blue-green and flecked with hazel. Clear. Not bloodshot. *Stupid*, I thought, but Emma had made me promise to look carefully.

"I was thinking, maybe you want to stop in at our place? You must get a few days layover?"

"That's awfully nice, but—"

"Come on. Lilly would love it. We could grab a few beers. Let me repay you for the upgrade?"

I noticed his eyes kept looking over my shoulder. I stole a glance. Ah.

"Yeah, you know," he said. "Back out on the prowl."

He'd noticed the redhead who had almost run into us on the sidewalk. Very attractive in an exotic sort of way. Not American, I guessed. She'd changed into street clothes, traded the lab coat for yoga pants. Nice legs.

She was cradling that package from outside like an infant in her arms.

In the lounger behind her, the jackass with the fancy cufflinks stared—slack jawed—into the distance. His homeless-Viking-looking friend was nowhere to be seen.

"And who's this beautiful lady?" Josh knelt, his face taking on a mock-quizzical look.

Lilly hung back by my leg and hid her face behind her hands. "I'm Lilly," she said finally.

"You can't be Lilly. Last time I saw her, she was no bigger than a peanut."

My daughter giggled. "I'm no peanut."

"Now you're a *big* nut." He ruffled her hair and stood.

Salutations finished, Lilly ran off in pursuit of the chubby-cheeked boy again. The same one we'd seen in the lineup outside.

"Conditions in Tibet are worsening as local rebels refuse to recognize the new Dalai Lama," the news anchor said in the background. "Authorities are now searching for monks who claim—"

"How are you doing?" I said to Josh.

His smile slid away. "What did you say to Emma?"

"What?"

"You heard me."

I made sure Lilly was out of earshot before replying. "I didn't say anything."

As a pause became awkward I added, "Don't blame me."

He remained aggressively silent.

I said, "Are you being serious?"

"Like I was the only one talking to those girls."

"*You* were the only one that took them to a hotel room."

He snorted. "Only because they weren't interested in you."

"I was not interested in *any* of that."

Two years ago, Josh had had a layover in New York. Emma suggested the two of us have a boys night out, to bond and get to know each other. Josh took me to a bar in the Meatpacking district, his uniform on, and picked up some women. He got hammered almost right away. I was trying to be polite and hold up conversation, but he wanted more than that. I refused his invitation to come back with them to his hotel.

"You cost me my marriage," Josh said. "She's taking the kids, the house. I won't have a pot to piss in after this."

"Look, I'm sincerely sorry for whatever is happening, but I didn't say anything. I had nothing to do with it."

And I didn't. I hadn't said anything to anyone. It wasn't that much of a surprise for me when Emma said Josh was getting a divorce—his marriage seemed like it was over two years ago.

Josh said, "This thing with my mother, the house in England that Alasdair won't give up? What did you say to Emma? Did you talk to her father?"

I stood in dumbfounded silence. Lilly ran past a few seats away.

It dawned on me that his being here on this flight wasn't an accident. It certainly wasn't him being friendly. He wanted to find out who had said what to whom.

From the corner of my eye, I saw the chubby-cheeked boy's massive father appear and sweep the kid into his arms, shushing him. I didn't understand what he said, but whatever it was, he wasn't happy. Lilly ran back and grabbed hold of my leg.

Josh's smile returned. "So Emma decided to stay."

"Her mother's sick."

"I heard. Sorry to hear that."

I pulled my daughter into me. His aggressive tone vanished the second Lilly came near. On closer inspection, his eyes did have a glazed look to them. Maybe not drunk, but was he high? He seemed off, not quite right.

He knelt again and took Lilly's arm. "I'll come and see you after we take off. I have a present for you."

▼▲▼

"Would you like another?" the flight attendant, Suzanne, asked.

I considered the ice cubes left in my glass and nodded. "Thank you."

The overhead mood lighting of the 777's cabin had shifted to a soothing blue. Each First Class pod was about eight feet long and three wide, all of them entering directly onto an aisle, with the odd-numbered ones closer to the sides with two windows each.

Lilly and I had one behind the other on the left side of the aircraft.

We'd already explored the amenity kit—a retro-747-themed package with toothbrush and paste, earplugs and noise-canceling headphones, a real goose-down blanket to go with the wide seats that reclined into flat beds. Each pod had its own twenty-four inch screen, but the entertainment system hadn't been turned on yet.

Already an hour sitting on the tarmac.

Lilly was asleep in her pod.

Normally I would have been excited to get into one of these seats. I'd walked past them jealously on previous flights on my way back to economy. Today it felt dirty.

Why had Josh given us the upgrade? To get on Emma's good side?

She was supposed to be here with us. Sixteen hours stuck in a tin can flown by him now felt like a prison term. I trusted that he wasn't intoxicated, but a tiny nagging uncertainty remained.

Then again, I hadn't seen anything. I had considered trying to leave. Cancel the tickets and walk out of the airport, but what would I say to Emma? And a part of me didn't want to leave. I wanted to get back to New York. Have a week to myself.

Josh was upset. He was going through a bad time. I was overreacting.

And Lilly was excited. I didn't want to take that away from her, so pretended I was, too.

Suzanne returned with another gin and tonic. My second. She took the old glass.

"Would you like some water?" she asked.

I shook my head. "How much longer till we take off?"

"We had to make a last minute crew change."

"Is Josh still flying?"

"It was only the backup crew that changed. And there's some kind of mechanical issue."

As if on cue, the cabin door opened next to the galley two rows up. A blast of humid air assaulted the air-conditioned stillness.

Two thick-set men in overalls, loaded down with tool belts and electronic gear, shuffled down the aisle past us. I craned my neck to look out of my pod to watch them.

A young dark-skinned man with circular glasses had his head leaning into the aisle, too. He turned to me. "Did you get that error message as well?"

"Pardon me?"

"I turned on my laptop, and it said, 'New Bluetooth device detected: Boeing 777' - set, reset? I told it to reset." He laughed at his joke. "I think we should go for it. Whatever's wrong, screw it. Let's get in the air."

"I can wait a little while," I said. *That was odd.*

The young man shrugged and retreated back into his pod. He couldn't be more than twenty. How did people afford this stuff? I counted twenty-eight seats in our section in the front of the aircraft, right behind the galley next to the flight deck, with another galley behind us.

The homeless-Viking kid had reappeared and had a pod closest to the economy section, while the flashy-cufflink guy was in a seat on the opposite side of the plane. They didn't even acknowledge each other.

The attractive redhead was in a middle row, and the large Chinese man with his chubby-cheeked son in a set of compartments right beside Lilly.

I settled back into my seat and pulled up the BBC on a private VPN on my phone so I could read the uncensored news. A newsflash about the dispute in Tibet was the top story. A linked essay on dams in the Tibetan plateau, of Buddhist terrorists trying to destroy them. The Chinese authorities were trying to impose a new religious leader. I took a second to process. Buddhists could be terrorists?

After writing a few notes in my journal, I flicked through more headlines.

Two more about Hong Kong independence protests. I selected stuff to do with the Arctic and found a news story about record temperatures near Greenland that related it to global warming and thinning sea ice.

Another, again, about Russian bombers interfering with American war game exercises with the Canadian forces coming out of the Alert base on Ellesmere Island.

The report said that Alert was the northernmost inhabited place on the planet.

We were going to fly right over it.

▼▲▼

A jolt woke me.

Out the window, the jetway moved back. My gin and tonic empty again. The plane slid away from the gate.

The GE90 engines whined into life and each spooled up and

started. I'd read up about the 777 before getting on the flight. This was the 300-ER version. Extended range.

I checked my phone. How long had I been asleep?

It was a few minutes past noon Hong Kong time. Midnight in New York. We were leaving about an hour late. I must have been asleep for only a few minutes, but I'd been dreaming. Of Emma. My wife. She was telling me not to go. Telling me to stay. The image of her face was strong in my mind as the dream dissipated.

I unclasped my seatbelt to check on Lilly. Her seat was upright. She smiled at me, said she was okay and the nice Suzanne got her a KitKat when I was asleep. Her seat belt was fastened.

I sat down and strapped back in. The plane taxied to the runway. Josh's voice came over the intercom telling the flight crew that we were number one for takeoff.

I looked out my window. The skies were mostly clear, light clouds high in the stratosphere. The entertainment system was active now, so I turned to the WTHAW channel—the "where the hell are we" moving map—and studied the dotted line of our path from Hong Kong up over Russia. Almost as soon as I turned it on, the IFE screen froze and went blank.

I turned it off.

Two hundred thirty thousand pounds of force pushed me back into my seat and accelerated the four hundred ton machine along the northbound runway. Sooner than I expected, the aircraft rotated into the air for an upward thrusting climb out. As we ascended through the cloud deck, there was a bit of chop, but barely worth mentioning.

Don't go, I heard my wife's voice echoing from the dream.

CHAPTER 4

"Wow, that's beautiful," I said.

Through the four front windows of the 777's flight deck, luminous red-gold clouds bathed the sky to our left and faded into a purple haze on the right.

"We're cruising at forty thousand feet, that's almost maximum ceiling," Josh said.

He was strapped into the right-side pilot seat—*chair* was the correct term, he told us—and he spoke through an oxygen mask covering his nose and mouth. He glanced over his shoulder and pulled the mask down.

"You can see the curvature of the Earth from up here." He pointed forward.

The horizon had a definite line that bulged in front of us. Through the small cabin windows you couldn't really notice, but the curve was clear from the wide-angle view here. I'd never witnessed it before with my own eyes—something I'd always wanted to see.

Lilly was as impressed as me. "That's purdy," she whispered.

She stood in the left pilot chair, with me behind supporting her upright.

Josh's copilot had been strapped into the left-hand seat when we first arrived. She had gotten up and excused herself to the rear after telling Lilly how cute she was.

"Are we supposed to be in here alone?" I asked. "Isn't there a rule that two pilots need to be in the cockpit at the same time?" I wasn't really alarmed, more curious.

"Flight deck," Josh said. "Nobody calls it a cockpit anymore. And you're not even supposed to be here at all. Post-911, nobody but flight crew are allowed up front." He glanced over his shoulder again, his oxygen mask still down. "I'm bending the rules, but I'm the captain. Still, I could lose my stripes for it."

"We should go back. I didn't realize—"

"I'm kidding. The autopilot is engaged, nothing for me to do right now except sit here. It's okay, I'm making a special exception. Plus, I said you're doing some writing on this flight, maybe submit a story for the FAA? Makes you sorta part of the team, right?" He winked at me. "My copilot is hitting the head for a minute, and we're in process of changeover. There are two more pilots right behind you in the galley."

He had already explained that the second flight team was about to rotate in. Four-hour shifts up front, and this was the end of the second rotation.

Josh pointed at me—"One"—then himself—"Two"—and finally, Lilly. "That's three, right? So we're not alone."

"Three," Lilly said and nodded. She stared out the windows, mesmerized.

A few hours into the flight, Josh had come back and apologized about his earlier behavior. Said he was under a lot of stress and had wanted to speak with Emma, but insisted that we come up to the flight deck. Lilly asked every ten minutes from then on when we could go and fly the plane, so it wasn't like I could say no.

I checked my watch. Five past eight in the evening Hong Kong time.

Early morning in New York.

For eight hours the moving map on my entertainment system had slowly slid over China, past the gray-brown deserts of Mongolia I saw out of my cabin window, and into the rolling green steppes of the southern edges of Siberia.

From our seats on the west side of the plane, the sun had skimmed below the horizon at about 6 p.m. but seemed to remain out of view without really setting.

Persistent twilight as we hurtled northward.

It was as the last glimmers of the sun had disappeared that Josh had come on the passenger intercom to announce that we were passing the Arctic Circle at sixty-nine degrees north. In Siberia the landscape had been dotted and then covered with snow, but a blue ocean had replaced the undulating white sheet. An expanse of indigo water stretched out below us two hours after passing into the Arctic. I had expected ice by now.

In the distance out the left window, a ghostly range of jagged hills appeared. Barely visible were straight black lines and dotted structures near the edges.

"What's that?" I asked.

"A Russian air base."

"Is that Santa's house?" Lilly asked.

"Not quite," I said. I wagged my head from side to side and smiled. "But close."

"Hey, hey, look up there." Josh pointed straight ahead.

In the murky distance, a clean white edge appeared over the dark sea.

"That's the icepack," he said. "Ten years ago at this time of year it started right at the coast."

"Climate change?"

"That's above my paygrade." He shrugged. "Just know the ice has shifted. We're at eighty-five degrees north now." He indicated one of the displays with white concentric rings and a dusting of green speckles. "About forty minutes from the North Pole. It's three hundred-fifty miles that way."

He pointed not quite straight ahead, but slightly to the right.

"We're not going over it?"

I'd spent most of the flight reading my book about Peary's polar expedition in 1909, the first person to reach the North Pole—or claimed to have. I wondered how Admiral Peary would have felt knowing I was passing over the same landscape his men had fought and died every inch to cross while I enjoyed a glass of wine and canapes in a recliner, cuddled under a warm down blanket.

"We'll be flying about"—Josh checked the display again—"maybe fifty miles to the east of it. Normally we fly maybe a hundred and fifty miles west, so we're about two hundred miles off our planned course. First time I've gone east, actually."

"And why is that?"

"Strong winds. There's a big circulating air system over the Pole right now. It's been pushing us east on the way up, but will push us back west by about the same on the way back south. There's a polar hurricane brewing over the Beaufort sea right now, with another low coming up behind it."

"Polar *hurricane*? That's a thing?"

"It's a thousand miles away. Won't even feel a bit of chop from it. The North Magnetic Pole has been acting up, too. The fun never stops."

"Should I be worried?"

I peered low through the window to get a better look.

At the horizon, slightly to the right, a speck of light cut through the purple twilight. Venus. Off to the left, a fat yellow moon surfed twenty degrees into the sky.

I'd been watching it the past few hours. Instead of circling overhead, it had crept into the sky and then rotated northward at a constant height instead of circling overhead. Weird.

"Did you know," Josh said to Lilly, "that here in Santa's world that the sun disappeared two weeks ago already?"

Lilly scrunched her face up. "What do you mean? I saw it today."

"Not up here. The sun doesn't come up every day—sometimes it stays hidden for a long time."

"Like how long?"

"Six months. No sunshine for six months up here."

My little girl pursed her lips. "But it's not nighttime."

"You're right. Not quite night, but not quite day. Twilight stays for a month after the sun sets."

It was a bit much for Lilly to comprehend. She nodded seriously.

"Do you want to sit in the captain's seat?"

The slow nod turned into a frantic one. Josh smiled at me, saying it was okay.

I eased her down into the left-hand chair.

"Put your hands here, but gently," Josh said as he indicated the flight yoke.

Lilly leaned forward and her fingertips touched the control.

"See, you're flying a jet."

My daughter's eyes widened. She put her hands back into her lap quick, as if the flight yoke was red hot. She giggled and looked up at me.

I inspected the pilot seat in front of me. Gray-brown leather, but with white patches worn through it. The controls had an equally weathered look to them, the screens scratched. "How old is this plane?"

"Twenty years, give or take."

"Isn't that *old*?" From the interior in First Class, I'd thought we were on a new plane.

"It's been refurbished."

"But the actual engines and wings are *twenty* years old?"

When I was in college, I had a car that was almost twenty years old, and one day a wheel had literally fallen off. Holes through the floorboard. Had to start it down a hill sometimes. This airplane was that ancient?

"But refurbished twice," Josh said. "These planes are good for thirty years. She's got a lot left in her."

Thirty years?

"Special flight today," Josh said.

When he didn't add anything after a few seconds I asked, "What's special about it?"

"Well, you guys are here."

That was cryptic. "So we're the special part?"

Before he could answer, a stocky Asian man in a short-sleeved white shirt and yellow shoulder bars appeared in the flight deck entrance.

"Changeover," the man said with a thick Chinese accent.

The moment he uttered the words, the floor rumbled up and down. Lilly squealed.

The aircraft shuddered again. I pulled Lilly out of the seat and took her into my arms, her legs wrapped around my waist, and squeezed myself against the wall to wriggle back through the exit. The stocky Asian man—the new pilot, I assumed—gently pushed past me and put an arm around Josh. He whispered urgently into his ear.

The new pilot glanced at me.

"Mitch," Josh said. "Sorry, but you guys need to return to your seats."

"Already on my way," I said.

Another tan-skinned man came into the flight deck with a suitcase in hand. I took a step back through the door into the galley corridor to make room. His uniform seemed too small for his frame, the shirt bulging to contain his stomach. He smelled of sweat under cheap cologne. Josh unstrapped after one of the new men strapped into the left-hand flight chair.

"Our relief crew has arrived," said a woman in the same white shirt and blue tie as Josh. She stood behind me in the walkway.

Josh introduced her. "Mitch, Lilly—this is Irene, Captain Irene Hardy, my co-pilot."

We exchanged pleasantries.

"Come on," Josh said, "I'll bring you back to your seats."

The first man had pulled out a sheaf of paper and clipped it to the flight stick of the right-side pilot seat. The plane rumbled with passing turbulence again.

Out the front window, the white line of the ice pack was beneath us now. With Josh behind me, I shuffled one step at a time back through the galley with Lilly in my arms, careful of my footing as the plane shook.

"So that Russian airbase," I asked. "What was it called?"

"That was the Bolshevik Military Complex on the Kosmolets."

"Are they involved in those bomber flights?"

"Your guess is as good as mine, but the name fits."

"The name?"

"October Revolution. That's the name of the island we passed over. I mean, it is October, right?" He laughed a laugh only a pilot could at a joke like that in a plane at forty thousand feet.

Another jolt of turbulence, this one almost strong enough to knock me sideways.

Josh said, "Come on, you better get back to those seats. We don't want you to get hurt."

CHAPTER 5

"I s *this* the North Pole?" Lilly asked.

She pressed her freckled nose against my cabin window and tried her best to look down.

"Almost," I replied.

The bulbous moon skimmed the horizon in a cobalt sky. Eight miles below stretched the ghostly expanse of blue-veined ice. The sun had lurked just beyond the horizon for three hours now, the hurtling aircraft seemingly pulling it back from the brink as we slipped over the top of the world.

Beautiful desolation, that's what came to mind.

I scribbled that thought into my journal. Wait, wasn't that what one of the Apollo astronauts said when they stepped onto the moon? I crossed it out and wrote, *Magnificent desolation*, but then scribbled that out as well. I put my pen down.

Lilly traced one tiny finger around a feathering of crystals around a small hole at the bottom of the cabin window.

"This is where Santa lives?" she asked.

Was she wheezing again?

"That's right." I took a mental inventory. Her inhaler was in the backpack by my knees. It had a few puffs left in it. I hoped.

I shifted in the seat of my pod. The turbulence had passed. Lilly was balanced on my knee, my shirt sweat-stuck to my back. A bit less than eight hours to go.

"Can see?" asked the chubby boy in broken English. His cheeks were flushed.

Cute kid.

Lilly had made a friend, the kid we'd met in the lounge. She made friends easily. Something she got from her mother.

I glanced up at the boy's father—the enormous man sat in a pod in a center aisle seat across and two down from us. He had those narrow-flat-faced features of someone from northern China, but not that I knew much about northern China. His eyes met mine and he nodded, yes, it was okay. I was about to pick the kid up to let him have a look out the window when a voice came over the passenger intercom.

"Ladies and gentlemen, the captain has illuminated the seatbelt sign."

From three rows forward, the flight attendant, Suzanne, smiled at Lilly and me. She continued speaking into her microphone. "We have an area of high turbulence approaching. Everyone must take their seat immediately. I repeat, the captain has asked that everyone please take their seat immediately."

"The captain?"

"Uncle Josh wants to make sure you don't get hurt." Was he still in the flight deck?

I shooed the chubby kid back to his father, then returned Suzanne's smile to indicate I was getting up for a second to take care of Lilly.

Instead of coming to help, Suzanne lowered the jump seat in the galley and strapped herself in. I've never been a nervous flyer, but I hated it when the flight attendants strapped in. Meant something serious. At a minimum, no more gin and tonics for half an hour.

I should have taken that glass of water when she passed by. A headache brewed behind my temples. Dehydrated. My wife often compared me to a camel. That was how little I tended to hydrate myself.

These seats were a luxury beyond our means, but having Lilly in her own pod area meant I had to get up out of my seat to double check that she'd strapped in properly. I yawned as I triple checked her seatbelt clasp. *Take care of her*, I heard my wife's voice telling me in my head. I checked the seatbelt for a fourth time.

"You tired, Daddy?" My little girl giggled and mimed my open-mouthed yawn.

"Why don't we take another nap?"

My eyes drooped as I spoke, my arms and eyelids suddenly heavy. I collapsed back into my seat, and had enough time to check the flight map—frozen and not working again—and to strap myself in.

I didn't fight it. Sleep was good anytime you could get it, and nowhere more than on a sixteen-hour flight.

▼▲▼

It felt like I was floating. I blinked and then blinked again and tried to understand…

My backpack hung suspended halfway up the pod wall, my arms raised up to each side of it. My stomach lurched, the remains of the salmon dinner in the back of my throat. My writing pen trickled up the cabin window to my left.

A terrible moaning grated in my ears.

My arms slapped down against the seat rests. The backpack thumped to the ground. A shooting pain from my left elbow where it slammed into the arm rest. The noise gained pitch.

No other sounds. Only the grinding moan.

Like an engine winch straining against a massive load. An engine. *The* engines. Those were the *airplane* engines making that sickening wail.

My mind fought its way out of the sleep-fog.

The big Chinese man in the middle aisle glanced at me, his jaw muscles flexing. Was this the turbulence?

My head snapped back.

Blood rushed into the base of my skull.

A projectile slammed into the overhead bin. A human body. A man. His knee slammed into a woman's face as he pirouetted in a gravity-defying cartwheel before he tumbled to the floor and then flew past me into the air.

Jesus Chr—

The seatbelt cut hard into my waist. I grunted to breathe. My arms flung back into the air. A Coke can sailed past my head and clattered into the window. I looked out. The ghostly purple-blue twilight had lightened.

No.

That wasn't the sky. That was the ice. The horizon cartwheeled back around.

"Daddeeeee!" Lilly screeched a high thin wail.

I strained to lean forward to reach over the divider. I almost had my hand—

A splitting roar felt like it ripped my seat out from under me. The walls of the aircraft bowed in and out in a rippling pressure wave.

A screaming rush of air drowned out the warbling groan of the engines. Papers and napkins whipped into the air. I gritted my teeth, strained to keep a hold on the divider and focused my mind on Lilly's piercing shriek amid the yells of other passengers.

Something hit my head. I brushed it away.

It swung back again. Something yellow.

Masks.

They dangled overhead of the passengers in the next aisle. One fluttered over me. I struggled to breathe. *Breathe.* Air. Wheezing.

Lilly.

Ten feet forward in the aisle, the man who had rocketed into the ceiling was inert on the floor, his head a tangled mess of hair and blood. The horizon wheeled around outside the window. The man's body flopped against the seats and back into the air.

"Lilly, I'm coming," I yelled over the noise.

I gathered myself, said a prayer and tried to take in a lungful of air, then unstrapped the clasp of my seatbelt and lurched out. My body sailed airborne before I sprawled into a small business-suited man in the next pod. Keeping low I stumbled sideways into Lilly and wrapped my left arm under her seatbelt. My legs swept out from under me, my shoulder lancing in pain as it took the load of my body whipping sideways.

Screams of passengers muffled under a deafening roar. A maelstrom of debris sucked toward the back of the plane. My hands numb in sudden cold.

"Here, here, put this on." I pulled down the yellow mask and put it over Lilly's mouth and nose.

She held it and I stretched the elastic over the back of her head. I gasped, inhaled a lungful of burning nothing.

The cabin floor seemed to come up at me. Pushed me down so hard I had to strain to keep my head up. I gritted my teeth and looked out the window. The horizon high, the portal filled with ghost-blue haze.

Ice.

Undulating lines in it now. Cracks.

I did my best to wedge myself between Lilly's seat and the wall of the pod, tried to lean over her. Protect her with my body.

Her small fingers clawed at my chest.

Outside the window the lines in the ice grew bigger. Closer. In the weightlessness of the dropping aircraft, my stomach felt like it jammed into my throat.

Emma…images of my wife flashed. *I'm sorry, Emma.* My God. My God…

This is it.

This can't be it. *Don't hurt my little girl. Please, God, don't hurt her. Please.* The rushing, tortured landscape filled the window. I tensed and wrapped my body around Lilly.

The first impact ripped me away from her.

CHAPTER 6

My body felt like it was pounded flat into a concrete wall. But no pain. No sensation except the concussive impact, an indescribable violence of compression. Then release. For a beat the universe seemed to pause.

Hover.

My little girl's face inches from me, her wisps of golden hair a tiny halo. Her eyes wide. *Reach out. Grab her. Protect her. Save her.*

But I couldn't.

The second impact battered me down. This time I felt my face slam into the sidewall of the pod before rebounding off the carpeted floor. My right arm over Lilly twisted behind my body.

Thin shrieks of humans over a hollow booming of gnashing metal. Tearing and splitting. Overhead bins flapped and spewed projectiles.

The next impact flung me backward, jammed me corkscrewed forward into some crevice, the wind knocked from me as my body folded in half. I fought to raise my head, to catch a glimpse of my daughter.

A rumbling roar like an avalanche of rocks down a mountainside. My head pitched side to side.

The world careened, the metal and plastic walls bending like reeds in a shifting gale. On and on, seconds stretched like hours. I dug my nails into the carpet.

Unable to raise my head.

The world rotated up. My face slammed into my knee. The screech of a thousand fingernails dragged over chalkboards glutted the air in an assaulting crescendo, my eyes pressed into the back of my brain…

▼▲▼

Breathe.

Just breathe.

A rasping sucking sound as I labored to fill my lungs.

No pain. No sensation except a suppressed high-pitched whine. Like I was squeezed into the bottom of an ocean a thousand miles deep. Darkness. Not darkness. Emptiness.

The whine rose into a roar that filled my senses, seemed to tingle my fingers and toes and face. The roar subsided into another high-pitched whine, but different. Not inside my head. And below that, a whimpering.

Lilly.

Lillypad.

I knew that sound beyond any other sound. That tiny cry. My little daughter. Why was she crying? What happened?

The airplane. Images of the cabin window jolted my mind awake. The wheeling field of blue-white ice. *We crashed.* My mind reassembled itself from incoherence.

You're not dead. Get a grip. Calm down. Think. Focus.

The high-pitched roar was definitely outside my head, beyond the ringing slowly subsiding inside. Then the tiny whimpering again.

Lilly.

A bleary blue smudge appeared in my vision. A luminous blue line.

I had one eye open now. My left. I closed it and opened the other. Same luminous blue line.

My brain began a mental inventory. *You still have two eyes.* I groaned and lifted my head an inch. *You can move your head.* Good. Try again, try more.

I attempted to lift my left arm.

It budged an inch but the shoulder screamed in pain. I shifted onto my right—painless—and propped myself up on one elbow. Above me, in the dim glow of the blue light, I recognized Lilly's ballet flats, the shoes with the little string bows she'd proudly picked out for the special trip home today.

"Daddy, Daddy," she whimpered.

"I'm here, baby." The effort to say the words took what little wind I had out of me.

I had to rest for a second to pull in another lungful of air.

Cold air.

Blissful numbness gave way to a throbbing pressure in my back and head and sharp pain in my left side. My right forearm was against the carpeted floor. It felt cold. *Wet.* The ground slick. I pressed my neck upward, tried to unbend myself from the waist and pushed with my right arm.

I was jammed into the foot well in front of Lilly's pod.

With every fiber of muscle in my body I heaved, groaned, then pushed and dug my fingernails into the carpet and pulled forward. I twisted my knees under me and lifted myself a foot and then another from the floor.

"It's okay, it's okay," I whispered. I shuffled forward toward Lilly.

Her eyes wide as saucers in the thin light. Her hands shook.

"Baby, are you okay?"

I felt her tiny ribs, as delicate as an eggshell. Stroked her cheek. She trembled, too petrified to even cry.

Her face seemed almost black. It wasn't the light. She was soaked in something sticky.

Blood.

No. Please, no.

A fresh surge of adrenaline submerged the rising pain. With both hands I pulled up her shirt, leaned as close as I could, my face an inch from her skin. *No, please, no.* I bent her forward and scanned her back in a desperate panic but couldn't see any wounds, not in her skin, not her legs, not her head.

All of her arms and legs were attached. Her teeth intact. Eyes open and staring. Was she broken in some way I couldn't see?

"Baby, does it hurt? What hurts? Can you move your arms? Your legs?"

She kicked her legs back and forth and pointed at her midsection. "My stomach," she whimpered.

I pulled her blouse up again and looked as close as I could, tried to wipe the stinging liquid from my eyes. Her stomach. The seatbelt.

The spiking fear ebbed.

I realized I was on my knees. *You're not paralyzed.* I checked my eyes again, then my teeth. *Still there.* I wiggled my toes and moved my feet and then paused, pulled up my shirt and felt around my midsection. No gaping objects protruding from my body. I felt my face. *Ah.* My nose felt like it was gone. Not quite gone, but not in the right place.

In the blue-gray light I realized both Lilly and I were covered in blood.

But it was my blood.

My face leaked it like a sieve down my chest. I coughed out a mouthful, the coppery tang assaulting my tongue and throat. Little sensation beyond a pulsing throb in the periphery of my skull.

My fingers almost numb.

I staggered to my feet. The ground was tilted to one side, angled front to back like a ski hill. Blue strips of lights illuminated the floor to each side of the aisle. To balance myself I gripped the divider wall.

To my left, a small Latino businessman groaned and looked up. He was strapped into his seat. Arms and legs and head intact.

All the pods around me looked whole.

The bins overhead gaped open with debris and bags haphazardly strewn about the cabin. I was the only one standing up. A few heads visible over the dividers. Behind me, beyond where the galley had been, I couldn't see clearly…but…a dark mass of twisted angles and metal, as if the front of the aircraft had crumpled inward.

"Don't move," I said to Lilly. "I'm going to get help."

I said the words without thinking. Automatically. *We need help. Someone can help.* More than that, I had to know if we were safe here. Sort and prioritize. Should we exit the aircraft? Were we on land? Were we sinking?

That last thought stopped me in my tracks.

Shivering, I fumbled with a small door to the side of Lilly's pod. I'd watched the safety briefing Suzanne gave before we took off. Always did. I made sure I knew where the exit rows were. The small door swung open. I reached in and found it. The life jacket.

I put it around Lilly's neck—giant-sized on her. "Keep it on your head, okay? Don't touch it."

Shaking uncontrollably, she managed to nod.

Should I find one for myself? *In a minute. I need more information.* My own terror submerged under a priority to protect.

That loud whining noise was definitely not inside my head. It was coming from the back of the cabin. Four rows back the curtains that divided the sections flapped. There was an exit row back there, right behind the curtains.

Had someone opened it? Did we need to get out?

I took in another deep lungful of air. It tasted…hard, somehow, with an acrid stench of burnt plastic—insulation?—and a whiff of high octane…*Jesus Christ*…jet fuel.

Fire?

Adrenaline spiked again into my bloodstream.

I took a step to the back.

"Daddy, Daddy, no!" Lilly stretched out her arms and squealed.

"Stay here a sec—"

"Daddy, please, please, please."

Without another word I leaned back down and unstrapped her and she wrapped her arms so tight around my neck she almost strangled me, her legs almost as tight around my body. My left arm was useless. I didn't resist her but I staggered forward and reached out with my right hand to each divider to stabilize. In the next pod down, the large flat-faced Chinese man was unstrapping himself.

"Are you okay?" I asked.

He ignored me and turned in his seat to raise his body over the divider. His son was in the next seat. I managed one more step toward the divider curtains. The man's son looked unhurt.

The kid's eyes met mine. He looked calm somehow. Maybe terrified. The man yelled something in Chinese and the boy answered quietly. I shuffled another step.

The homeless-Viking kid in the frayed army jacket was in the next pod.

"You okay?" I repeated.

He nodded in mute response.

I repeated the process the next two pods down to the rear galley of First Class. Lilly clung tight to me and shivered. A flight attendant sat in the jump seat. She looked unconscious, her head sagged forward. Two of the heavy carts had wrenched free of their moorings and lay piled atop each other amid scattered bags of chips and soda cans.

An exit row to my right. The door closed and latched. A breeze blew open the curtains five feet in front of me past the folded-open door of a bathroom. I shuffled forward, almost slipped on the wet carpet. I pushed aside the curtains.

Tried to comprehend what I was looking at.

A pale blue band of light in the distance. Overhead a twist of angry frayed metal of the ripped fuselage. Torn open like an exploded tin can.

I stared into open space where the back of the aircraft had been. The indigo sky overhead melted into washed-denim blue with high pink clouds over the horizon. A still and alien landscape pierced only by a roaring whine.

I looked left.

Two hundred feet away? Three hundred?

A massive structure rose up from a blue-white sheet. An angular shape tilted upward at twenty degrees, a knife edge that blotted out a slash of the twilight sky. A wing. At its base the oblong shredded fuselage of the back half of the aircraft.

A third of the way along the wing, the huge circular hole was an engine. The noise emanated from it. The turbine screaming as if we were at forty thousand feet.

A wide blue-black gash in the gray sheet between us and the other part of the plane. I gripped onto the metal divider wall with my right hand and looked down.

Water.

Chunks of ice floated in water by my feet. A twenty-foot gulf of black water between me and blue-white ground.

Not ground.

Ice.

I backed up a step so fast I slipped and fell onto my rear, cursing as I tried to keep myself upright with Lilly. I dug the fingers of my right hand into the thin carpet, but then slid down again toward the freezing chasm.

"I got you." A strong hand grabbed the back of my shirt and twisted and lifted.

I scrambled upright with Lilly clinging to me. One of my socked feet had slipped into the frigid water but nothing more. I realized I didn't have shoes on.

"Thank…thank you," I stuttered and gripped onto the galley wall while Lilly gripped onto me. She was too terrified to even acknowledge anyone else.

The man's white shirt almost glowed. Thin tie. Glasses. It was the guy with the tortoise-shell eyeglasses from the lineup, the one who let us ahead of him.

"Gotta keep your feet dry and warm, that's key," he said. "Get back up and find your shoes. Bundle up your little girl."

"What happened?" I said.

"We crashed."

He said it matter-of-factly, but then what was there to say? My question wasn't really a question.

Straight in front of us—where the plane had impacted—was an undulating and shattered mosaic of white shards of ice between dark water in a trail that stretched into the murky distance. Scattered around us was debris and dozens—hundreds?—of multi-colored rocks.

Not rocks.

Suitcases.

The airplane had ripped open and disgorged its contents. A sharp breeze pierced my numbness. A painful biting cold in my fingers and face. The wind cut knife-like through my cotton shirt. Puffing clouds of white disappeared on each breath.

The ghostly blue moonscape around us was the ice and snow. We'd hit the ice pack.

We were *on* the ice pack.

TRANSCRIPT AUDIO 2
National Transportation Safety Board.
Mid-Flight Disappearance of Allied 695,
Boeing 777, NTSB/AIR.
Washington, DC

S hould I put a new one in?" Peter asked.

The first recording tape had ended. They did physical recordings rather than digital. Standard operating procedure—SOP—was to back those up again in magnetic tape, and *then* copy to digital, but an original physical recording was harder to change and mess with after the fact.

Richard replied, "Let's keep going."

He got up and changed the spool, pressed record, and went to get another cup of coffee. No windows in this conference room, but his body sensed the sun going down outside. Past seven at night.

"So it crashed on the ice. I could have guessed that," Peter said.

"We're not in the business of making guesses."

"I'm saying it had to come down somewhere. From Matthews's description, it was within the Arctic Circle. Makes sense from what we can piece together from radar data."

Richard sat back down. "Sounds like there was an explosive decompression. There were five hundred pounds of lithium batteries transported in the hold. That's not within NOTOC hazmat limits for the US."

"It is for China."

"Not for US flights. Can you look into who authorized that?"

"Will do. Mitch did a detailed job on describing the accident. He must have had a lot of time afterward to write all this down. So if the plane tore in half on impact..."

"And didn't ignite," Richard added.

"Had to be half full of fuel, at least at cruising altitude. So they must have dumped it." Peter scribbled some notes. "Ballpark dump rates for triple-sevens are five to six-thousand pounds a minute, so a hundred thousand pounds would take twenty minutes."

"Which doesn't make sense," Richard said.

"How so?"

"If we believe this narrative, means someone landed it. Ninety-eight percent chance they went gear up to get down on ice. If they had time to dump fuel—twenty minutes, as you say—then whoever was piloting would have gone through the crash landing procedures: notify flight attendants, briefing of passengers on life vests, getting everything stowed, telling passengers with dentures to take them out, you know the routine...and at a minimum, at fifty feet the BRACE, BRACE, BRACE command. From Mitch's account, none of that happened."

"Maybe they didn't have time."

"But they had twenty minutes to dump fuel? Do we have a recent psych profile of Captain Joshua Martin?"

Peter leafed through his papers. "I'll have to check with Allied."

"I think maybe we need to interview his family."

"You know how that will look?"

"There was no activation of the emergency transponder from the flight deck."

Peter said, "Maybe it was the Russians who shot them down."

Richard closed his eyes, pressed his palms into them and sighed. "Wouldn't be the first time they took down a commercial airliner, but then where is the wreckage?"

"You think maybe..."

"Captain Martin? A suicide grudge?"

"Also wouldn't be a first time," Peter said. "I'll get his files, look for anything on alcohol and drugs, get the psych reports. If what Mitch Matthews wrote down is true, then Captain Martin was already breaking the rules."

Richard scanned the notebook. "I'll keep reading…"

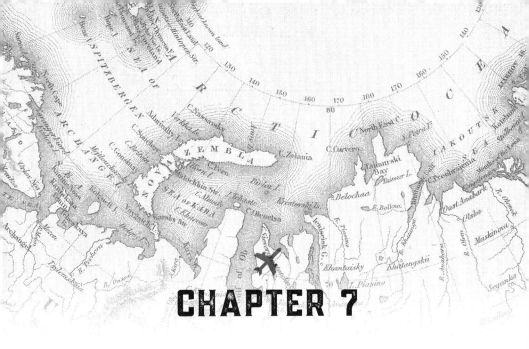

CHAPTER 7

The tortoise-shell eyeglass man said, "You okay?"
He held me upright by the scruff of my neck, with Lilly clinging
to me. He was surprisingly strong. At the check-in counter, all I had
noticed was his cool outfit. Now I saw muscles bulging under his white
buttoned-up shirt.

"Think I broke my nose." I couldn't feel it. Couldn't feel much of
anything.

"She okay?" He said more softly.

Lilly's arms tightened around my neck, her body shivering. I
nodded.

"Nothing else? How's your head?"

"Ringing."

"Mine, too. Goddamn miracle."

"Miracle?"

"That we're alive. Otto. Name's Otto Garcia." He let go of me slowly,
made sure I had my balance.

"Mitch Matthews." I didn't risk letting go of the galley wall to shake
hands.

"And your little one?"

"Lilly."

"Nice to meet you, Lilly." Otto ducked his head to try and catch her eye, but she kept her face buried in my neck.

I felt one of her fingers tickling the skin of my shoulder. She traced a letter. A skin sign. Back and forth. An "S". She was scared. Of course she was scared.

"It's okay, Lillypad, we're safe," I whispered. "Don't need to be scared."

"Okay, Mitch," Otto said. "I'm going to need you to get back up and take care of your little girl."

I nodded. He didn't need to tell me, but it helped somehow.

There was only so much the adrenaline could mask. Dipping my head sent shooting pain through my neck. I grimaced. My hands—my whole body—shook, and only half from the cold. Shock started to set in. A dull throb blossomed in the back of my skull and lanced into my temples. Did I have a concussion? Internal bleeding?

"Mitch, hey, Mitch, stay with me," Otto said.

"I'm okay...I'm just...ah..."

"Keep focused. Your little girl is depending on you. Get back up there and look through the overheads, empty all the bags and find anything you can to put on. Loose layers. Get something on your feet and around your neck and head. Wrap your little one up. She's small and loses heat faster. Once you and your girl are comfortable, see what you can do to help everyone else. Group them together to share body warmth."

"Okay." I checked my watch. 10:55 p.m. Hong Kong time.

"I'm going to make sure we're stable," Otto said. "See what the situation is. I'll see what I can retrieve down here, find out what supplies we have and do a first check for the injured."

"Okay, okay."

I started back up the aisle, glad someone was taking charge. I grabbed what handholds I could with my right hand, struggling with Lilly with my left. My socked foot was sopping wet and painfully cold. Tiny LED lights had come on in the ceiling, not the gentle mood lighting, but hard white pinpoints casting everything in monochromatic shades.

I passed the homeless-Viking kid two pods down from our seats. He was strapped in, his fists clenched.

I'd read that in accidents some people sprang into motion while others were rendered almost catatonic. Maybe it was the rapid shift in circumstance, like entering a room with people you didn't know. It took time for the brain to assimilate the new information, for fear of the unknown to subside enough for action to begin. If we had sunk under the waves, the people still in their seats would all be dead by now.

"What's happening?" Homeless-Viking asked.

"Back half of the plane ripped away—"

"The *back* half?"

"Tore away. It's a few hundred feet away over the ice. Goddamn miracle." *Calm down. Calm down.* "My name's Mitch."

A beat of silence before he responded, "Bjorn."

The small Latino man in the seat across from Lilly was on his feet now. "Are we sinking?"

"I think we're stable." I used Otto's words. "We're on the ice."

In the middle of the aisle in front of me, the man who'd crashed into the ceiling on the way down was inert on the floor. A blond woman was bent over him.

"On my god, oh my god, oh my god," she whispered, and then in a louder voice, "Is anyone a doctor? Can someone help?"

"I'm a…I can help," answered a voice from the other side of the cabin. It was the red-haired woman.

I climbed up the incline to our seats and deposited Lilly into her pod. She resisted and fussed and squirmed, but I talked to her softly and said it was okay and stroked her hair and kissed her forehead, told her to close her eyes. I bundled her up in the down blanket we'd been given, but she shivered from the cold. Wheezed.

What was the temperature? Freezing. *Below* freezing.

I hauled myself into my pod and found my bag. I had an extra shirt in there I was going to change into upon arrival. I leaned over the pod wall and gave it to Lilly, told her to put it on. I gave her my own blanket and foam mattress padding and wrapped her up in that as well. Retrieved my shoes, pulled off my sopping wet sock and replaced it with one from my bag, pulled off my shirt to put a t-shirt under it.

The frigid air stung my bare flesh.

When I pulled the t-shirt down, it came away with a dark smear of blood from my face.

I had some extra sets of socks—had to throw them in my carry-on after forgetting to pack them in my checked luggage—and some boxer shorts in the bottom of my bag. *Lucky.* I laughed. Sure, lucky. After thinking for a second, I leaned over Lilly and pulled one leg band of the boxers around her head, fashioned them into a kind of hat and gave her the socks to wear on her hands.

I gave her the puffer.

"Only use if it gets really bad," I said. "You understand?"

I retrieved my phone from the front pocket of the seat and turned on its light. It worked. I put it in my pant pocket.

Thankfully, the nose of the plane was angled up, so the seats were angled back to create a safe cradle to lie in.

"I'm going to look around," I said to Lilly. My teeth chattered and I clenched my jaw to stop them. "See if anyone needs help. You'll be able to see me, I won't go far."

Her eyes were barely visible under my boxer-shorts-headgear, her face ringed by the yellow-gray plastic of the life jacket. At first she shook her head but then she nodded.

"That's my big girl."

By my feet was a leather gym bag and a ballistic-shelled carry-on. I lifted them up. "Are these anybody's?"

When no one answered I took it as an implicit invitation to proceed. The gym bag had another t-shirt which I pulled on, and a long sleeved shirt that was too small for me. A pair of thick socks which I put over my hands.

The carry-on was full of women's clothing. This had to be someone's from the cabin, but I needed something right now. I counted at least six women in seats nearby. I put it aside, but then thought better of it and grabbed two pairs of black yoga pants—one I tied around my head and covered my ears, the other I pulled around my neck.

If anyone asked I'd return them.

The cold was intense.

I fished the life jacket from the side door of my pod and put it around my neck.

"I thought you said we weren't sinking," said the Latino guy in the seat next to me. He had found a few new layers of clothing as well.

"I said I *think* we're not." I turned to the red-haired woman who knelt over the unconscious man in the aisle. "How's he doing?"

"Not good." Her accent was French. "Can you help me move him into a seat? My name is Isabelle."

"Mitch." In the next aisle over there was an empty seat right beside Isabelle's. "Over there?"

As gently as we could, we turned the man over. His face black with blood. His wife—I assumed his wife—cried and tried to cradle him.

Isabelle took his feet while I lifted under his arms and we waddle-stepped through the galley to the aisle on the other side.

Halfway through I saw Suzanne, our flight attendant. Her jump seat had been almost cut in half by a metal sheet protruding from the front of the aircraft. I'd never seen a dead person before, but there was no way she wasn't.

Further up the aisle I glanced again to where the flight deck was.

A mass of twisted metal. No way anyone survived that. Jesus Christ. Josh. I'd been chatting with him what seemed like minutes ago. Now he was gone. My wife's brother. *My* brother-in-law. It didn't make any sense. His kids. My God.

I edged myself to the empty pod to deposit the man onto the bed.

"Hey, no, *nyet.*" The asshole with the flashy cufflinks stumbled toward us from a corner of the galley. One arm had a pile of blankets, and the other wrapped around a full white garbage bag. "That my seat."

"Are you serious?"

"Get out." The man barged past us and shoved me back and slumped into his seat.

"*C'est pas possible,*" Isabelle whispered, and then louder, "Use my seat, *la*, right behind."

We maneuvered into the next pod and deposited the bleeding man.

I took a long look at the asshole, who busily arranged the blankets he'd found around himself. The white bag he'd taken from the galley was full of chocolate bars and chip packets and water bottles. *What the f—*

"Hey, come look," someone yelled from the back of the cabin.

I checked Lilly on the other side of the cabin. A woman from two seats up that I'd checked on earlier had come to sit with my daughter. The two of them looked at me and the woman waved. I nodded back—that was fine, my nod said. "Lilly, are you okay?"

She nodded a tiny nod.

The voice again called out from the back of the plane, "Hurry up, come and look!"

My pulse sped up. Was it a rescue? Already?

CHAPTER 8

"Come on, come and see!"

I stepped down the inclined aisle toward the back of the cabin. Easier this time with my sneakers on. The throbbing in my head was getting worse.

I cleared the curtains. Open sky greeted me.

Twenty feet away on the ice two people stood and waved me forward. The black gap of water at the edge now had some sort of bridge across it. Galley carts pushed onto their sides and stacked end to end.

"Water's not deep," Otto said.

He was one of the men on the ice. Neither of them had life jackets around their necks.

"Did you see a plane?" I remained where I was. "A helicopter?"

"Look," said the other man.

I recognized his frayed army jacket. It was Bjorn, the homeless-Viking kid. He pointed at the horizon toward the left of the still-undulating-waves of the wrecked sheet of ice. "It's the sun."

A thin band of blue-white sky. A tiny glimmer of brilliant gold.

"You know what that means?" Bjorn said, his accent halfway between Scandinavian and British.

He had a wool hat on, and with the bushy beard and boots looked like he'd stepped out of my Arctic explorer book. My brain had a scattered thought: *Had he planned to be here on the ice?* Who the hell would have a wool hat and boots in their carry-on coming from Hong Kong?

I held up one hand and tried to soak some warmth from the cold rays. "Is someone coming?"

"It means we are somewhere south."

"South?"

"Not at the North Pole. The sun won't rise there for another six months."

"So where are we?"

"Somewhere south of the North Pole."

"Isn't everywhere south of the North Pole?"

"What I think he means," Otto said, "is that we're quite a bit south, toward the Arctic Circle somewhere."

Quite a bit south? From what I could tell, they stood on a twenty-foot-thick slab of ice.

"We've got variations in light and dark," Bjorn said. "If we were at the Pole, the bright spot on the horizon would circle three hundred-sixty degrees without changing appearance. This is good."

"This is *good*?"

"And we're on ice," Bjorn added. "Which means we're not east of Greenland or near Russia." The way he said 'Russia' he almost spat the word out. "We must be straight along our flight path, maybe near Canada. They have bases up here."

Bases.

When I was in the flight deck with Josh, I'd seen a Russian airbase. That was what Josh said. The October Revolution. Maybe this wasn't an accident? The sudden decompression, the rushing wind. Had it been a bomb? Terrorists? Or had a missile hit us? Had we been shot down out of the sky on purpose?

I shivered and considered the galley-cart bridge. It looked stable enough. I rubbed the plastic of the life jacket around my neck and took a step. Two more and I was out on the ice. I paced out another careful twenty feet and turned around.

For the first time I saw the whole thing.

There was a ridge of ice rising up thirty feet from the sheet, looked like an iceberg frozen into it. The nose of the plane had collided with it and flattened the flight deck. We'd come to rest against this. It was why the cabin was tilted back.

About fifty feet to either side were cracked edges of ice and gulfs of black water between us and the next ice sheet. Our floe was maybe three or four hundred feet in length, from what I could judge, maybe a hundred and fifty wide.

The almost-full moon was near the front of the crumpled nose of the aircraft. The moon was about the same angle into the sky as I'd seen it out my window a few hours ago. It hung in the purple-blue but starless sky.

I scanned for Venus.

Nothing. Just the moon, and a speck of the sun fighting to rise. The sky went from baby blue near the sun to indigo on the opposite horizon.

Three hundred feet away on another platform of ice, separated by at least fifty feet of black water, was the back of the 777. One engine and wing attached to that part of the fuselage. No sign of the other wing or engine. Something moved in the darkness at the edge of the aircraft's shattered hull.

Not something—but some*one*.

Bjorn waved and yelled a greeting. They waved back, called out something we couldn't understand before disappearing back inside the wrecked hull. So there were survivors in the rest of the plane.

Otto said, "We didn't explode into flames on impact. Nothing at all. Don't smell jet fuel, not much anyway."

"Is that lucky?" I said.

"Wasn't luck. We were only halfway through the flight. Had to be a hundred thousand pounds left, so someone must have jettisoned it. Means the pilots *tried* to land."

"But we came down on ice and water."

"Still would have burst into flames—that much damage, and a wing torn off?"

"What do you mean, they *tried* to land?"

"They had some control. Wasn't an uncontrolled descent, otherwise we wouldn't be having this conversation."

I considered that for a few seconds. "So they had time. To radio."

"Priority is to get control of the aircraft before communicating. Doesn't look like they had control."

"I thought you said they did?"

"I said *some*."

"How do you know so much about flying?"

"Had some experience with it."

"How long do you think it will take them to get here?"

"Who's 'them'?"

"Rescuers. Coast Guard. I don't know."

Was there even a Coast Guard up here? Whose coast exactly? Massive icebreakers could get into this, couldn't they? Planes? Could they land on snow and ice? If they had skis or something?

"We're thousands of miles from anywhere inhabited."

"But they must know we're here?"

Otto said, "I don't know if there's radar coverage this far north."

"But there's like"—I searched for the right word—"transponders or something in the plane? You can't lose an aircraft like this."

Nobody answered.

Bjorn said, "They will search along our flight path."

I paused before saying, "We were two hundred miles off course before the crash."

"How do you know that?"

"I was in the flight deck before we came down. The pilot is my wife's brother." Probably dead brother now.

"You were in the flight deck?" Otto took a step toward me. "That's not supposed to be allowed anymore, is it?"

I didn't reply.

"What did you see?"

"The sky. Not much. My daughter wanted to go."

"Anything else?"

"The relief crew came in. We hit some turbulence. Josh said there was a polar hurricane."

"Josh?"

"My wife's brother."

"Hurricane?" Bjorn said.

"That's what he said."

"That's all you saw?" Otto said.

"I don't know. I fell asleep."

Bjorn said, "Your brother-in-law. Did you go and look? Up front?"

I realized that I hadn't. Maybe Josh wasn't in the flight deck. He'd been relieved. That's right. Maybe he was in the back. I looked over the ice at the other half of the aircraft.

Otto shook his head. "I had a quick inspection. They look dead. Four of them."

"Four?" I said. "There were *four* people in the flight deck? All pilots?"

"Couldn't tell if they were all pilots."

I closed my eyes and tried to remember. When we were up front with Josh, he said it was forty minutes to the Pole. The relief crew came in and we went back to our seats. I checked the IFE as we slid over the pole, then Suzanne said there was major turbulence, and…I fell asleep.

So why were that many crew up in the flight deck together for more than an hour? Maybe both pilots went back up front for some reason.

"Something must have gone wrong," I said.

Bjorn snorted. "No kidding."

A gust of wind blew a sheet of hissing ice crystals around our feet. I wrapped my arms tight around myself. I couldn't stand out here for much longer. Then again, where else was there to go? The only way to get warm was back in the shattered cabin.

And was it my imagination, or had a foot or two of the plane slid into the water since I first came out here?

"Stay in place," Otto said. "Secure shelter. Those are the priorities for cold weather accidents. Keep your feet warm and dry, and get on as many layers of loose clothing as you can. And water. We need to do an inventory of fresh water we have available. Make sure that hoarder asshole doesn't grab everything."

He leaned over to grab two suitcases by his feet. The ground was littered with them.

"Take as many as we can. We'll empty them out and use the clothes to keep warm, see what else we can find. Batteries, light, food. Stack the bags into the gap and cut off the wind. The higher we stay in the cabin, the better we'll trap warm air. Doesn't look like it's sinking."

I wasn't so sure.

▼▲▼

After a head count of survivors in our section, for three hours we collected everything we could find on the ice around us. The guy from the seat next to me—he introduced himself as Manu Bermudez—came to help, as well as two women, Ling and Gerarda. The rest stayed inside.

We worked in shifts, in pairs—buddy system, Otto said, for safety—stopping every half an hour to warm up at the top of the cabin. Everyone wore life jackets around their necks.

Scattered among the bags were six bodies still strapped into their rows of seats. Otto checked them. None of them alive. We gently disentangled them from the wreckage and stacked them by the front of the plane. Otto took their wallets and personal effects.

But someone had survived.

On another ice floe, two hundred yards back in a jumble of debris, a whining sound. Crying. There was no way we could get to them across the open water.

At first we strategized about building a bridge, but the cold bit into our fingers and toes until we couldn't feel them. Dropping into the frigid water would be a death sentence. I did my best to ignore the pleading cries, but the incoherent whining tore deep into me.

Was it someone's wife? Husband? Tears froze on my eyelashes. Someone's daughter? Little girl?

Bjorn estimated it was only five to ten below freezing. About twenty Fahrenheit. Not too cold, he'd said, but I didn't agree.

The sun didn't clear the horizon. Its disk never fully rose, and at about 3:30 a.m. on my watch the last of it slid away beyond view. Barely three hours of glancing rays. It wasn't a sun-rise-and-sun-set, more like a white-bellied whale turning over in the far distance.

No signs of any rescue crews. No planes. Nothing in the sky. Dead silence pierced by a heartbreaking whimpering that eventually died down.

I was exhausted. Beyond exhausted.

After doing our best to seal the gaping hole of the open fuselage, I climbed into the pod-bed with Lilly, into a nest of clothes we'd scavenged from the bags. I'd left her alone for too long, and needed to be close to my daughter, to hold her for a while.

Three hours of sun? I checked my watch again. Three-forty-five. We were supposed to be landing in New York right now.

▼▲▼

"Help, come and help me," a woman's voice called out. "He's alive."

"Who's alive?"

In my dream, I was sitting with my wife at the kitchen table before we left that morning. Having hot coffee.

"The pilot," said the voice.

That wasn't Emma's voice. I opened my eyes. Shadows against shadows. I realized Lilly was wrapped up in my arms, fast asleep. She wheezed as her lungs tried to take in a breath.

The dream became a nightmare.

"Please. Come. Help me." The voice gained pitch. A French accent. That was Isabelle's voice.

I did my best to turn my head, but shooting pain lanced down my spine. "What's wrong?"

"Your brother," Isabelle said from the darkness. "Your brother-in-law Josh, he's alive."

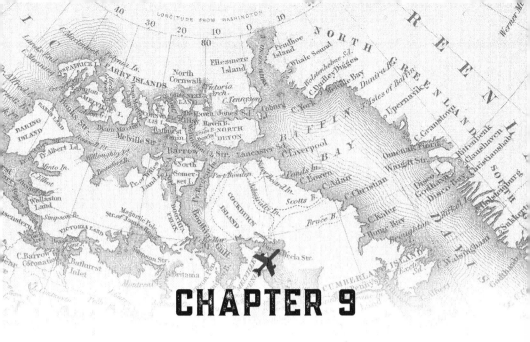

CHAPTER 9

"J osh, can you hear me?"

We carried his body as gently as we could and placed him in my pod bed. Without any electrical power, Otto ripped the seat into the flat position and propped it up on some bags. Josh's legs flopped as if they were made of string. A bone protruded through his shirt on his left arm. His face a mass of congealed blood.

But he'd opened his eyes.

The blond-haired man had died a few hours ago, and Bjorn and Isabelle had carried his body out onto the ice. They'd decided to do the same with Suzanne's body and the flight attendant from the rear galley. Then they'd gone and pried fully open the flight deck door. They'd been trying to extricate Josh's body when he screamed in pain.

"Josh," I repeated. "Can you hear me?"

I had my phone's LED light on.

One of his eyes was swollen shut, but the other fluttered open.

"Mitch? Mitch, don't…the crew…"

His eye closed.

"What did he say?" Otto hovered next to me, so close he squeezed my body into Josh's.

"Back up a bit," I said.

Isabelle was next to me, with Manu and Bjorn crowded around as well.

"He said something about the crew," said a dark-skinned young man from ten feet away.

I hadn't talked to him yet. He'd stayed in his seat. It was the guy who had joked about the 777 being connected to his laptop's Bluetooth before we took off. The twenty-year-old kid with the circular glasses.

"He needs some water," Isabelle said. She had a finger to his neck. "Pulse is very weak."

Otto stood up straight and squeezed out of my pod. "Hey, who's got some water?"

"What can we do?" I said to Isabelle.

Her hands trembled as she felt down Josh's body. "He's got internal injuries. I don't...I can't do much. Keep him hydrated. There's some Prednisone in the kit. Maybe bring down inflammation. Treat the pain." She'd found the emergency medical kit earlier. "I'm not really a doctor."

"Tell me anything—"

"Hey, do not touch!" someone growled.

It was the asshole in the pod in the next aisle over. Otto had a bottle of water in his hand, but the guy had gotten up out of his seat and was trying to grab it back.

"I need it." Otto tried to push the guy back, but he was huge.

Fat but with muscle beneath. A real Russian bear.

"Get your own." He grabbed the bottle and tore it from Otto's hand. "This mine."

"One of the pilots is alive. I need some water."

"There is more up front."

"Are you serious? He could die."

"Who put you in charge?"

The Russian stood a good foot taller than Otto, but the smaller man didn't back down.

Otto said, "I was a Navy SEAL. I know how to keep people alive.

And I don't see you helping."

"I help myself. And I was GRU. Not impressed. Go find your own water."

"*Christ*," Otto muttered under his breath, and then louder, "What's your name?"

"Roman."

"Otto. Roman, look, we need to work together."

"Go and get water from the galley," I yelled. "Hurry!"

Why hadn't I gone to check on Josh in more detail before? Tried to take a pulse? My brain was scrambled, one thing jumbling into the next.

"We need to share what we've got," Otto continued, ignoring me. He glared at Roman. "You can't hoard supplies."

The Russian sat back down without saying anything. Water still in hand.

Josh gasped and sucked in a raspy lungful of air.

"Can someone get some goddamn water?" I repeated.

▼▲▼

Josh didn't wake up again, but he didn't die.

"Will he be okay?" Lilly asked.

I had her wrapped up in my arms. The woman from the pod in front of me—Vera Zelenko she said when I asked her name—had been sitting with Lilly. We had taken out Lilly's coloring books, but it was too dark and the crayons too hard to hold with the sock-mitts. After a half hour of fussing I'd managed to get her to sleep, or at least to close her eyes and stay still, with her teddy.

Vera had lodged herself under Lilly's seat when I returned, and Bjorn and Manu joined her. It felt odd having unknown people so close, but it made sense to share body heat. On the other side of the cabin a few people had congregated around Roman, and there was another knot of people further down from them.

Otto said that human bodies gave off about a hundred watts of energy. The same as an old incandescent light bulb. Twenty six of us meant almost three thousand watts of heating power, and we had to trap it in the higher reaches of the cabin.

In the next seat across from us, however, the large Chinese man remained alone, with his chubby-cheeked son in his arms. They both seemed impervious to the cold.

The boy smiled at me again. Somehow the kid's calmness gave me relief.

"Is Uncle Josh going to be okay?" Lilly asked again. She wheezed in another breath.

"I don't know, honey. He's hurt pretty bad."

Normally, I tried to treat Lilly as a little adult, not as a child, and I expected the same from her—to treat adults and everyone else with respect. But under these extreme circumstances, I didn't want to overwhelm her. She was already terrified—as I was—but then again, I didn't want her to get careless.

She needed the right amount of scared, but not too much. I needed her to know we were safe, that there was a plan, but I also needed her to be on her guard. I needed her to be more adult than ever. A tough thing to ask of a five-year-old.

She paused before asking, "Is he going to...die?"

"People will be here soon. To help us."

After getting the water for Josh, I'd taken four bottles for Lilly and myself. I drank half a bottle before thinking I'd better conserve it. For Lilly. My headache throbbed dully. I'd tried taking a few ibuprofens I had in my carry on, but nothing seemed to help.

"Sweetheart, can you drink some more?"

"I'm not thirsty."

"Please?"

She gave me her grumpy look but opened the bottle and took a few sips. She'd almost finished the bottle I'd started. I had to make sure she stayed hydrated. "And eat a bit more of that granola bar?"

Another frown and she shook her head.

"Okay, but in a little while? Yes?"

I checked my watch. Past 10 a.m. Hong Kong time.

Twelve hours on the ice.

Six hours since we were scheduled to arrive. One way or the other, we were missed by now. They had to be coming for us. I listened for sounds of engines. Outside it had darkened, the bright patch on the horizon rotating to the right of the cabin and dimming to an azure blue.

The first stars had appeared. Polaris, the North Star, had shone straight overhead when I went out two hours before. My dad would have been proud, or at least not disappointed. I remembered the stars.

Polaris was within a degree of true north. I had stood out on the ice and watched it. Did it move in the sky? Not by much, but I couldn't stay long to observe.

The moon continued its lazy circulation—never setting, staying the same height in the sky—the fullness of it casting shadows over the ice. Bright enough to see by lunar light, although the light gave nothing an edge.

Lilly took in another wheezing breath.

"Baby, get your puffer. Where is it?"

"It's all used up."

A tingling prickled the base of my scalp and radiated into my fingertips. "You finished it? I told you—"

"I tried. I only used it twice. It's empty."

This time she really had to force it to get the breath in. Slowly suffocating. The air was freezing. A flare up? Goddamn it, why didn't I go to the pharmacy before we got on? I wish we had something—

I sat upright.

"Daddy, are you okay?"

I began to unwrap myself from the folds of blankets and clothes. "Stay here."

After doing my best to step over the people around us—they weren't sleeping anyway—I retreated to my pod next door.

I held my ear next to Josh's mouth. Still breathing. I clicked on my phone's light and located the medical kit Isabelle had brought over, opened it up and scanned the foam packaging at the top.

Two vials of adrenaline were missing—three remained—and the Lorezepam bottle was gone. Something called Haldol was gone, too… and…damn it. At the bottom corner was an empty L-shaped space with *Ventolin* marked underneath.

"Everything all right?" Bjorn whispered.

He'd followed me when I got up.

"Did you see who took this stuff out of the medical kit?" I held it up.

He shrugged. "Isabelle was working on that guy earlier." The one who died, he didn't need to add. "She's asleep." He pointed to the other side of the cabin next to Roman.

"What are you guys doing?" It was the dark-skinned young man.

He had skin like chocolate and tight curls of black hair visible beneath two or three pairs of women's tights wrapped around his head that pinned his wire-framed glasses to him. "Is he alive?" he whispered.

"What's your name?" I asked.

"Howard." He extended his hand.

I shook it. "Mitch, and this is—"

"Bjorn. I know." Howard squatted in the aisle. "Is he alive?"

He meant Josh. "As far as I can tell."

I sat down on the floor as well, felt the frigid metal beneath the carpet.

"Your brother-in-law did a good job," Howard said. "He was strapped into the pilot seat. He must have been the one that got us down."

I didn't know why Josh was in the flight deck a good hour after he was supposed to have been relieved, but I didn't say anything. "I guess he did."

"And we're lucky we're on the ice," Bjorn said. "Twenty years from now, there won't be any ice here. It'll be blue Arctic. You'll be able to kayak to the Pole."

Howard snorted. "Seriously? The Earth's usual state is no icecaps.

Most of the last hundred million years there's been no ice up here."

"Yeah, but what's happening now isn't natural," Bjorn countered, his voice a low whisper.

"Not natural? You're saying humans aren't natural? That we're outside of nature?"

"You know what I mean." Bjorn's voice gained in volume.

Howard didn't miss a beat. "There's no evidence that what's happening now isn't part of a natural cycle—"

"Guys, seriously?" I had to stop them. "You are *seriously* having an argument about climate change right now?"

"He started it," Howard said.

I asked, "Do you guys know each other?" Who had Bjorn been talking to before we left? Wasn't it Roman?

"Never met before," Bjorn said. "I was saying it's good we landed on ice. The polar ice pack is at the annual minimum right now. Not much of it left in summer. Ice this thick means we're within ten degrees of the Pole, somewhere toward the Western hemisphere. I mean, chances are. I guess there's still some ice sheets toward Russia."

Howard seemed like he wanted to add something. His head bobbed up and down for a few seconds before he said, "And that's what I wanted to talk to you guys about."

"What?" I asked.

"Our location." He pulled out a cell phone, keyed something into it and held it up to us. It was the map app.

I squinted to get a better look. "Does that say we're in Hamburg, Germany?"

"Obviously we're not, unless Hamburg has changed a lot since I was last there." Howard pulled out another phone and held it up. It had the same location on its app.

"Does GPS even work this far north?" I asked.

"No reason it shouldn't. These planes fly using it. Which is what worries me. What do you remember about the accident?"

I closed my eyes. "I came back from the flight deck—"

"When was that?"

"About half an hour before the Pole."

"Everything was normal?"

"Josh was in the process of changing over to the new flight crew."

"So why was he in the pilot chair?"

"I don't know."

"What else?"

"I watched a movie for a bit, then checked the IFE to see if we were over the Pole. It froze up. Stopped working."

Howard said, "The flight tracker was freezing up the whole way."

"And then I went to sleep."

"Me, too."

"Me, too," added Bjorn. "And then all hell. What are you getting at?"

Howard pulled a string with a small piece of metal attached from his pocket. "GPS satellites orbit at twelve thousand-six hundred miles up. More than halfway to geostationary. There's thirty one of them, and they all should be within thirty-odd degrees of the horizon. Easily line-of-sight visible from here. Maybe some issues with DOP—"

"Dee-ohh-what?"

"Dilution of precision due to high angle."

"How do you know all this?"

"I know stuff. Look, it's not just GPS." He fiddled with his phone some more, his face lit blue in the glow. "The iPhone and most Androids have been able to track Galileo satellites for a few years."

"Galileo?"

"European GPS system." He frowned like I was an idiot. He held up the phone. "Nothing. I tried using the GNSS app view to triangulate the satellites, but there's nothing there. Twenty four satellites in that constellation."

"I'm not following."

"That's fifty-five satellites that seem to have disappeared, as far as I can verify right now. I checked using my phones and two other people's. Same thing. I need to find someone with a Huawaei or Xiaomi—the Chinese manufacturers plug into the Beidou Chinese

GPS and Russian GLONASS positioning systems, but I'm betting all this isn't a coincidence. Have you been outside?"

"About an hour ago."

"What did you see?"

"A few stars. The brightest part of the twilight rotates around the horizon with the moon."

"What *didn't* you see?"

Howard held up the string with the metal attached to it. The tiny piece of metal rotated back and forth in front of our eyes. He waited but it was a rhetorical question. "Auroras. Did you see any auroras?"

The Northern Lights. The giant displays of light in the extreme northern skies. I'd never seen them with my own eyes, but was sure I'd recognize them. I'd seen them on TV. Had I seen any? I shook my head. Bjorn shook his as well.

"This is a magnet I scavenged from one of my old phones, from the little motor inside. You see, it just keeps spinning."

"A compass," Bjorn said. "You're saying that's a compass."

"Right. So either we're right on top of magnetic north…" The little piece of metal spun back and forth. "Or there's no magnetic field."

"Wait a second," I said. "What about the compass app?" I turned on my phone and swiped to a folder. I clicked the app and it opened—but it asked for access to our location first.

"You think I'm that dumb?" Howard held up his phone again. "Of course I tried the compass app, but how do you think it works?"

I hadn't really thought about it.

"You need a magnetometer in the phone for it to work. They used to have them in older models, but they got rid of it in newer ones. Yours doesn't have one. Neither does mine."

My compass app indicated that north was somewhere behind me.

"And mine says true north is that way." Howard pointed about forty-five degrees away from where my app said it was. "We can switch between true and magnetic north in the app, but they're working off differential GPS. Any of you have a phone three or four years old?"

I closed my compass app. I purchased this phone two weeks ago. Bjorn shrugged.

Howard added, "Even if GPS was working, we'd need to be moving to get a good direction signal, which usually isn't a problem."

He held up the spinning magnet attached to the string again. "Riddle me this. What could knock out fifty or a hundred satellites all at once—all over the planet—and bring down an airliner at the same time?"

Howard had a kind of manic intensity in his eyes. I wasn't sure if it was that, but hairs rose on the back of my neck. The kid sure knew his technical stuff, or did an awfully convincing job of it.

"I have no idea," I said after a pause.

"Magnetic field reversal."

Silence. Only the sound of the wind outside against the metal hull and someone snoring.

"I've been thinking a lot about it," Howard said. "Did you know that the north magnetic pole moved a thousand miles from Canada almost to Russia in the past twenty years? Something's been up, man. I think it happened. I think we had a magnetic field reversal."

"The *Earth's* magnetic field?"

"Yeah. I think it flipped. North to south. Or somewhere in between. No magnetic field means no Van Allen belts keeping us safe—we're bombarded by solar and cosmic radiation, man. Could have fried all those satellites, knocked down this plane. It happens every few hundred thousand years, regular as clockwork. Just never when humans had civilization before. Not when we had power grids and electronics."

"Explain to me," I said, "slowly, what that means? Exactly?"

"Means the whole electric grid out there is fried. No more grid, no more communications. Means humanity out there might have been thrown back into the Stone Age. Means nobody is coming to get us."

CHAPTER 10

*N*obody *is coming to get us.*
The thought circled around and around in my head in the darkness.

There wasn't much to do except wait, but were we waiting for something that wasn't coming? I'd gone into the galley and decided to do an inventory. They'd already gone through the second service before the crash but there were fifty-one half-frozen meals left, seventy-three bottles of water and ninety-six soda, and one garbage-sized bag of pretzel snacks. A tray of small bread buns. Twenty-two of them.

Not much to keep twenty-six people alive for long.

There were more people alive in the back section of the plane—across the open water between the ice—but so far we hadn't managed to talk to them. We had no idea what shape they were in or how many had survived. I couldn't imagine them having any more food or resources than us. I hoped they had a satellite phone or some communications with the outside world.

If the outside world still existed.

Howard had explained more. How the Earth's magnetic poles flipping would mean everything would be bombarded by naked solar radiation and how this could wreck power grids and electronics. I didn't even know the risk existed, didn't realize how vulnerable the global network was to something like this. Otto dismissed it, said that Howard was exaggerating, but the young man made a convincing argument—and Josh had mentioned something about the North Magnetic Pole acting up when we were in the flight deck..

I crept back into the nest of people cradled around Lilly. The best thing to do for now was keep warm and to think. It was all I could do, really, apart from check on Josh from time to time.

At least the LED strip lighting was on in this shattered part of the cabin. That meant batteries somewhere, right? How long would they last? At that thought, I switched off my own cell phone. Turned it off.

I laughed grimly to myself. Off. Not airplane mode.

My attempt to laugh ignited a fit of coughing that erupted into a thudding pain in my face. My nose was smashed off center, my sinuses clogged with blood and snot. Isabelle had tried to take a look at it, but I'd waved her off. Not important, I'd said. Painful, though.

I couldn't smell very much.

My left shoulder ached as well, but I'd regained some use of it.

No matter how many layers I tried to wrap around Lilly and myself, the cold seemed to seep in through every crack. I became obsessed with thinking of what we could light on fire. Some clothing? Maybe a seat cushion? But the soot of it would rise into the cabin and asphyxiate us. We needed a chimney.

Eventually all the circling thoughts came back to a central one. Armageddon. Was Howard right? Had the world out there been destroyed? What about Emma? What was happening out there? Why had nobody come for us yet?

I woke up to the sound of Lilly's wheezing.

"Sweetheart...?"

"Sorry, I was trying to be quiet."

"Keep your face under the covers, okay?" She needed to breathe air as warm as she could.

"Did you drink some more water?" I asked.

She nodded.

"Are you sure?"

She rolled her eyes but accepted the bottle from me and took a sip.

"And eat more of that granola."

"I'm not hungry."

"Lillypad, please? For me?"

She relented and fished out the bar and nibbled on it.

I checked my watch. 12:45 a.m. Hong Kong time. I'd been drifting in and out of fitful sleep for ten hours. Listening to Lilly's breathing the whole time. It was getting worse. A familiar woman's voice echoed on the other side of the cabin.

It took me five minutes of negotiating with Lilly until she let me slip from the blankets, telling her that I wouldn't go more than ten seconds away from her at any point. After I got out, I pulled on three pairs of jeans. The cold made them stiff.

Bjorn was gone from the floor near us. Otto looked up at me but didn't move. The big Chinese man and his little son seemed asleep. I checked on Josh. Shallow breathing but alive. I crept as quietly as I could to the other side through the front galley.

While our side of the cabin had congregated together in a bunch, the other side had kept separated in their individual seats. I found Howard on the other side, in an empty pod bed in front of Roman. Isabelle was talking to the Russian, but the moment they saw me they both went quiet. Roman had his face turned away from me, pretending to sleep.

"Isabelle, were you the one who opened the medical kit yesterday?" I asked.

She was wrapped head to foot like a caterpillar in a chrysalis, alone in her pod.

"Call me Liz. That's what my English friends use. It was up there."

Her chin flicked in the direction of overhead bins toward the front. "Next to the defibrillator. I administered an adrenaline shot and Toradol to the injured man."

"Did you take out the Ventolin inhaler?"

She shook her head. "I didn't touch it."

"Where did you open the med kit?"

With her head she indicated the pod Howard was asleep in. As quietly as I could, I crept into his area and clicked on my cell phone, turned on its light. I checked the floor, in the corners, in the aisle. I turned my phone back off.

"Was the inhaler in there when you opened the case?"

"I don't remember."

"And you didn't take it?"

She shrugged, again—no, she hadn't.

"How many of the adrenaline vials did you use?"

"One."

"There are two missing. I checked last night. You didn't use another one on Josh?"

"No."

"What's Haldol?"

Her pencil-thin eyebrows furrowed together. "An anti-psychotic."

"That's missing, too. And the Ativan and Valium." I'd looked. I could use some.

"Somebody is stealing the medical supplies?"

Was it really stealing? If someone needed them, that was fine—maybe—but everyone had heard Lilly wheezing. They knew she needed an inhaler. Who would make a child suffer?

"Hey," I said, and then louder, "Hey! Everyone. Wake up. Did anyone find an inhaler? Did anyone take anything from the medical kit? I don't care what happened, or maybe if you need it, too…but my little girl needs it."

Muted replies and mumbles around the cabin. Some whispers in other languages, I assumed asking for translation.

"So nobody has an inhaler? Nobody found one in a bag?"

More mumbles of nothing.

"Goddamnit…"

Past the curtains, twenty feet down the cabin from me, spots of light on the carpeted floor.

"Thanks, anyway," I whispered to Isabelle.

"I will keep the kit with me," she replied. "*Des maintenant.* From now on."

Why didn't I think of the emergency medical kit yesterday? Where else could I find an inhaler? I made my way down the aisle. Eyes followed me from occupied pods. I swept back the curtains. A wall of suitcases stacked to the ceiling greeted me. Through gaps in them, tiny dots of yellow.

▼▲▼

"I think that's sunrise," Bjorn said. "About an hour later than yesterday."

It was 1 a.m.

Sunrise had shifted a whole hour later in a single day. That was how far north we were. In another day it might not rise at all. Not for months.

A tiny sliver of gold at the horizon below a blanket of white above and below. The moon a bright patch behind high clouds opposite in the sky from the feeble sun. The moon circled, but lower over the horizon than the day before.

I'd come out on the ice by myself after putting on another two layers of sweaters and a second pair of socks over my hands. We hardly needed the galley-cart bridge anymore—a layer of ice had formed between the fuselage and surroundings. Maybe this would stop the backward slide of the cabin into the water?

I walked to the edge of our ice floe in the purple twilight and found a point as close as I could get to the other half of the aircraft. No motion over there the past few hours.

White boulders of ice like rocks strewn over the hard packed surface. It wasn't ice, but it wasn't snow either. It squeaked underfoot.

Bjorn had followed me out after I'd been staring at the other half of the plane for a few minutes. I scanned the horizon. Nothing but empty desolation as far as I could see, flat nothingness into a hazy distance where ice met sky.

From the corner of my eye I saw something move. "What the hell is that?"

About a hundred feet from us, at the edge of our ice drift, it looked like a pole bobbing up and down. Many poles, jabbing at the sky. Was it some part of the aircraft?

Bjorn looked where I was looking and said, "Those are narwhals."

▼▲▼

I couldn't resist the urge to go and get Lilly. I made sure she was bundled up, made sure we kept back from the edge of the ice, but I had to bring her out.

"Are they unicorns?" she said, her little eyes wide with wonder.

The massive dark speckled-white animals rose and fell in a seething mass in the gap between the ice floes, the single horn protruding from each of their heads longer than a human's body.

"They are whales," Bjorn said. He came out to stand beside us, a lifejacket around all our necks now. "The impact of the crash must have opened the ice up to make a big breathing hole for them. And we call that their tusk."

It was almost hypnotic to watch the huge mammals sliding up and down—dozens of them—their tusks needling into the Arctic sky. I held Lilly in my right arm. We'd only been outside for a few minutes, but both of us were already shivering.

The whining cry from the other ice floe started up again.

"We'd better go back," I said.

▼▲▼

I returned outside with Bjorn after tucking Lilly into bed.

The wind had picked up. The day before it had been dead calm, but now there were blustery gusts between a steady wind from the left of the aircraft—and a slow rolling motion under our feet that hadn't been there before. The horizon seemed to undulate.

The heart-rending whimpering sound drifted on the wind.

"It's not a person," Bjorn said.

"I know."

It had to be a dog, some poor animal trapped in a crate that had been disgorged with the rest of the luggage. That didn't make it any less heartbreaking to listen to. No way to get there. It almost made it worse. I couldn't stand animals suffering. How had it survived this long out on the ice?

The gap was narrowest here between the ice floes. Maybe twenty feet. The gray ice beneath our feet dropped about a foot into the black water, but which now was covered by a dark sheet of slick-looking ice.

"Is that jet fuel?" I said.

"That's called grease ice," Bjorn said. "So thin and smooth it looks oily in refracted light."

I looked at the other half of the aircraft. Two hundred feet away. The light dusting of snow around it disturbed by footprints. There weren't as many bags scattered on the ice near it as yesterday. Someone had been busy.

"Can we walk over the ice yet?"

"Doubt it's more than half an inch. *Maybe* an inch. Good news is that the water is quite calm. Nilas will form soon—"

"Nilas?"

"That's the next stage of ice formation. On calm water it doesn't granulate. Next few hours it should thicken at this temperature, but to get across we will need to distribute our weight. We need skis or snowshoes."

We hadn't found any of those. Not much use for that sort of equipment in Hong Kong.

"How do you know so much about ice?"

"I'm a climate researcher. I work for Greenpeace. Was on my way to a conference in New York."

"Researcher?" I let that sink into my brain for a second. "What do you think of Howard's theory?"

Bjorn rubbed his beard with one hand. "Fantastical, but, I don't have better ideas. Not yet."

"Is what he said true? About the magnetic north moving that much? About magnetic reversals in the past?"

"All true. A fast reversal of the magnetic field would cause havoc."

"Jesus…"

"Are you religious?"

"It's an…I don't know, I just say it."

"Would be a good time to be religious." He gazed across the chasm to the other ice floe. "I think we might be on the edge of the Odden Ice Tongue. The ice here is about five to ten feet thick. Maybe we are even in Norway. Probably Denmark."

"Denmark?"

"Greenland is owned by Denmark. They claim a good chunk of the Arctic all the way to the Pole. Same as Norway."

"I thought up here was all international"—I searched for the right word—"water? Land?"

"Up here, my friend, are oil and gas and resources beyond imagining. The Russians planted a flag on the North Pole sea floor a few years back to claim it for themselves. There's a big argument over what constitutes a continental shelf and who—"

"How can you tell how thick the ice we're standing on is?" Geopolitics didn't interest me right now.

Bjorn shrugged. "I only see about a foot above the water line. About fifteen percent of floating ice is above the surface, so I'd guess we are on seven foot ice."

"So how does that tell you we're on…this 'Ice Tongue'?"

"It's thicker than single year ice which tops out at five feet, and we're at the end of the minimum ice pack. The big ridge the front of the plane hit looks like captured drift ice. Much thicker. Might have saved us. A lot more buoyancy."

"Do you think we could use the suitcases as snowshoes?" I said. "Open up the big plastic-shelled ones and put a foot in each one? That would distribute the weight, right?"

"Take the empty ones and close them up, they would float. We could form a bridge maybe."

"Tie together some fabric to make ropes?"

"I wouldn't want to be the first one over, but sure. Maybe."

I stared at the other shattered half of the aircraft. "Shouldn't somebody have been here by now?"

Bjorn looked up. Dense white clouds. "Maybe they haven't seen us."

"Could we make a sign or something?"

"You mean like spell out 'HELP'?"

"The aircraft is white and covered by snow. Couldn't hurt, could it?"

"Not hurt, but in these clouds? Darkening twilight? Not sure. There has to be transponders."

"But what if Howard is right?"

"You mean, could we get out by ourselves?" The Norwegian laughed. "I have been to the North Pole. Did I tell you that before? We flew from Longyearbyen on Svalbard aboard a Russian Antonin An-74 to Barneo."

Somehow I wasn't surprised by this revelation. "Barneo?"

"It's a camp an enterprising Russian outfit sets up each spring at eight-nine degrees north. For tourists. Barneo is a joke—it means 'not Borneo.'"

"Antonin An-74…that's that huge transport?" I'd heard of it. The world's biggest airplane. That could land up here? The thought gave me hope. Tourist camps and massive aircraft landing strips made the landscape seem less alien and remote.

"You're thinking of the An-225. Not the same. The An-74 is smaller, specially designed for polar flying. The engines are on top and in front of the wings so the exhaust goes over the airfoil surface to increase lift for short take off. Clever. Russians are the masters of Arctic equipment. When we got to Camp Barneo in April it was minus forty, and we had to take a Russian Mi-8 military helicopter to our drop-in point. We wanted to ski the last hundred kilometers to the Pole ourselves."

"Hold on. You work for Greenpeace, and you flew First Class?"

Bjorn continued to stare straight ahead.

I asked, "Are there any other camps up on the ice? Like a North Pole Station? Is this Camp Barneo still there?"

He shook his head. "Trust me. We are not getting out of here by ourselves." He patted me on the back and walked away. "But I'm going to see about your idea. Make some sleds."

"Nobody goes out on the ice alone." Otto had come out. "Did you hear me?" He stood ten feet away as Bjorn passed him. "Buddy system, always a buddy system."

"Bjorn was with me."

"You were out here five minutes by yourself."

"I'm not going to fall in."

"That's not what I'm worried about."

"Hey, you're not wearing glasses?" I said to Otto. "Did you lose them?"

"I put in contacts. My glasses fog up in the cold."

Contacts? He managed to put in contacts in these conditions? I wrapped both arms tight around myself. Ten minutes and I couldn't feel my toes. My cheeks burned.

"Polar bears," Otto said after a pause. "That's why we use a buddy system."

A tingling in my scalp. I looked left and right. "You saw a polar bear?"

"Doubt you'd ever see one before it attacked you. Apex predators. This is their world."

"There are polar bears here?"

"Everywhere on the ice. They hunt seals, walrus, even whales. They're the largest land carnivores on the planet, a metric ton of claws and teeth and muscle. Not afraid of humans. Not afraid of anything. To them, you're lunch."

"What point is a buddy, then?" I looked around nervously again. How did everyone seem to know so much about the Arctic? Was it me who was ignorant?

I hadn't even imagined that we weren't alone out here in this desolation. Of all the ways to die, my most private terror was the thought of being *eaten* by something. Usually this involved nightmares of a giant shark. I couldn't wade into ocean deeper than waist-high without having an excuse to go back to my beach towel.

So far I'd been worried about keeping warm. But...polar bears? Come *on*.

"Safety in numbers. Bigger groups gives them something to think about. Maybe less aggressive—unless they're hungry, in which case, we're lunch and dinner."

▼▲▼

I hurried myself back inside. For two hours I scribbled notes in my journal while Howard meticulously taped together sheets of paper against the opposite wall of the cabin and constructed a polar-view map of the world. He'd found supplies in one of the bags we'd opened, and an LED flashlight that he said would last for hundreds of hours.

"We definitely flew over the Pole," Howard said. "Or fifty miles to the east of it, right?"

He pointed at me—I nodded and shrugged at the same time—then he used a marker to draw a dotted line past the right side of the North Pole on his map.

"Even if our plane's transponders aren't working," Howard continued, "there's gotta be radar coverage up here. Mitch, you said we passed a Russian airbase forty minutes before the Pole?"

I nodded and shrugged again. I didn't want to be sucked too far into Howard's orbit. Lilly wheezed in my arms. The chubby-cheeked kid had gotten out of his blankets with his dad and came to sit with us. The kid was snuggled beside me and had Lilly's hand in his. It seemed to calm her.

"Maybe the Russians are the ones that blew us out of the sky," Bjorn said.

"Maybe." Howard drew a fainter line forward on the map toward New York. "A straight path would take us toward Ellesmere Island in Canada. How long did we fly past the Pole?"

"I fell asleep," Bjorn said. "No idea."

I was asleep as well. How long, I wasn't sure.

"Me, too," Howard said. "But I don't see any land. We can't have reached Ellesmere."

"Horizon isn't more than ten miles, even from top of the ice ridge," Otto said.

"But they have to know where we are," Howard said. "It's not like that flight that went out over the Indian Ocean that nobody ever found. The north must be bristling with military radar."

"That's designed to detect ballistic missiles," Otto said. "Not commercial jets."

"How would that be different than bomber aircraft? Why is nobody here yet? We didn't even sink."

"Maybe it's some big fight between the Russians and us," I said. "But there's no way they'd leave a commercial jet full of civilians sitting on the ice to die…would they?"

"Nobody even knows we're alive."

"But they have to know we're missing."

Otto said, "Do you know how many times a commercial jetliner has been shot down on purpose?"

"On purpose? By military?"

"More than thirty times," Howard said. "Look it up on Wikipedia."

"I thought you said there was some magnetic anomaly—"

Otto groaned. "Stop with this magnetic anomaly thing. It's making a bad situation worse to start inventing more stuff to worry about, and we've already got—"

"Hello?" a voice called out.

Everyone froze in place like mannequins in a store window. The voice came from beyond the curtains. Out on the ice.

The unfamiliar voice called out again. "Hello? Is anyone there?"

CHAPTER 11

W e have two hundred and fifteen survivors but we're losing more every hour," the man said. "I'm the flight purser. We need help, anything we can get."

"Purser?" I said.

"The cabin manager. I'm in charge of the flight staff. Name is Adrian Petruchio. How many survived up here?"

"Twenty six."

Adrian advanced up the aisle to me and Otto. Most of the people in the cabin lay immobile. Their eyes followed the newcomer. A few people jumped out of their seats to follow him and ask questions, misshapen mounds of clothing converging like flies to meat. Adrian kept silent as he walked toward us. He assumed we were the ones in charge.

Even in the sub-zero conditions, a fetid aroma had spread through the cabin. We used the toilets, but there was no water to flush. Twenty-six people over a day and a half accumulated a lot of waste. Good thing we had four toilet stalls, and one mercy was that the cold kept it from festering. Otto said we better start going to the bathroom outside the front of the plane, but then that meant near the dead bodies stacked out there.

"Is there a rescue operation?" My heart felt like it leapt into my throat. "Did they contact you yet?"

Adrian held my gaze. "So you haven't heard anything?"

Silence for a beat before the man cursed under his breath.

The last glancing rays of sunshine had disappeared over the horizon half an hour ago. 3:30 a.m. The sky deep-cyan twilight.

I asked, "So you *didn't* talk to *anyone*?" even though I already knew the answer from the way his face creased up.

He asked, "Did any of the pilots survive up here?"

"Captain Josh Martin. He was the one flying when we hit. He was strapped into one of the flight deck seats. He's alive, but he hasn't been able to say anything yet. "

"Nothing?"

"Not about the accident."

"About what then?"

"He hasn't regained consciousness."

Adrian's face remained blank. "Did Suzanne tell you his first name?"

"She's dead."

In the waxy light and speckled shadows, I saw the way Adrian's facial muscles sagged. "Where is she?" His voice caught on *she*.

"With the others." Otto inserted himself between myself and Adrian. He sensed what I did and added, "Sorry, we didn't have time to do much more for her."

"He's my brother-in-law. Josh, I mean. That's how I know his name."

"Oh." Adrian's eyes narrowed. "Right. You're Mitch."

The way he said it, I was going to ask what he meant when Otto cut in again. "What did you hear in the back? What happened?"

"There was an explosive decompression—I think one of the rear doors blew out."

"How the hell did that happen?"

"No idea. Almost everyone was asleep, and the passengers near the back didn't survive."

"Do you have any Chinese phones?" Howard shuffled forward in the aisle and tried to press between myself and Otto. "I need to test some Chinese phones. Maybe some older models, ones with magnetometers in them? Do you guys have any GPS signal?"

Adrian replied, "You either?"

"Nothing. Do you have a Chinese cell phone?"

"Only my iPhone."

"I'm going to give you an Android." Howard took out a phone. He said he sideloaded an application into it. "Use the FireChat app. Connect to my network. We can chat using Wifi—I've got a portable Wifi router in my backpack with a signal booster that should cover the distance. I'll turn it on for five minutes the start of every hour. To save the battery."

Adrian took the offered device and let Howard explain how to use the app. It was simple enough.

"So you don't know what happened either?" Adrian asked.

He posed the question to the group, but it was Howard who answered in a hushed voice, "I think it was a magnetic field reversal."

"A what?"

"The Earth's magnetic field. We think it reversed, that's why there are no—"

"Adrian," Otto interrupted, "how did you get over here? Can I go back with you?"

"We made a sled by tying suitcases together. I laid on my stomach and dragged myself over the ice."

"That's what we were going to do," Bjorn whispered to me.

"Do you have a radio?" Adrian asked. "Is any of the equipment working in the flight deck?"

"Everything is totally smashed, at least as far as we've been able to tell so far," I said. "Isn't there a satellite phone or something?"

"All of that was up front in the flight deck. What about the survival suits?" Adrian said. "There are two of them stowed in the front First

Class stowage bins. Did you get them out?"

"Survival suits?"

"Yeah, they're orange, like big onesies. Supposed to be in the forward bins for this situation."

"We went through everything," I said. "Didn't see them."

"That's not possible. You didn't look."

"I looked," Otto said. "Trust me, no survival suits."

"What about emergency kits? There are knives, rope—"

"Didn't find anything like that."

"You're sure?"

He pushed past us and stood on a pod-bed to inspect one of the front bins. He checked the next one and the ones around it and cursed. He got back down.

I said, "Why hasn't anybody come yet? It's almost thirty hours. Aren't there transponders on the plane? Shouldn't they have activated?"

"There are four ELTs—emergency locator transmitters. Two in the life rafts that activate if deployed, one in the cabin that's activated by crew, and one in the rear door airframe that's activated by high g-forces. There's also a transponder in the black box."

"They work like an EPIRB, right?" I asked. They were the emergency beacons on boats. It was about the only thing I liked about my dad's sailboat. The rest had terrified me.

"ELTs are different. These go straight to satellite. The rear one should have fired, and we didn't sink." Adrian shook his head and shrugged at the same time. "Maybe it's a big search radius? And if there's something wrong with GPS…maybe the ELT isn't hitting the satellites. I don't know."

"We were two hundred miles off course. To the east," I said. "I was in the flight deck with Josh before the accident."

"Off course?"

"He said we were flying fifty miles to the east when usually they go a hundred fifty to the west."

"But air traffic would have known of the course adjustment. They would have radioed it in and changed the flight plan. In fact, they knew the winds. They knew we would be pushed onto a different course. There are planes flying over the Pole constantly. Probably are right now."

"We haven't seen any other planes. Nothing in the sky."

"Nobody is coming for us," Howard said quietly. "I'm telling you, the magnetic field—"

"Please," Otto said, "can you please stop with that for now?"

"I need to see the flight deck myself," Adrian said.

"Sure." I turned on my phone's light. "Come on."

"Did someone say they needed a radio?" asked a voice. It came from my aisle behind Lilly. The small Middle-Eastern-looking man named Rasheed. "Because I have one. A small shortwave. In my luggage."

▼▲▼

"Does *any*one else have *any*thing they think might be useful?" Otto shone his phone's light around the cabin on each person's face one by one. "Come on, people. Batteries. Flashlights. Radios. Anything you've found in the opened luggage. We need to start working together."

Rasheed got out the small radio.

A digital unit with shortwave transmit and receive. He didn't think of it, hadn't realized he was carrying equipment we could use.

He said he had been waiting for the authorities to arrive, that he had been too terrified to think properly. He said he was bringing it back as a gift from an uncle to his son. Said his family lived in Kolkata, that it was normal for people in the countryside to use shortwave.

Idiot. That was my first thought, but then again, the fear and cold made it hard to think straight.

Rasheed said he knew how to use it. It took ten minutes of scrambling to find four triple-A batteries to power the thing up, scavenged from a suitcase with a kids toy in it. I couldn't imagine that we could transmit very long distances on four tiny batteries, but Otto figured we'd be able to receive. He said he could hook up a big antenna by running exposed wiring around the cabin.

That being said, we got five minutes of nothing but static across all frequencies when we turned it on.

"Doesn't mean anything," Bjorn said. "The ionosphere needs to be cooperating to bounce the radio waves back."

"Does it work up here?" I asked.

"In the north? Sure, it was important in a lot of early polar exploration. Night is the best time for reception—this endless twilight isn't working in our favor. The darker it gets, the better reception and transmission."

Great. So we needed colder and darker to communicate. It seemed like something Bjorn would know.

Despite being housed in one of the most technologically advanced machines humanity had ever created, our lives depended on a tiny radio the size of two packs of Kraft dinner taped together.

"You're wasting your time." Howard hung back in the shadows, a doom-mongering wraith. "If the fields reversed, it's the tipping point for an extinction level event…"

"See if you can hear anything," I said to Rasheed. "Like music, whatever."

I tried to ignore Howard, but the fear was infectious. I wanted to know if the world out there still existed. That would be something. More than something. Everything. It meant Emma wouldn't be in danger. The thought sent me into another spiral. She knew. That we were missing. That her little girl was gone. An airliner down. As she'd feared. Why did I go?

My stomach flared into a knot. *I'm getting us out of here. It'll be okay. Stay calm.*

"I need the medical kit," Adrian said from the other aisle.

He'd searched every storage bin, went through all the piles we'd accumulated but hadn't found the survival suits or emergency kit he said had to be stored up here. He'd cursed a few more times during his rummaging. He said it was impossible. More than once he asked if we were hiding it from him for some reason.

After giving up, Adrian went into my pod where Josh was laid out. "You did recover the medical kit up here, right?" He inspected Josh's face and body. Tried to rouse him again and again. Nothing.

"*Oui*. Yes, we have the medical kit." Liz had it under her blankets with her. As she'd promised.

She was right next to me. I saw she cradled another package under her other arm. The same package I'd seen her with in the lounge. And on the street.

"I'm going to need to take some things from it," Adrian said. His face was inches from Josh's.

"What about us?" I said.

"There are only two medical kits on board. One in First Class, and one in the rear. We recovered the one back there, but we've got dozens of seriously injured people. We need as much medical supplies as we can get."

"Do you have Ventolin in the other one?"

"Pardon?"

"An inhaler. The one from this kit is missing. My daughter needs it. It's an emergency."

"We've got a lot of emergencies going on." He didn't even look up from Josh. "Can we inject him with adrenalin?"

Liz said, "He is very fragile."

"You're a doctor?"

"I did medical school but never practiced. I went into research."

"We have two doctors in the other side," Adrian said. "So we can't wake him up?"

"It might be fatal."

"Might be worth it." Adrian muttered this low enough that I was sure it wasn't intended to be heard. In a louder voice he said, "I'm going to need as much clothes, jackets and food as I can drag back with me. We are freezing to death back there. We have ten times the people."

Silence in the cabin for a second and then two and three.

Just the sound of Lilly's wheezing breath. I had to get back over to her. Against his father's protests, the chubby kid had transferred himself over to Lilly's pod again. They whispered together. He seemed to be trying to help her breathe more slowly. Anything to calm her down was good.

"Well?" Adrian's voice gained a notch of volume. Of aggression. "Do I have to go and look myself?"

A pause of one more beat before I answered, "I'll collect what we have."

▼▲▼

"Give them water," the big Russian said. "Keep Coke cans for us."

The moment I began to root through the galley, the bear of a man materialized out from under his mass of clothing. He still stank of cologne but with a strong undercurrent of body odor and the sour tang of day-old alcohol. He'd been steadily working his way through the mini-bottles of whiskey and scotch.

"I don't like Coke," I said. "Doesn't it dehydrate you?"

Dehydration obviously wasn't a concern of his, but my lips were cracked already, my tongue pasted to the top of my mouth. I kept most of the water assigned to me for Lilly. I couldn't imagine a hangover in this hell, but I could sure understand the need for a drink.

"Better to keep the water," I said, and put a soda can into the collection bag.

He grabbed it, replaced it in the rack and put in a water bottle instead. "Coke has sugar. Calories."

"Isn't caffeine a diuretic?"

The Russian looked at me with unblinking eyes. Either didn't understand or didn't care.

"I mean, it makes you piss more." I was going to say, "pee", but it felt silly from one man to another.

"Myth. Trust me, you want the caffeine. Stimulant. And the sugar. Keep soda. Give water."

Discussion over, the Russian opened one drawer and then another and tossed the water bottles into the garbage bag. We took food trays and buns from another locker and tossed them in as well. I held the light, he did the work while I did the counting in my head.

"Okay." I held up the mostly full bag. One of those large white kitchen garbage bags. "I filled up a sack. I think I'd better come…"

I stopped mid-sentence and scanned the cabin. Where was Adrian?

"I notice you don't go to your private stash," the Russian whispered into my ear. "You keep your pile secret, yes?"

After I'd seen Roman hoard his own pile of drinks and food, I'd done the same—quietly—for Lilly. I mean, I had to protect her, right? I didn't think anyone had noticed.

Static hissed on the radio as Rasheed cycled through different frequencies. Beyond that, another noise. Something thrumming against the walls.

"Come up here," Adrian said from behind me. "Look at this."

He was at the flight deck.

▼▲▼

Otto and Adrian and Bjorn crowded around the forward door. Each jostled for position against the stove-in walls ten feet up the corridor from the galley.

After we got Josh out, we'd left the other three bodies up there. They were definitely dead. All were male—Irene Hardy, the pilot I'd met, wasn't up there. The others I wasn't sure I could identify. Might have been the two relief pilots. Their bodies were badly damaged. We couldn't get them out. Not in one piece anyway. We did our best to jam the door shut and wedge clothes into the gap to stop warm air drafting out through the smashed front of the aircraft.

Otto and Bjorn had their phones out. Lights on. Heads down.

"Yeah, I see what you mean," Otto said. His face was away from me. Voice muffled.

My feet were numb. They hadn't warmed up in the past hour since

I'd come inside. It wasn't that much warmer in here. Or was it getting colder outside? Or both? The gnawing chill ached deep into my bones. I didn't even notice myself shivering anymore.

Something more than that bothered me.

"Adrian, when you got here you said, 'Did any of the pilots survive up here?'" Was it his figure of speech? "What did you mean, 'up here'?"

"Captain Hardy is in the rear of the aircraft."

"She's alive?"

He nodded.

The cold slowed my brain down. "So Josh came up here, but she didn't?"

He nodded again.

"Weren't they relieved an hour before the crash?"

Adrian kept his head close to the flight deck door. Inspecting something. "All of my flight crew except the three pilots have been accounted for. None except for them and Suzanne and Jennifer were up here."

And Suzanne and Jennifer were dead. Which meant…my mind clicked forward in slow motion before the half-frozen light bulb went off. "So who's the fourth person in the flight deck?"

"I have no idea."

Otto waved me forward and stepped back. He shone his light on the right side of the twisted frame of the flight deck door. "What does that look like?"

It was almost pitch black up here. No strip lighting or emergency overhead LEDs. Just the sharp light and weaving shadows of the tiny bulbs in the phones each of them waved around. I took a closer look.

A small hole near the right door latch. A puncture. Two more near it.

Otto's hand shook and the light flickered. "Bullet holes, right?"

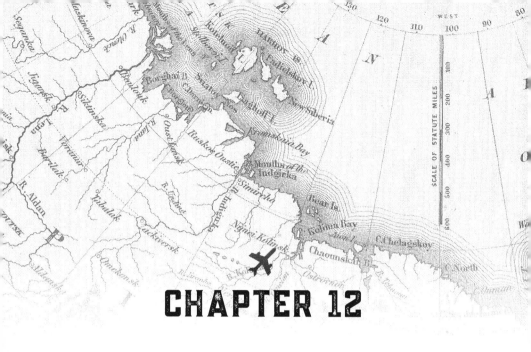

CHAPTER 12

Ice crystals hissed past me, the blue-black ice inches from my face. *This was a bad idea.*

A fresh gust of wind—Bjorn called them williwaws—pushed me sideways. The bags I was flat against caught like sails and threatened to tip me over.

"Use the forks!" Otto yelled.

I felt a tug on my left leg attached to the thin cord of ripped clothes—our safety line. I jammed my left arm down and tried to stabilize myself. I had a fork in each hand. The only thing we had we could use as ice picks, Bjorn had explained. Thank God we were in First Class and at least had metal ones. Plastic wouldn't have been much good.

I can't feel my hands.

A bubble slid by under the ice below me. How thick was it? The air pockets lazily slid by what looked like millimeters under the surface. I was on my stomach, balanced on a raft of tied-together suitcases. I released pressure on the left fork for fear of cracking the surface.

I didn't tell Lilly I was coming over the ice. I waited for her to be asleep, left a small LED light next to her as a nightlight. Waited ten minutes while I listened to her wheezing deep breathing before I crept away. Told Liz to make sure to stay with her.

Ten thousand feet of frigid water below me. Maybe twenty thousand.

I can't swim.

My God, what am I doing? How the hell did I end up face down on a half-inch of ice over an abyssal chasm on top of the world? I could have sent someone else to get an inhaler from the other side of the plane, but...

"Pull me!" I yelled. "Pull, pull, pull..." The words came out in a frantic tumble.

It looked so easy when Adrian had crossed first, spread-eagled on six suitcases lashed together. Someone had appeared on the other side and we threw them a rope. We improvised a contraption like one of those Wild West ferries across some river in Missouri. Ropes to each side and pull the raft across.

Simple.

Until you're the one over two miles of nothing.

Calm. Stay calm.

A tug under my arms and the suitcase-raft slid a foot forward. Fifteen feet to go. Maybe twenty. It could have been a mile.

Another gust of wind threw me up and back down in a stomach-lurch-inducing panic. My broken-nosed head slammed into the ice beneath me. Splintering pain shot through my face and radiated into my fingers. I must have screamed because I stopped moving.

"Pull," I yelled through the agony and dug both forks into the thin ice.

Gunshot holes. Were those gunshot holes? It was hard to tell, and I was no expert. Otto was, and said he couldn't tell either.

My dad had tried to share his love of guns with me when I was younger, and I had learned to shoot but never liked it. The metal of the door and walls in the flight deck had been shredded and twisted by the impact, but what could have punctured a sheet of metal like that? Maybe a lot of things.

Maybe a bullet.

Maybe not.

The sled inched forward. Squeaked over the ice.

Who was the fourth person in the flight deck?

It wasn't one of the pilots.

Not one of the crew members. Adrian said all fourteen were accounted for, only eight still alive and that included Josh.

Then again, could we trust Adrian? I didn't know him from a hole in the wall. I didn't know *any* of these people. And when Adrian heard who I was, why had he made that face?

What had Josh told him?

What the hell was Josh doing flying the plane an hour after he'd been relieved? What had happened? Explosive decompression, Adrian had said, but he said he'd been asleep until it woke him up. Back cabin door blown out. Adrian said that if there was an emergency, the captain—Josh—would have come right to the front to fly the plane. That could explain it. But still.

The Russian airbase.

Had we been shot down? Was that why nobody was here yet? Was the world at war? Did we have to get out of this hell by ourselves?

More than thirty hours on the ice and no sign of the outside world. Was Howard right? Had the world outside ceased to exist? Had we passed into some netherworld?

Another merciful tug under my arms. Another few inches to safety.

Why did Rasheed have a shortwave radio? Who in the hell has a shortwave these days?

Please God, don't let me die.

▼▲▼

Straps and knotted-together curtains billowed and flapped in the gusting air. A makeshift barrier, across the ripped open hull of the back half of the aircraft, was almost useless at stopping the frigid wind from driving straight into the cabin.

I had my arms wrapped tight around my body. Thirty minutes in the open with the mounting gale cutting through me. Couldn't feel my fingers, my toes, my face. No sensation in my face was a small mercy. I'd left spatters of blood out on the ice where I'd smacked into it.

At first I thought they had wood stacked up by the entrance before I realized they were bodies, the frozen skin brown and black with only the scantest of clothing remaining. Beside the morgue pile someone squatted, relieving themselves next to a yellow patch of ice surrounded by dark mounds.

Overhead the sky was a deep royal blue, the brightest spot on the horizon directly to my left. Ahead of the aircraft—behind the intact tail section—a mauve-blue horizon. To my right, the full moon hung about fifteen degrees in the sky. No stars yet.

I pulled back the curtains. My eyes adjusted to the gloom inside as I stepped forward.

Nobody got up from their seats to mob me. Adrian announced that he'd been over to the front of the aircraft, that two of the pilots were dead, one injured and unconcious. A few people got up to speak to him. Nobody had any new information, he said, but he said we had a radio working. He said it wouldn't be long now.

I wanted to believe him.

Everything inside the cabin was a monochrome gray, the only illumination from the reflected twilight from the snow outside. The air was sharp, cold on each inhalation, but not clean like outside. An animal musk permeated the cabin.

Next to the windows, people huddled in clumps every few rows under checkered collections of clothing—but not piles like we had. When the plane ripped apart, the main luggage compartment had spewed bags onto our ice floe as the plane pirouetted away. We'd taken all the luggage from probably half of the two-hundred-odd people back here and used it for ourselves.

Even in the dim light, I saw patches of frostbite on exposed skin.

Bjorn had explained what it would look like.

Nothing I could do.

The mounting gale outside cut straight into the main cabin here, whereas on our side the nose was pointed into the wind. Our section was angled up and captured what heat we generated, where here it was open and flat. We had two galleys of First Class food. Adrian said they'd already eaten everything they could find.

The flight purser kept two steps ahead of me, Otto two steps behind. Only the three of us had crossed over to the other side.

"Hello?" Adrian said into the phone Howard had given him. "Can you hear me?"

At first static but then I heard Howard's voice reply. So his app worked. The kid wasn't all crazy talk. He knew how to get tech stuff done. At least we were in communication with the others. I asked Adrian to ask about Lilly, and heard Howard's voice saying she was fine.

"Excuse me. Could I get everyone's attention?" I held up one arm, self-conscious in my thick layers of clothing. Five socks over my hand in the air. "I've got water and some candy bars and pretzels. Don't get up, I'll walk around and distribute them."

I made my way over to the nearest group. Three men and three women huddled on two chairs by an exit row. They mumbled thank you.

"Does anyone have an inhaler?" I handed out water bottles. "For asthma? My little girl needs one."

Everyone shook their heads. I made my way to the next group. Otto followed behind me, asking people if they had Chinese brands of phones—one of which someone volunteered—and if anyone had any GPS. Nobody had been able to get any signal of any kind, including maps. Most said their batteries were already dead.

We'd already made it most of the way to the back of the plane. Adrian was supposed to join us at the back with Captain Hardy, but he was talking to people halfway to the front.

The medical kit on this side of the plane was missing the Ventolin as well. Nobody here owned up to taking it either. My frustration mounted with each row we passed. We were the ones handing out our water, risking our lives to help them. Why wasn't anyone in this group ready to help me?

It wasn't only that I hadn't found an inhaler that made me uneasy. The steady thrumming of the wind against the hull was louder. A sickening rolling motion beneath our feet gained intensity.

That newly formed scrim of ice between the floes couldn't last much longer.

"I've got an inhaler."

A thin young man in a dark suit pulled away the shirt covering his head. He had buzz-cut hair and wire-framed glasses. He took my offered water bottle and fished around in his pocket. "Here, go ahead."

"Thank you."

I took the inhaler and went to put it in my pocket, but the guy jumped from his seat.

"I meant take a puff, you can't take it with you."

"But I said my daughter needs it."

"So bring her here."

"I'm in the other half of the plane."

The man shook his head and grabbed the puffer from my hand. "No way. I'm sorry."

Otto pulled my shoulder and inserted himself between us. "Come on, friend. Let us borrow it, we'll bring it back." He turned to me and said in a lower voice, "Let me handle this, okay?"

The guy got more hysterical and some of his friends advanced. I stepped back. What was I going to do? Fight him for it?

"Mitch."

I was so intent on the struggle for the inhaler I almost didn't hear my name. I turned.

"Mitch," said the voice again. A woman's voice.

It was almost pitch black in the final rows. I reached into my pocket, turned on my phone and clicked the light on. Blond hair. Blue suit and tie.

"Irene?" I took three steps down the aisle.

She was by herself in the very back of the plane, in an empty row of three seats in the middle.

"Captain Hardy?" I said as I sat in her row. "Is that you?"

Her face was a congealed mass of black blood, one eye swollen shut, but it was the same woman Josh had introduced us to when we went into the flight deck. I turned my light off. In the background, I heard Otto swearing at the guy I'd been trying to get the inhaler from. He wasn't backing down.

Captain Hardy said, "Is Lilly…is your daughter alive?"

I nodded.

"She's all right?"

"She's not hurt. Needs an inhaler, but she's safe."

"Thank God," Irene said. "Thank God. This was all…this is…"

"What happened? After I left?"

"We came to the back. You went ahead of us, but we were right behind you. Didn't you see us pass you?"

"I saw you pass. We said goodbye."

"Josh came with me into the back of the plane to rest. We were supposed to be off for the next four hours."

"He was the one strapped into the pilot seat in the flight deck."

"Josh went back up to the front when the turbulence started. He said he wanted to make sure you and Lilly were okay."

He never came to see us. "What happened after that?"

"I don't know. I fell asleep."

Same as us. Same as everyone. How could *everyone* have been asleep?

"When I woke," Captain Hardy said, "we were spinning out of control."

"Adrian said the back door blew out. Was it that one?"

I pointed to the other side of the cabin. The back of the plane must have hit hard, because the seats had been pressed almost into the ceiling. The extreme rear of the aircraft was underwater. A pool of black enveloped the last twenty feet. She was lucky to be alive.

"I don't think it blew out. Adrian seems to think so, but I asked people to look and I'm not sure now," Irene said. "There *was* an uncontrolled decompression."

"Were we...I don't know, hit by a missile? Was it a bomb?"

She shrugged and shook her head. "I'm not sure." She paused. "What happened between you and Josh? When he said you were coming on the flight, he didn't seem happy about it."

What did that have to do with anything? But I answered anyway. "He was getting a divorce, looking for someone to blame. What else could cause something like an uncontrolled decompression?"

"Lots of things. There are thirty or more on commercial flights every year—rarely a bomb, and by that I mean, something that someone did on purpose. Sometimes it's something in the luggage, a pressurized container explodes, or sometimes an engine part pierces the cabin."

The way she said it seemed to hint at something. "But you have an idea?"

"We had five hundred pounds of lithium batteries in the back hold. I told Josh I had safety concerns, but he checked the NOTOC hazmat limits from the manual. He said it was legal."

"That could cause a decompression?"

"Lithium batteries can explode and catch on fire." She groaned. "My legs are both broken. I haven't been able to do a lot of investigating."

I looked over my shoulder. Otto kept back a few rows and seemed to be listening, but was more focused on arguing over the puffer.

"You know Adrian?" I said to Irene. "You trust him?"

"Sure."

I looked back at Otto again.

"It didn't feel like a bomb," Irene said. "But a missile? Did Josh say something? Is he alive?"

"He hasn't woken up yet. Why was he flying?"

"That's a captain's prerogative, especially if there's a problem."

She hesitated.

"What?"

"He was getting divorced," she said. "He hadn't been himself lately. We shouldn't have even let you onto the flight deck, but he was the captain. I was thinking of reporting him."

I held her gaze in the gray light. "What are you saying?"

"That he wasn't himself," she repeated. "That's all."

I lowered my voice. "You think he brought down this plane on *purpose*?"

She didn't answer.

The ground beneath us rocked with the mounting waves and wind. "Josh told me there was a polar hurricane in the Beaufort Sea."

"That was a thousand miles from our flight path. A whole series of circulating lows that changed our course to the east by a few hundred miles."

"So we weren't blown off course by the winds?"

"The winds did change the flight plan a bit, but that's normal over the Pole. It uses less fuel to go with cross winds than fight them, especially when they push us back on course later in the flight."

"Would the emergency locator transmitter, the ELT back here, have activated? With the impact? It's at the back door, right?"

"There's another in the Main Equipment Compartment. That should have fired as well. There's no way the outside world doesn't know where we are. There are transponders on the flight data recorder in the rear and voice recorder up front. If Josh was flying us, there are two more ELTs he could have activated manually."

"So why haven't we heard anything?"

The wind beat hard against the window and shuddered the metal beneath our feet.

"Did Josh tell you anything about who was on the flight?" Captain Hardy looked over my shoulder.

Why was she hesitating? "Whatever you've got to say..."

"Is there a guy named Roman in the front?"

I nodded.

"That's Roman Kolchak."

"Is that supposed to mean something to me?"

"The Siberian super-billionaire? He's about the richest guy on the planet. There's an arrest warrant out for him in Russia. He was escaping and asking for refugee status in America. It was a secret, or was supposed to be."

▼▲▼

The asshole wouldn't give up his puffer. I almost wanted to beat it out of him, but Otto held me back, told me it wasn't worth it. What did he know? He didn't have a little girl waiting on him. Suffocating. But by that point the guy was ranting and wheezing himself.

We had spent over an hour in the back part of the plane. Already too long.

When we crossed the ice, the sky had been clear, the moon visible—but when I stepped past the tattered curtain now, the moon was gone.

The sky slate-gray.

Wind howling.

We hurried back to the edge of the floe. Our half of the aircraft barely visible not two hundred feet away. The ice heaved under our feet.

Figures materialized from the gloom and shuffled past us. I didn't stop to see who they were. I was too cold. Too scared.

We spent five minutes screaming into the wind before Bjorn appeared on the other side. Thankfully the wind was coming from his direction and he let it carry the suitcase-raft and rope across. Three minutes later and Otto had made the traverse.

The raft rattled its way back to me.

I got flat onto my stomach on the suitcases. The black ice in front of my face heaved up and down in mounting swells.

"Okay!" I yelled. "Pull!"

I didn't bother with the forks. Didn't bother with finesse. Held on with both hands to the tied-together sheet-rope. Gritted my teeth and closed my eyes.

Not five feet onto the ice, the front suitcase-sled caught on something. I shot forward. Scared to smack my face again, I reared up and jammed both elbows down.

They went straight through the ice.

The rest of my body followed.

I tried to scream, but my lungs filled with an ice-cold slug of saltwater. With one hand I let go of the rope and clawed at the life vest around my neck. Reached for the red handle.

I thrashed.

Black all around me.

Falling and flailing into the frigid darkness.

CHAPTER 13

*D*on't leave me, Mitch. Don't leave.

My wife's eyes were wide, but black as coal. Black as the deep cold depths. I reached for her, but she pushed me away as she begged me not to leave.

"Emma, I'm not going," I muttered. I held her tighter. Felt her body next to mine.

I was cold. So cold. One warm spot. A spreading heat from the center of my forehead.

I realized my eyes were closed, so I opened them. The chubby kid, Jang, had his nose an inch from mine. His right hand was pressed against my head. It felt incredibly hot, almost burning, like an energy was flowing between us. The kid smiled.

"Mr. Mitch?" he said. "Feeling better?" He let go of my forehead.

"Daddy, Daddy, you okay?" Lilly was bundled up next to me, her face white in the half-light.

"I'm…I'm f…fine…"

My whole body shuddered as it tried to warm up. With both arms, I squeezed Emma, tried to stop the trembling by holding on tighter. Her face was fresh in my mind, her presence clear.

"Hey, oh, okay, *bonne*," whispered a voice in a lilting French accent. From very close.

I blinked and Emma's face came into focus. Except it wasn't Emma. Large brown eyes. A sprinkling of freckles over a button nose. Red hair.

Red hair.

"Liz?"

"*Nom de Dieux*. You are feeling *mieux*, yes?"

Her face was close. As close as Jang's had been a second ago, and close enough that...I felt the skin under my arms, the flesh my hands gripped. Smooth. Warm. A lingering scent of expensive perfume over stale sweat.

With a jolt of realization I released my hands. "Liz? Are you..." I felt her smooth skin against my body. Against *all* of my body.

Something else. A scratchiness on my neck. Other arms around me. *Hairy* arms.

"*Hej hopp i blåbärsskogen*," Bjorn said.

His breath was warm and smelled of onion and tickled my left ear. "Means we are taking a jump into the blueberry forest together. Seems you are better."

The Norwegian disentangled himself from behind me. A crinkling sound like cellophane wrapper being balled up. I was cold, but now felt a clammy sweat sticking my body to Liz's.

"We had to get in naked with you, mate," Bjorn explained.

His accent still confused me. Continental European-sounding yet faintly British at the same time.

"Your lips were blue. Otto took the emergency space blanket from the medical kit." Bjorn balanced himself on top of the pod-bed and hopped into the aisle and looked down. "Not quite naked. I kept my skivvies on. I mean, we both did."

Liz kept her arms around me and didn't let go. I hadn't been this close to a woman who wasn't my wife in years, even well before we were married.

"Your core temperature isn't quite up yet," Liz said.

I squirmed but gave up. The second or two of effort had depleted what little energy I had. My mind slid back.

The water.

The terror of it slipping over my head. I swallowed a whole mouthful of it, then managed to pull the tab on the life jacket. It popped me back to the surface. By then I was scrabbling madly in an adrenaline-fueled frenzy. Everything was hazy after that. Bjorn's face on the ice. A numb sensation of being dragged.

I slowed my breathing. *Calm. Calm down.* That's what Emma would tell me.

Beyond the thumping of my heart in my ears—they'd wrapped something tight around my head, and sounds were muffled—but a steady drumming sound rose in my senses. That had to be wind against the hull. More than that, there was a keening wail. A howl that pierced the gale.

"Come here, Lillypad." With one shaking hand I pulled my daughter between Liz and myself, wedged her between us. I was shivering, but could talk without chattering.

"You're okay, Daddy?"

"I'm fine, baby. Cuddle me."

I checked my watch. Almost 9 a.m. Hong Kong time. When did I go back over the ice? Six? Seven? So I'd been semi-conscious for two hours.

I looked out the cabin window to my left. I was in Lilly's pod-bed. I heard Josh's soft regular breathing behind me in my pod-bed. The light outside was dim, twilight but waning.

2 a.m. was my best guess at midday here, when the twilight was brightest, so 2 p.m. would be darkest, right? I wasn't sure. The mechanics of the days were alien. Everything about this place was alien. I'd have to ask Bjorn.

I held my daughter against me. Squeezed her tight. Thank God. I shouldn't have gone out there. Shouldn't have risked it.

Lilly's tiny body wheezed on each breath. I didn't even get the goddamn inhaler.

"Glad to see you're back. That was close."

I looked to my right. Otto stood in the next aisle and nodded to me. He went back to talking with the big Russian.

Roman. Roman Kolchak.

I straightened up. The Russian billionaire trying to escape. I *had* heard of him. In the news. On BBC. A big fight with Putin. They were going to lock him up. I heard on the news that he had spirited away tens of billions, that Putin was furious about it.

And here he was, in a downed airliner.

Who else knew? Irene knew, so Josh had to have known as well. Nobody had said anything. A special flight, Josh had said in the flight deck. Was that what he meant?

The sad wailing sound increased in pitch into a primal scream. Lilly put both of her hands over her ears and pressed. Her face scrunched up.

Liz cooed and tried to calm my daughter.

"Somebody should do something about the dog," I said without thinking.

"How the heck is that thing alive?" Bjorn whispered.

"I agree." Roman stood up from his pod-bed. First time I'd seen him get up apart from when he'd raided the galley.

He pointed at Bjorn who had sat down in the next pod. "You, come with me."

"Where?" Bjorn looked equal parts confused and scared.

"Outside." Roman had a huge metal bar in his hand, something he must have scavenged from outside. He began pulling shirts over his head. None quite fit his huge frame.

"Don't hurt it," Lilly mewled. She sat upright and looked straight at Roman.

The Russian ignored her and pulled one last shirt on. He growled at Bjorn and the younger man acquiesced. The two of them disappeared down the aisle together. The animal's wail degraded into yelping howls.

"Keep your head down," I whispered to Lilly and pulled her back to me.

Two seats up from me, Howard's head bobbed up over the divider.

"Hello? Hello?" he said into his phone.

I heard a muted response acknowledging. Adrian's voice. He was talking to the other cabin using the mesh network he'd set up. At least that was worth part of the trip over.

The chubby kid, Jang, had retreated to his father's embrace. The boy's eyes met mine. He was so calm, but I found it odd the way his father seemed to have an almost reverence for the child. He kept his eyes down and away when he looked at his boy. It was odd.

Something else was odd.

I didn't hear the now-familiar shush of static on the radio.

"Where's Rasheed?" I whispered, and then louder, "And Manu? And Vera?"

Usually they were jammed in a nest around Lilly's pod, but the area around us was almost empty.

"Manu and Vera went to the other part of the plane," Liz said, her voice a whisper inches from me. "Most of them left."

"Most?"

"Eleven of us stayed this side, and that includes Josh."

"I don't understand. Why would they leave?"

"Rasheed is here somewhere, but when you were gone, fifteen of them decided to go to the other side. Adrian said that the emergency transmitters were all on that side of the plane. He said that the black box was in the rear, too, plus the two life rafts. We messaged with Howard's phone, talked back and forth. With the storm coming, Manu and Vera and the rest decided to go."

Those were the people I saw out on the ice when I was returning. I hadn't realized.

"Why didn't you go?"

Liz didn't reply but shrugged. In the dimness I saw her precious package right beside us. She never went anywhere without it.

"Why were you on this flight?" I asked.

"I think this is a question we are all asking."

"What do you do back in the world?"

It felt incredibly intimate talking to her like this, our bodies slick with sweat and intertwined. I felt warm for the first time since we'd been here.

"You mean work?" she said. "I suppose I am a *missionaire*—a missionary. I was on my way to Africa after New York."

"I thought you said you were a doctor?"

"I have a PhD, so it gives me a name."

"In what?"

"Genetics."

"And you're a missionary?"

"Tell me, Mitch, what did you find on the other side?" Her voice was low and sultry.

I paused. "Lots of injured people." I glanced at Lilly. She seemed asleep. I lowered my voice. "A lot of dead people, but the others are toughing it out."

"Did you talk to this other pilot? Irene Hardy that Adrian spoke of?"

"Yeah."

"And...?"

What did I want to tell her? And why didn't I want to tell her everything? "She said Josh came up to the front when the turbulence started. To make sure Lilly was okay, to make sure the plane was okay."

"And did you see him come back up to the front?"

"Not since we left the flight deck."

Howard put down his phone and peered over the divider. "What else did she say?"

"That Josh wasn't himself—" I stopped mid-sentence. I hadn't wanted to say that, but now had no choice but to explain. "He was going through a divorce. He blamed me. Family stuff."

"That explains the weird look Adrian gave you," Howard said.

He noticed that? Bright kid. And *I* noticed that he had an empty pill container in his hand. He put it away when he saw me looking. Was he the one pilfering the med kit?

"Was his separation bad?" Liz whispered.

"His wife was getting everything—the house, the kids. My wife's father was even taking away the family home in England. I guess none of that matters anymore…"

"You're not serious." Howard got out of his pod and advanced toward us. "The pilot—your brother-in-law—blames you for his nasty divorce, and he's the mystery guy in the hot seat when the plane goes down?"

"It's not like that."

"Then explain what it is like. Adrian sure gave you a weird look."

"What else?" Liz interrupted. "What did this Hardy say? Was it an attack? Terrorists?"

"I think it was this asshole." Howard flicked his chin at the inert body of Josh in the next pod.

"Be quiet," Liz said to him.

I continued, "Irene said there were five hundred pounds of lithium ion batteries in the hold. She said that could explode or cause a fire. She said the decompression could have been a lot of things."

"Adrian said the back door blew out," Howard said.

"Irene said she wasn't sure that was true."

"Then what did?"

"She doesn't know. She fell asleep before the crash."

"I was asleep as well," Liz said.

So were we. Me and Lilly. Maybe that was why we missed seeing Josh. We were all asleep. I glanced at my watch. What time did we impact the ice? I remembered 10:55 p.m. on my watch just afterward. It seemed odd that everyone was asleep.

I looked around the cabin. The wind buffeted the fuselage enough to begin rocking it back and forth almost in sync with the rolling motion under our feet. Waves. In the past few minutes the cabin had darkened. I noticed the LED lights weren't on anymore. One last system failure. Just the light through the windows which had gone dark in a hurry.

The pleading whining had stopped. Maybe a minute ago. What had Roman done out there? I dreaded telling Lilly that they'd killed the dog. I would tell her something else.

And where was Rasheed?

Otto went out with Roman and Bjorn, but I hadn't seen Rasheed. Maybe he went over with the others? But Liz seemed sure he had stayed. I was about to ask her again when I heard a fumbling and banging.

Otto appeared first and stamped his feet against the deck. "Goddamn freezing. That's a serious storm."

Bjorn followed him. He blew onto his hands.

Roman came last and walked up our aisle. He had his fists up, clutched around his chest. "You not want me kill dog?"

I held a hand over Lilly. "Look, I didn't—"

He dropped something on me. Something cold and white. Something that shivered and burst into a frenzy of licking. A tiny bulldog.

Lilly woke up and squealed with excitement and took the puppy into her arms.

"Now your responsibility," Roman said. "Any food comes from your food. Stupid. Will drain what we have, but you say what you say. I am not asshole."

Bjorn added, "Dog was lucky. It was buried under a mound of what looked like insulation and bags ripped out from the plane. Kept it alive in this cold. Roman went across the ice by himself to get it."

Liz reached a hand out and held the Russian's hand. "That was sweet and very brave."

He held her hand for a second, then shrugged and made his way back to his side of the cabin and wrapped himself up.

Otto stood in front of us and smiled. "I got a present for you guys, too."

I was about to ask if he had dog biscuits when he produced a blue plastic nozzle from his pocket and held it out.

"Holy…Otto, where did you get that?"

I took the Ventolin inhaler from him and shook it. Full. Totally full.

"After we argued with that guy? I waited for him to calm down, then snuck back and stole it from the pocket of his coat. He didn't need it as much as Lilly does."

Otto shrugged at his indiscretion.

"Thank you," was all I could think of to say.

"What I really wanted to get over there was some jet fuel from the wing," Otto said. "There still had to be a few thousand pounds left. Could have used in pot burners, but I couldn't figure a way to get at it." He went back to his seat and rummaged with his covers.

Gripping the inhaler, I pulled both Lilly and the dog deeper into the nest between myself and Liz. The Frenchwoman looked bemused and wrapped her arms around the little girl and the dog. It took me a few seconds of watching the puppy lick Lilly's face before my brain returned to its previous thought.

All asleep.

Ten fifty-five.

"Howard, were you asleep before the crash?"

"Yeah."

The puppy licked and licked my daughter under the covers.

"And Liz, you were asleep as well." It wasn't a question.

She nodded, yes, and I asked everyone else. Everyone was asleep.

"Howard, did you look at the time after the crash?"

"Didn't think of it."

"I did. Ten fifty-five. At eight-thirty we were supposed to cross the Pole, right?"

Howard paused to consider. "That sounds right."

"That's almost two and a half hours before we crashed."

Complete silence in the cabin. Nothing except the mounting roar of the wind buffeting the walls.

"Does anyone else remember actually passing the Pole?"

No answer. I remembered tucking Lilly in, thinking I'd take some pictures out the window and write some notes when we crossed zero latitude. It was a big part of this flight, and yet nobody remembered it?

"So nobody recalls passing the Pole. We were all asleep? Every single person? And nobody remembers *anything* from the next two and half hours?"

"That does seem odd," Howard said quietly.

We were missing two and a half hours of flight time that nobody remembered.

What was going on all that time?

And why was everyone unconscious?

CHAPTER 14

D addeeee!" Lilly screamed and dug her little fingernails into my neck.

The ground pitched both sideways and up beneath us, rolling the entire fuselage until we were almost suspended sideways in the air. A driving gust of wind beat against the hull.

I grabbed the sidewall and tensed for a sudden free fall if the cabin rolled upside down. The squall abated and the whole assembly rocked back, metal groaning under the strain. Everything swayed back and forth with the motion of the swells under the ice.

A cracking thunder reverberated through the cabin.

Lilly pressed her face into the small of my neck. Another crack like a pistol going off. The cabin shuddered and then dropped down, first inches and then more. Black water sloshed not more than ten feet down the aisle from us. Already past the curtains. Already a foot closer than an hour ago.

We were sinking.

And it was dark.

Lilly was terrified of the dark.

The churning maelstrom raged over the ice and sea, and with its arrival, the temperature had plummeted. The cold had returned with a vengeance, penetrating deep into my bones under the blankets and layers of sodden clothing.

Liz had disentangled herself from the nest they'd created to warm me up after my near-death plunge twelve hours before. She hadn't gone back to her side of the cabin, but taken all her things and wedged into the floor by the still-unconscious Josh.

Even Roman had abandoned his side of the cabin to join the knot of people on our side, taking the pod beside Howard, right above Jang and his father, across from us. Otto and Bjorn had moved into the floor of our pod. Something about the threat of death made people clump together.

"Jesus, God, please," I muttered under my breath, not loud enough for Lilly to hear me. "Please help us." I wasn't much of a church-goer, but I couldn't help it. "It's going to be okay," I said to Lilly in a louder voice.

A light dangled over our heads.

Howard strapped his LED flashlight to the overhead luggage bin, and I had another smaller one I kept as a nightlight for Lilly. The cabin was almost pitch black apart from the single light that swung back and forth, around and around as the cabin and ice floe pitched on the growing waves roiling beneath us. Stark shadows swept along the walls like ghosts driven from the raging storm.

The wind abated from a roar to a low rumble.

"*Det blæser en halv pelican,*" Bjorn said. "It is blowing half a pelican out there. How far do you think we could have come in two and a half hours? I mean, our missing time on the airplane?"

Bjorn didn't like to keep quiet. Couldn't keep quiet. He was scared. We all were.

"Fourteen hundred miles in that time." Otto sat beside Bjorn, just below us.

"That's the whole distance from the North Pole to the edge of the Arctic Circle."

Howard's polar-oriented map was taped against the underside of the overhead bins above us. A line was drawn down the center—the path from Hong Kong to New York. Bjorn had added a dotted line around the circumference, and the new radius of uncertainty of our position. The light swung around in a circle and illuminated the map for an instant before casting it back into darkness.

"So we might not even be in the Arctic," I said.

"We're definitely in the Arctic." Bjorn steadied himself. "We wouldn't have sea ice like this—"

"You don't know that," Otto said. "This could be drifting pack ice that went south. We can't see any further than the horizon."

"We definitely didn't land in the Beaufort Sea area. We would have come down in this storm if we had. That's where this storm was back then. Right? Mitch, that's what Josh said when you were in the flight deck?"

I should have taken Lilly over to the other part of the plane with me. This section was much smaller. It didn't have any of the emergency transmitters in it. No life rafts. What was I thinking? I was an idiot. For leaving Emma. For coming here. Punish me, but not Lilly. Please.

Under the noise of the howling wind, a shushing hiss. Howard had spent the last three hours busy playing with Rasheed's radio, plus fielding calls to the other half of the aircraft. So far they'd been getting battered as bad as we were. Every hour he turned his phone back on to give them a call.

"You're not going to get any shortwave signal in a storm," Bjorn said.

"I'm not using the radio," Howard said. "That's my messaging app. I can't get anyone on the other end."

"It's probably the storm."

"It is not the storm."

"I'm telling you—"

"You think I'm an idiot?"

Bjorn stared at him without saying anything.

"You really think I'm an idiot?" Howard's voice edged upward.

Bjorn hung his head down. Howard went back to fiddling.

Rasheed had never reappeared.

Maybe he had gone to the other side with everyone, but he'd left all his things here. His bag. All of his extra clothes and small pile of supplies. The radio. We'd left his things where they were for now, all except the radio—but why would he have just left like that? Maybe he had to rush. The ice had been disintegrating. Maybe he went through the ice, like me.

I didn't even want to think of what it looked like out there now.

Glanced at my watch.

Past 1 a.m. Hong Kong time. October eighth. Third day on the ice. No sign of the outside world, but in these conditions, that would be a real miracle.

A fresh squall of deafening intensity buffeted the fuselage. We heaved to one side and then back, the metal groaning and creaking.

How much more could it take?

Better not to think.

Everybody had taken on tasks to occupy the mind. Roman collected and stacked the remains of the frozen dinners and chocolate bars and cans of soda. Bjorn drew maps. Otto fashioned tools from scrap metal and parts he'd scavenged from luggage. Liz was in charge of Josh.

I had my own personal project.

I found a sewing kit and some gift-wrapping tape, and had a dozen or so needles lumped together. I took apart a kids toy from the same luggage and stripped out thin wires.

As the cabin rocked back and forth and Lilly clung to my chest under the mass of sodden blankets, I concentrated on wrapping one coil after another carefully around my stack of needles. I had to wait for the light to swing back over me for each wind of the coil.

Bjorn scribbled on a piece of paper in his lap. "We need some way to narrow down our location."

"Why?" Otto said. "What's the point? You think we can walk out if we know where we are?"

"*Det ligger en hund begraven här*—means there is a dog buried here. Something fishy is going on. It will help us figure out what happened."

"How will that help us?"

"I need to know what happened in those two hours."

I didn't say anything but kept winding my coil. I alternated between that and trying to take notes. Another blast of Arctic fury quivered the walls. Lilly's body shivered against mine.

"The Russians did this," said a deep voice.

It was Roman. He didn't lean out of his pod or address anyone. His raspy voice filled the space between the howling wind.

I hadn't said anything to anyone else about Roman. About him being the mysterious billionaire on the run. I was waiting and watching. Seeing how people acted toward him. Was he about to admit something? "Why do you say that?" I asked.

"One way or other, this was Russians."

"This was an accident." Otto adjusted himself below me.

"No accident."

"You know that for sure? Based on what?"

"Oil, the gas. The Russians own the north, but nobody else realizes it yet."

"Norway has more claim than Russia," Bjorn said.

"If anyone owns the North Pole, it's Canada," said a female voice. It was Liz, from the next pod over. "I read up on it before the flight. We claimed it in 1925."

Despite myself, I laughed at that. I'd thought she was French, but apparently she was French *Canadian*, and she was sticking up for her country. It wasn't their usual apologetic approach.

"Ha," Roman said. "Even your friend the United States doesn't recognize your rights to northern waters. You know they swim nuclear submarines between your islands without permission?"

"That's because they're trying to lay claim to the Northwest Passage," Bjorn said. "As the ice melts on the North Pole, the ice between Canada's northern islands will open up a route in the north for shipping. Means they won't need the Panama Canal anymore to get from Europe to Asia. And bigger ships, too."

"And Canada would stop that?" I asked.

"They wouldn't stop it, but they could ask for transport duties. The US doesn't want to pay anyone, even if this goes against three hundred years of maritime law."

"Money, money, money," Roman growled. "It is always all about money."

"He's right," Bjorn said. "The north is warming up five times faster than anywhere south. Means all the oil and gas and natural resources that were under all that ice are now up for grabs. Norway, Denmark, Canada, the US and Russia are all arguing about who owns the Pole."

"Only two of those are actually able to fight about it," Roman said. "Rest of you grovel for scraps."

"You mean, Russia and us?" I said.

"Yes, *you*."

"Roman," I said, "so you think the Russians shot down the plane. But why?"

"To control the north. They do not want people flying up here anymore. They only open the airspace after Perestroika, biggest mistake of twentieth century. They need reason to close again. Mystery airliner goes missing. Good reason to stop."

"You don't think it's about *someone* on the airplane?"

The wind howled in the silence, but I noticed the rocking motion wasn't side to side like it had been the past two hours. Had the wind shifted directions?

"Why you say that?" Roman asked.

"You think it was a random choice to shoot us down?"

"Who said anyone shot us down?" Otto interjected.

"Let him answer," I said.

"I did not say we were shot down."

"Then brought down? You think there was someone on the aircraft?"

It bothered me. Everything bothered me. The holes in the flight deck door. The unknown person up there with Josh—nobody could ID him. Was it a passenger? If it was, why? I sat with Josh and tried to ask him, but all he did was mumble nonsensically.

"I think not accident, but I not know why."

"It was the Chinese." This voice was even lower than Roman's.

It was Jang's father, Shu. He stared right at me from across the aisle. He hadn't said more than two words this whole time, barely more than introducing himself to me.

"It is pride, you and the Russian arguing," Shu said. His English was halting but perfect. "Russia is a faded power, and America is going as well. China is the one who wants control. The Belt and Road, have you ever heard of it?"

"That's the Chinese plan to build like a new Silk Road around the world," Bjorn said.

"Around the *whole* world. Through Asia, Africa, South America, they are building all roads and seaways so everything leads back to China. And that includes the north. Even they want to control all the water. In Tibet they are building dams to block water from glaciers—"

Shu stopped mid-sentence. His boy Jang had his arm around his father's neck and seemed to squeeze it, but then Lilly was squeezing me as well with each new blasting squall outside.

"How would the Chinese have brought down the plane?" I asked. I had the image of the Russian airbase in my mind.

"We took off from China, didn't we?"

"Hong Kong."

"That is China. Who were those men who came on before we took off?"

The men…it took me a second to understand what he was talking about. Before we took off, we'd sat on the tarmac for an hour. Technicians had come on board—and Suzanne said they had to make a last minute crew change. Adrian said they replaced the second set of co-pilots.

"You saw the men do something?"

Shu shrugged. His boy tightened his grip around his father's neck. "I don't know," Shu said finally. "I know the last flight that disappeared, it was going to China. Don't trust them."

The flight that had disappeared over the Indian Ocean a few

years back. Never to be seen again. Nobody had ever found out what happened to that plane. Was it the same fate for us?

He said he didn't trust the Chinese, but wasn't he Chinese?

I was about to ask Shu where he was going, where he came from, when Howard said, "It wasn't the Chinese." He held up two phones. "I tested these, and none of the Chinese Beidou chips and GPS satellites work on the Chinese phones either. This is more than geopolitics, this is something—"

"I'm tired of your theories," Bjorn said.

"My theories? You're busy talking about the Chinese or Russians bringing us down."

"Nobody brought this plane down," Otto said quietly. "It was an accident."

"Why would it have to be a country?" Liz said from the next pod. "Maybe it was terrorists, stupid people with a bomb."

"They still need a reason," I said.

"They need no reason."

The light swung back and forth and circled overhead. I'd almost finished coiling the wire around my pack of needles.

"I know why," Howard said.

A blast of wind wailed against the hull, a rising screech.

Bjorn yelled over the noise, "We are not interested, Howard."

"You should be." The kid almost screamed the words. He stood up straight and held something over his head.

"You think 9-11 was terrorists? You think it wasn't an inside job?"

"Shut up," Bjorn said.

"You want to know who brought down this airliner? It's the deep state. The CIA, the ones who control the CIA, the—"

"What the hell are you talking about?" I pulled Lilly tight against me.

Howard's face contorted into a maniacal leer. "It's in here."

He pointed at a small metal box in his hand.

"Snowden has nothing compared to what I've got in this. Ten terabytes of bringing the deep state to its knees. I stole the American intelligence agencies' combined data snooping across all Asia. I have a meeting next week with the *New York Times*, man. The deep state don't want me coming back to the States. I'm the reason this airliner came down. It's the United States of Goddamned America that stuck us in this hell and we're never getting out alive."

CHAPTER 15

I opened my eyes. Something woke me. It was quiet, the cabin dark—but not black, and not monochrome in its dimness. Glimmers of yellow fluttered across the overhead bins. I blinked and raised one hand to wipe my eyes.

The flashlight was off.

Red reflected through the cabin windows on the other side. I bolted upright.

Absolute silence. Stillness. No wind. Almost no motion in the floor.

And it felt warmer. Much warmer.

Lilly was wet-sweat stuck to me under two layers of down blanket. Her breathing regular and soft. The tiny bulldog puppy nestled against her. A loud snorting-snore broke the silence. That had to be Roman from the sheer volume of it. In the aisle across from me, Jang's eyes were wide open in the semi-darkness. He looked straight at me.

Again a glittering light, this time out the cabin window next to me. A searchlight?

My heart skipped a beat and I listened hard but heard nothing beyond the snoring and snuffling of the sleepers around me. A soft reddish light glow returned outside.

The last thing I remembered was Otto trying to calm down Howard in the middle of one of his fits. Everything was quiet now.

I unwrapped myself from the layers of blankets and clothes and tiptoed to avoid Otto and Bjorn beneath us. I pulled on another pair of jeans—stiff with cold. I selected another pair of shoes to put on and wrapped them in white garbage bags from the galley.

The multi-hued light reflected off the ice outside, bright enough to cast shadows inside.

I made my way a few paces down the aisle and had to step onto a new galley-cart bridge that Otto had erected during the storm. The fuselage had slipped another few feet below the ice but had held—wedged in place, Otto had confidently announced. We weren't going to sink, he said. I needed to believe him.

I pushed past the curtains and pulled away a layer of suitcases stacked as our bulwark against the elements. Behind them was a wall of wet snow. I used one of the cases to shove it away into the slurry of ice at my feet as I balanced on the two galley carts Otto had jammed together as a bridge. Cascading radiance glistened just beyond.

▼▲▼

"Beautiful, isn't it?" Bjorn trudged through the knee-deep snow behind me.

I hadn't heard him come out.

"Incredible," I replied.

I sat on a suitcase and gazed straight up.

A banded ribbon of haunting greens and yellows with arcing violets hung high in the sky. It spanned three-hundred-and-sixty degrees around the horizon into the distance behind us past the nose of the aircraft where it faded into a dark blue. When I came out the air was clear, but a hazy fog crept over the ice behind us.

5 a.m. on my watch. Deep twilight but not quite night.

"We might say to this, *å være midt i smørøyet.*" Bjorn dropped a suitcase next to mine and deposited himself onto it. "Means being in the middle of the melting butter in porridge. When you are somewhere unbelievable."

"I'll be back in a second," I said.

▼▲▼

I held Lilly tight in my arms. "It's called an aurora."

"A roar?" she whispered.

"Ah-roar-ah."

"It's purdy."

"Pret-*tee*," I corrected.

The air was almost warm. A thick fog swept in almost the moment I'd gotten Lilly out with me.

"Is this heaven?" Lilly held out one tiny hand.

A haze of gold and red shimmered around my daughter and me. The colors shifted to violet and then pink, enveloped us in a humid blanket. I held my hand out next to hers—our arms fading into the mist—outstretched my fingers and then wrapped them around hers.

"It's beautiful," she said.

And it was.

The iridescence pulsed and surrounded like a living thing.

"Are we dead?" She whispered so low I could barely hear her.

"Of course not."

"How would you know?"

"Mommy is waiting for us. We're going back to her."

"Are you sure?"

"I'm sure."

The light dimmed and flickered.

"I'm frightened," she said.

Me too, I thought, but I held her tighter and said, "Everything is going to be okay."

"But you're worried."

"So you don't have to be. We're waiting. People are coming. No need to be scared."

The green glow brightened into red and gold, and a fresh breeze blew the billowing fog to reveal the sky. The spell was broken.

I took her back in.

▼▲▼

The spectacular aurora hadn't been the only shock of coming outside.

The other half of the aircraft was gone.

Disappeared.

We hadn't heard anything from Adrian on Howard's messaging app after a few hours into the storm. We weren't sure what to think, and the storm so ragingly intense and loud that there was no way to go outside to see what was happening. The ice around us had broken into a patchwork of channels and floes jostling quietly in what remained of the swells from the storm.

"You think the other part of the plane sank?" I said.

The fog had dissipated.

Bjorn said, "I think that wing sticking up acted like a sail. Had to be blowing at more than a hundred kilometers an hour for a day. Bet it pushed them miles away. Hard to say."

Or tipped them over into the abyss, but I didn't push the point. I didn't want to think about it. Didn't want to imagine what could have happened to Adrian and Irene and the hundreds of desperate people back there. Despite my efforts, my mind filled with images of rushing cold water, of fingers clawing against metal.

Otto told us our section of the plane was stable, but Bjorn and I had discovered a huge new crack in our ice floe. It ran straight through the middle, right down the center under the fuselage. Both edges of the ice now visibly angled inward. It probably wasn't a new crack. The impact of the crash must have caused it, but the storm had made it worse.

At any moment, the two halves of our ice-raft could split and send the nose section of the plane—and us—plunging into the frigid waters. We could abandon it, but then do what? Try and sleep in the open, in the new wet snow? And what would happen if the cold returned? The fuselage was our only shelter.

All the life rafts were in the other half of the plane.

I closed my eyes in silence for a few seconds before opening them again.

The iridescent light cast dappled shadows over the mishmash of ice and dark water that stretched to the fuzzy horizon. More than a mile away, and I doubted we would see the other half. They had just been blown further away. In a few hours it would lighten up and we'd get a better view.

It had warmed up—it didn't even feel cold— but the terrible headache gnawed behind my eyes. My tongue felt like it was attached to the top of my mouth. I needed to remember to drink some water when I got back inside.

"I'd say it was a few degrees above freezing, eh?" Bjorn said. "Maybe even six or seven? Terrifying, isn't it?"

The warm air was a welcome relief, but now I wished it was colder. We needed the ice to hold together, not melt apart. I couldn't even swim, not that it would help.

Bjorn continued, "Last winter temperatures in the Arctic were forty-five degrees Fahrenheit warmer than normal. Imagine if that translated into lower latitudes, if Phoenix had summer temperatures of one-sixty. It's coming in Lilly's lifetime...half of America will become uninhabitable, whether you believe humans are causing it or not."

"I'm more worried about the next few days than decades."

Bjorn looked me up and down. "I noticed you haven't been drinking much water, my friend."

"I have been," I said, but he was right. I'd been keeping it for Lilly.

"You know the air is so dry up here, it's more like a desert than anything else. And being dehydrated will hasten frostbite, lower your blood pressure, a whole lot of bad things. You want to keep your little girl alive, you need to stay healthy."

He produced a bottle of water from his pockets. "I've been stuffing it with snow and melting it down. Come on."

I took a few sips. He encouraged me to drink more so I finished it.

The moon hung behind us—it hadn't set in four days—but it wasn't full anymore. Maybe three quarters. A shimmering red dot below it—Mars—with Venus almost opposite in the sky right at the horizon. Venus was the third brightest object in the sky after the sun and moon.

Straight in front of us the sky was darker—almost purple-black—and the aurora was brightest. Overhead the sky was deep blue, dark enough for Polaris to shine through. A few other stars pricked through the heavens with it, Aldebaran in the Taurus constellation barely visible near the moon.

The horizon-to-horizon view was massive, unfettered by trees or buildings. Seemed ten times bigger than any sky I'd ever seen before. The glowing ribbon of green fluttered and stuttered, shifted one way and then back and then began to undulate against a brightening red background.

The scale was impossible to comprehend—like a wall into heaven—the speed of transitions in the light show breathtaking. How could something so massive and quick be absolutely silent? The blues and purples and gold and greens reflected against the rolling horizon-to-horizon snowscape—like we'd been transported into some other dimension.

"Same principle as neon light tubes," Bjorn said as he watched me watching the aurora. "Charged particles from the sun—the solar wind—are funneled into channels by the Earth's magnetic field. When they hit atoms in the atmosphere, it gives off light. The red"—he pointed high overhead—"is from oxygen atoms way above two-hundred kilometers, the blue over there from nitrogen, and the big green"—he traced the warbling ribbon—"is oxygen at about a hundred kilometers."

"You know what this means?" I said. "Howard's theory of magnetic reversal isn't true."

"Unless we switched north for south."

"Really?"

Bjorn laughed and shook his head at the same time. "Howard has *han har roterende fis i kasketten.* Rotating crap in his cap. Not all quite there. He's off his meds. You know that?"

"Off his mind is more like it."

Bjorn lowered his voice. "I saw him scatter pills onto the floor. I picked them up and asked Liz. It's Haldol. An anti-psychotic. Used to treat schizophrenia."

"Those pills were missing from the med kit," I said.

Why would he steal pills from the med kit and then throw them away? Then again, if he was psychotically delusional, he might think we'd try to use them on him—and if he was psychotic, then what else was he doing? Was he the one who took the Ventolin? And the missing adrenaline? He didn't seem dangerous, but then again...

I took my phone from my inside-jean pocket and turned it on. I flipped to the map app. It still said we were somewhere near Hamburg. The battery was redlining. Almost gone, despite me only turning it on once in a while as a light. I turned it off. Another shred of our technological bubble disappearing.

"No GPS," I said. "Howard checked those phones from the other plane, the Xiaomi brand? Said no Chinese or Russian GPS satellites working either."

"Not sure you should trust Howard."

Trust. "You and Roman seem to get on. How did you know him?"

Bjorn's face creased up in the green glow. "Roman?"

"You knew him?"

"Never met him before."

I paused a beat and then two and waited for him to explain. I was sure I'd seen him arguing with Roman in the lineup before check in.

"So you two don't know each other? Don't know him at all?"

"No."

Tingling across my skin and up the nape of my neck as I realized he was purposely lying to me. Why would he lie? He didn't even say he knew who Roman was. How could a climate researcher not know who one of the world's biggest oil and gas oligarchs was? Someone like Roman had to be a public enemy number one for Bjorn.

"Daddy?"

I turned. Lilly waded through the deep snow toward me. "Honey, sweetheart, you can't just—"

"But I wanted to see more of the pretty lights."

A few steps behind Lilly was Jang, and twenty feet away his father hung back at the edge of the shredded fuselage. The little white bulldog was gamely trying to navigate the snow and follow the two kids, but barked once and then twice before going back inside.

I took Lilly into my right arm and wrapped her up. My left shoulder was sore but getting better, and the dull pain in my face almost forgotten. Liz had done her best to clean up my smashed nose. I had looked at it in the bathroom mirror, but there was nothing to be done.

"The lights are beautiful, aren't they?" Lilly and I both gawked at the glimmering heavens.

"I'm going to scout around the plane," Bjorn said. "I won't be far."

He got up and Jang took his seat on the suitcase beside me. The little guy smiled at me and then turned his face up to the sky.

"Are we going to die?" Lilly said in a quiet voice.

Emma and I hadn't had time to have a talk about death and dying with Lilly. Not that we hadn't had time, but it wasn't something you wanted to talk to a five-year-old about. I didn't even know how to approach the topic.

"I told you," I said in my most soothing voice, "people are coming for us. We're going back to Mommy soon. The storm is over. Everything is okay."

"Who is coming?" She looked down and kicked her feet.

After wrapping her feet in six layers of socks over her shoes, I'd double-bagged her whole lower leg below the knee in plastic bags and wrapped it tight with elastics.

When I didn't reply right away she added, "Because Howard said we're all going to die."

"Don't listen to Howard, he's not...he's not right in the head. Do you understand?"

"Is Nanny Zhen going to die?" Lilly started to wheeze on each breath.

This caught me off guard again. "I...uh..."

"Dying is not the end," Jang said.

The kid's voice was soothing. His English surprisingly clear. He looked at me to make sure it was okay before he continued. "You see that star up there, Lilly?"

He pointed at Polaris.

My daughter nodded. She wheezed in and out on each little breath.

"The star's light takes thousands of years to reach us, and the star might be dead already right now, but we see its light. Its light never goes out, never stops being a part of this universe, and it is the same for all of us."

What did they teach these Chinese kids in school? Even I was spellbound and looked up.

I couldn't help thinking of my own father. When he died I felt like I'd been cut adrift. As much as I'd felt like I didn't need him anymore—when he was gone, I realized how much of my life revolved around him, how many things I wished I'd said but never could anymore. Was he up there, somehow looking down on me?

Lilly's wheezing pulled me out of my daydreaming.

I decided to get her puffer from my pocket.

"Please, Mr. Mitch, let me try," Jang said.

The kid asked me to sit Lilly down by him, and he led her through some breathing exercises. Within a few minutes, her breathing returned to normal. I put the puffer away, even more impressed than before.

CHAPTER 16

The start of our fourth day on the ice.

For nine hours I'd watched the auroras glowing in the sky until twilight had washed them away. The air was still warm but cooling.

We had stripped away some of the snow to inspect the crack down the middle of our floe. It seemed stable, as long as the wind and swells didn't increase.

Every few hours I would undress Lilly and try to clean her up, find some fresher clothes and blankets from the diminishing supply and make sure she ate something—and more importantly, drank something. I made a show of doing the same myself, but even after Bjorn's warning I held back and left most of what we had for my daughter.

I was tucked back in with Lilly, checking my watch every few minutes as time crept past. She squirmed and I felt her tickling me.

Not tickling, but writing. A skin sign. I played along. Two downward strokes. One in the middle.

An "H."

"You're hungry?" I whispered.

She nodded almost imperceptibly.

"Want some pretzels?"

Now she shook her head, but much more animated.

"Me, either."

She wriggled closer into me. I knew what she meant. "When they come get us, you know what I'm going to eat? A big, juicy hamburger. And some fries. You want some fries, too?"

She nodded.

Imagining a hamburger set off the saliva glands in my mouth, and it hurt.

"And milkshakes," I said. I knew they were her favorite. "Two big chocolate milk shakes. Even three. You want three?"

She nodded even harder.

"In a day or two, you can have anything you want, Lillypad. You rest."

▼▲▼

Curled up with a sleeping Lilly, I borrowed the LED flashlight and scribbled down some notes in my journal. I tried to make sure to do a little bit every day. A part of me wanted to write down the emotions, wanted to believe I could use this when we were rescued, to write a book, maybe. Like I'd been telling Emma I would.

But another part of me I didn't even want to admit felt like I needed to record what had happened. In case we didn't survive. In case someone found it, like the journals of countless doomed polar explorers before. Something about this wasn't just an accident—Roman Kolchak being here, those bullet holes, the two hours of missing flight time.

I checked my watch again for the millionth time, but I'd finally had enough of feeling like the time on my watch wasn't the *right* time.

"Hey, everyone," I said, careful not to speak too loud to wake Lilly up. "I have a suggestion. Can we all please set our watches twelve hours ahead? Set to 2 p.m. right now?"

I was tired of feeling upside down with the time. Right now my watch said 2 a.m. Hong Kong time, but the sky was about its brightest.

I'd decided I wanted to make this the middle of the afternoon to regain some small sense of normalcy.

Roman had come by and shown me some of the Coke cans. They'd frozen solid the night before, as well as all the food we had stacked in the galley—he told everyone we'd better start storing the bottles of water and soda under our covers.

Bjorn went outside and stuffed all the empty water bottles with fresh snow and brought them inside. Otto made a point of telling everyone not to eat snow—it would lower our core temperature and give us diarrhea and dehydrate us.

An inventory of food was even more worrying.

I had a jacket pocket full of peanuts and pretzels that I'd been trying to feed to Lilly, but this was almost empty—and the fourteen people who went to the other side took a lot of what we'd had left.

We had sixteen frozen meals, twelve buns and forty-three chocolate bars plus a collection of pretzels left between the eleven of us. Less than five thousand calories each, Otto had whispered as I catalogued it to him. Not including the soda, Roman had pointed out. Sixty-odd cans of soda added another thousand calories each.

I hadn't really eaten in at least two days.

My headache was getting worse, but I only had one bottle of unfrozen water left—which I made sure Lilly drank, and she insisted we give some to the puppy.

I had some words with Howard when I came back inside. Told him to keep quiet, to never talk to my daughter. He said he hadn't, and then he asked me about the lights in the sky.

Howard said that they were watching us.

He said not to trust anyone who came here. He told me we had to escape, to leave.

I told him again not to talk to my daughter. More forcefully this time, with more naked aggression, but I wasn't sure if that was the right thing to do or not.

Bjorn and Otto had more words with Howard, mostly out of

earshot, but I heard them asking about his medication. He was getting more and more agitated.

I decided to keep away from him.

I checked in with Liz who was taking care of Josh. He was asleep, or in a coma. She wasn't sure. She tried to give him water, and considered sticking a tube down his throat, but she wasn't sure she could get it right. She said he didn't need intubating as much as he needed a nasogastric tube for feeding or an IV for saline fluids. She didn't feel qualified enough doing any of them. Not yet, anyway.

Over the next few hours the sky lightened and the aurora bled away. Yellow light reflected on the snow outside my cabin window.

I painstakingly wound the coils of wire around my needle stack, and used some tape to connect six batteries together end-to-end. I finished by taping the stripped ends of my coiled wire to the positive and negative ends of the battery stack. I had to leave it for a few hours and let the current run through the whole assembly.

Otto had gone out to see if he could spot the other half of the plane.

He had only just gone out when he yelled, "Hey, come and see this."

I jumped up and spilled my science project onto the floor. "What is it?" I yelled back.

Was it the ice? The crack opening?

The sun was clear over the horizon.

Not high in the sky, but the disk of the sun was fully clear in an almost blue sky.

I'd taped a fresh set of garbage bags around my feet before coming out. The snow was slushy, and puddles of water formed in the bottom of footprints in the knee-deep snow. The air warm. The crack unchanged.

But the wind was picking up.

I said, "The sun didn't even rise two days ago, did it?"

Liz had come out to see for herself. "Have we been driven that far south by the wind?"

Were we drifting into a warmer region? The air, the melting snow—it all made sense—but we had no life raft, I reminded myself for the dozenth time.

The entire front section of the plane was covered in a layer of snow now. There was no way anyone flying over—or even a satellite taking images—could discern us from the snowscape.

"I think it is a mirage," Bjorn said. He held one hand over his eyes and squinted. "It happens sometimes in the north."

"Why is it so warm?" Liz said.

Bjorn shrugged. "It happens. Last year it was above freezing at the North Pole in the middle of winter. I'm going to look on the other side, to see if I can see the other part of the plane."

We inspected the central ice crack again. Nothing we could see had changed.

He traipsed through the deep snow away from us.

"Was it possible for the wind to push us that far?" I said to Otto. "In one day?"

"We don't even know where we are."

"I know where we are."

Otto, Liz and myself turned to find Howard standing at the edge of the fuselage. He pointed something at us and had a sack over one shoulder.

"Hey, hey." It was Bjorn's voice, on the other side of the nose of the aircraft. "My God, come now, I've found…" his voice trailed off.

"Nobody move." Howard pointed the thing in his hand at us.

It took me a second to realize what it was.

A gun.

"Guys, I've found Rasheed," Bjorn said. "Come now, I think he's—"

A loud crack.

Howard fired the gun once and then twice into the air and pointed it back at us.

"Didn't you hear what I said? I told everyone—"

Something moved behind him. A shadow rushed forward. Shu dove straight into Howard's back, tackling him face-forward into the snow.

CHAPTER 17

I t hurts. Stop hurting me!" Howard screamed.

"Maybe you should loosen it a bit," I said to Otto.

"You want him to escape?"

I didn't want him to get loose, but escape? To where exactly?

Otto cinched the strip of cloth tighter around Howard's chest.

"Please be quiet," he said to him, his voice polite yet aggressive.

I said, "So that's your gun?"

"I told you," Otto replied. "I'm the Air Marshal. *That* is my gun, yes. And it wasn't fired before Howard pulled the trigger."

"Why didn't you say something before this?" Bjorn demanded.

Otto switched on the flashlight and inspected his knot-work. He clicked off the light.

Even with the sun clearing the horizon outside, it was dark inside the cabin. We'd secured Howard in his pod, but it was awkward. The seat didn't really have a back—the whole thing was integrated—and it took four of us to carry Howard's writhing body up here. I'd gotten soaked up to my waist when I slipped in the ice slurry by the entrance.

With the rising temperature, the whole cabin now smelled fetid. Waste from one of the upper toilets had seeped down the aisles and soaked the carpets. I itched under my layers of clothing.

After subduing Howard, Shu had come straight to Jang and collected his son into his arms. I asked him to take Lilly with him, and the three of them were sequestered away in the corner of the cabin as far from us as possible.

She kept the tiny LED light we'd found. She was scared to be in the dark, so I made sure it was never fully dark for her at any time.

Roman hadn't participated at all in the melee.

Howard whined, "Don't let him take those."

Otto had removed his precious disk drive and put it into the pocket of his jacket. For safe keeping, he said.

"Not another word," Otto said to Howard, his nose an inch from his, "or I'll stuff a rag in your mouth. Do you understand?"

Howard glared at Otto and nodded in silence.

"I made a mistake. I should have kept the gun with me at all times. I only put it down a few minutes when I was changing." Otto had secured the gun in his waistband now.

I saw the menacing bulge under his clothes. *Those holes in the flight deck door.*

"You haven't answered me." Bjorn stood ten feet away, his arms crossed.

"I have my reasons."

"I think we deserve to know those reasons."

"And I told you, I'm not—"

"Looked like Rasheed was bludgeoned." Liz pulled back the curtain and took off her wound-up head covering. Her cheeks flushed from the relative heat inside.

She had gone outside to inspect Rasheed's body. When Howard came outside brandishing the pistol, Bjorn had just found the poor man's body under the snow near the ice wall at the front of the crumpled nose of the aircraft.

"You sure of that?" Otto said.

"The whole back of his head is purple. Looks like blunt trauma to me."

"You've got to be kidding me," I muttered. "So you're saying he was killed? By who?" I kept my voice down.

Otto said, "Could he have fallen onto the ice? Could that have caused the injury?"

"It is possible," Liz admitted.

I looked at Howard first, at his skittering eyes, then Bjorn and Roman and Liz. I didn't turn to look at Shu and the two kids, but finished by looking straight at Otto.

"Can you prove you're the Air Marshal?" I said.

"I have the passenger manifest—"

"You can show us?"

"Memorized. You want me to tell you all something about yourselves?"

Bjorn's crossed arms dropped to his sides. His face went slack.

"Everyone needs to remain calm," Otto said. "Liz, with all due respect, you are not a real doctor. You have a PhD in microbiology after doing medicine, but never practiced, from what I read in your file. So you can't go telling me what happened to Rasheed. Maybe he slipped and hit his head on the ice, maybe a lot of things. That was one hell of a storm we survived. Maybe he had an argument with someone going over to the other plane. Maybe a lot of things. It's no use getting ourselves worked up."

"They're coming, I'm telling you, they're coming for us." Howard squirmed in his seat and tried to get free. "Don't listen to this asshole, he's one of them. I can hear them. They're coming. Check his bags. I looked through them. He has equipment, I don't know—"

"Didn't I tell you to shut up?" Otto held up a sodden rag of clothing.

"I bet this asshole is the one who killed Rasheed," Bjorn pointed at Howard.

"Or maybe Rasheed was the terrorist. Or Shu." Howard spat the words back. "Maybe that other guy, Manu? Where the hell is he? Why did he leave in such a hurry with the others? He went over to the other side, now that part of the plane is gone."

"Did you take the Ventolin?" I said to Howard. "Did you take the stuff from the med kit?"

"I didn't take anything."

"Look at this." Bjorn had Rasheed's radio in his hand and held it up. "Look, look what he did. The 'transmit' button on the radio has been ripped off."

Howard was the only one who'd been trying to use it.

"I didn't do that," Howard said quietly.

"What else have you done?"

"I didn't do it."

"Why hasn't anyone come yet?" The words came out of my own mouth, yet they sounded like it was someone else speaking. The room wobbled in my vision. "We're stuck on this melting ice cube in the middle of the ocean, no life rafts, no emergency beacons, and now we have a homicidal maniac—"

"Calm down." Otto put his hand on my arm, the same way Emma used to do. "You're hyperventilating. Liz, we have some Lorazepam in the med kit…?"

I took a deep breath and exhaled, then took a few steps down the aisle past Liz to my pod-seat and the mess of dirty blankets and clothes. I sat down and put my head into the palms of my hands. "I'm fine."

Liz put a hand on my arm. She had put her small backpack on, the one with her package in it.

"I'm fine. I'm good." I said it loud enough so Lilly could hear me.

The wind had picked up some more outside. The floor rolled slightly on the swell.

I felt something under me as I sat down and pulled it out. My needle and battery experiment. I inspected it to give my mind something to focus on. The battery was probably dead by now. It was as good as it was going to get.

"Everyone, calm down," Otto said. He stood up at the front of the cabin next to Howard. "I can guarantee that there are a lot of good people out there right now, searching for us, and I bet they're not far away."

"How can you know that?" Bjorn said.

"I know it doesn't feel like it, but the entire world is out there looking for us right now. There are probably four different navies and half the world's air forces and satellites—"

"Then why isn't GPS working?"

"We do have a working transponder."

I had finished undoing the package around my needle and battery pack. "We do?" I looked up at Otto.

"The flight deck voice recorder is up in the front. I've had a look a few times and it seems like it's intact. That thing is transmitting our location right now."

"How do you know it's working?" I said.

"We've been here for four days," Bjorn added.

"Three days," Otto corrected Bjorn as he looked at his watch. "Three days and six hours. That's seventy-eight hours, and for almost half of that we had a massive storm overhead. I'm sure there's a big search grid, but we're not underwater, either. There are visuals. The sky is clear today. Be patient. They're coming."

"But you don't even know where we are," Bjorn said. "We could be thousands of miles away from where they're looking. We had two hours missing that we don't even know about—how do you explain that? And—"

"I think I know where we are," I said. "Or at least I have a better idea."

I held up my little experiment in front of me. I suspended the pack of needles on a single thread, balanced at its middle. The needles swung back and forth, but wavered in a determined and focused way. They pointed in a definite direction, about forty-five degrees to the left of the nose of the plane.

▼▲▼

"I figured Howard's experiment with those tiny magnets he pulled out of the cell phone wasn't good enough. We needed a bigger magnet."

Bjorn was busy drawing a new polar map on nine sheets of paper on the forward bulkhead of the cabin. "That was a good idea, Mitch. Excellent."

Where he was excited, Otto seemed annoyed. Our Air Marshal sat down, shaking his head, convinced that our obsession wasn't going to get us anywhere. He said we had to conserve our energy and stay calm.

Roman listened to him, but then the big Russian never did anything but sit. Shu had gotten back into his seat with Jang. Lilly with the dog in our pod area. Liz attended to Howard—he had a few cuts and scrapes. Our prisoner glared at Otto but remained silent, his mouth rag-free.

I got my idea from doing the same thing in science class in high school many years ago. Create an electromagnet by wrapping coils of wire around something with iron in it and then attaching to a battery. Leave the current going through it for long enough, and you turned the lump of metal into a magnet itself. So I made as big a magnet as I could, and then hung it from a string and—boom, it pointed in a definite direction, no matter how many times I knocked it off course.

Except we weren't quite sure which end was north.

Bjorn took out a marker—we'd found a pack of children's Crayola coloring markers—and drew a large circle. "So this is the Arctic Circle," he explained.

"What difference will it make knowing where we are?" Otto said.

"And we know we passed the Pole," Bjorn continued, ignoring him.

"We flew for two and a half hours after that," I said, "and we have no idea where."

"*But*, two days ago the sun didn't rise—which means we are quite a bit inside the Arctic." Bjorn drew a dotted line a few inches inside his Arctic Circle and marked it seventy-five degrees north, and then another a few inches outside the North Pole and marked it eighty-seven degrees. "And we're not exactly at the Pole, since we have variation in light and dark. We're inside these two circles, more or less."

So we were somewhere inside a two-thousand-mile-wide donut.

"The Magnetic Pole is located here right now." He made a dot slightly to the left and down from the geographic North Pole. "We can approximate south as the halfway point between where we saw the sun rise and set three days ago, so the nose of the plane is pointing more-or-less toward the Geographic Pole."

He drew a dotted line about two-thirds of the way down the circle at a slanting angle which went through the Magnetic Pole. "But your compass is pointing about forty-five degrees away from the nose of the plane, which means our location is somewhere along this line."

"But only the part of the line inside the donut," I said.

"That's right."

He started scribbling in islands and land masses—at the top, Russia, and the bottom, Canada. Top-right was Europe and Svalbard Island, and in the bottom left he wrote, *Alaska*. At the other lower corner he made a more detailed scribbling of Greenland.

"See, our line of probable location passes right through Greenland and Ellesmere Island."

That part of the line was on the bottom of the donut.

"Either that or the East Siberian Sea," I pointed out. The line within the donut also extended toward the Russian coast on the other side of the Arctic Ocean.

"But we saw the sun come up today, which means we're drifting south."

"You said that was a mirage," Otto said.

"Maybe I was wrong. If we're drifting south, it means we have to be in the Transpolar Current." He drew arrows on the map pointing down between Greenland and Ellesmere, and down the east side of Greenland. "The currents from Russia all head north, and the one through the Bering Strait comes north past Alaska and gets caught in the circulating Beaufort Gyre."

He drew a circle to the left of the pole with arrows going around and around. "They used to call this the Pole of Inaccessibility." He pointed at the center of the Beaufort Gyre.

"Why is that?" I asked.

"Because the old polar explorers thought this spot would be the hardest spot to get to. A never-ending rotating mass of ice, even more remote than the North Pole—but we're not anywhere near there."

"How can you possibly know that?" Otto sat up in his seat. "We're drifting. You said it yourself. You're making a lot of assumptions and a lot of guesswork. We can't get a location fix. We're under a lot of psychological—"

"The warm air. It's above freezing today. We have to be somewhere here." Bjorn pointed to the north of Greenland again. "It's the warm air brought up by the North Atlantic current. If we're in the top of the West Greenland current, then we'll be brought south, down into the shipping lanes—"

"That will take months"—Howard's voice a disembodied whisper—"we'll all be dead by then."

Otto held up a threatening lump of rags. "What did I tell you?"

A loud crack.

This time it wasn't a gun going off.

The floor juddered under my feet. Lilly shrieked as the cabin pitched to the left, a booming thud echoing as the ice shattered below the fuselage and the ground fell away.

TRANSCRIPT AUDIO 3
National Transportation Safety Board.
Mid-Flight Disappearance of Allied 695,
Boeing 777, NTSB/AIR.
Washington, DC

Take a bathroom break?" Peter said.

"Sure," Richard replied. He needed to stretch his legs anyway.

Peter got up and unlocked the door to the conference room and exited, but before it closed, Richard noticed his new partner pulled his phone from his suit jacket. The door thudded shut.

Past 10 p.m. already. They had ordered in some sandwiches, the scraps of which were dumped into the trash. Richard went to inspect to make sure no notes had inadvertently made it into the garbage. Reporters weren't above dumpster diving to get a scoop.

Then again, what did they really know so far?

He took the opportunity to change to a new recording tape and start a fresh pot of coffee. He dumped the remains of the old one into the sink and refilled the machine.

The door opened. Peter reappeared.

"No phone calls, in or out," Richard said. "Not without my say so."

Peter affected a surprised look but then admitted, "I just called my wife."

"Call her in here next time."

"Sure. Sorry."

They sat back at the table across from each other, the recording machine in the middle.

Peter looked at his notes and said, "So commercial GPS wasn't working after the crash. You think maybe that had something to do with it?"

"With what?"

"The crash. Maybe a magnetic anomaly? Solar storm? Different rules for this stuff that far north."

"I think we need to focus on the two-plus hours of missing flight time. Mitch was very specific. 10:55 p.m. Hong Kong time after the crash. We have them on radar track as they passed the Pole?"

"Russians tracked them all the way up. It's right after that all signals go dark."

"Yet this account claims they didn't hit ice for almost three more hours."

"If this account is accurate."

"Let's assume it is."

Peter shrugged, okay. "That much flight time could put them anywhere within the Arctic Circle, all the way from Russia to Canada. What we *think* was Allied 695 appears on US military radar over the Beaufort Sea about an hour after it disappeared from Russian scopes."

"Which is where we've been looking, but that can't be right. A huge storm was over the Beaufort Sea at that time, and they didn't land in heavy weather. That only came a day or two later."

"There were two big lows circulating in the Arctic at that time."

"Right," Richard admitted. "But they didn't land in either of them, which means we know where they weren't. We need to start checking satellite images of the whole goddamn Arctic Circle, not just the Beaufort area."

"That's eight million square miles. The Russians have already—"

"I don't think we should trust the Russian data."

Peter rocked onto the two back legs of his chair. "Now that is a loaded statement."

"And I need you to contact the TSA. Find out who Otto Garcia is.

Get all the information on this Air Marshal that we can."

"What about the rest of them? Howard? Isabelle? Bjorn? Roman Kolchak?"

"Start with Garcia."

"What about Matthews?"

"What about him?"

"Shouldn't we investigate him first?"

The new pot had finished brewing. Richard got up.

"Of course," he said. "Start a file on Matthews." He poured two cups. "And Kolchak. Find out exactly how he ended up on that flight." He sat back down and offered the coffee to his partner.

"You want me to continue reading?" Peter asked.

Richard picked up the journal and took a sip. "Thanks, but I'll do it."

CHAPTER 18

The fuselage had dropped at least another two feet deeper into the water. A ten-foot-wide gap of water where the ripped metal rested against the submerged ice. We tested the depth of it, and it wasn't more than five feet until we hit something solid beneath, but we had a hard time illuminating the gap to see what was down there.

For a terrible second I thought that we were going straight into the Arctic Ocean.

But the ice held.

For now.

How much longer was impossible to tell.

"Can you hear that?"

Bjorn turned up the volume on the radio. Below the static something garbled. Definitely a human voice.

"Keep trying," I said.

Another victory.

Bjorn had taken over the shortwave. It worked, despite being sabotaged by Howard. Maybe Howard hadn't even been trying to find a signal on it. It only took Bjorn a few minutes of playing with the controls to hear some warbling voices.

I'd tried to get some sleep and had cuddled up with Lilly, but my mind kept circling around and around. I went outside with Otto and attempted to make an "X" in the fresh snow using black suitcases we could spare from our wall. It was well above freezing. I was soaked. It was warmer than before, but that seemed to make it colder as the wet chill penetrated the layers of clothing. When we came back in, only one thing was on my mind.

The transponder.

The flight deck voice recorder had a transponder in it. If that wasn't working, we were as good as dead. It was the only way the outside world would find us.

▼▲▼

I strained to pull back the flight deck door.

A rancid stench assaulted us. We had strips of clothing around our noses and mouths, but the warming had accelerated the decomposition of the three corpses in the twisted metal coffin of the nose. A thick blanket of snow up top hadn't helped by trapping the humid air. Everything melted. A slick layer of water covered everything.

"It's down there and to the right," Otto said. He held the flashlight up and shone it through the gap. "It's orange, but you can't quite see it from this angle."

"But you have?"

"I got in further with Bjorn earlier. The CVR looks intact."

The right side of the flight deck looked as destroyed as the rest of it. I wanted to see it for myself, but there was another reason I needed to get Otto away from the others.

"Do you know who Roman is?" I whispered. I let go of the flight deck door.

Otto nodded. "Roman Kolchak. The Russian billionaire owner of Rosomakha, the huge oil and gas company. They do most of their business in the Arctic—which is ironic. Or at least, he *was* the owner."

"What in the world is he doing on this plane? Why isn't he on a private jet?"

"He couldn't get authorization to leave Russia—some sticky business with the Politburo—so he smuggled himself out. He's applying for asylum in the US."

"You knew who he was the whole time?"

"We flag any persons of interest on the manifest, and I usually look through profiles of the First Class passengers. Technically, he's under my protection."

"Is it possible Russia brought us down because he's on the plane?"

"I have considered that possibility."

"And you didn't say anything?"

"I was watching."

"Watching?" I said incredulously. "And Bjorn—he lied to me. I saw him talking to Roman before the plane took off. He told me he didn't know Roman. Said he had no idea who he was."

"Are you sure?"

"He's lying. Why would he lie?"

"He's not lying about working for Greenpeace," Otto said.

"Is there anything else you're not telling us?" I tried to keep my voice down. "Anything at *all* about any other passengers on this plane? What about the five-hundred pounds of lithium batteries?"

Otto exhaled and rubbed his head with one hand. He shrugged, no, nothing else.

"Why did you take Howard's disk drive?" I asked.

"So I can control him if something happens. You want it? Might be better if you take it, in case he gets loose and comes after me."

Otto handed it to me. It wasn't much. A small bit of metal three inches by four. I wasn't sure I wanted it, but took it anyway. I put the disk drive into my jean pocket.

Something else didn't make sense. "When Adrian came over—the flight manager—he didn't seem to know you."

"That was the plan."

"Plan?"

"He was under instructions—is *always* under instructions—not to give up my identity. Standard operating procedure with respect to the Air Marshal." Otto turned off the flashlight. "We've gone somewhat beyond SOP."

It was almost pitch black. I remembered he had a gun on him. Did he have any other weapons? I tensed, sensing him moving in the darkness.

"You shouldn't leave Lilly with Shu," he whispered.

"What?" I could hardly hear him, his voice was so low. I moved closer.

"Mr. Shu, Jang's father. Or, he says he's the kid's father."

I waited in the darkness for him to explain.

"Shu and the boy came onto the plane under false passports. The man's real name is Pemba Ldong."

"Why did they let him onto the plane?"

"I only got an update once we were underway. They didn't catch it at the airport. Not right away."

It took me a few seconds to process. "Why is he on the plane?"

"We don't know, but he's on our watch lists. Pemba Ldong is a known terrorist, and he doesn't usually work alone."

▼▲▼

Exhausted but unable to sleep. Clammy itchy heat under misshapen layers but bone-numb cold tingling fingers and toes. Pastel-gray light draped itself over the aisles and pods in the tomb-like silence of the cabin.

I collected Lilly and the puppy from the pile of blankets she'd burrowed in together with Jang. Shu—or Pemba Ldong, if what Otto told me was true—gave me a curious look when I came to collect Lilly. I said that it was time for us to take a nap together, but then, she was already asleep and mewled and complained when I took her.

I noticed that Jang didn't immediately cuddle into Shu. Or Pemba? What should I call him? *I'd better call him Shu*, even in my head.

I didn't want to slip. Didn't want to let the secret out. My mind skittered from one thought to another without touching down, my body and mind exhausted but real sleep impossible. Night never fully wrapped its soothing black-blanket around us in this ashen-twilight purgatory.

Fear wormed at the pit of my stomach in the bone-chilling weariness.

Otto said that Pemba/Shu was a Tibetan terrorist, was red-listed on Interpol by the Chinese for blowing up dams high in the Himalayas. A Buddhist terrorist. I'd seen them in the news before we left. I'd asked, *Had he killed people*? Otto wasn't sure. Was Jang his son? He doubted it. Otto said the kid was just cover, a way to make Shu blend in.

Blowing up dams wasn't the same as taking down airliners.

Or was it?

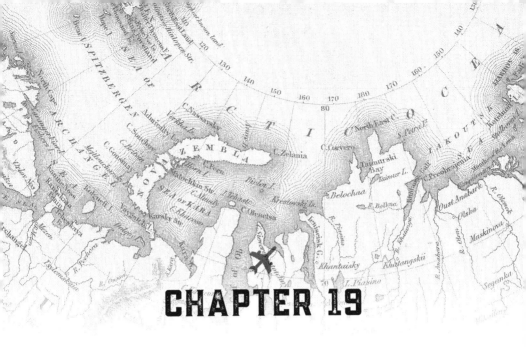

CHAPTER 19

It dawned on me that everyone who remained on this side of the aircraft had a reason for wanting to stay separate from the main cabin. Roman, the Russian billionaire—who knew what he was afraid of? Pemba/Shu and Jang—what were they escaping? What had they done? Otto the guardian. Bjorn the liar—why exactly was he here? And Liz? I hadn't figured her out.

And me? And Lilly? How did we end up here?

It was my fault.

My headache pounded. When had I last eaten? I gnawed on a frozen KitKat and tried to get Lilly to eat some.

She refused.

When had she last eaten?

I fantasized about a hamburger. Big and thick, hot off the grill. Piled with grilled mushrooms. My stomach grumbled and tightened. My brain a raw-frozen-molasses of neurons.

Liz had encamped herself in the pod with Josh at the top of the rows and tended to him. Lilly and I below them, with Jang and Shu one pod below that on our side of the cabin. We'd all moved as high as we could, away from the slush of ice and water now at the edge of the curtains.

Roman remained alone on his side of the cabin. Away from everyone else.

Howard slumped forward, tied up in his seat in the middle row, every now and then looking around with bleary eyes to mutter obscenities. He cried out that his hands were cold and Liz checked on him and said soothing words and encouraged him to take his meds.

Otto installed himself above Howard, with Bjorn in the pod-bed below playing with the radio, static crackling, every now and then garbled words coming in and out—cricket scores in India was the best he'd been able to manage.

But that was enough.

The outside world was still there.

At least we'd regained some rough idea of where we were. People were looking for us—Otto had managed to convince me of that. Convinced *us* of that.

Hope was what kept people alive, he said.

The voices in my head talked to me, too. Somewhere Emma was out there thinking that her daughter was dead, the voices said. That her husband was dead.

But we weren't.

I'm not going to let that happen.

I had managed to fall asleep.

Eight hours? I checked my watch.

8 a.m. on my newly adjusted time zone, now twelve hours ahead of Hong Kong Time.

I rubbed my eyes.

The start of yet another day on the ice. How much longer could we survive?

Ten hours of a fitful waking nightmare of fidgeting and itching. In more than four days I hadn't changed my underclothes. A rash burned between my thighs, and in more private places.

The temperature had dropped since I'd laid down for this last misery-sleep.

The cold was one thing, but the newfound dampness with the mercury dropping was a whole new creeping terror of what the next hours might bring. The cabin smelled sickly sweet of meat-rot and faintly of ammonia. Static hissed on the radio from Bjorn's pod, and then the chatter of voices for a few seconds before static again.

An iron twilight hung immobile outside my cabin window like a steel wool cap pulled over the world's head. A silver three-quarter moon skimmed motionless over a monotonous-gray-white horizon. Water, water, everywhere…yet…

Those holes in the flight deck door. I'd looked at them again when I was with Otto.

The bulldog puppy squirmed in the space between Lilly and I. My daughter's eyes were open and looking at me.

"We're going to be okay," I said.

She closed her eyes. The puppy licked her. She giggled. I smiled. Whatever Roman said, this puppy was worth her weight in gold.

Gold.

Which would only be valuable if we could eat it right now.

I was hungry. Beyond hungry, if I was being honest. Tired of rationing these damned snacks. Not for the first time I felt the puppy's meaty warmth and tried not to. Putting the thought away, I extricated myself and left the two of them nestled—almost invisible—under the mound of fabrics.

▼▲▼

My pants were loose around my waist. Not that I couldn't lose a few pounds. The headache never seemed to go away.

Something new, though. It felt like my feet were swimming in mud inside my shoes each time I took a step. Tingling. Prickly. Squishy.

I strapped myself into the jump seat against the bulkhead above Josh's pod where Liz was half-sleeping. I undid the elastics and plastic bags and pulled off the last of the layers around my feet and peered at them.

I muttered aloud to nobody, "What is that?"

Was it another layer of plastic? My feet were a different color from the rest of my leg. I wiggled the toes but didn't feel any pain. I scratched the skin…it felt…numb? Tingling.

In the semi-darkness I rooted around in the bags of clothes against the upper bulkhead for more socks. Something dry. Nothing was. Otto had parked himself against the upper bulkhead next to me, right above Howard. The jailkeeper's position.

I turned on my phone's light and tried to inspect my right foot. Chalk-white.

The rest of my leg tanned-pink.

"Trench foot," Otto said.

I didn't know he was awake. "Trench what?"

"Like the poor bastards in the trenches in World War I."

I strained to look at the bottom of my foot. Water-wrinkled like I'd been in a bathtub for a week. Not quite white, but grayish. The toenails, too.

"You have to take care of that," Otto said. "Try to wash and dry them. Don't cut off circulation with wrapping too tight."

"Wash? Here?" I tried not to sound incredulous.

"Do your best. You need your feet. Without feet, you're not getting anywhere."

"Is it that bad?" I tried to get a look at my left foot. The same thing. They didn't hurt. Tingled. Cold.

"Skin goes necrotic if it continues—the flesh dies. Gangrene. Infection that'll kill you. That bad enough? Do your best to dry them off and wrap up loose. Don't keep them in plastic bags all the time. Let them breathe. Change your shoes. We have enough."

I found the least-damp pair of socks I could find. "Thanks."

He leaned in close and whispered in my ear, "And what I said before?"

"About what?"

"Shu."

I turned my phone's light off. "Yeah?"

"Look, who China puts onto an Interpol Red List—it's not all the same. One person's terrorist is another's hero. Half the people on China's list are people they don't like politically. Maybe he's a good guy. I don't know. But he did use a false passport."

Which someone who was a political dissident trying to escape China might do.

"That's all I wanted to say." He pulled away.

I rooted around some more and—jackpot—found a new pair of sneakers, two sizes too big, and put them on over the two new layers of sort-of-dry socks I'd found.

The odds-and-ends pile was almost empty.

▼▲▼

"Can we wake him up?" I asked Liz.

We both bent over Josh and tried to listen to his breathing. Ragged. Uneven.

He hadn't eaten at all in the past three days. Liz had been barely able to get any water into him for fear of flooding his lungs. She had toyed with the devices in the med kit, but she wasn't sure. She didn't want to risk killing him.

There was still the chance that he was the one who crashed the plane. Maybe on purpose? It seemed impossible—how could he do such a thing? But it had happened before. I felt like the possibility implicated me as well. One way or the other, he'd been at the controls, but it felt too extreme. Was something else happening to him as well?

Money problems?

What had happened in those missing two hours? Why was he at

the front of the plane instead of in the back with Captain Hardy?

Liz wiped Josh's forehead. "We could inject him intravenously with adrenaline. There are still three vials in the med kit."

"But?"

"In his state he might not even wake up—and his heart might fail."

"You think it would?"

"*C'est possible.* It's possible."

"Likely?"

"What are you asking me?"

I paused. "Is he improving?"

"His eyes open sometimes. He mutters, but not anything I can understand. Maybe getting better and dying at the same time." She shrugged. "Like us all, *j'suppose.*"

Liz had her small backpack on. She always had it on, without fail, even when she slept.

"Will he get better if we wait?"

She didn't know and affected again that type of Gallic shrug and head tilt.

"You're Canadian, right?"

"I was born in Nantes—France—but live in Montreal."

"What do you do for work again?"

"Infectious diseases. We've been working in the Congo."

"That's why you said you were a missionary?"

"And what do you do, Mitch?"

What did I do? I didn't do much lately, if I was going to be honest. "A writer. At least, I'm trying to be. I used to work as an analyst."

"Analyst?"

"Mostly financial stuff. My contract expired. I decided to try writing."

"And writers often get First Class?"

"That was Josh. This"—I motioned around the cabin—"was a gift." If the sarcasm was understood or not I couldn't read from her expression.

"Ah, *bien sur.* I forget. *You* and Mr. Josh. If you inject him, he might die. Yes? You understand? So you want to?"

Very businesslike. "What about Howard?" I didn't like the intonation in her voice. "Did you get him to take his pills?"

"I think so. I watched him take them, tried to make sure he swallowed."

She'd been tasked with getting some of his medication down his throat.

"I can hear you," Howard said quietly from the next aisle.

I ignored him and whispered as low as I could, "Is he dangerous?"

"I think he is...how do I say? I mean, if you were a schizophrenic and your airplane crashed for mysterious *raisons* with these people on board—so you do not think you might be pushed over an edge? We are all under stress, no?"

My own mind was a crumbling mess. I kept thinking I saw things moving outside the cabin windows. "What do you think of Roman?"

"The billionaire man?"

A pause.

"You knew?"

"Who does not know a man such as this? *Fameux.*"

So I was the only idiot. Maybe I was seeing shadows in the fog.

"What's in your backpack?"

"*Pardon?*" She didn't look up from Josh.

"I saw you before we even got on the plane. You won't let anyone touch it. What is it?"

"Ah...."

I waited.

"It is my work."

"Work?"

"A biological sample."

"And that's allowed on an airplane?"

"As long as it is alerted with the authorities. In a Dewar container or vacuum flask. It is the safest way to transport such materials. By hand. I followed all processes with the authorities."

"And that's on its way to Africa?"

"*J'espere.* I hope. I needed to go to New York first. We are in need of funding. It will save many lives, yes. Many people's lives more than ours depend on a rescue. And it needs to be soon."

"So what kind of biological sample are we talking about? It's going to save lives?"

Liz hesitated. "It is"—she searched for the word—"horsepox? A modified virus like smallpox but not the same. Modified as a vaccine against a retrovirus. We used—"

"We?"

"I work in a lab, yes? With other people? *We* used something called CRISPR *technologie* to insert new code sequences—"

A voice interrupted us. A British voice I'd never heard before said, "And today the Senate Judiciary committee of the United States will be voting on whether to allow evidence in the Burt Denessey case."

"Guys, guys," Bjorn yelled. "I've got something on the radio."

"In a few moments on the BBC World Service we will be listening to experts with the latest on the disappearance of Allied Airlines flight 695."

CHAPTER 20

A ir crews from Canada, Russia and the United States today are resuming the search for Allied Airlines flight 695 that went missing over the Arctic on October fifth on a flight from Hong Kong to New York," the BBC news anchor said.

"A massive storm—a polar hurricane as it has been described—hampered search efforts for the first few days. Today we enter the fifth day of the search. The United States and China and Russia and the European Union have all diverted satellites to aid in the..."

"See, Howard, no magnetic reversal," Bjorn whispered. "The satellites are working."

"Then why no GPS?" Howard whispered back.

We all crowded around the small radio in Bjorn and Otto's pod.

The BBC announcer continued, "The question is, why was there no radio contact before the plane went down?"

Another voice, an American, answered, "I think there was a fire on board. There was a large load of lithium batteries in the hold—"

"Nope, no fire, guess again," Bjorn said.

"Shhhh." Liz put a hand over his mouth.

"My theory is that this was a hijacking gone wrong," said a different voice on the radio. This one sounded Asian-accented. "There was a hundred-million dollars' worth of diamonds being transported by one of the passengers."

"One thing that is not speculation," said the BBC announcer with his British accent, "is that another major low is heading into the Beaufort Sea in the next days, so crews are working to take advantage of the clear weather as temperatures are set to plummet from the extremely unseasonable highs sweeping across the Arctic right now. The high temperatures have given hope for possible survivors, but with bitter cold returning—"

"Jesus Christ," I said aloud. I pulled my rags tighter around my body. "At least they haven't said anything about Russians shooting us down."

"Please be quiet," Otto said.

"—could it have been terrorists?" the BBC anchor asked. "A hijacking?"

"Possible, but unlikely given what we know. We're optimistic that we'll find wreckage above the water. There is a lot of sea ice forming off the coast of Barrow—"

"What?" Bjorn said.

"Shhhh."

"With the search centering on a point a hundred miles east of Wrangel Island—the last suspected radar contact with flight 695—off the coast of Russia in the Beaufort Sea, tensions are rising between the two military powers who had squared off only days before..."

"Wait a minute." Bjorn got up and went to his map on the forward bulkhead. He clicked on his flashlight. The radio broadcast went back to commercial.

"They're saying we are here." He indicated straight into the middle of the circle he'd identified as the Pole of Inaccessibility. The center of the Beaufort Gyre. "That's more than a thousand miles away from here."

He pointed at where he had estimated we were, nestled between Greenland of Denmark and Ellesmere Island of Canada.

Otto shrugged. "What did I tell you?"

Bjorn stared at his map. "That is not possible."

Roman chuckled, a deep rumbling laugh from his corner of the cabin. "Unless Mr. Mitch's compass isn't really compass, and unless we are adrift, and unless—"

"They're looking in entirely the wrong place." Bjorn cut him off. "They're looking for us on the wrong side of the Arctic."

▼▲▼

Six hours since we'd heard the broadcast on the radio. The signal had faded in and out before dying.

It was now 2 p.m. on my watch. The new adjusted time. This was supposed to be the brightest part of the day, but it barely qualified as twilight.

I was back outside with my new sneakers wrapped in new plastic bags. No stars in the slate-blue-gray sky with a three-quarter moon near the edge of the horizon. No Mars. No Venus.

No clouds.

A dome of near nothingness in three hundred and sixty degrees around our fuselage-cave covered in drifted snow. Black patches of water between the undulating floes near us. In the distance the sky merged seamlessly with the matte blue-white below.

Utterly alone.

The view was hard for my mind to comprehend or process. Like a thousand-pound slug of lead pressed against the top of my brain. My thoughts oozed forward through time—no day, no night, no signal that hours went by except the digits on my watch.

I kept looking up for blinking lights. I stopped high-stepping through the new snow every few seconds to listen, my head and ear and body going up to the sky like a prairie dog coming out of its hole.

We came out to arrange a larger visual sign in the snow with the suitcases. The air was quiet so we didn't need as much of a wind break.

There were satellites overhead. Looking for us. That's what the BBC said. British people were smart, right? They knew what was going on.

The broadcast had mentioned speculation that Roman Kolchak had been on board the flight, had connected this to the reports of the diamonds and maybe other valuables. Of course they had talked about Captain Joshua Martin—a reporter had dug up his divorce filings in California. Nobody had mentioned me, nothing about Lilly. A few frantic words from family members pleading for answers, but I hadn't heard Emma's voice. What I would have given to hear my wife's voice, for some tiny connection back to her.

"How can they be looking in the wrong place?" I said. "Maybe we're not where you think."

Bjorn replied, "You're the one that made the magnet and compass."

"But if they're looking in the wrong place," I said, "then the transponders can't be working. None of them."

"The cockpit transponder looks intact," Otto said from the other side of the floe. "It has to be working. There will be someone here soon, trust me."

Never mind the buddy system—I made sure to only come out in threes now, and never left Shu with Lilly anymore. I'd asked the big Chinese man to come out with me and Bjorn and Otto to help, and left Lilly with Liz.

Did we have a killer in our midst? What happened to Rasheed?

I kept my distance. From everyone.

"How can you be so sure where we are?" I asked Bjorn.

"Wrangel Island?" He dropped a suitcase near the edge of the floe and sat heavily on it. We were all exhausted. "Do you see any land around us?"

"They said *near* there. Near Russia."

"Have you ever heard of Ada Blackjack?"

I shook my head and inspected the plastic bags around my feet for breaks.

"She was an *Iñupiat* woman—"

"A what?"

"An Eskimo. Born in Alaska in 1898. She was hired as a cook on a polar expedition in 1921 with a bunch of Canadian and Norwegian explorers—they went to Wrangel Island. Owned by Russia at the time, and still is."

"What was so important about Wrangel Island?"

"It was the last place that wooly mammoths existed. Less than four thousand years ago there were some living there, until we killed the last of them off. When the Egyptians were building the pyramids, there were mammoths roaming the north. Did you know that?"

I did not, but neither did I care. "So what was on Wrangel Island in 1921?"

"Nothing."

"They went there for nothing?"

"They wanted to try and claim it, but things turned bad," Bjorn said, "as they often did on these expeditions. After getting stranded, most of the men tried to venture back across the seven-hundred miles of the frozen Chukchi Sea to Russia. You know what happened to them?"

It was a rhetorical question. I scanned the horizon. I thought I saw something move.

"They all died. All the men died. All except for Ada."

"And her?"

"She survived out here, in a place like this, for two years by herself. Hunting and trapping on the ice. Two years later a whaler pulled up to Wrangel and found Ada there by herself."

Bjorn dragged himself up off the suitcase and walked ahead of me back to the fuselage.

"Why are you telling me this uplifting story?" I asked.

"Because we're not walking out of here. Not without help."

I tried to imagine making my way across the fractured landscape. Getting from one floe to the next had almost already killed me.

"But you don't think we're there?"

He picked up two more suitcases and shook his head.

"How can you be certain?"

"I just know." He trudged back to the edge of the ice and dropped the cases. He had a life jacket around his neck like the rest of us when we came outside. "The temperature, for one. It wouldn't warm up like that near Russia."

"What's the temperature supposed to be?"

"More like minus twenty this time of year. Maybe minus twenty-five."

I was aching-numb cold already. *Minus twenty?* We wouldn't survive a day. My inner layers were sweat-soaked through. Already I felt the outside layers of my clothing stiffening—freezing hard—with the cooling temperature.

On the positive side: one more connection to the outside. They said the temperature would be dropping, and it was dropping. That meant the other things they said had to be true as well, right? The satellites? The world could see us now? My internal dialogue went around and around inside my head.

"There's another storm coming," Bjorn added.

That's right. They said that, too. I stopped and scanned the sky, listened again.

Hurry.

Hurry. Please, *hurry.*

Nothing but creaking ice and the breeze's soft hiss as it carried snow crystals over the drifts. I checked my phone.

Battery dead.

I cursed.

Bjorn stepped through the two-foot-deep tracks on his way fifty feet back to the fuselage.

I stayed in place and cursed a new and more inventive slur at my phone. "Can someone check to see if we have GPS?"

Shu was with Otto on the other side of the floe a hundred feet from me. "Will be a waste of time," the Chinese man said loudly.

Damn it.

We only had the one flashlight left to share between us.

Howard said he had a phone charger.

"What happened to her?" I listened hard and looked skyward.

Bjorn picked two more cases. "Who?"

"Ada Blackjack."

"She died in 1982. At home in Alaska. Famous. A bunch of books about her. She hated all of them. The books, I mean. She didn't like to talk about it."

"In the Eighties? Are you serious?"

The thought defied sense. A woman stranded out here alone for two years, back in the golden age of polar exploration about the same time as Peary slogged up to the Pole for the first time. They had leather boots and wool scarves back then. *She survived.* She survived and lived all the way to the age of MTV and Cabbage Patch Kids. Almost unbelievable, I couldn't imagine—

I literally stopped in my tracks.

There was a low groan in the air that wasn't there before. Was it the storm coming?

Otto and Bjorn argued about something near the cabin.

I held up one hand. "Hey. Quiet!"

That sound again.

From my left.

I squinted.

Was something moving? Was it my shadow hallucinations again? In the dim light, a small black shape. Two of them. One of them raised something and wagged it side to side. Was it a seal? Narwhals again? No, no, it was...

I raised both arms and waved back.

"They're here!" My voice cracked with shrill excitement. "Boats. There's someone here!"

CHAPTER 21

O ver here!" I yelled and jumped and waved my arms. How far away? A mile? It was hard to judge.

A thumping concussion and sputtering hiss. The snow around me lit up in reflected red. I turned to see the shimmering spurt of a flare arcing into the slate-blue sky. Otto had one hand straight above his head, the flare pistol pointed skyward.

Liz stood in the gaping-wound of metal of the cabin opening, balanced on one of the galley carts. Roman had already climbed onto the roof and stood in knee-deep snow, one hand shielding his eyes. Shu stood to one side of Liz with Jang in his arms.

I watched the flare flash as it trailed a crescent of dark smoke behind it. It flickered out.

The boats—two?—had stopped. The people in them had gotten out and spread onto the ice.

Was I sure I was seeing this? I glanced back. Everyone else was transfixed as well.

A flash in the corner of my eye. A flickering light rose into the sky in the distance above the boat people. The flame went almost straight up, supported by a pillar-strand of gray. As it started to sag toward the ice, I heard a soft thump and hiss.

How long was that? A few seconds until we heard the noise? Three or four seconds of lapse between the visual and the sound. So they were about a mile away. They'd fired their own flare less than a mile away.

They were pulling the boats over the ice. That's why they got out.

Their *own* flare.

My stomach felt like it dropped through my knees into the watery depths.

Was this the other half of our aircraft who disappeared two days ago? Maybe this wasn't a rescue. Two life rafts. The other half of the plane had two life rafts. We hadn't seen them in days. Had the other part of the plane capsized on the ice? Was this tiny struggling band the last of the two-hundred-odd people I'd last seen freezing to death in the hull of the plane?

Maybe *they* needed *us* to rescue them.

▼▲▼

I scanned the sky. No blinking lights. No sounds up there. No motion.

If this was a rescue, wouldn't the rescuers have planes swarming around us? Dropping off supplies? Helicopters? Icebreakers? The distant flare trickled down into the snow and winked out.

Maybe five or ten minutes since we'd first seen them—whoever *them* was. They got back into their boats. I heard the groan of the engines again.

Engines.

Life rafts didn't have engines.

They were closer now. The boats were dark. Not yellow like I imagined the life rafts. Those were Zodiacs. Like ones I'd taken Lilly whale watching on in Canada one time, on the West Coast. My stomach wobbled somewhere back into the middle of my body.

It wasn't the people from the other plane.

But…

"They'll be here soon," Otto said as he put an arm around my shoulder.

"Yeah."

We both watched for a while in silence.

"Liz, where's Lilly?" I asked without looking around.

"She's with Irene."

"Irene?"

"*Le petit*…the puppy."

The noise of the boat engines reverberated in the hollow fuselage shell. My eyes had to adjust to the relative darkness inside the cabin.

Everyone else was outside, but I'd come back in.

Lilly was asleep, burrowed under a dozen layers of dirty blankets and shirts with the puppy. I assumed she was with the puppy. I remembered the warmth of our family dog when I was a kid. Like a hot water bottle. Dogs had body temperatures higher than humans, somebody had explained to me once. It was why they felt so warm to cuddle up to.

I paused and leaned in close to her to listen for her breathing. Nice and regular.

I tiptoed around the divider and into Josh's pod area. I put my ear next to his mouth. Was he even still alive? After a second I heard a raspy breath.

I glanced at Lilly.

My child.

Who I'd do *anything* to protect. Anything.

I looked back at Josh. He'd been incensed with rage when he talked of his wife taking the kids. Had seemed almost deranged. Had he put us here? Was this his fault? I didn't like Josh very much, but I had a sense of him. I was good with people, right?

Wrong.

Emma said I was a terrible judge of character.

The groaning engines grew ever louder.

I felt around under Josh's bed for the medical kit, then opened it near the cabin window. Three vials of adrenaline. With one shaking hand I retrieved a syringe from the case at the bottom. I'd never stuck a needle in anyone in my life, but I'd given blood a dozen times. How hard could it be? I'd watched nurses give me injections at least as many times. Make sure no bubbles in the syringe, right?

What about his kids?

What about *mine*?

I upturned the vial, pulled the cap off the syringe and plunged the needle through the rubber stopper. I had to lean against the window to get enough light. I pulled back the plunger.

We had to know. Not just me. Everyone here. They had a right.

Josh was the captain of the plane. It was his responsibility to get everyone home safe. That's what he'd told me on one of our drunken nights out. He had told me how he shouldered that responsibility, how he took it seriously.

How much? How much should I take out? What was a lot of adrenaline? I drained the whole vial into the syringe, then tapped it like I'd seen nurses tap it. Like I'd seen druggies do on TV. No bubbles. I squirted a tiny bit out of the top of the needle.

The grinding noise of the engines louder and louder.

My hand shook holding the needle.

I put it down and capped it and filled another syringe. I had no idea how much I needed. I put the capped syringe and the remaining vial into my jacket pocket and sat down next to Josh.

"Buddy, I know we've had our differences." I took his right arm and tied a length of a shirt under his armpit and cinched it tight. "I know you were mad at me, but this isn't about that. You're family, and I do love you—if I find you a bit...doesn't matter."

What the hell was I doing? Did I want to do this? No. Did I have to?

The engine noise growled and echoed ever louder.

I held his arm up to the light. I was supposed to inject it into a vein. That was right, right? What had Liz said? Damn it, damn it…

With gritted teeth and shaking hand I did my best to slide the needle into my best guess of where the blue line of his vein was at the inside cusp of his elbow. I squeezed about a quarter of it into him, then half.

Waited a second.

And…

I squeezed the remainder out.

The engine noise grated in my ears.

Josh's eyelids flickered. His arm in my hands flinched. I realized the needle was stuck in his vein but before I could remove it, his whole body jerked upright.

He sucked in a gasping lungful of air, his eyes wide and white in the dim light. "Mitch?"

I held out both hands to his shoulders to hold him back. He looked like he was about to jump out of the pod. "It's okay, keep calm. I injected you with adrenaline."

"Where are we? Where's Lucy?" His wife. "What happened?" His head swiveled left and right, his eyes open but not seeing. Not comprehending.

"The plane. It crashed. Onto the ice."

His hands gripped my forearms like vise-claws. The needle bobbled, stuck out of his arm. "We crashed?"

"Onto the ice. Josh. I need you to calm down and to think. Remember. What happened? You were in the pilot seat when we opened the flight deck. The only one strapped in. You were flying."

I let go of his arms and gently removed the needle.

"That's…that's right." He wobbled back but caught himself. "I was trying to bring it…"

"Were you the one flying?"

"Yeah."

"Why?"

"I was trying to bring us down."

"On purpose?"

He blinked and shook his head, but not answering the question. Trying to clear his head, I guessed. His eyes rolled back up in his head but he fought to remain conscious. "It was…I…what happened to the other pilots?"

"They're dead."

"Hardy?"

"She survived. I met her in the other half of the plane."

"Other half…?"

"We split open on impact. No fire, though. Did you drain the tanks?"

The boat engines outside warbled, seemed to separate as if going in different directions. I craned my neck to look out the window.

He said, "Yeah, I dumped the fuel."

"What happened after we passed the Pole? There are two hours nobody can remember."

"The cabin was depressurized," Josh whispered and then coughed. "Knocked everyone out. They…they reduced the pressure."

"Who's they?"

He coughed again. His eyes rolled up.

I shook him. "Josh, who's 'they'? Who did this?"

"The two Chinese pilots—I mean, I think they were Chinese—I didn't know them, but there were other men…"

He panted for breath and closed his eyes.

"Stay with me, buddy."

"I need to speak to my kids. Can you get me a phone?"

"We have no phones. No connections."

He blinked a few times in succession and his eyes seemed to gain focus. "Wait, you mean…has there been any contact with the outside?"

"We heard a radio broadcast, but it said we were last seen a thousand miles from where we think we are."

"That's because that's what they wanted."

The boat engines seemed to roar just beyond the cabin's opening.

"There are people coming, Josh. I need to know what happened.

Who is 'they'? Was this an accident?"

He looked straight into my eyes. He seemed fully awake now. "This was no accident. Those two pilots who came on late? They hijacked the aircraft. They must have flown it west for an hour and brought it up into radar contact, then doubled back and flew below coverage. They somehow shut off all communications and transponders."

"Why? How?"

"I…I woke up. Found an emergency oxygen canister before I blacked out." His forehead was slick with sweat. His eyes bugged out of their sockets. "They must have put something into the ventilation system…"

"Josh?"

He had trouble focusing. "I waited, pretended I was unconscious. Heard them saying they flew west for an hour and were doubling back. Taking the plane somewhere. One of them went into the back, so I waited. They left the flight deck door unlocked. I got the knife from the emergency kit, went in the cockpit…"

His voice trailed off again. I slapped his cheeks.

"I took back control and locked the flight deck door, but they had guns. They…"

"Why? Josh, why did they want to hijack the plane?"

The boat engines roared. I heard Otto yelling greetings.

Josh gripped my arm again and pulled me closer. "There's something on the plane that they want. They wanted to land it and get something on this plane. Something in the First Class cabin."

CHAPTER 22

"Josh!"

His eyes rolled back up into his head again. I grabbed him to stop him from keeling over onto the floor.

"What were they looking for? Diamonds? We heard on the radio that there was a shipment of diamonds." I shook him. "How many were there? Only the two pilots? There were three people in the flight deck with you."

His face went flaccid. His cheeks drooped.

Someone was panting. Was that Josh? No, it was me. Breathing in and out, in and out, in quick gasps.

"I told you," said a disembodied voice in the darkness.

I turned my head. Howard's face loomed a few feet away in the next pod.

"I told you this was no simple accident," he said.

"I forgot you were here." I said it as much to him as myself.

"Hmmm…maybe. *Maybe* not. Very few things are really coincidences. Especially here. Especially now." His face contorted. "Untie me."

I lowered Josh back into his pod-bed and put an ear to his chest.

Still breathing. His heart hammering away in his chest, faint but quick, trilling and missing every few beats. The boat engines roared. Ever closer.

Should I hit him again? With the other syringe? I had no idea about adrenaline other than fight or flight, but if I was a betting man—which I wasn't—I'd bet another dose right now would kill him. His heart was already going like a staccato jackhammer.

Give him a minute, maybe he'd wake up again. I gently let go of Josh and picked up the med kit again, fished out a bottle and dumped a few pills into my hand.

"Swallow these," I said as I stood. Two Haldol. "Then we can talk."

"She already gave me some."

"I'm giving you more." Liz hadn't come back in yet. Usually she kept close to Josh and hovered around him.

"I told you this wasn't an accident. I know things."

"You said a lot of things."

"But I knew. I knew." Howard's voice gained pitch. "Who is outside? Who are they? You can't leave me tied up like this."

"You tried to shoot us."

"I tried to save you."

"From who?"

"Otto." He spat the second syllable out like phlegm.

"I have your disk."

"That's what they really want. What they need from First Class. You know how many times I've stolen a billion dollars?"

"Come again…?"

"I made a living doing penetration tests. I'm a hacker, but a white hat. Good guys. I'd break into banks and steal a billion dollars. I gave it back. I even broke into nuclear reactors."

A ballooning sense of unreality gripped my mind. How much should I believe from this guy? But there seemed to be kernels of truth in the chaff of his mind. "Howard, we don't have much time. Tell me what you know." I moved closer and proffered the pills again.

He nodded. I put them into his mouth. He swallowed and opened wide enough for me to inspect.

Outside, the engines cut off—or one of them did. The other sounded more distant. Were they circling us? Or was that another boat?

Howard said, "You said you haven't seen any airplanes? No helicopters? No boats? I mean, like big icebreakers?"

"Only the two Zodiacs."

"Could be a sub, then. They can break ten feet of ice, and it's already broken up from the storm."

I hadn't even considered that.

Howard said, "But how would these rescuers know where we are?"

"The CVR. The voice recorder. It's got a transponder."

"Josh said the replacement crew turned off all the transponders somehow."

"Can you turn that one off, just like that? In flight?"

"I don't know."

An admission that there was something technical that Howard didn't know was almost jarring. It made him sound honest and reasonable.

"Maybe these are rescuers." My stomach roiled in a painful knot. Saliva flowed in the back of my throat.

"You're right. Josh could be lying. I mean, he admitted he crashed the plane."

"Forced to crashland," I pointed out.

"With him at the controls. A drunk, you told me. Raging mad at his divorce. Maybe broke. Maybe"—Howard rolled his eyes up at the ceiling before looking back at me—"mad at you."

"This has nothing to do with that."

My head tipped forward as I considered retching. My cheeks burned, my stomach lurched into my throat but I gagged and steeled myself. The spasm passed after a second.

"I hear things, you know. You all think I'm stupid."

"We're a bit scared of you."

"Of me?" He cackled what began as a laugh but turned into a sob. "Please. Untie me, goddammit. Please."

My brain swam and I sucked lungfuls of air. *Calm down. Calm down.* The boat engines started up again. More yelling from outside.

"Your friend Liz, she has smallpox in a jar. Do you know what that is?"

"I know what it is," I said, but really had no idea. I wanted to run but had nowhere to go.

"That's a weapon of mass destruction, my friend."

"She said it's a vaccine."

"And I heard we have a terrorist on board."

I didn't say anything. Had he heard all this because we'd forgotten about him? We didn't notice the quiet gremlin we'd tied up in our midst? Or had someone told him?

I took a few steps back to Josh's pod and shook him gently. Listened to his breathing. More steady. His pulse not hammering, but his eyelids didn't even flutter as I shook him again.

Howard continued, "Whoever hijacked us, they want something on this plane. That's what Josh said. Why did all the people on this side—the ones left—stay here?"

It was a question I'd been asking myself.

"You know what I think? The radio said we're close to Russia."

"Bjorn doesn't think so."

"You trust Bjorn?"

I didn't answer.

Howard said, "Who's the only Russian on board?"

It was a rhetorical question. The billionaire trying to escape from Putin; and the billion-dollar follow-up: Whoever "they" were, why would they risk it? Down an entire airliner?

Howard answered my inner monologue without needing to be asked. "You know the KGB was caught trying to cyber infiltrate the MH17 crash investigation? That was one airliner the Russian military brought down recently. You know how many others they have? How many other airliners have been shot down or brought down on purpose by terrorists or militaries?"

"Daddy?" said a small voice.

Calm down. "Lilly, it's okay."

"What's the noise outside? Is everything okay?" She sat upright in her pod-bed holding the little puppy, her shoulders hunched inward.

The boat engines went silent.

I took a few quick but unsteady steps around the divider and put an arm around her. "It's going to be fine, Lillypad. Don't worry." I tried to make my voice as steady as I could.

"They are here," said a deep voice behind us. Roman stood in the entranceway of the cabin.

CHAPTER 23

I wrapped both of my arms as far around Lilly's little body as I could. She smelled of Lilly—a faintly sweet funk I could sense anywhere— but also of sweat and damp and now also of dog.

"There are some people here," I said as I adjusted her makeshift head covering. I made sure her feet were wrapped and considered sitting down to put another layer of plastic around them.

Roman hovered by the ragged curtain entrance in the half-light. Liz stood behind him.

How long had the Russian been there? What had he heard?

"Liz," I said. "Could you check on Josh?"

"Why? What happened?"

"Nothing," I said before Howard could say anything. I glanced at him and he looked at the floor. "I…we have visitors?"

"Two boats. They just landed."

"So then we're going to have to move Josh."

I had to go outside and see who was here, and I decided I needed to keep Lilly in my arms. Keep her close. Protect her. Muffled voices from outside. Otto? Bjorn? But someone else as well. The voices were excited. Yelling.

"Come on, sweetie." I made my way down the aisle and edged my way past Roman. "You coming?"

"I need something." He walked past me up the aisle.

I didn't ask. Liz slid by me on her way to Josh.

The ice-slush near the curtains had frozen over again with the returning cold but I stepped across the galley-cart bridge anyway to be sure. The puppy followed at my feet. The voices grew louder. A thin wind bit through my layers the second I stepped into the hardened snow pack.

My breath heaved out a cloud of white vapor.

"Come, come here."

A man in a bright orange space-suit-looking coverall waved an arm at me. His voice had a strange flat intonation, faintly British—like Bjorn's accent—but something else as well. He stood twenty feet from the twisted metal of the cabin entrance, in a growing pile of boxes at the center of the ice floe.

They had already put down two layers of blue tarp over the uneven frozen snow and secured the corners each with a heavy black case.

The man unfurled his heavy orange suit by pulling on an off-center zip that ran the top-half of it, uncovering his black sweater and hat. He pulled his hands from the integrated gloves and tied the two orange arms of the suit around his waist and knelt in the middle of the tarp.

Two boats, one on each side of the floe. Large black Zodiac-style inflatables each with two benches and an oversized outboard engine. They had secured them halfway up onto the ice.

I counted eight people. All men.

Two remained in each of the boats, one at the stern near the engine and one at the bow handing off equipment to other men who lugged boxes and bags to the center. One man stood off to one side of the growing pile of equipment and talked to Bjorn and Otto who were busy explaining the crack in the middle of the floe. The man said not to worry.

The guy talking to me bent over and worked on something.

A stove.

Steam curled from its top.

"Come, come," the man urged again and waved to me. "Where are the others?"

The gunmetal gray cathedral sky was rimmed bluish-purple. The pin prick of Polaris straight overhead. A few others pierced the vault. My dad had taught me this was nautical twilight—not civilian, when no stars shone through, but when the first of them appeared. The moon was lined up with the nose of the aircraft behind us. Its crescent hugged the ice, a gray scimitar almost hidden in the distant mists.

"The others?" the man asked again. He had a strap around his chest attached to an automatic weapon slung across his back. Each of the men seemed to be armed.

"There are a few inside. One of them injured. One we had to restrain. Who are you? How did you get here?"

"Okay. Okay. Come. My name is Gunnar." He waved me forward again and turned to the man talking to Bjorn and Otto. "Jules, get them suits."

It was hard to resist the smell of whatever was in that stove. Lilly waved at the man and said hello. The puppy followed us forward. Someone opened one of the black cases and produced another orange suit like theirs and indicated that I should sit and change into it. They said we didn't need the dirty old life vests around our necks anymore, that the new suits had them integrated.

Gunnar took one look at Lilly and a second later produced a miniature survival suit.

"They said there might be children," he explained.

Who exactly is "they?" I felt stunned.

The men pulling equipment from the boats had propped up a wind break. We sheltered in its lee, sat on the two empty cases we had pulled the suits from. Bjorn and Otto already had orange suits on as well. One of the men, Jules, helped me get Lilly into hers.

Bjorn said, "Mitch, drink some water. A whole bottle."

Gunnar offered up a plastic bottle from a crate and unscrewed it. I put it to my lips and drank some down. Bjorn waved at me and encouraged me to drink more. I did my best and offered some to Lilly.

The next thing Gunnar handed me was an aluminum mug with steaming liquid inside. "We are so happy we found you," he said in his peculiarly accented English. He accentuated the first syllable of "happy".

"Where are you from?" I asked.

Elation and fear competed for space inside my mind. Was this it? The rescue? I took the steaming mug. A sheen of unreality unbalanced my senses, made everything look two-dimensional and heightened the bright new colors. I hadn't seen anything but drab and gray in days.

"We are Coastal Jaeger brigade. Finnish Marines. Part of the European expeditionary force. We located you ten hours ago but could not reach you due to the fracture ice." He waved a hand in the direction they'd come.

He didn't pronounce his words quite right.

"No airplanes?"

"Yes, earlier. Very high."

"I didn't see any."

"Well, we are here, yes?"

His smile was infectious and Lilly beamed one back. He held up one finger and stood and turned and a moment later came back with two gray wool blankets for Irene the puppy, who by this time was shivering.

After giving us some steaming foil-wrapped meal packets, he turned again and spoke to Jules. Otto had gone to the nearest boat. To my right, near the fuselage, Roman and Liz had appeared and another of the men ran over with two survival suits. Liz pointed inside and said something I couldn't quite hear.

This whirlwind of situational change seemed to happen within seconds. My mind felt shell shocked—but the tight knot in my stomach eased a bit. These men didn't look dangerous.

They didn't seem to be looking for something. Didn't hold us at rifle point and demand anything. They weren't digging through the cabin.

Josh said whoever downed the plane wanted something on it.

Could I even trust what he said? Should I tell them what he said? *Not yet*, a voice cautioned in my head. Make sense of things first. Get warm first. Eat something. *Calm down.* The voice in my head sounded like Emma.

Lilly looked up at me and took a bite of her foil-wrapped sandwich. The puppy had already shaken free of the wool blankets and ran toward Liz and Roman, while Gunnar was deep in conversation with Jules a few steps away. They spoke into a walkie-talkie.

"Is that a satellite phone?" Bjorn asked Gunnar.

The Norwegian sat behind me.

"Can I call my wife?" I asked.

Gunnar made a sour face. "I am very sorry, not possible. This is communication only to our ship."

"You mean, we can't call someone?" I said. "Can you call the ship and have them call out? I need my wife to know our daughter is safe. Right now."

"Very soon," Gunnar said. "But we do not have the right tools now."

"What ship?" Bjorn asked. He squinted in the direction they had come.

Gunnar pointed into the distance. "Very hard to see. We need to leave very soon. As soon as possible."

"Why?"

"The storm is coming."

Gunnar pointed the opposite way. We both followed his arm. Where the horizon was purple blue straight ahead, it was iron gray in the direction of Gunnar's outstretched finger.

"How many are you?" he asked.

"Ten."

"Many injured?"

"Only one, like I said, in the cabin. One of the pilots. And one man restrained."

"Restrained?"

I made a hand gesture like tying a knot tight. "Dangerous."

Gunnar's mouth was half-open and he nodded as he deciphered my meaning. "Any other injured?"

"There are some bodies under the nose."

"We will see if we have time. We need to get as many of you as we can in that boat." He pointed to where Otto was talking to the two men in the Zodiac closest to where they'd come from. "We need to get the voice recorder out. Fast as possible."

I said, "Did you find the other half of the plane? The other survivors?"

Gunnar stared at me as if I'd dropped from the sky. Another second pause before he replied, "Yah, yah, of course. The other plane part."

"So you found other survivors?" I nodded in the direction of his ship. "Did they get the black box from the back half?"

"Yah, we found them."

"How many?" The uneasiness in my stomach knotted tighter.

He turned and said something to Jules before turning back to me. "We have not much time. I was not with the other boats."

"Mr. Rasheed Tumeris?" Jules said. "Vera Zelenko?"

He had a sheaf of paper encased in plastic in his hands. He was also halfway out of his survival suit. The two men seemed unconcerned by the cold.

"Rasheed didn't make it," I said quietly. "He's up at the nose. Vera went to the other half of the plane before we got separated." He must have a passenger manifest, I assumed. "You'd better talk to Otto"—I pointed in his direction at the boat—"if you want to go over the manifest."

Jules nodded. "Yes? Okay?"

Gunnar got up and joined him and walked over to the closest Zodiac.

An incredible sensation of warmth permeated deep into my feet, at first a dull throb but now fiery painful tingling. My fingers buzzed as blood seeped back into them fully for the first time in days. I hunched inward to cup the warmth of the survival suit and pulled Lilly close next to me in the pocket cover of the tarp windbreak. I took a sip of the warm soup from the aluminum cup. My feet burned, but it was pure bliss to be warm. Or *warming up*, at least.

Someone had set up four floodlights on tall tripods at the corners of the center area. Two focused on the boats to either side of the floe, with two casting harsh white light on the twisted remains of the aircraft.

"I do not think they are Finnish," Bjorn whispered.

I counted the survival suit cases. Six. Seven. Eight.

"They said European."

"He said Finnish."

"They're not speaking Finnish?" It sounded Scandinavian to me.

"Not very well. Then again, the Coastal Jaeger units of Finland are more Swedish than anything else. But they're not speaking Swedish, either."

Was he lying again? I took another sip of the hot drink. What if he wasn't?

The knot in my stomach tightened again. I moved an inch away from Bjorn. He'd lied about knowing Roman. Where was the Russian now? I stood and looked back and forth. Roman and Liz were already in the closest Zodiac, where Gunnar had said we needed to go.

Were they kidnapping Roman?

The rescue guy in the back of the boat was engaged in small talk with the Russian. Everyone seemed at ease. Otto was talking to Gunnar and Jules now, the three of them walking toward the ripped-open fuselage that had been our home for the past five days. They waved two of the other men forward who carried what I assumed were cases of tools to take out the flight deck voice recorder.

If someone had hijacked the plane, then Josh had saved us. I could describe the whole story when we got onto the ship. Someone else could decipher what had happened, dig into the details and untangle the web. Right now I needed to keep Lilly safe.

"Hey, Mitch," Otto called out from the edge of the opening to the cabin. "Have you seen Shu?"

Shu. Pemba. The terrorist. I'd been so focused on the lure of warmth of these massive survival suits that I hadn't noticed not seeing the big Chinese man getting into one.

I had seen him as the boats had first appeared, but after that? In the cabin? Only myself and Josh and Howard. When I had noticed Howard there, I'd looked around for anyone else. Roman had shown up after I'd been talking with Howard. Maybe before that.

"Haven't seen him since the boats arrived," I yelled back.

I looked the other way, about four hundred feet or so to the end of the ice floe where the black waters from both sides converged. It wasn't like there was anywhere to hide. Not for a three-hundred-plus linebacker of a man.

And what about Jang?

"Jang!" I called out. "Lilly, did you see where Jang went?"

"I don't know," she said.

I looked at Roman again. He was right next to the guy at the back of the Zodiac. The other guy in that boat had gone to the aircraft cabin.

"Mitch!" Otto yelled out again, this time slightly muffled.

"I can't see Shu," I called back.

"Mitch, you better come here."

He had gone into the aircraft cabin and now came back out. When I didn't move, he wiped his face for a second before saying, "Captain Josh Martin is dead."

CHAPTER 24

The cabin's interior was murky, punctuated by scissoring beams and flashes of the LED headlamps we held in our hands as we waddled up the left-hand aisle in our new survival suits.

Liz had stood up in the boat when Otto had announced Josh's passing, but Otto waved her down, said they would take care of it. There were two Finnish Marines in her Zodiac, and one of them got up and joined me at the entrance to the cabin.

He said he was an emergency medical tech and led Otto, Gunnar, Jules and myself inside. I brought Lilly with me despite protests from Gunnar. I said that Josh was my brother-in-law, that he was Lilly's uncle. The Marine shrugged and said it was my choice.

The emergency tech leaned over Josh with a light in his face. Gunnar knelt beside him, unstrapped his weapon and set it on the floor.

The pilot's mouth was shut, but his eyes were open and already opaque. I blocked Lilly from seeing him. She squirmed in my arms. The puppy followed us in and jumped around our orange-booted feet and yapped to be picked up.

Howard kept his eyes steadily on me all the way up the aisle. Had he said anything?

"I asked Liz to check on him when the boats got here," I said.

Had I killed him? He seemed stable when I left. I looked on the floor of the pod. The med kit was gone. The cabin was quiet. Should I put Lilly down? I felt like I was going to fall over but gritted my jaws and tightened my grip around my daughter.

The emergency tech pumped Josh's chest a few times in quick succession.

Howard caught my eye and looked down.

The tech shook his head as he held two fingers to Josh's neck.

"Damn it," Otto muttered.

Gunnar got up and said, "Jules, go with them and look at the flight deck."

Something flickered in my peripheral vision and flew through the darkness.

Gunnar dropped to the floor. Thudding steps thumped away from us and someone yelled from outside. Jules jumped across the dividers and sprinted down the opposite aisle.

Otto angled his flashlight down and swore. Gunnar groaned, a metal rod beside him. He was splayed on the floor, his wool hat gone, his blond hair spattered black with blood.

▼▲▼

"Where is the child?" Jules demanded.

The man stood over Shu while three more of the Finnish Marines tried to restrain the massive Chinese man. The face of the one behind him—that had Shu in a headlock—was smeared red. One more Marine to each side as they struggled to keep him pinned on his back. Dark spatters of blood covered the snow around the men.

Shu bared his teeth and struggled to break free.

I had exited the cabin behind Otto and kept my distance from the writhing knot.

"Where is he?" Jules had something in his hand now. A box cutter knife flashed in the glare of the floodlights.

Shu tried to kick at him.

"His name is Pemba Ldong." Otto stepped forward to join them.

Everyone froze at a piercing scream that emanated from the cabin behind us, interspersed with snarling curses—recognizable even in Finnish or Swedish or whatever these guys were speaking. Shu grunted and struggled some more.

With Lilly in my arms, I stepped over the slippery hard-packed snow away from the cabin entrance. The puppy barked inside. Liz and Roman were in the Zodiac to my left, and from the boat to my right, the remaining Finnish Marine jumped out to help.

Bjorn stood in the middle of the equipment at the center of the floe.

Everyone turned to watch Gunnar limp out of the cabin entrance, followed by the med tech who had a squirming Jang in his arms. Without a word or explanation, the two of them walked toward the boat with Roman and Liz in it.

The yapping puppy followed them as Jang wriggled to get out of the Finn's arms.

I took a cautious step forward. "What the hell is—"

With a bellowing roar, Shu yanked the two Marines to either side of him forward in one quick motion, got his legs under himself and stood straight up with one man dangling behind trying to choke him. Shu jammed his hand into the man's face and lifted him up as he turned and flung him away.

Crack.

Another crack.

Gunnar stood in front of Shu, one arm outstretched with a handgun in it.

Shu dropped to one knee, but then bellowed again and charged forward. Gunnar managed to get off one more shot before the raging bull plowed into him, scrabbling at his arm. With surprising speed the Chinese man had the weapon out of Gunnar's hand.

Two of the other Marines already had their weapons out.

I ran. Shielded Lilly from the men and guns with my body.

I sprinted away from the fuselage, past Bjorn who took cover behind stacked crates. Beyond the floodlights it was dim and I slipped and almost fell. More sharp cracks of shots behind me, but echoless in the vast expanse.

My next step caught a rut and I fell awkwardly forward and spun in the air to hold Lilly away from the ground as I crashed into it and skidded.

A stuttering burst of gunfire.

Not a handgun.

An automatic weapon.

"Stay there," said a voice. "Don't move."

I wasn't sure if they were talking to me or someone else. Panting, I held Lilly's trembling body against me. The dog had scampered after us and stood defiant in the snow. I looked back.

Howard stood on the left side of the fuselage, a compact weapon in his arms.

"Mitch," he called out. "Come on, get—"

A boat's engine whined to life. Gunshots cracked overhead. Ten feet in front of me the snow erupted in a puff of chunks and mist. Were they shooting at me?

"Mitch, over here," yelled a woman's voice.

It was Liz, motioning at me from the Zodiac. Roman was at the engine, speeding the boat along the water gap. I glanced toward the plane. Howard and Bjorn were twenty feet away. They stumbled and slipped backward toward me, yelling obscenities.

Stay away from me, I wanted to yell. Lilly breathed in quick sharp gasps below me. Was I crushing her? Without thinking I got up and ran toward the boat. Pure instinct. Get away from the guns. Protect Lilly.

Roman angled the Zodiac to the ice edge, which was three feet above the water line.

"Quick, hurry," the Russian said as he idled the engine. The boat coasted to the edge.

I didn't dare to look back. I handed Lilly over to Liz. Jang cowered in the bottom of the boat near Roman. I tried to jump to one side of Liz and Lilly but slipped and tumbled hard into the front seat plank as Bjorn and Howard jumped into the boat from behind me.

"Go, go, go!" Howard yelled.

I was face-first in the plastic bottom. Spat out a mouthful of diesel and tried to turn. Lilly shrieked. The boat engine roared to life and I tumbled sideways. A yelping squeal as I fell onto the puppy who had somehow gotten onto the boat as well.

Someone yelled, "Wait!"

Not a Swedish or Finnish voice. American.

I pushed myself up from the floor. Otto ran along the edge of the ice, chased by two of the Marines. One of them had a gun raised and shot at him. Otto fired back two shots and then jumped awkwardly in his orange suit and landed half on the edge of the Zodiac. Bjorn grabbed his hood and heaved.

We pulled away from the edge.

Gasping for air, I searched for Lilly. She squirmed toward me over the seat.

I grabbed her and desperately looked for holes in her small orange suit. "Are you okay?" She wrapped her hands tight around my neck.

We rocked backward as the boat accelerated forward.

I managed to sit upright with Lilly in my arms in time to see two of the Finnish Marines standing on the ice, not twenty feet away, their automatic carbines raised and pointed at us.

But they didn't shoot.

Roman turned the boat into open black water between the next floe and gunned the engine.

CHAPTER 25

The boat engine grumbled throatily between yowling high-pitched whines as Roman wound his way back and forth between chunks of ice. Bjorn sat on the bow and kept watch ahead and called out instructions. Stubbled ice-slush stretched before us in a widening gulf under the gloom.

Mute silence as we coasted past a purple-green wall, a small iceberg that reflected the faint glow of a warbling aurora in the sky. Beyond the green glow, a carpet of stars prickled the black-blue sky.

For two minutes I did nothing but check and recheck Lilly's body and jumpsuit. No holes. No blood. Just a trembling child who kept telling me she was okay.

The temperature was dropping faster than what remained of the fading light.

Liz coaxed a terrified Jang from the floor of the boat and into her arms, but the frozen kid had wriggled away from her to me. I didn't refuse him. He had no survival suit, but only the ragtag of dirty clothes we'd scavenged in the cabin. Compared to the rest of us in the new high-tech suits, he looked like a street urchin, curled into a fetal ball against the cold.

I unzipped the front of my suit and brought him inside. His small hands were literally as cold as chunks of ice, his entire body trembling uncontrollably. He was cold—but more, he was mute with fear. I couldn't blame him. Having two little lives to protect and coddle submerged my own fear, at least for the first few minutes as I made sure they were okay.

The mound of snow on top of the 777 cabin—and the dark figures of the Finnish Marines watching us—disappeared into the gloom.

Jang wasn't the only one without a survival suit. Howard sat in the middle bench of the boat and gripped the automatic carbine he pointed high.

Nobody tried to take it from him.

He shivered and tried to wrap his arms around his body. He had on a few layers of shirts and pants we'd had him wear in the cabin, some boxer shorts wrapped around his head and the weapon held in his double-socked hands. His wrists red from the chafing against the ropes.

Nobody offered to share their warmth with him and he didn't ask.

Finally I said quietly, "What the hell just happened?"

Roman answered with a soft voice, "Why don't you tell us?"

He kept his eyes straight ahead on the floating ice debris. He'd taken the puppy into his suit. A small lump on the left side of his body that squirmed every few minutes.

"*Att lägga lök på laxen.*" Bjorn had two of the LED headlamps and kept them pointed ahead, sweeping the light back and forth in the semidarkness. "Means to put onion in the salmon. I think maybe we made things worse. From the frying pan and into the fire, as you would say."

"Where are we going?" I asked Roman.

"Away."

He didn't qualify his statement.

"Turn around." Otto stood up from the front bench with one arm out of his halfway-unzipped survival suit. He pointed his handgun straight at Roman. "Turn this boat around," he repeated.

The Russian didn't acknowledge him and stared straight ahead.

"Don't test me. I will shoot you. Turn us around."

After a tense pause Roman said, "You know how many bullets I have in me already?"

"I'm not going to say again—"

"Sit down." Howard had the muzzle of his carbine pointed at Otto. "Sit the goddamn hell down. We're not going back. I told you we were being hunted. I told you they were watching us, waiting out there."

Otto glanced down at Howard and bared his teeth then swore under his breath. "You better know how to use that thing, asshole."

"I already shot a couple of those Marines with it." Howard shook but kept his automatic weapon trained on Otto.

I backed away as far from the two of them along the middle bench I shared with Howard and pulled Lilly to the other side of me.

Otto swung his gun down and trained it straight on Howard's head. "You lower that right now or—"

"Can we please not shoot each other?" I waved one arm between them and kept Lilly away with the other. Jang clung to me inside the suit. "Roman, please turn the engine off. For a minute? They're not chasing us."

The two men kept their guns aimed at each other.

The boat engine grumbled. One second passed and then another. Roman capitulated and shut off the engine, muttering curses in Russian under his breath.

"Put the guns down," I said more calmly. "Are you going to have a shootout in front of my five-year-old daughter?"

Otto slowly lowered his arm.

Howard lowered the carbine. "Why the hell did you jump into the boat?"

"Because I'm in charge of keeping you idiots safe," Otto replied, "as much as I'm thinking now it was a stupid idea. I'm an Air Marshal—"

"Don't go getting delusions," Howard interrupted. "You're not a US Marshal. You work for the TSA, home of the Freedom Tap." He grabbed his crotch with one hand. "Chair Marshal is more like it."

"You are my passengers," Otto continued. "My responsibility. This trip is definitely not over. And this guy"—he waved his gun at Roman—"is in my care. He requested asylum. I'm a law enforcement officer of the United States. That makes him my charge."

"By shooting him?"

"If that's what it takes to make him safe."

"Did you tell those Finnish guys that you were the Air Marshal?" I asked.

A pause for a beat. "No."

"And why not?"

The boat coasted to a standstill.

I answered my own question. "Because you didn't trust them. I didn't either."

Otto sat down and put his arm back into his suit. "Goddamnit. We're going to die out here, you know that? We've got no shelter. That was the number one thing we needed to survive. The other was the transponder in the voice recorder. That was our only contact with the outside world."

"We've got these." I pulled at the hood of my survival suit. "I'm a damn lot warmer now than I've been in four days. And if they are from the outside world, then there will be more people coming to find us— but personally, I don't want to bring my daughter back there. Not with men shooting guns at each other, like you morons are trying to do."

Ahead of the boat was a dark channel bordered by three-foot ledges of ice and wind-blown drifts edged in steps above that. A hundred feet away the black channel opened up to a sea of flat slush that disappeared into the dim distance. No horizon, just a fading gloom that ended a few thousand feet away with the pinpricks of early stars and the greenish-yellow aurora.

"And they're not chasing us," I said—not a question but a statement.

"They can't. I put a few rounds into their boat." Howard's teeth chattered as he spoke. He tried to hold his gun upright, but it quivered in his grip.

"And how did you get loose?" I asked him.

Roman said, "I untied him."

"You did *what*?"

"I know you injected Josh with the adrenaline," Liz said quietly. She hadn't said a word yet. She didn't look at me as she said it.

"Is that true, Mitch?" Otto kept his eyes down.

"I didn't kill him."

"You injected him with adrenaline? What else?"

I remained silent.

"What was going on between you guys?" Otto said.

"Nothing." What should I say?

"Did you want to quiet him before the rescuers arrived?"

"Are you kidding me?"

"I'm not kidding." Otto's eyes met mine. "Now's not the time for secrets—"

"Seriously?"

Jang squirmed inside my survival suit and I held him and Lilly to me. I swiveled on my bench to look around at each person in turn. "You're asking me about secrets?"

Bjorn looked straight ahead over the bow. I said to him, "I know you and Roman knew each other. Before this."

I kept one eye on the wobbling barrel of Howard's gun. The guy had one of his cell phones out now and tried to operate it with one trembling finger. I had his disk in my left coat pocket and he knew it. I sensed him edging closer to me.

Bjorn adjusted his position at the bow but didn't turn around. "He paid me. He was paying me to alter Greenpeace reports to give his Arctic drilling projects a favorable light. When he got into trouble, he asked me to smuggle him out of Russia. On our boat."

Roman shrugged an admission. "Nobody would suspect a Russian oil oligarch of hiding on that greenie rust bucket."

"Why were you on the plane?" I asked Bjorn.

"He insisted. He didn't trust that I hadn't ratted him out for more money than he offered."

"So that something like this hijacking wouldn't happen."

"That's right."

"And *did* you rat him out? Is that why we're here?" My voice grew louder. "Is this all about goddamn money? Some Politburo grudge against an oil tycoon?" Had we finally gotten down to it? "Don't you think maybe you should have told us? Was it worth killing all those passengers? Risking all our lives?"

Bjorn stared ahead as he shook his head. "It wouldn't have changed anything if you knew."

"Did you, though?"

"Rat him out? Are you insane?"

"That's not an answer."

"Of course I didn't."

"Or maybe he betrayed me before I forced him onto the plane," Roman said. "You were not cooperative about coming."

Roman and Bjorn arguing at the check-in had looked like it almost came to blows.

"But I did. I got on the flight. Do you think I'd come on a flight where I knew I'd die?"

"Perhaps you didn't know what they would do."

"I didn't say *anything* to anyone."

"I do not trust him," Roman said.

I heard Otto mutter under his breath, "I don't trust any of you."

"And yet here you are," said Howard back to him.

Howard was playing with his phone. What was he doing?

"We don't know what just happened," Otto said in a louder voice. "Maybe the rescue was a mix up with the Finnish Marines. Not properly trained."

I said, "They were shooting at you."

"Because this idiot was shooting at them. He shot first." Otto zipped his survival suit back up and waved an orange-gloved hand at Howard. "He shot at least one of them. How the hell did you get that gun?"

"The one that got hit in the head. He put down his weapon. And I didn't mean to hit that guy, I was just trying to scare them."

"They were defending themselves."

Howard stood his ground. "They attacked Shu. I was trying to save him."

"His name is not Shu," Otto countered. "Did you know that guy was a terrorist?"

"According to who?"

"Did you tell them?" I said.

Maybe that was why the Marines had reacted the way they did. If they knew there was a Red List terrorist on the manifest and tracked him down as one of their first orders of business. Maybe he'd kidnapped Jang.

"I didn't tell them, but maybe they knew. They had a passenger list."

"And what happened to him? To Shu?" I'd run off when the first shots were fired.

"He died."

"You know that for a fact?"

"They put a half dozen rounds into him."

Jang's hands gripped me tighter under the suit. I hadn't realized what I was saying. Was Shu—or Pemba?—Jang's father? Was Otto telling the truth? Were we detailing the death of this kid's dad in front of him? Which made me think...

"Jang," I whispered and did my best to look down into his eyes. "Are you okay?"

He trembled but nodded.

"Can I ask you a very important question?"

He nodded again.

"Was that man your father? The man we're calling Shu—was he your dad?"

The kid's eyes were wide. He started to bob his head but then shook it in a trembling denial.

"Was his real name Pemba Ldong?"

Jang buried his face into my chest and nodded.

"Pemba? You're sure."

"Pemba was his real name, yes." The boy barely whispered the words.

"Where are your real parents?" My throat tightened up.

"I do not know." He hid his face from me.

"Did Pemba take you from them?"

His head bobbed up and down. "He did."

I brought one hand into the center of the suit and stroked his black hair. "Okay. Okay. That's enough for now. Rest."

Everyone looked at me. Otto met my gaze and held it.

So he *had been* telling the truth about Pemba. I hadn't really doubted him.

In the silence, just the sound of water lapping against the boat. Then something else. Voices. Very low, almost inaudible. Roman heard it as well and looked back the way we'd come.

Where were the voices coming from?

I looked right.

Bjorn stood up.

But Howard looked at his hands. The noise—the voices—came from his phone.

"You want to know who those guys were?" he said. "I gave them a little present. My other phone. I left it on and dropped it in their gear. I have that phone-to-phone app enabled and we're in range of my booster."

A moment of dumbfounded silence before I said, "Turn it up."

"And you know what else?" He turned to me with a big smile after tapping his phone.

"What?"

"GPS is working."

CHAPTER 26

The mesh networking app—FireChat, you remember?" Howard said.

"It can work from this distance?"

In the half-light I couldn't see much more than five hundred feet before any definition faded into the gloom. I couldn't get my Bluetooth speaker back home to work more than fifty feet.

"I had a Wi-Fi booster and antenna in my pod attached to a battery. I bring one when I travel. Outdoors that's good for a thousand feet, maybe a thousand five."

Howard's mind often seemed to have only one oar in the water, but it was an excellent one when he got it going in the right direction. The voices were garbled and low.

"Russian, they are speaking Russian," Roman said.

Bjorn had come from the bow to crowd around Howard with the rest of us. "Yeah, maybe, but they're Finns—half of them speak Russian. They're mostly Russian to begin with."

"I'd like to see you say that to a Finn's face," Roman grumbled.

"What are they saying?" I asked.

"Be quiet and I will tell." He moved forward and knelt in front of

Howard, who kept one arm hooked around his carbine and held the phone up with his other sock-covered hand.

I listened for a few seconds. The only word I could make out was "telco," or something like that.

"Does anyone else have a working phone?" I asked. Mine was dead.

Everyone shook their heads.

Great.

I stood up to get a better look and felt Jang slide down inside the suit. He clung to my midsection. It felt like I was pregnant, carrying a child—which I was. I angled between Bjorn and Otto to get a better look at Howard's phone.

About fifty percent power left.

"Do you have a charger?" I asked.

"I used them all up. Left the last one attached to the booster."

"You could have told us."

"Are you *kidding*? Roman was the only one who trusted me. At least *he* untied me."

"Be quiet." Roman had his ear as close to the phone as he could.

"Why do they keep saying 'telco'?" I asked. I heard it again.

"Can you switch it to the map app?" Bjorn whispered.

That's what I wanted to see as well. If the GPS was working, then...

Howard had to take off the layers of socks from his right hand to tap on the phone's screen. Even in the faded light, I saw a pale line across the middle of his index finger. He put the sock-mitts back on.

I leaned closer.

Bjorn unzipped his suit to bring one hand out the front. He leaned in and expanded the image on the screen with two fingers.

"I told you," he said. "We are right next to Greenland. About eighty-five degrees north."

"That spot looks closer to Ellesmere Island," I said.

But he was right.

The spot on the map app was nowhere near Wrangel Island or Russia, and at least a thousand miles or more from the edge of the

Beaufort Sea. So Josh had told the truth as well. That the hijackers had diverted the plane but doubled back.

"So which way is south?"

He rotated his phone back and forth, then pointed off the left side of the boat.

"And how far is that?" I indicated Ellesmere Island.

"A hundred miles, maybe more." Howard zoomed in to try and get the scale more accurate. "Maybe one fifty to the Canadian town of Alert on Ellesmere."

"How do we know this is right?" I said.

"What…what do you mean?" Howard's teeth chattered.

"I mean, last time I looked at my GPS, it said we were in Germany. All of our phones had the same wrong location. Maybe this is another wrong location."

"And why would it start working now?" Otto pushed in to sit beside Howard.

"I thought about that. It must be a GPS transmitter. I can't believe I didn't think of it before."

"Care to explain?"

"GPS signals come from sixteen thousand miles away. You need to set up a transmitter locally that broadcasts a GPS-frequency signal that's a little more powerful and you'll swamp the one coming from orbit. Could be a device as big as a pack of cigarettes. There must have been one in the flight deck of the plane."

"So now we're away from the plane—"

"We get GPS back. On that ice floe we couldn't get far enough away from whatever it was."

"But the other passengers had the same problem in the back of the plane, too. No GPS."

"So there must have been two of them, or a few. Like I said, small device."

I considered that for a few seconds. "But our phones never said they had no GPS signal. The signal said we were in Germany."

"That's what I'm saying."

"But what's stopping them—whoever 'they' are—from giving us a new false location? Like, if we've escaped, they might think—okay, let's broadcast a GPS signal so they go where we want them to go. Leading the lambs to the slaughter house."

Nobody had an answer for that.

Static hissed and the voices came clear for a second. Russian. Even I could tell it was Russian they spoke. And there was that word again.

"What does 'telco' mean?" I asked Roman.

He ignored me.

"But hold on," Otto said. "If the Russians knocked us down out of the sky with a missile, how—*and why?*—would they stash a bunch of GPS blocking devices on the plane?"

"Because we weren't knocked down out of the sky. We were hijacked."

Otto turned from looking at the phone and had to manually pull back the hood of his bright-orange survival suit so he could look at my eyes. "You say that like you know for sure."

"I talked to Josh. That's why I injected him." I glanced at Lilly. Her eyes were closed as she clung to me. "He was fine when I left him. Breathing regular."

"Care to share?"

Otto's voice didn't insinuate but his eyes narrowed.

The boat rocked ever so slightly as everyone leaned in toward me. Howard tilted to get a look at me around Otto who sat between us. Bjorn stood with a hand resting on each of Howard's and Otto's shoulders, and Roman knelt in front of Liz.

"Josh told me the plane was hijacked."

Otto said, "By who? Did he see them? I mean, white, black, brown? How many? Any names…?"

"He said the two replacement pilots hijacked the plane. They shut down the cabin oxygen so all the passengers passed out, or put something into the ventilation."

"I saw those guys come on board," Bjorn said. "They looked Chinese."

"Every Asian looks Chinese to a Norwegian." Roman muttered this comment loud enough for everyone to hear. "You know how many Asians we have in Russia?"

Of course all of Russia was in Asia. Nobody rose to the bait.

Otto pressed, "So Josh didn't see any faces? Anything specific?"

I explained how I thought the missing two hours were when we were all passed out, that we must have flown into radar coverage near the Beaufort Sea. That it was a purposeful deception before they doubled back.

"Doubled back to where? Where were they going?"

"To Russia," Roman said.

"I don't know. He passed out. That's when the boats arrived."

"Why didn't you tell us?" Otto said.

"Tell you? Christ, Josh tells me we were hijacked, the crazy Finns get there and I barely have time to put on this survival suit before you idiots start a reenactment of the OK Corral with my daughter in the middle of it."

"That wasn't my fault."

"I'm telling you now."

"That's it?" Otto said.

"That's it."

"Daddy?" Lilly tugged my right arm. "I need to pee."

▼▲▼

The first order of action was handing off Jang. Otto offered but the kid didn't want to have anything to do with him, so Liz took Jang and bundled him into her survival suit.

That done, I unzipped Lilly's suit and slid her out like a crab molting its shell. She began shivering right away. We pulled down her layers of dirty clothes beneath—mostly shirt-arms ripped up and improvised as leggings with double-wrapped adult clothes up top—and I held her bum out over the side.

Her pee dribbled into the dark water, splashing and burbling over the distant voices the others tried to listen to on Howard's phone.

Bjorn said it was maybe minus ten Centigrade. Maybe minus twelve, and getting colder. How much further could it drop? Anything was possible up here, he said quietly, with the sun gone for six months. Down to minus thirty. Minus forty.

With wind chill, exposed like this, that would feel like sixty or seventy below. And that was in Celsius. In Fahrenheit it converted to more like minus one hundred. It was possible to survive in such temperatures, he said as a half-joke, but only if you were a Muskox.

The water was calm. The fifty-foot gap between floes opened into a slushy sea maybe a hundred feet in front of us. Not in front, but toward the *bow*. I'd better start using nautical terms.

I held Lilly off the port side—I remembered it was 'port' because 'port' and 'left' had four letters in them—and watched the oily water undulate.

Ten thousand, maybe fifteen thousand feet deep?

I'd been terrified of water as a kid. My dad had thrown me into the community pool when I was an infant, my mother had told me, and where most kids doggy paddled up, I'd swallowed a mouthful of chlorinated poison and sunk straight to the bottom. I guess he meant well, I guess he'd wanted a son like him. An adventurer. He'd loved the water. He took me out sailing before I could walk.

I'd hated it, but wished I hadn't.

Water and I had a tortured relationship, like me and my dad. He died years before I met Emma. Before Lilly even existed. If only he could see me now, out here. I looked up.

"I'm done," Lilly chirped.

I shook her a little to get rid of the last pee drops and then stopped. What the hell was I going to dry her with? "Does anyone have...ah... cloth?"

When nobody answered, I wiped her bottom with the sleeve of my orange suit. She was shivering violently from the cold now, her lips turning almost blue. I deposited her on the bench and she pulled her covering back together and jumped back into the suit and zipped up.

I watched her and had another realization: We had no bathrooms on this thing. No toilet paper. And then another thought: do we even have any water?

The throbbing-but-familiar headache had returned. With the spike of adrenaline fading, I felt my stomach aching again. I still tasted those delicious sips of that hot soup the Finns gave me, my first warm drink in almost a week.

"You hear?" Roman said. He had his head next to the phone. "They said they wait for backup. We need to go."

"Nobody else here speaks Russian," Bjorn countered. "How do we know that's what they said?"

"Because I told you."

The Norwegian said, "You're the reason I'm stuck in this hell. You think I trust you?"

"You want go back?" Roman indicated the water of the starboard side. "I throw you in and you swim back like worm."

"Worms don't swim, you idiot."

"I think we should test that idea."

"Guys, guys, please," I interjected. "Can we focus?"

I looked at the back of the boat, at the engine. A single outboard. A Honda BF100. Meant it was a hundred horsepower. Looked very new. The gas tube led to a built-in reservoir under the back bench. Maybe six feet wide.

Two red plastic canisters next to some other cases. The red ones were definitely reserve gas tanks. Probably twenty-five liters.

Inside my survival suit, I pulled my two arms from the sleeves and into the middle area. These things were more like spacesuits or miniature shelters. Otto said they floated like boats and could keep you alive for days on the open ocean. I hoped he was right.

I felt around inside, in the jacket pockets of the coat I had on underneath. I felt the vials of adrenaline and the other syringe I'd already filled and capped. Next to them was my homemade compass and attached string. I fished it out and unzipped my suit and held up the magnet by the wire.

The taped-together stack of needles rotated side to side, but began to settle in a direction pointed toward the port side of the boat. It was 10 p.m. on my watch.

"We need a plan," I said as I put the magnet away.

"We need to go back," Otto said immediately. "The botched rescue had to be a mix up. The temperature is dropping. We have no shelter. No food. No water. Even if that GPS is correct, do you know how far we are from nowhere? This place kills even the best equipped explorers, and we've got two kids—"

"I know that. You think I don't know that?"

"I'm saying, no matter what happened, our only chance for survival is heading back to those guys. We hold our hands up. Pemba was a Red Listed terrorist. Those Marines must have recognized him, but they didn't know who else they were dealing with. They didn't know we were just bystanders."

"We can't...can't go back," Howard stuttered. His forehead had white patches.

"*Nyet*," Roman said.

Liz shrugged. "We have to go back. We cannot survive out here."

"They will kill us," Roman said.

"They didn't shoot at us when we left," I pointed out. "Didn't you notice that? If we were the last remnants of evidence of some international conspiracy, don't you think they would have mowed us down with their machine guns when we coasted by not twenty feet in front of them?"

"There is another storm coming," Otto said quietly. "Do you want your daughter out here when it hits?"

I remembered the wind screeching against the hull of the aircraft. The rolling waves cracking and tearing the ice. I looked to the bow of the boat—west, as best as we could estimate. The horizon was much darker there than to the east. Had to be thick clouds. The wind picked up and pushed the boat back a few feet against the ice edge.

After a pause, I said: "Let's head for Canada."

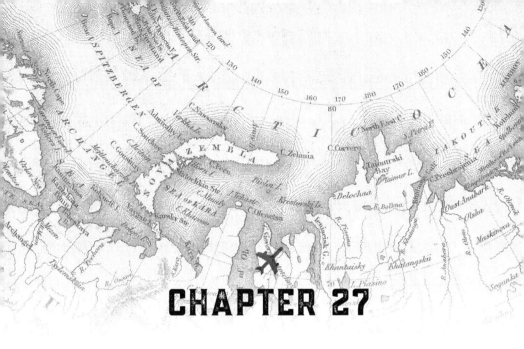

CHAPTER 27

"A re you insane?" Otto stood up straight and towered over me. I held Lilly close to me. "Could you keep your voice down?"

"Do you know what you're saying?" he said in a lower voice, but one equally shot through with exasperation.

"I know one thing."

"What's that?"

"I don't know much about Canada—"

"So why do you want to try and get there?"

"—but if I had to bet who brought this airliner down—*and why*—it would have nothing to do with Canucks. And if I was ever in a bad jam, I'd want a bunch of Mounties on the charge coming to help out."

Bjorn wagged his head up and down. "I have to say I agree with Mitch on this."

"And what else do you know about Canada?"

I shrugged. "Hockey?"

"Which is violent as hell."

Bjorn offered, "Ya, but more of a kind of *gentlemen* violent."

I unzipped and took out my magnet again and let it spin. I pointed off the port side. "Look, that's south—"

"-ish," Otto said. "South-*ish*. Maybe."

The needles swung back and forth slowly within a forty-five degree arc.

"You don't even know that's south and not north," Otto added. "Or how close we are to the Magnetic North, which would throw that off and have it pointing any direction. And how are we going to get to Canada? You know how big it is?"

"Five thousand miles wide?" Something like that. Canada was the massive frozen hat of America. "That gives us pretty good odds. Almost half of the Earth's circumference up here."

"With the other half Russia," Roman grumbled.

"And we head for that...that...t...town. Alert." Howard's teeth chattered as he tried to speak.

"It's not a town," Bjorn said. "That's a Canadian Armed Forces base."

"Even better," I said. "And we have flares, right?" I'd seen two survival boxes in the bottom of the boat.

"You said yourself the GPS suddenly working might be a trap," Otto pointed out.

In a short silence, the voices on Howard's radio became louder.

"They say someone is coming," Roman said.

We listened. Was that a low groan of engines in the distance?

"I want to get back to my wife, Mitch," Otto said.

"As do I."

"Are we going to walk to this Canadian Forces base?"

"We don't have to. The map says we're about a hundred and fifty miles from Alert." I pointed at the back of the boat. "That's a hundred horsepower engine. Looks new, must be an efficient four-stroke. You divide horsepower by fifteen to get gallons per hour for newer engines."

"I know all that, Mitch, but if we head out there"—Otto pointed off the bow—"we are going to die. You will kill your own daughter. I am going to die. I can't let that happen."

"We can leave you here on the ice with a flare," Howard offered.

"If we throttle down to seventy-five percent maximum," I

continued, "that cuts fuel consumption by half and optimizes output. So that engine is going to suck three to four gallons an hour." I pointed at the built-in fuel tanks. "That's gotta be twenty-five gallons."

"If it's full."

"So check it. Please, just check it."

Otto sighed but then stepped forward down onto his knees, unzipped his suit and began to unscrew the cap of the fuel tank.

"Plus those twenty-liter reserve tanks, the two red ones." I paused to do a mental calculation. "That's thirty seven gallons of fuel. Eleven hours of run time. And I bet this thing, loaded like this—"

"How do you know so much about this?" Liz asked.

"My dad. I would guess we can do twenty knots if we trim right. No waves." I turned to Bjorn. "You think this ice is cracked up enough for us to get close?"

"If we are where we think we are, there's a lot of new ice. Thin. It was shattered in the storm. We saw how far those guys came. From the horizon. As far as we could see."

I didn't understand how they were able to find us. Unless the flight deck voice recorder's transponder was firing—in which case, half of the world would have already descended on us with supplies and helicopters. I tucked the thought away in the back of my mind.

"Twenty knots is about twenty-three miles an hour. Eleven hours will get us two hundred-fifty miles. That's twice what we need. We get close to that Air Force Base and we fire off flares."

"That's the plan?" Otto knelt over the open fuel reservoir.

"I say we put it to a vote."

"First things first." Otto leaned back and outstretched one hand. "Howard, can I borrow your phone for one second? I need the light to see if this tank is full."

Howard could barely hold on to the phone himself. He nodded and handed it over.

Instead of looking into the fuel tank, Otto pocketed the phone in his suit with his left hand. His right hand shot straight out and caught the hacker flush in the side of the face. So quick nobody else had time to react. Howard crumpled sideways and Otto leapt forward and grabbed the automatic weapon.

For an instant I thought he was going to open fire. I turned to protect Lilly with my body. Roman was already on his feet.

Instead of shouldering the weapon, Otto simply tossed it a few feet over the side. It plopped into the water and disappeared.

Howard righted himself and rubbed the side of his face. "What the hell was that for?"

Roman moved stomach-to-stomach with Otto, bent over six inches so that his nose about touched the American's. "You give phone back or you go into that water, no suit." He shoved his hand into Otto's pocket.

The Russian looked twice the size of the American.

Otto didn't resist. "I'm trying to keep us safe." He held his hands up at his sides, palms out, in surrender.

"Can you please sit," Liz said. "The boat is rocking. I don't want to have to resuscitate anyone else from cold water immersion."

Howard trembled violently as he tried to raise a hand to his face.

"Jesus Christ," I muttered. "Somebody needs to volunteer to let Howard borrow their suit."

"I have the dog," Roman said.

I'd almost forgotten about the puppy, Irene. The Russian sat on the back bench awkwardly and I saw a little lump squirm up his chest and a small white face appeared.

"We should let Howard freeze to death." Otto whispered it low, but loud enough.

"I thought you were protecting him?" I said. "Your charge, right?"

Otto's head slumped between his shoulders. "We need to go back."

"I think we put it to a vote."

"You know I've got a gun, right?"

"We should head south," I said. "If those guys were really good guys, then they'll come looking. And more will come looking, not just them. Let's give ourselves some space for now."

Otto closed his eyes and seemed like he was counting to ten. "Okay, a vote."

"Guys," I said in a louder voice, "I'm going to take off my suit and share it with Howard. We need him if we're going to make it out of here."

Bjorn said, "And what is the catch?"

Roman handed the phone back to the shivering Howard.

"Before I do, I want a vote. Who wants to go back, and who wants to head for the Alert Canadian Forces base on Ellesmere?"

The boat rocked on rippling wavelets whipped up by a breeze.

"A show of hands. Who wants to go to Canada?"

Roman's hand shot up right away.

Howard said, "Can I vote that we leave Otto on the ice right here with a few flares?"

Liz shook her head. "I'm not sure about trying for Canada."

"You know what my vote is," Otto said.

Bjorn took a deep breath before saying, "I don't know."

"You mean, you're abstaining? Or you need more time?"

The noise in the distance was louder. Definitely another engine. Or several engines.

TRANSCRIPT AUDIO 4
National Transportation Safety Board.
Mid-Flight Disappearance of Allied 695,
Boeing 777, NTSB/AIR.
Washington, DC

Do you believe him?" Peter asked. "About what the pilot said before the attack?"

"You mean, do I believe Mitch? Or what Mitch said Josh said?" Richard stretched his neck forward and groaned.

They'd been at this for nine hours and were three pots of coffee deep. Past midnight already. He needed some antacid. His wife had left two voice messages. He texted back that he would sleep at the office. He got up to make yet another pot.

Peter said, "So you see the problem."

"This isn't a courtroom. We're trying to find the truth, not assess guilt. If not the truth, then I'm looking for a cause. We find causes, then we suggest fixes so it doesn't happen again. That's what the NTSB does."

"You're not looking for justice?"

It was a leading question.

One thing Richard knew for sure was that Peter wasn't here for justice or truth. The past few hours, going over this, it had become clearer what his *newly* appointed partner, Peter Hystad, was here for.

He was here to babysit.

No, that wasn't right. This guy was here to spy, but for whom Richard wasn't sure, and maybe he was here to do more than just spy. Or maybe Richard was just too tired, seeing conspiracies everywhere.

"Not our job to find justice," Richard answered. "Only causes. I need you to contact the Finnish government and European teams, see if they had any units go missing."

"Wouldn't we have heard something?"

"That's why I'm asking to check."

"So do you think it was hijacked?"

"I don't disbelieve anything at this point."

"Maybe somebody was going for the diamonds? Not just terrorists, but hijackers—criminals?"

Richard paused to consider before saying, "The South African conglomerate is reviewing its records, but their insurance company isn't buying the story. I don't think there were any diamonds on that plane. I think that was a fabrication."

"This whole journal could be a fabrication. I just got an email about Mitch Matthews."

"And?"

"Did you know he was a contractor for Tree Capital Group?"

"Former contractor." Richard had already dug that up from his contacts. "He stopped working for them five months ago. He was a financial analyst. Wife said he quit to try writing. Explains this journal."

But he saw the implication. Tree Capital's parent company was the Constellation Group, a big international government military contractor. It wouldn't take long for conspiracy websites to circulate theories once this journal became public.

Another tape had finished, and Peter indicated that he'd make the change to a new one.

Richard observed his new partner to make sure he put the completed recording into the evidence folder. Watched him for some sleight of hand.

"Even if this journal was somehow faked—and I don't believe it is,"

Richard said. "We could still find the reasons behind the fabrication to discover the real truth."

"So we're back to truth."

"I know you weren't talking to your wife on the phone outside."

At first Peter's eyebrows furrowed together in mock confusion, but then his face went slack. He said, "I'm trying to make sure we don't get into trouble, here. Don't get ahead of ourselves."

Richard sized up his new partner, stared at him with unwavering eyes. "And I want to make sure that whatever happened to Allied 695, does not happen again."

CHAPTER 28

Like the ancient mariners, we navigated by the stars.

I had been the point-man guiding on the bow for an hour now, and had just gotten my survival suit back. For the first three hours, I gave it up to Howard. I endured three hours without its protection, sandwiched between Liz and Otto and covered by anything else I could find. It was an hour since I'd gotten the suit back on, and I hadn't warmed up yet. My feet bricks of ice. My body shivering.

At first, the vote on whether to head for Canada had been split—myself and Roman voting to go, with Liz and Otto thinking it better to head back. Roman convinced Liz to change her mind, and then Bjorn came down off the fence. It ended up five to one, or seven to one if we counted the kids.

Otto didn't want to be left alone on the ice, and he still felt responsible for protecting us. So despite his protests, we headed away from the plane wreck and off on our own.

Roman and Bjorn had taken the first shift driving for three hours, and now it was myself and Otto. The engine droned from behind me, the quiet shush of the waves breaking from the bow under me. I perched on the front of the Zodiac. Otto's face was a moon-white orb barely visible twenty feet behind me as he operated the outboard engine.

I had explained that we didn't need to keep using Howard's phone to figure out the direction. We just had to follow the heavens home.

Even so, once an hour we'd turn the phone on and check our position and adjust. We needed to save the battery. Less than half charged now. Without it, we'd be dead.

Straight ahead was the darkest part of the sky, the blue-black firmament cloudless. No moon. No Venus. Only the hard pinpoints of the stars. Air so clear that we could almost navigate by the light of them. Straight overhead, at the end of the handle of the Little Dipper, was Polaris—the polar king, the North Star. The constellations rotated perfectly around it like a stellar merry-go-round.

So far on my watch I'd been aiming us at Leo, at the bright dot of Regulus at the lion's foot. Over the next hour I'd switched to Arcturus at the tip of the herdsman's plow as it swept around left to right across the invisible horizon in front of us. Halfway into the sky ahead was the Big Dipper in Ursa Major.

The Big Dipper.

It felt like the constellations tugged me forward, a familiar and even familial connection from this alien world to the universe I was desperate to get back to.

Somehow the pull felt backward in time.

Back to when my father had first detailed the heavens to me when he took us camping at Saranac Lake in Upstate New York. He made me memorize the formations, quizzed me on them. Told me that one day my life might depend on it when I was sailing.

I knew even then that I'd never be a sailor. Not like him. A part of me had had a kind of resentment, like I wasn't the son he'd hoped for. But today I was my father's son, leading an expedition home by the stars.

Something thudded against the bow and rocked us sideways. We hit smaller chunks of submerged ice every now and then. Two hours ago we had gotten stuck on top of a large wedge we managed to push away.

I clicked my headlamp back on.

A murky gray wall lurked in the middle distance. Sheeting layers of pancake ice broke and slithered sideways over each other and away from us as the boat plowed forward. My heart felt like it lurched into my throat. I swept my light to the left and searched for a gap in the growing frozen facade.

"Left, turn left," I said and pointed.

The four-foot embankment of ice ended maybe two hundred feet off to one side. The ice had been trashed and ripped by the storm and weakened by the recent bloom of warmth. Merciful channels of slush-filled black water appeared somewhere as a way through, but the ice was reforming on the surface in the vicious cold.

Somewhere out there was home, but somewhere closer was a frozen wall we wouldn't be able to pass. Not in the boat.

▼▲▼

I pulled my head inside my survival suit and used it as a cocoon to bring myself out of the damn wind for a few seconds. A slurry of ice chunks ahead as far as my headlamp could illuminate. I checked the glowing dials on my watch. Past 1 a.m. on October 12.

Two more hours of facing this infernal wind before Bjorn would take over the piloting.

For maximum efficiency, we had to keep the trim right—the nose up at three or four degrees and fast enough that she would plane. I figured my twenty-knot estimate was about what we were managing. Twenty-three miles per hour.

Sounded good.

Except this wind.

Bjorn told me the wind chill factor was non-linear. I'd watched him grimacing in the front and not quite understood what he meant. Wind chill was something the weather anchor would tell me, and maybe it stung on December days when the breeze cut between Manhattan's skyscrapers. But sticking your face out—even covered as best you could—into a twenty-three mph wind when it was already twenty below freezing?

He said the effect was like minus fifty. The colder the air, the effective wind chill dropped exponentially.

I could cover my forehead and cheeks and pull my survival suit hood tight, but the wind cut straight into my eyes. My eyelashes instantly heavy with icicles that I had to wipe away from my stinging eyes each few minutes, frozen tears stuck to cheeks I had to rub every thirty seconds to make sure weren't solid with frostbite. I lashed the headlamp onto the orange integrated glove of the survival suit and tried to keep it focused forward.

And these were survival suits, not *Arctic* suits.

They were designed to keep someone alive in frigid water, not to explore the frozen wastes of the north. Water temperature was rarely below freezing. The air here was much below that. The warmth I'd felt when I first put it on dissipated as the air temperature dropped and I faced down this wind. The cold a tiger whose claws ripped into me.

I shivered even inside the suit.

I poked my head back up and glimpsed through the opening.

A ghostly apparition loomed and grew.

"Right, go right!"

The boat swerved to clear a bobbing ice sculpture. Bjorn said the icebergs were good. Meant we were closer to land. The sheets of ice were cracked up and dislodged. A silent crystalline menagerie. My head jerked sideways as the Zodiac thudded into a submerged ledge and for a heart-stopping instant I thought we'd stick, but Otto gunned the engine and we surged clear.

Open water ahead. At least for two hundred feet. I tucked my face back down into the suit.

Our seventh day out here.

A week that my wife had suffered. Wondered. *I'm coming, Emma.*

I'm coming home. With Lilly. I promise.

My little girl was asleep—I hoped she was asleep—in the nest assembled between the middle two benches. Six humans and a dog wedged as close together as possible and covered with everything we had.

Roman had taken Jang into his survival suit while Liz cradled Lilly, and Bjorn had given me his suit for this shift while we let Howard keep his. Everyone else in the middle piled around the Norwegian who huddled away from the wind.

Howard had frostbite on his fingers. That's what the telltale white lines were, Bjorn had explained. He'd tapped a finger on my cheek and I tried to scrape away something—it felt like a bit of gum stuck there. He said that was frostbite as well. I'd never experienced it. It didn't hurt. He said it wouldn't hurt until it defrosted. Then it would burn.

We had to be careful, he said.

No kidding.

I told Lilly to stay inside her suit with the hood pulled shut. Told her to use as little of what remained in the inhaler as possible.

We'd checked the crates in the boat. Six plastic-shelled cases each about two-by-two foot.

One case of MREs—Meals, Ready-to Eat, as Otto described them. Thirteen hundred calories each. Twelve packs. Twelve bottles of one liter water, half of which was already frozen. A box of tripods and lights but no batteries. One box with a night vision scope, the rifle gone. A case filled with synthetic blankets, all of which were now wrapped around the nest in the middle.

Two cases were survival kits: lengths of nylon rope, flare guns with three flares each, mylar space blankets, fold-out shovels, water purification tablets and first aid kits. The final item in each kit were serrated knives about six inches long. Otto took the knives.

My tongue felt like it was pasted to the roof of my mouth, but I kept most water rationed to me for Lilly. Bjorn reminded me to take a sip every now and then. My brain ached deep between the temples, the pain blossoming into the base of my skull.

Another ghost appeared in the night.

"Right, to the right," I croaked, but now Arcturus was to port. "And then swing around to the left after that."

"What?" Otto yelled over the noise of the engine.

I made a circling motion with my hand. "Around that way."

"Got it."

I waited for us to clear the berg before I tucked my head back in.

The initial euphoria of setting off—of escaping, of not sitting still—had worn away into a gnawing fear. Where the hell were we going? We had less than a day of food or water, and we were slowly freezing even in these suits. Not just that, but it was my idea.

What if this whole escape was a convoluted trap? Or worse. What if we were heading nowhere?

We followed the stars, but I had no real idea if it was the right direction. With a sextant, it was possible to figure out your latitude—how far north—by measuring off the North Star on a clear night. Figuring out our position east or west was impossible. That technological solution took centuries to solve. If the phone was wrong, we were dead.

The Alert base was the most northerly permanently inhabited place on the planet, Bjorn had explained when we decided to go. It was a tiny speck in a massive and unforgiving wilderness. The next nearest settlement was two hundred fifty miles south, the village of Eureka at the lower edge of Ellesmere.

He said the island was more like a polar desert. At least that would make it easier to walk.

If we could get there.

Soon we would hit the "fast ice," he said. The sea ice that is fastened to the shore. The polar current slipped south here. Meant no warm blooms of water. Meant the fast ice might be miles thick before the shore. Might be tens of miles.

When the plane crashed, we were twenty-six people huddled against the cold. Then we were eleven after most of them left before the storm.

Were the people in the other half of the plane even still alive?

Now we were down to eight. And one dog.

Was this how it happened? One by one, until we were all gone? Disappeared into the frozen waste?

In the book I'd read about Peary, they'd talked about the doomed Franklin Expedition of 1845. Two ships had set sail from England to explore the Northwest Passage—the HMS *Erebus* and *Terror*. They were never heard from again. One hundred and twenty-nine men lost.

A dozen ships had tried to find a trace but none succeeded.

Over the decades people heard stories, and twenty years later in the 1860's, they found the remains of an encampment and a journal detailing the horrors. The ragtag of dwindling survivors had gone from one island to the next, burying their dead as they went. Cut marks in human bones detailed the final sad chapters of cannibalism.

I felt for my journal in my pocket, then poked my head back out of the opening in my suit and stared bleary-eyed into the frigid wind.

▼▲▼

My feet were almost knocked out from under me by something. I had my head down in my suit so I couldn't see what pushed me sideways. My left hand gripped the cord attached to the bow to keep me in place. I struggled upright, pulled down my hood and stuck my head out.

A body slumped itself into the nook at the bow of the boat below me. Their back to the wind and protected by the lee of the inflatable wall. Howard's face glowed in the light of his phone he held up, inside his suit, inches from his nose.

"You're doing great," he said and held up the phone.

I did a quick check ahead, then leaned down to block the wind and get a better look.

"I was a bit off in my first estimate." Howard used two fingers to expand the screen. "We were more like a hundred-sixty miles from Alert CFB to start with, but we're only one-ten to one-twenty now."

The dot had moved closer, but that was after five hours.

We'd already emptied one of the twenty-five-liter containers into the main tank, which was now only three-quarters full. The other container would fill it. That would give us another eight hours at this pace. I did some mental calculations. In five hours we should have crossed a hundred and twenty miles, but Howard was saying we had only gotten sixty miles closer—we'd had to wind back and forth and slow down a lot.

"You're sure?" I said.

"We have more than enough fuel at this rate. I'm doing my calculations, too."

"Turn the phone off." It was down to one-quarter charged.

The screen's glow winked out and left us in darkness. I angled my head up and stole a glance forward. Squinted into the wind. Nothing but slush ice as far as I could see.

"I noticed you left one thing out when you spoke to Otto," Howard said.

"What's that?"

"That Josh said the hijackers wanted something in First Class."

The boat slapped up against some ice and back down. I didn't answer.

"They wanted something and tried to crash a plane onto the pack. A downed plane on polar ice. You know what laws apply?"

I had no idea and it was rhetorical, so I let him continue.

"Floating ice might look like land, but we're on the high seas. We're subject to the ancient rules of salvage and retrieval. Anything found out here can be claimed by salvage law, did you know that?"

I hadn't thought of that. "I wanted to tell Otto in private that the hijackers wanted something in First Class," I said.

"You don't trust Liz or Bjorn or Roman, either?"

"I don't trust you, that much I can say." That was a bit infantile, so I added, "Look, I wanted to keep a few details to myself. This isn't personal."

"I can understand that."

"Good."

"Can I have my disk back?"

Silence for a beat as the boat bounced up and down.

"I'm keeping your disk safe for you."

"You know I need it, right?"

"I know."

"Black hat, black hacker. You know how hard it is to be a man of color in my job?"

What was I supposed to say? I didn't reply.

Howard continued, "Of course Snowden even has the word 'snow' in his name. Snowflake. White as hell. Of course he's the famous hacker." He paused. "I can feel it, you know. Even when I'm sleeping. I can feel where my disk is."

"Make sure you keep taking your meds."

"I didn't disable the radio."

Liz was behind me with Lilly. We avoided having her do a shift with Howard—we said so she could take care of the kids, but it was more to keep an eye and babysit Howard.

"I had nothing to do with the radio," Howard repeated. "That was Otto who did that."

"Otto did not disable the radio."

"Rasheed. Have you forgotten about Rasheed? How did he end up dead?"

"I don't know. He went out with the others in the storm."

"There is a killer on this boat. You know that, right? I can feel them. My thoughts can sense their presence."

I had my head down but peeked forward again. Tears streamed from my eyes. Nothing ahead. If someone was a killer, I had a feeling it was the guy talking to me. I felt for the fork I kept in one of my pockets.

"Adrian didn't know Otto," Howard continued. "Didn't you notice that? The cabin manager didn't know the Air Marshal. What does that tell you?"

"They're trained not to acknowledge the Air Marshal."

"Even after an accident?"

"I don't know much about it."

"But I do." Howard's face appeared again from the darkness. He'd turned the phone on again.

"Turn that off."

"Okay, okay." His face disappeared. "But did you look at his gun?"

"Whose?"

"It's not a Sig Sauer P229. That's the standard issue gun for an American Air Marshal. His isn't one. That's a Glock in his pocket."

I put my head up in time to see a gray wall materialize from the gloom. I turned awkwardly in the thick suit and yelled, "Left, hard left!"

The boat angled almost forty-five degrees to swerve around.

"You need to go," I said to Howard. I shone my headlamp right into his eyes.

He began to inch his way along the bottom, back to the middle. "Someone's a killer on this boat. You remember that."

CHAPTER 29

H ead more toward Vega now," I said to Bjorn.
"That one?" He pointed into the sky—more like fisted at it with the mitt of his suit.

"That's Deneb. The shiny one to the right. That's Vega."

He shifted his arm in response.

"Between there and Arcturus," I said. "The brightest dot straight ahead."

Almost two hours into Bjorn and Roman's shift. Ten minutes to 5 a.m. Bjorn nodded that he understood and I slid back into the relative warmth at the floor of the center of the boat.

At the end of my rotation at the bow we came to a wide floe of ice we had to get out on foot and explore. For a few terrifying minutes I thought we would have to trek a hundred miles across the ice to try and get to the Alert Canadian Forces base. We eventually found a way through to open water to the south but it took most of an hour.

Otto had reluctantly given up his survival suit at the end of our shift. Gave it to Bjorn who had managed the three hours curled in a fetal ball in the middle of the boat covered by the blankets and surrounded by the others. I'd done the three hours before that with no suit and hadn't managed to properly warm up even after I'd gotten it back.

For the first half hour without an orange suit on, Otto had sat up defiantly clothed in only the ragtag collection of shirts and coats from the plane, but after that the former SEAL assumed the same curled-up fetal position in the middle of the boat out of the wind.

I wasn't looking forward to my turn again.

The cold was terrifying. Nowhere to escape it. It crept under the skin and refused to leave.

I was glad to have Jang's small body clung tight to my midsection inside my suit now. An extra source of heat. Maybe we'd need to get two adults into one of these things soon when we slept.

In fact, the more I thought about it, there was no way I was spending any more time exposed like that. Could I fit in Liz's suit with her? Not possible for me to get in with any of the men, except maybe the slight frame of Howard.

Or we leave him to suffer the cold. I didn't trust him.

I decided I wasn't going to give up my suit again. I doubted I could survive it, and my little girl needed me. I curled up at the front of the pile next to a shivering Otto and held Lilly.

"We are more than halfway," I heard Roman say over the droning engine.

He wasn't speaking to me.

"Do you think we'll get the whole way in the boat?" Liz replied.

She was beside me, but sat upright. She'd volunteered for a rotation at the bow, but we preferred keeping her closer to Howard and tending to whatever needed fixing.

"*Nyet*. There will be thick ice near the shore. I have spent a lot of time drilling in Arctic."

"But close?"

"You work for United Nations?" Roman asked her.

"Not exactly. I work for a lab that is working to help them."

"With this viral outbreak in Africa?"

"That's right."

"I often wish I had done more of this."

"Done what?" Liz said to Roman.

"Helped people. You know, like Bill Gates does. So this is what your package is?"

Liz kept her precious Dewar container in her small backpack wrapped up inside her survival suit. Everyone knew what it was by now.

"That's correct," she replied.

"Go right," Bjorn yelled from the front.

Roman stood up. "We go left," he said. "I can see." He turned the boat.

It was dark, but not quite full nighttime.

The two men began to argue.

Liz moved next to me and curled up. "So you know the stars, Mitch?"

"A little," I replied.

"Sounds like more than a little."

"My dad taught me."

"So what is that one?" She pointed straight up.

She picked the easiest one. "That's Polaris. The North Star."

"Tell me more about it."

"It sits directly above the North Pole," I said.

"What does that mean?"

"The Earth spins like a top. You take that central axis of rotation straight up, and that's the North Celestial Pole. The North Star sits within one degree of it. This far north, it seems to sit straight overhead."

"Doesn't the Earth wobble on its axis?"

"It always points the same direction," I said. "But it's tilted about twenty-four degrees on its axis with respect to the sun. That's what gives us the seasons as we go around it."

"Of course."

"The technical name is Alpha Ursae Minoris. It's a yellow star about a hundred times bigger than our sun."

"I must sound stupid. I'm supposed to be a scientist."

"How did you end up on this flight?"

"Bad luck. Like all of us. I was supposed to be on a different route."

"So how did you get on this one?"

"The ticketing agent got me on when mine was canceled."

I wasn't supposed to be on the flight either, not until Josh had announced to Emma that he was flying that day.

"I have another question."

"Yes?"

"How long does it take to get scurvy?"

She laughed. I hadn't heard her laugh before. "That takes months. Even years. Your American body is more than full of enough vitamin C for now."

The boat knocked into something and we shifted sideways.

"I'll tell you something else you don't know," she said.

I waited.

"Scurvy caused the rise of the mafia."

"How's that?"

"When the English discovered that lemons could stop it, the best place to get lemons was Sicily back in the 1800's. They charged a high price and it led to the creation of farming cabals that became the mafia."

"Tell me something else I don't know," I said.

"Like what?"

"Like more about what's in your container."

"I've already told you."

"Howard said it could be used as a weapon of mass destruction. Is that true?"

The engine rumbled. I waited a second and then two.

"That is not true," she finally answered.

"So it's not a smallpox virus?"

"*Techniquement*, an orthopoxvirus. Related to horsepox, but not the same. It was reconstructed synthetically. It cannot hurt people."

"You're sure of that?"

"I am sure."

The way she said it, I could tell she wasn't, but not in a way that she *was*, either.

"Could it be turned into something that could?"

"Only by someone who was very skilled."

"Into smallpox?" It took humanity decades and untold resources to wipe this disease from the face of the planet. I did a project on it in high school.

"What's in this container is harmless."

"Can we open it to look?"

"Why? And no, that would destroy it."

"Could *you* turn it into something harmful?"

I'd almost forgotten that Jang was curled up inside my suit. "Elizabeth would not hurt anyone," he said.

"But maybe someone would force her to," I said to the both of them.

Liz sighed and sat upright. "Can I volunteer for bow duty?"

"You want to come up here?" Bjorn said from the front.

She stood, bent low, and began to make her way toward him.

"Mr. Mitch?" said a small voice.

Jang's face was invisible in the interior darkness of my suit even when I tried to look down at him. A tiny disembodied voice.

"You okay?" I asked.

"It is more you that I am worried about."

He was curled into a tiny ball, balanced on my stomach under the suit.

"You should not worry about the things you cannot change," he said.

"You don't understand, Jang."

"I understand perhaps more than you think."

Maybe the kid knew something about Pemba? About what happened? "Tell me then," I said.

"We are all exactly where we are supposed to be, Mr. Mitch."

"You know where we are?"

"I know exactly where I am."

"And that is…?"

"With you."

My flicker of hope that the kid might know something useful about Pemba or the accident faded, replaced with the constant gnawing uncertainty clawing at the back of my thoughts, the mind-gremlin that refused to let me sleep.

"You should not fear death," Jang said after a pause.

What kind of thing was that for a Kindergarten kid to say? "We're not going to die," I replied.

"We all die, Mr. Mitch, but it is only the ego that is afraid."

I didn't know what to say. In the semi-darkness, Bjorn wriggled on the floor. Otto cursed and told him not to move the blankets. From the front, Liz called out to turn right.

"Do not be afraid," Jang said.

Somehow the kid's voice put me at ease. Not only his voice, but his *presence* so close to me had a kind of calming effect that was hard to describe but as enveloping as the cold. Lilly mumbled that she was okay when I checked on her, and I cupped her next to my body with Jang between us. A few minutes later I drifted off to the droning of the engine.

▼▲▼

"I think we need to get out."

Emma stood over me and leaned in the window of our car.

"I don't want to," I mumbled.

"Wake up," she said.

I opened my eyes. I couldn't see anything so I tried to wipe my eyes. It felt like I was wrapped in plastic. "Emma, I can't—"

"I'm Isabelle," Liz said.

I blinked and blinked again. I wasn't blind. It was dark. A light turned on and illuminated Lilly's face below me. I felt Jang squirm.

"Come on, Mitch, you need to wake up."

I groaned, held onto Jang and sat half upright against the wall of the boat. The sky blue-black above to gray-blue at the horizon. Straggler stars remained visible, with Polaris pinpointed aloft.

"What's going on?" I asked. "Are we stuck?"

My mind was groggy and disconnected. Nobody seemed upset, the movement around me slow. Bjorn jumped from the front of the boat and I was about to yell out, but he levitated into the air. My eyes adjusted. He stood on a ledge about a foot above the bow.

"How long?" I said to Liz on the bench to my left.

Howard was to my right, sitting upright and illuminated by the glow of his phone's screen. "About twenty miles."

"To what?"

"We've been following the edge of the ice for three hours," Liz said. "We went an hour east and cut back. This is the closest we can get."

"Twenty miles to the Alert CFB," Howard said.

I noticed he was cocooned in a swaddle of the blankets and crinkling mylar. No survival suit.

A figure crunched across the snow and materialized from the gloom to be side-lit by Liz's headlamp. It was Roman. "Now we walk," he said.

CHAPTER 30

More you want to carry, more you *have* to carry," Roman argued. "We need to think about this," Otto replied.

Roman added, "We need to move light and fast. Twenty miles I do in one day by myself."

"So then go."

"Give me the gun and I go."

The two orange-suited men stood toe-to-toe in freshly drifted ankle-deep snow.

"You know I can't do that."

"Then give me a knife and I stay."

Otto relented and reached into the pocket of his suit.

"How come I don't get a knife?" Howard said.

Even shivering on a frozen slab of sea ice a thousand miles from nowhere, this kid had a sense of humor. He had both Mylar sheets around himself like a shawl, his sock-mitted hands pulling them tight. He cast me a sideways grin and hopped from one foot to the other.

Roman had refused, in the rotation, to share his survival suit with Howard, and nobody else had volunteered. Liz had said she wanted to, but she was suffering from the cold worse than the rest of us. Maybe not worse than Howard, whose fingers were so frostbitten he couldn't operate his phone anymore.

After declining to relinquish his survival suit, the Russian had volunteered to transport Jang.

I knelt in the snow and did my best to tie a knot in a length of the nylon rope. Bjorn had fashioned two sleds by opening the six plastic cases to carry what supplies we had—which wasn't much. Bjorn said he'd tow one set of cases, Otto said he'd pull the other. Even bringing my hands out of the suit for a minute made my fingers painfully cold.

"You walk as far as you can," I said to Lilly.

My daughter nodded bravely, her breathing short and shallow. She stared at the ground.

"Leave the dog."

Roman stood over us. Jang peeked over his shoulder from inside the suit.

The puppy was wrapped up in two of the synthetic blankets in one of the half-open cases tied up in the sled formation. It had run around yapping on the snow when we disembarked, until it began hopping around with one little leg in the air and then the other. Its paws were freezing.

"We can't leave Irene," Lilly said in small voice.

The puppy shivered and looked at me with its big black eyes. I picked it up and stuffed it into the opening in my suit into my top layer of clothes.

"We're bringing the dog," I said.

"Waste of time." Roman stomped off twenty paces, stopped and said, "We go?" without turning around.

I took one last look at the Zodiac gently rocking in the black water at the edge of the ice. We had considered trying to drag it across the ice with our supplies in it, but the thing must have weighed three hundred or more pounds.

The sky had lightened into a waxy twilight that hid the stars. The horizon to the south was almost pale blue, a hazy red ringed the horizon behind us that faded into gray. Scudding low clouds became visible as the twilight brightened, puffy white interlopers that skimmed the ice-bound plain.

"You know what's funny?" Bjorn said as he wrapped a length of cord around his waist and attached it to his three-case sled.

I took Lilly's hand and stood.

"The Arctic gets as much sunshine as the tropics." The Norwegian trudged forward and followed the Russian's footsteps. "It's the angle of the rays. Funny, no?"

It wasn't. Not at all.

The gray light was a welcome relief from the darkness—I turned my headlamp off and followed in Bjorn's footsteps—but no amount of twilight could make up for an unobstructed view of the beaming star that seemed forever beyond our horizon.

▼▲▼

"Do you know who my grandfather was?" Roman asked.

"No idea," I replied.

Talking kept my mind occupied.

For two hours we had wound our way across the fractured landscape. The first three hundred feet had almost forced us back to the boat as we tried to cross a ten-foot ridge of ice with a yawning crevasse a foot across that opened and closed with the slow motion of the waves. We gave up on the sled idea almost immediately and rejigged to carry what we needed on our backs, and instead used the rope to tie us all together in a seven-person caravan.

In case one of us slipped in.

Roman went first, carrying Jang inside his suit, followed by me and Lilly and Liz, with Bjorn and Howard and Otto in the rear. I offered to carry Lilly, but she was determined to walk as much as she could herself. I kept a careful ear listening to her breathing. Her inhaler was almost empty again.

"My grandfather was Aleksander Kolchak," Roman said.

"During the Russian Civil War in 1918, he established an anti-communist government in Siberia—later the Provisional All-Russian Government—and was recognized as the 'Supreme Leader and Commander-in-Chief of All Russian Land and Sea Forces' by the other leaders of the White movement from 1918 to 1920. His government was based in Omsk, in southwestern Siberia. He died in 1920, killed by Bolsheviks by firing squad."

We had fashioned a sling across Roman's back for Jang. The kid kept quiet while we talked, almost as if he wasn't there. Maybe he was sleeping? I hoped so.

"Why are you telling me this?"

The dog squirmed in my clothes to find a more comfortable position.

"So you understand," Roman said.

"What?"

"That I am not a Communist. You do not see it?"

"See what?" I replied.

"What the Russians are doing? What Putin's goal is?"

"Tell me again."

Twenty miles.

How long could that take? Two miles an hour was half of normal walking pace. At that rate it would take ten hours. We had to tough it out for less than half a day. That was my thinking. It was optimistic, I had found out.

A hundred feet forward, then a hundred sideways, followed by hauling each other over never-ending pressure ridges of ruptured ice. Then fifty feet back through the maze. Without stars to guide us, we had to consult Howard's phone every fifteen minutes only to find we were going in the wrong direction. We'd hit a merciful patch of flat ground and set our heading on a bulbous lump on the horizon.

I slipped and shuffled forward.

The cold seeped into my suit, into my teeth and into my brain. I couldn't remember the last time I'd felt my feet or fingers. If these survival suits weren't designed for Arctic conditions, they most definitely weren't well constructed for Arctic *exploration*, not for trekking across the open ice. We needed boots and crampons, not these rubber soles that froze and slipped.

I kept checking on Lilly who soldiered forward, but I heard her wheezing.

Soon I'd have to carry her.

Or one of us would.

Roman seemed invulnerable to it all.

"Putin sees Perestroika and the collapse of the Soviet Union as the greatest disaster of the twentieth century," he said. "The Russian population and economy was keeping pace with America until the 1980's but now has collapsed by comparison."

"What does that have to do with us?"

"Everything. It is this whole frozen wasteland"—he spread his arms wide—"that Putin lays claim as his own. We planted a Russian flag on the seafloor of the North Pole."

"Yeah, Bjorn mentioned that."

"The northland has always been ours. This is how we Russians see the world."

I noticed how he was inclusionary. Even hunted by his country, he wasn't separate from it.

"What does that have to do with us?" I repeated. My teeth chattered.

"This climate change that Bjorn speaks of? This is how Putin will defeat the great American enemy. He is sowing seeds of uncertainty, using the social media, using his own scientists—enough to delay, to give the greedy a reason not to do anything."

"So he crashed an airliner?"

"He wants to claim the whole of the Arctic as his when the temperatures rise. In fifty years, half of America will be uninhabitable and most of its great cities flooded under the sea, but Siberia will warm enough for farming and become the breadbasket of the world. Not everyone loses with the changing climate—Russia wins, America loses. The north will open up for travel and shipping and resources. I know. I was participating in Putin's machinations. I am a part of it. It was what

I didn't want to be doing anymore. It is why I contacted Bjorn."

"I thought he helped you fudge ecological impact studies?"

"I needed a cover for contacting the Greenpeace people."

I didn't say anything.

"Trust me, Mitch. Misinformation on climate change will win Russia the future of the world, the advent of the new Russian Empire. We've been around for more than a thousand years—what's fifty years of waiting in this?"

"But why down an airliner? To get to you?" There had to be easier ways than this.

"Do you know of the War Scare of 1983?"

I shrugged to indicate I'd never heard of it.

"The West ran war games in the Arctic, like are happening now. In response, the Soviets mobilized nuclear submarines and bombers. A Korean commercial airliner flying from Alaska was shot down by the Soviets—and it had an American Congressman on board."

"I didn't know that."

"It almost started a war. Perhaps this is the same. A replay of history. It is not diamonds or even me they are after. It is the entire world."

Had he heard Josh tell me that the hijackers were searching for something in First Class? Why was he trying to convince me?

Roman lowered his voice. "I think it was Howard who disabled the radio. So we could not transmit. Yes, they search for us, but in the wrong place. That radio could have transmitted our location. He could have also been the one to disable the GPS."

"You think he was one of the hijackers?"

The Russian stumped forward.

I followed in his footsteps. That didn't make any sense, I thought. Who would risk being out here in this? Why? I turned to glance at Howard, who looked more than halfway dead already as he stumbled forward one step at a time, attempting to keep the blankets and Mylar wrapped around him.

▼▲▼

"We dig in here for the night," Otto yelled over the noise of the wind.

I let Lilly slide off my back and knelt to turn and block a gust of crystalline snow. I checked my watch. Eight p.m. Ten hours of slogging torture and we were only five miles closer to the little dot on Howard's screen.

His phone's battery was in the red. Maybe ten percent left.

A biting wind sprang in the last hour as the first stars pierced the sky. It was too dark to continue walking safely even with the headlamps, but we had a bigger problem: what looked like a hundred-foot-wide chasm of oily black in front of us.

No end to it within visual range, but in the light-sucking darkness we couldn't see much more than a hundred feet.

Otto stopped us at a wide ridge with a depression this side away from the wind. He dropped to his knees and with one of the shovels began to dig. Roman joined in and hacked away huge chunks of packed snow and tossed them behind us and around us.

We did our best to cut away a cubby hole big enough for the eight of us and spread the blankets across the raw ice at the bottom. Bjorn volunteered to take the puppy into his suit and I pulled Lilly close. Liz took Jang. The rest crowded around in a tight knot while Otto piled snow and ice chips against the survival suits.

▼▲▼

"Mitch, hey, Mitch."

I roused from my almost-slumber and looked up through the opening of my suit.

Otto shone his headlamp into his mitt to reduce the glare. "You awake?" he whispered. Thick plumes of white vapor from his mouth as he spoke.

I nodded, doing my best not to groan as I shifted position.

Quiet. No wind. Lilly in my arms, her breathing regular and soft but wheezing slightly. I had had my face tucked down and could smell myself—we hadn't had a chance to change clothes before putting on the survival suits, and a week of sweat and grime was now trapped inside this shell.

My tongue felt pasted with sawdust. The blissful semi-conscious dozing replaced with a blooming headache and desperate thirst and sharp stab of fear in the pit of my stomach. Or hunger. That might be hunger, too.

"How are your feet?" Otto squatted in front of me.

"Fine."

"Fine how?"

"Can't feel them."

"Let me see one. Quick."

I shifted the hood of my suit sideways. Everyone seemed to be sleeping. I let go of Lilly into the knot of Liz and Jang and Bjorn and edged my backside a foot or two toward Otto. "Do we have to?"

"Unzip and let me have a look."

Without the wind it felt warmer. I awkwardly pulled the long transverse zip down the front of my suit—it went from the neck all the way halfway down the right leg for easy entry and exit. The cold rushed in right away.

"Can we make this quick?" I said and pulled my right leg out.

It was encased in two layers of sweat pants with an under-layer of jeans. Otto fixed his headlamp around his head and unwrapped the four layers of sodden socks.

He muttered a curse and began rubbing my foot with something. I still couldn't see.

"What?" I said.

He had a dirty white towel around my foot. "We gotta dry this off."

"Why?"

For a second he pulled the cloth away. In the harsh light of his headlamp my foot looked distended. Gray and brown, the toes dark.

He continued rubbing then got out something from his pocket. "I got a few extra pairs of socks," he said.

He repeated this with my left foot.

By the time he was finished I was shivering cold again before I zipped my suit back up.

"That's the trench foot?"

"Made worse by the cold. Wet and frostbite don't make for good feet." He glanced at the knot of the others almost buried under the ice and snow beside the ridge. "We gotta get moving."

"I need to talk to you," I said.

"Can it wait?"

"Josh said the hijackers were looking for something in the First Class cabin. Maybe that hundred million dollars' worth of diamonds? Howard's digital stuff? Liz's biological package that might be used as a weapon. I don't know—"

"It doesn't matter."

"Did you know?"

"I suspected, but that doesn't matter anymore."

"Do you think a 777 could be hacked?" I lowered my voice to a whisper. "Maybe Howard had something to do with this? Turning off the transponders, getting off the radar. You need technical skills for that. What are the chances of him being on this flight, along with those diamonds, Roman the billionaire, Liz's thing?"

"Where we're heading is one of the listening posts for NATO's North Warning System."

"Alert?"

"Think about that name for a second."

I did. "Ah."

"Don't you think it's odd we crashed less than two hundred miles from a NATO listening post and nobody came to find us?"

The hairs on my neck prickled. "What are you saying now?"

"I'm saying I don't think any of this is a coincidence, but it doesn't matter. We're committed now. Your brother-in-law, Josh, did an amazing job getting that airliner down. I'm trying to finish the job he started and get you out of here alive. And I want to get back to my wife, too."

Ice creaked against ice in the distance. I looked up and saw the fading dot of Polaris pinpointed in the center of heaven.

"It's my fault I'm here. That my daughter is here," I said.

"It's nobody's fault."

"You know why I took this flight?" I bit my lip.

He waited.

"Because I wanted some time to myself."

"That doesn't sound so bad."

All the things I desperately wanted to say to Emma. To tell her that we were still alive. All the things we had wanted to do together—that *she* wanted us to do but I always put off. Taking her on an adventure somewhere. Learning to swim with Lilly. Finding out if we were going to have a son or daughter. What had I done?

"My wife is *pregnant*. Who leaves their pregnant wife by herself on the other side of the planet?"

"You think it better if she was here? She would probably be dead by now."

"Her mother is sick with cancer, and her family was…I just didn't want to stay. Didn't want to deal with it. I was being selfish. I pulled my family apart. Put my daughter in danger and left my pregnant wife. I should have stayed."

"It doesn't matter."

"What the hell is wrong with me?"

Silence.

Just the ice moaning in sadness. I was so thirsty I didn't think I had a spare drop of fluid in me, but a tear leaked down my cheek. *Asshole.* I rubbed it away with the back of one orange mitt. I was such an asshole. I hadn't even admitted the truth to myself—not really—but I needed to get it out. I needed to confess.

"Did you know that there are five types of brothers?" Otto said.

"What?"

"Do you know"—he repeated more slowly—"what the five types of brothers are?"

"You mean, like brother-in-law?"

"Real brother. Wife's brother. Sister's husband. Wife's sister's husband."

I counted in my head. "That's four."

"So what's the fifth?" he asked.

"No idea."

"Brother from another mother. That's what we are now, Mitch. I'm going to get you out of here. Don't start blaming yourself, it's a way of giving up, of giving in. Your daughter needs you strong."

"Okay...okay," I stuttered.

"But we need to get moving. And I need you to take this."

He pressed something into my hand. It was the knife from the emergency kit. Roman had the other one.

"I've got the gun," Otto said. "I need someone I trust with this."

I glanced left and right. "You want to leave now? It's dark."

Not pitch black, but not twilight either.

"Someone is following us," he said and got up.

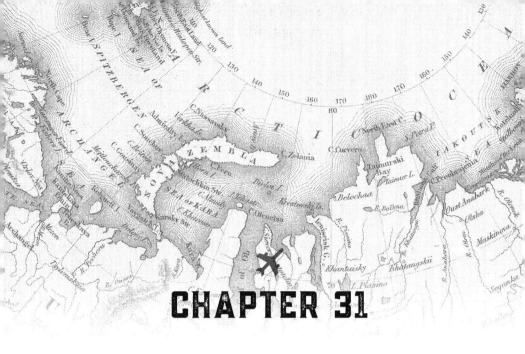

CHAPTER 31

"Are you crazy?"

My hand holding the headlamp shook. I tried to angle the light to get a better look at the submerged ledge of ice thirty feet away across an undulating oily blackness.

Otto steadied my hand. "This is the narrowest part and we can pull ourselves up on there."

"I'm not doing this."

"I walked a mile back and forth while you slept. This crack could go for miles."

Bjorn stood beside him. "I'd bet this is part of an ice shelf. Or it was. And by that I mean, attached to land. But he's right. A crack like this could be twenty miles long. Might never end."

"We need to swim across," Otto said.

"I can't swim." I couldn't stop my hand shaking and it wasn't only the cold.

"Float then. You don't need to swim."

I shifted my wobbling light beam to the middle of the inky abyss. They wanted me to step into that? Swim thirty feet through glacial ocean water and haul myself onto ice?

"I almost died last time we tried this, and we don't have the life vests." Everyone had discarded them when the Marines arrived.

"We didn't have these survival suits then."

"You said the ocean here is fifteen thousand feet deep."

"Doesn't matter how deep."

"I realize that I can drown in ten feet of it."

"More like only two or three thousand this close to land," Bjorn pointed out.

Otto muttered, "You're not helping," and then added in a louder voice, "Mitch, these suits float. They're mini-lifeboats all by themselves. This is *exactly* what they were designed for."

"As long as you don't let water into them," Bjorn said.

Otto turned to him. "Could you please shut up?"

"Daddy, I'm hungry." Lilly pulled on my arm.

I couldn't drag my eyes away from the dark water for another second or two, but then I blinked and looked down at my daughter. "We don't have anything more for now."

After Otto got us up, we huddled together and opened half of the MRE food rations—six of the packets—and shared the contents in a semi-religious ceremony by the lights of our headlamps. I ate a pack of curried chicken and another of beef stew, together with Jang and Lilly. The packs had chemical heaters which we used to warm the food and then cup in our hands. A side dish of mashed potatoes. I let Jang and Lilly eat the crackers with peanut butter and jelly and pocketed the M&Ms.

It was by far the most delicious meal I'd ever eaten, but it was half of all our food remaining. Maybe a thousand calories each total to start the day.

Otto wanted to get something in our stomachs to kick start our final push. Said that we only had a day left to reach the base. Howard pointed out that we only made maybe five miles toward it the day before, and Bjorn said that polar explorers used up more like ten thousand calories of energy a day to fight the cold.

Otto ignored them both in his pep talk.

I drank a careful few mouthfuls of water from one of the bottles I'd kept in my interior pockets to keep from freezing. The kids finished off the rest.

▼▲▼

I stared again at the dark water before me.

As much as it terrified me, another part of me wanted to dive straight in and drink it. To soak in it and let it down my throat. My mouth was parched. Otto again warned us not to try and eat the snow. We needed to melt it first, he repeated over and over. Eating the snow would give us cramps and diarrhea.

A huge split now in the bottom of my middle lip where it had cracked. It bled and froze.

"Can I have some more water?" Lilly asked. "My throat is dry."

I paused a beat before answering, "Sure, honey," and took out my last water bottle. "Take a few sips, okay? Be careful."

She held the bottle in her mitts. I unscrewed the cap.

"Let me see again," I said to Otto.

"Roman's got it."

Behind me, the Russian stared through the night vision scope we'd scavenged from the boat. "I think it is one," he said in a throaty growl.

Everyone was hoarse.

He handed over the scope and I closed one eye and looked through it. Nothing at first. Blank darkness.

But.

There.

A green dot hovered in the middle of my field of view and then disappeared.

"Are you sure?" I said.

Otto replied, "The scope picks up infrared. Body heat. I saw two dots earlier. Maybe more. They're getting closer."

It had to be the Finnish Marines. Didn't it? Or someone else?

Should we run away from them—or toward them?

"We either wait for them to get here," Otto said, "or we cross the water. Fifteen miles that way"—he pointed over the water—"and either we're safe, or we wait for whoever it is. You choose."

I handed the scope back to Roman and noticed Jang's eyes peering at me from behind the Russian. He'd taken the child in his suit today again, in that sling we had rigged.

I turned to face the ice chasm again.

"Okay...okay...okay..." I muttered under my breath, not really agreeing or disagreeing but more trying to convince myself.

"Daddy, Daddy." Lilly pulled on my arm again.

"Give me a minute, sweetie?"

She dropped to her knees in the thin snow. "But Daddy!"

She had knocked over the water bottle. Before I could recover it, half of the precious contents drained into the snow. I bit my tongue and held back the curse words erupting in my head. It was my fault. I had to pay more attention.

▼▲▼

"Slowly...slowly..."

Otto backed himself into the water. We'd tied one end of a nylon rope around his waist and Roman lowered him, rappelling-like, down a forty-five degree angle of ice four feet over the water.

Otto had his suit cinched up tight around his face. The rubber made a seal, he said, and he said that he could have jumped into the water and floated to the top like a cork. That's what these things were designed for, he kept repeating. He liked using the words, "designed for," as if that made this less terrifying.

Up to his midsection in the water, Otto pushed away from the ice. He sank down.

Then floated, up and down, at about chest-level, then rotated onto his back. The three of us with headlamps kept them focused on him.

"Look, watch," he said.

He unzipped half of the front of his suit and sat halfway upright, his arms pulled out of the sleeves. The arms of the suits remained to the side in the water, while he waved his hands at us from the middle of the suit-boat. It was more for my benefit than anyone else's.

It did work.

I felt my heart rate subside a little.

Otto zipped himself up and back-paddled across, flopped over awkwardly onto the opposite ledge and pulled himself up with the cord around his waist. Liz went next with Jang stuffed into her suit. We tied her up, she dropped into the water and Otto eased her across.

She made it look easy.

Bjorn offered, "I'll take Lilly?"

"Yeah, sure."

From here I could watch and jump in if there was any problem. Definitely safer if she went with him.

"Honey, you listen to Uncle Bjorn, okay?"

I knelt in front of her and zipped her small suit up tight. It didn't quite seal the way the adult ones did. She didn't appear scared at all.

With Liz and Otto on the other side, Bjorn held Lilly in one arm while he slithered down the ice edge and held the rope with the other. They were both tied to the rope, and bobbed like corks the moment they were halfway in. I kept my headlamp focused on her. A few seconds of holding my breath and my daughter was on the other side.

No going back now.

We ferried over the two remaining cases we had carried—sealed up—and Bjorn volunteered to slither out of his survival suit which they sent back across for Howard.

"Your turn," Roman said to me as Howard suited up.

"Yep." But it was difficult getting my feet to move forward.

"Come on, Daddy," Lilly urged from the other side.

My arms shook so bad I had a hard time gripping the rope. I almost forgot to tie it around my waist before Roman reminded me.

My breath heaved in and out in great white plumes that dissipated into the darkness around me.

The air sharp in my nostrils.

I slipped on my first step down the ice embankment and fell heavy against my side. I yelled out something, my mind filled with an image of me tumbling in headfirst and flailing and sinking as my suit inundated—but at least I'd be able to drink it in. Satiate the terrible dryness in my mouth before dying. Stupid thoughts competed inside my head.

My heart jackhammered.

Unable to breathe, I gulped for air.

I took another step.

Now a vision of my father at our community pool on Long Island. *Get in, he told me, float into the deep end and swim. It's natural. Do it. Step forward.*

My left foot hit the water and I felt it immediately. Pressure around my leg as the water pressed in. The immediate coolness. I looked up and saw Jang's little eyes peering at me from behind Roman's head as the Russian manhandled the rope I held onto.

Jang's eyes were so calm. The child smiled at me. Don't worry, Mr. Mitch, his eyes said. We are all exactly where we should be.

I'm sorry, Emma. I'm so sorry.

I let go and dropped into the Arctic Ocean.

CHAPTER 32

"Eleven miles." Howard turned to show us his orange mitt with the phone in it, his face illuminated in its glow.

"Turn it off," I said.

He wiggled his left hand free from the neck of the suit. Then dropped the phone.

I jumped forward and unzipped to pick it up and turn off. Frigid air flooded my suit and I swore. "How about I keep it for a while?"

Howard stumbled and almost fell over an outcrop of ice. "I can't work it anymore anyway." His fingertips were frozen. He made a noise I thought was a giggle but became more like a donkey braying. Was he laughing or crying?

I was tied directly to him and now regretted my choice. If anyone was going to fall through the ice, it was Howard. The kid was half dead. Delirious. More than his usual crazy.

The wind gusting. And getting stronger. It whipped tiny ice crystals across my face like sandpaper.

Our ragtag band wound through jumbled blocks and pressure ridges and flat patches of black ice that Bjorn said were most dangerous.

We were all tied together, all seven of us, except for Jang who rode strapped inside of Otto's suit this afternoon.

Afternoon.

The word conjured up images of lazy summer days and slanting sunshine. It was 2 p.m. on my watch but almost as dark as when we left. No stars. No sky. No horizon. Just the tiny patch of light cast by our four headlamps in the daisy-chain of humans scrabbling across the frozen wasteland.

The darkness seemed to feast on the feeble rays of our lamps.

Roman took the lead. He had the puppy wrapped in a blanket in a case strapped to his back. He'd complained about the dog, but Liz had taken a liking to Irene. He'd stopped complaining. She was tied to Roman and followed him. I heard them talking up front. They talked a lot lately, even slept next to each other on breaks.

I carried Lilly on my back in a sling. Bjorn was behind me with Otto and Jang bringing up the rear.

Already five hours of forced marching. I felt as dead as Howard looked. Crossing the water had filled me with a rush of excitement that made the first hour disappear. It had felt like a baptism, floating there over the abyss.

But that adrenaline was long gone.

Adrenaline. Not for the first time I remembered the vials in my pocket. The syringe.

"Eleven miles," Howard repeated from in front of me, his head down. "You know who else had eleven miles to go?"

I didn't bother to respond. He had a habit of speaking with questions.

"Robert Scott. The famous British polar explorer who was the second to reach the South Pole. Or maybe I should say, infamous."

"That's right," Bjorn said from behind me. "He only had eleven miles."

"That's how far Scott was from safety—from reaching camp—when he gave up. Sat down and froze to death. They said his skin was clear like yellow glass when they found him. After one thousand six hundred miles of walking through hell like this, he gave up with only eleven to go."

"Be quiet."

"I bet it was the voices in his head, too." Howard turned to me with a leer. "Told him to stop. Told him he'd be more famous if he stopped. Yellow-glass skin. Maybe that's how they'll find us."

"Keep walking."

I felt for the knife in the side pocket of my suit. He'd been off his meds for at least a day, and the pressure had to be cracking his mind. It was affecting all of us, but I sensed Howard flailing as his psyche spiraled away. I didn't want to let him take us down with him. I wouldn't let him. I couldn't. I had to protect my daughter.

"It is getting darker," Bjorn said.

I tried to crane around to look at Lilly. "Is she asleep?"

"Looks like it."

"You think it's getting darker?" I said.

"Day by day, the light falls faster. We're heading into the full polar night. Pitch black for five months."

My lower legs felt like numb tree stumps I balanced on like stilts. Both cheeks hard lumps of ice. Frostbitten. I didn't dare look at my feet again.

Bjorn shuffled up to walk beside me. He'd gamely volunteered to go a shift without a survival suit. He said Howard would freeze to death if he didn't. He wasn't wrong. We did our best to wrap Bjorn in as many clothes and blankets as we could, sealed under layers of Mylar and tied together—but he had to be frozen.

I was frozen. So cold.

So *tired*.

I daydreamed about lying down. For a minute. To sleep.

"To early theological writers," Bjorn said, "the north was the abode of the Antichrist. The Goths, the Vandals, the Vikings—they all raided Rome from the north."

I felt like I could feel the Devil lurking in the darkness around us.

"In *Dante's Inferno*, the ninth level of hell—the final one—isn't fire, but a lake of ice. No hellfire burning but ice freezing. The Far North was literally hell."

I couldn't argue with that.

"Do you have any water?" Bjorn asked.

I shook my head. None to share. I only had maybe a half bottle left in my pocket next to my journal.

He laughed a giggle that bordered on a sob. "Water, water, everywhere, yet ne'er a drop to drink."

I knew that line. From *The Rime of the Ancient Mariner*. An old book. A poem.

Bjorn said, "I'm dying of thirst and surrounded by water. Walking on water. Like Jesus did, but this is no miracle. If this was old ice—ice more than a season frozen—we could melt it down to drink. That's what the old polar explorers did a hundred years ago, but we can't anymore."

"We can't drink this?" I scuffed the ice underfoot and slipped and took a jarring step. I tasted copper in my mouth. Blood from my split lip. It immediately congealed in a frozen lump.

"Too young and thin. This is salty ice." He trudged forward another few steps in silence before adding, "You know that while we've been arguing about climate change the last thirty years, the Arctic has lost ninety-five percent of its old ice?"

"I didn't know that." *Didn't care.*

"I saw you getting all friendly with Roman."

"How much did Roman pay you?" I asked. *Was it worth it? To betray your beliefs?*

"We're all here because of him. You shouldn't trust that asshole."

"But I should trust you?"

"I could say the same."

I bent my head down.

"I think Roman is the one who downed the airliner," Bjorn said. "Hired the hijackers. I'll bet there's a lot more than a hundred million in diamonds with us in one of these cases."

This wasn't a new angle and I was too tired to respond.

Bjorn continued, "He's being hunted by the Russian Politburo. Dead no matter where he goes in the world. So he downs an airliner. Everyone disappears. Roman is presumed dead—but he's not."

"He said he wanted to change," I said. "To get into environmentalism. That's why he contacted you."

"And maybe Santa will come save us on his sleigh."

"What projects did he fund with you?"

"What projects didn't he?"

It wasn't an answer.

"Maybe that Chinese guy was his partner," Bjorn said. "Maybe Roman got to him like he got to me. Shu or Pemba or whatever his name was. That guy was Tibetan. He was fighting the good fight. Like I was trying to do. He was trying to stop their government diverting water from the Himalayan glaciers. Their Dalai Lama died a few years ago, did you know that?"

"How do they pick a new one?"

"I think the Chinese are trying to do it for them."

In front of us, Roman struggled over a six foot ridge of ice. I stopped and tried to breathe.

▼▲▼

Seven miles.

I checked the phone. Only a hair of power left. Only seven miles to go, but every step forward a superhuman effort.

One step.

And then another.

Repeat.

For the past hour the nature of the ice had changed. A brief gray light from an opening in scudding clouds had lit up the landscape enough to see what looked like a field of sandpaper before us as I crested a ridge and pulled Lilly up. On closer view, the dots of sand were chunks and jumbles of ice crisscrossed by pressure ridges only a few feet high.

Bjorn said it was a good sign.

We'd made good time.

So close now.

Otto tugged on the cord around my waist. "We should stop for a few minutes. Drink what water we have and eat."

Seven miles.

Couldn't we fire off some of the flares? We had six in one of the cases. The Alert base was a NATO listening outpost. Would they miss flaming signals fired into a dark sky from seven miles away? Just fire the damn flares.

"Mitch, stop. Take a rest." Otto's face loomed in my field of vision.

I dropped to my knees.

Then to my side.

"They're getting closer," were the last words I heard before blackness descended.

▼▲▼

Dark wet eyes looked deep into mine. They glistened in the beam of my headlamp.

Whiskers twitched.

The head bobbed up and down and came closer. The eyes huge and inquisitive. Smooth skin that I wanted to reach out and caress.

"Mitch, you with us?"

Two sharp cracks and the shining eyes disappeared with a plopping sound.

"Mitch."

Someone grabbed my shoulder and pulled me around. I squinted into the glare of a headlamp. Something touched my lips and a hand held my head up.

"Drink," Otto said.

I gulped in a mouthful but the effort was painful. My lips burned. I swallowed.

"Easy, easy." He pulled the bottle away. "You liked the seal, huh?"

I'd regained enough of my senses to prop myself up on one elbow. "Where's Lilly?"

"She's fine. Over with Liz and Jang getting something to eat. You need to eat, too."

"How…how long was I…"

"Maybe an hour."

"The seal?" I said.

He nodded and thrust his chin out to indicate a spot behind me. "There's a hole in the ice. Little buggers have been coming up every now and then to inspect us. They took a particular liking to you."

I groaned and sat upright. I could barely feel anything. My body cold-numb. No sensation at all from my feet or fingertips. I rubbed my face with the back of my hand. It felt like my cheeks and nose were covered by a hard plastic mask. Which they weren't. They were frozen solid.

"How much further?" I asked.

"Seven miles. Maybe six till we hit land."

If we were going in the right direction. If we weren't chasing a ghost-signal. If this wasn't a trap, or worse, a random artifact of some digital system gone wrong.

"Seals?" I said again. Was there some meaning to them?

"We're probably closer to land," Otto said.

I noticed the wind had increased. A constant buffeting that I had to turn my back to. I checked my watch. Nine p.m. Coal black outside of the pools of light from our headlamps. No stars. Had to be heavy clouds overhead, I imagined.

"I think another storm is coming," Otto said. "We need to get moving."

"Can I get a minute to eat?" I staggered to my feet and almost fell right over.

"But hurry," he said.

"Hurry?"

Roman and Bjorn were already loaded with gear and motioning to me.

I asked, "Are those people following us getting close?"

Otto took a deep breath. "I'm not sure those are people."

CHAPTER 33

W hich way?"

Otto said, "Keep scanning back and forth till you see a green dot."

We'd climbed to the top of an eight-foot pressure ridge. It took about all the energy I could muster despite Otto hauling me most of the way up. I had to sit down and gave the scope back to him.

"Do you not want to look?"

"Give me a few minutes."

I pulled my head and headlamp inside my suit, into the comparatively warm cave-like interior away from the wind, and took both hands from the sleeves into the middle as well. There was a half-portion of warm beef stew in my left jean pocket, which I took out and forced into my mouth. I knew I had to eat—I knew I was starving. I forced it into my mouth and swallowed.

Why did I decide to climb the ice ridge and then eat? I wasn't sure. My mind was muddled. Events and decisions seemed to spring out of nowhere in the frozen darkness.

My journal was in my left jean pocket as well. The pen there as well, warm enough that the ink hadn't frozen. I finished the stew and paused, took out the pen and journal and scribbled a few notes. It might be all anyone would know of us if we didn't make it.

I took a careful sip of water.

A few drops of the precious last trickle. My mind didn't even seem to want the water anymore. My skin flaked off the back of my hand, sloughed off my body under the layers of clothes. When did I last go to the bathroom? I hadn't even peed since we got into the boats, and that was two days ago.

"Give it back to me." I pulled my face back to the suit's opening. I wriggled both arms back into the suit's arms and used the left mitt to grip the scope again.

"That way." Otto pointed.

I closed one eye and pressed the scope against my cheek. Felt the solid chunk of ice growing into my skin there. I scanned back and forth slowly but only saw flickering gray through the night vision device. Otto gently guided it.

A fuzzy green dot appeared.

"Zoom in." Otto clicked on the magnification.

Still fuzzy but looked like two dots now. Bobbing up and down.

"Could it be a person?" I said.

"Could be, but the gait? The way that's moving? I'd bet that's a bear. Almost invisible in infrared except its face and eyes."

"How far?"

"Thousand yards at most."

"It can follow us?"

"I tried shooting one of those seals."

I'd heard the two shots.

Otto continued. "Thought we could leave a bloody carcass behind as a gift and slow it down—but might be better to keep the ammunition."

"Can't you shoot it?"

"With this?" He pulled out his handgun.

It was a Glock 19, I noticed. Like the one my dad used to have, a gun I'd fired more than a few times. Not a Sig. Howard was right.

Nineteen rounds in the magazine. How many had he used already? I counted backward in my head.

"That's a ton of teeth and claws coming this way," Otto said. "Biggest land predator in the world. No fear of humans. This gun is a toy compared to a polar bear. A round would bounce off its skull. We need a big caliber rifle, or a shotgun."

"Like the one that was attached to this scope?"

"Exactly."

"Which we don't have."

"Wish we did, but wishes are just that."

I scooped some snow into my water bottle, packed it in and then put the bottle back into my interior jean pocket with the phone in the outside pocket. We slid down off the ridge to join the others.

Bjorn offered to carry Jang, on the condition that he get his survival suit back. Bjorn had been exposed for most of the past few hours, so we transferred all of the extra clothing to Howard, who accepted his punishment of losing the survival suit.

Nobody else volunteered.

▼▲▼

My foot went straight through the black ice and I yelped as I dropped in and splayed sideways. Lilly squealed from my back.

Bjorn yanked the rope behind and pulled me as Howard tugged from the front.

I wrenched my leg out of the water, from the hole I'd punched through with my foot, and crawled forward on my stomach. Wind whipped frenzied snow devils into mini tornadoes.

Roman was clearing another ridge in front of us. He hauled Liz up.

We were all tied together again. Roman and Liz in the front. I'd discovered that Liz had been some kind of marathoner back in the world. While the rest of us fell apart, she remained almost constant. She kept her precious biohazard container inside her suit.

Howard came behind Liz.

Easier to stick him there as he trusted Liz, the only person he didn't complain about in our party, and she was able to better help tend to him.

Lilly and I came after Howard. I had her on my back for speed. What little I had left.

One foot in front of the other was the refrain in my head, but beyond the pain and delirium was a new fear of whatever was chasing us. *Hunting* us.

Otto and his gun brought up the rear.

"Sea ice is only half as strong as fresh ice," Bjorn said as he helped me to my feet. "At this time of the year, the new ice is maybe"—he made a mental calculation—"nineteen centimeters. That's like only two inches of fresh ice. Barely enough to hold a person. Tread as lightly as you can between the pressure ridges."

I mumbled thanks and checked on Lilly. She said she was okay and asked if I wanted her to walk. I said no, I was fine, but I wasn't. I didn't tell her about the polar bear, either.

I couldn't look straight ahead, but had to turn my face to one side to keep it out of the biting wind and unending stream of sandpaper ice crystals. My eyelids heavy with encrusted ice.

"I love the north," Bjorn said from behind me. "And did you know, polar bears almost always come in pairs?"

I didn't have the energy to tell him to shut up.

"It's completely devoid of humans up here, and almost all life, really. Of five thousand species of mammals, twenty-three live above the tree line in the north. Nearly nine thousand species of bird, but only six up here. Even fish—maybe fifty thousand species worldwide, yet just fifty in the Arctic."

"And you love that?" Otto said from behind me.

"I have respect for the simplicity, the elegance," Bjorn replied. "It is so fragile, this world up here. Assholes like Roman are the ones destroying it. We think we are separate from the environment, but we're not."

"Not everyone thinks that," Otto said.

"You're right. The Saami people, the Inuit of Scandinavia, don't see themselves as separate from animals, so maybe there is some hope."

We reached a ledge too high to step over. Roman was on his belly and offered a hand up. I took it and the man levitated me into the air. His strength was incredible. One by one we got to the top, and, careful not to get caught in the ropes, we slid down the other side.

Another ridge loomed two hundred feet away in the darkness, illuminated by our headlamps.

"Have you ever seen a muskox?" Bjorn asked.

I shook my head.

"They're the only large animals that have survived from the last Ice Age. They are perfectly adapted for life up here. The wooly mammoth, the dire wolf, the saber tooth tiger, the North American camel and short-faced bear—they were all survivors of the Ice Age, and yet all extinct. Wiped out by humans. The list goes on. Giant armadillo, ground sloths that stood on their hind legs as tall as giraffes…"

"What's your point?" Otto asked.

"Every other place on the planet, humans have used their technological prowess to displace animals—all except for the far Arctic, but it is starting here as well. This pristine wilderness is endangered. All that will stop man is a virulent virus or our own weapons technology turned against ourselves."

"There is one more thing that would stop it," said a small voice from behind Bjorn, from inside the man's survival suit.

It was Jang.

"What's that?" I said. The poor kid. I made an effort.

"Wisdom," Jang said. "Wisdom could stop humans from destroying."

Bjorn laughed heartily. "Wisdom? No way. What we need is an apocalyptic war or pandemic."

He had been going on like this for three hours. Raving like Howard.

The more this place seemed determined to kill him—the worse he suffered frostbite and dehydration—the more he extolled the virtues of the frozen wasteland like a self-flagellating acolyte drinking in the pain on his way to Valhalla. Almost like he was excited polar bears were hunting us.

"We're in their environment, you know," he said. "We're the intruders. It's perfectly normal for them to want to eat us. We're food here."

Maybe you are, but not me. Not my daughter.

At first his ranting was a welcome distraction, like the radio playing in a car on a long road trip—something that used up mental space without being listened to. After three hours of it, a new thought had percolated to the top of my mind.

Eco-terrorism.

He said he had a link to Pemba Ldong. That both he and Pemba were fighting the good fight, trying to stop the powers that be from exploiting nature. And he was constantly trying to convince me that Roman was the instigator of our disaster.

But.

Were Bjorn and Pemba the hijackers? The thought percolated around the edges of my mind. Did they bring the aircraft down to spur a war between America and Russia, the East and the West? War games were ongoing right now and tensions were already high. Maybe Roman was right. This was like the War Scare of 1983, and maybe Bjorn was an eco-terrorist, urging on the final conflict between the superpowers by crashing the airliner.

He didn't even seem to want to survive. He wanted to become one with the wasteland. Maybe that was the plan. Maybe the two pilots were working with Pemba and Bjorn. They wanted to crash the airliner and didn't want to survive. That would explain why Pemba attacked the rescuers, and that would explain why the rescuers were so quick to bring out weapons when they got to our section. They knew the hijackers were in the First Class section.

They just didn't know who they were.

And now here *we* were.

Wandering the frozen landscape, with this idiot leading us to our deaths. I gripped the knife blade in my pocket now every time Bjorn opened his mouth.

▼▲▼

"It's not working," I said.

Shivering, I did my best to hold the phone and pull the icicles from my eyelashes. I had my head inside my suit away from the driving wind. So strong now it buffeted me back and forth even in the lee of an outcropping of ice.

The phone's screen remained blank.

A new terror gripped and twisted what remained of my gut. Last we checked, we had three or four miles to go. The blue dot of our location on the screen was almost on top of the red marker for the Alert Canadian Forces base. I'd zoomed to look at the locations of the buildings. An airfield to the left, separated by a mile and a half. Some outbuildings there with the main collection of the town arranged along a main street.

A town.

Out here.

A few miles away.

It didn't seem possible.

The wind built in force, bringing with it whipping snow. It was rare to see snow up here, the insufferable Bjorn had pointed out. This place had more of the precipitation profile of the Mojave Desert, he said. I'd almost wanted to strangle him.

Otto said to stop and check the phone, so we huddled together in a tight knot against the growing maelstrom. Pitch black and beyond cold. No food left. Little water.

Two of our headlamps had frozen so we were down to two left. The light from them barely pierced ten feet into the angry sucking darkness. We tried to keep heading in the same direction, but after crossing two or three pressure ridges our heading invariably began to shift without visual references beyond a few dozen yards.

Robert Scott crossed a thousand six hundred miles of this and stopped eleven miles from camp, sat down and froze to death when he could have made it. *That won't be me.* I kept Lilly close at all times and checked on her. She didn't have to walk, but her breathing was wheezing and forced. No more inhaler. Jang tried to calm her down, but she was in distress. *That won't be us.*

Just a few miles.

In clear weather we might even be able to see this damn town. In clear weather with light, but then didn't they have lights at this place? Floodlights? Warm food. Warm beds. Maybe I should lay down. Only for a minute. Gain some strength and sleep for a minute.

I didn't even feel cold anymore.

I had to use the knuckle of my hand to try and poke the screen. My fingertips were frozen and the screen didn't interact with them. Needed warm, unfrozen flesh.

"Warm it up," I heard Howard suggest, his voice muffled and distant from outside my suit.

I stuck the phone between my thighs, right into the pit of my groin. It was the only part of my body that even resembled warmth, and I could only tell because the phone felt like a chunk of ice when I stuck it there.

A minute later I retrieved it, and lo and behold—angels singing!— the screen winked on when I pushed the power button. I angled it back and forth and then pointed in the direction of Alert. Maybe two miles.

"That way!" I yelled as loud as my hoarse voice would let me.

A brief thought. Two miles? Did this town have cell reception? But I didn't see any connection bars. I turned the phone off. A red whisker of power left, but that was all we needed.

▼▲▼

"Which way?" Roman called out over the wind.

We'd been making slow progress almost straight into the howling wind. Even in daylight, I doubted we would have more than a dozen feet of visibility in this white-out, as Otto called it. This was a black-out, Bjorn had cackled, midnight of the polar night. He guessed the temperature was under fifty below with this gale.

If the place didn't kill him, I was sure one of us would.

I ducked back inside my suit and tried the phone but the screen remained stubbornly blank.

For the past ten minutes or so I'd noticed that we hadn't had to cross any pressure ridges, but that meant no visual references. We'd been going up a steady incline it seemed, and Roman wanted to make sure we didn't miss our mark. I put the phone in my crotch and took it out. Still nothing.

Walking up an incline.

I stuck my head out of my suit, my headlamp attached around my temples. Roman had the only other remaining headlamp and looked straight at me.

"Which way?" he asked again.

"We're on an incline."

"We're what?"

"Incline."

"What!"

I made an angle with my hand. "We're going up."

It took him a second to realize what I meant. Even in the frenzied whipping darkness I saw his eyes go wide at the realization.

We were on *land*.

My jolt of excitement dribbled away, replaced with a bolt of pure terror.

Right behind Roman, a wall of what I'd assumed was ice shifted, but it wasn't ice.

A throaty growl filled the air. The animal roared, more like a lion than any bear I had ever imagined, and the nine-foot-tall beast reared up onto its hind legs.

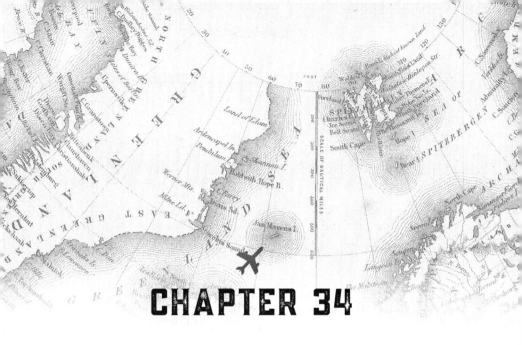

CHAPTER 34

The polar bear dropped to its front feet and made a hissing and snorting sound, its head lowered. The fur was mottled gray in the light of our headlamps, the skin seemed to droop from its bones, and not even all the massive animal was visible. It bounced from one paw to the other.

Roman backed away and to the left. He was ten feet from it and the only other person with a headlamp. The bear shied away from the light. Liz scuffled backward as well but got caught in Howard who was so frightened he stuck in place. She shoved him back and they got tangled in the rope and fell into a heap.

The rope tugged me forward. I was tied to it. Tied to them.

Two quick shots cracked the air, so close I felt a flash of heat. A high-pitched whine in my ears. Three feet to my left, Otto's gun was up, his arms extended. He fired again as I tried to back away, but the cord held me in place to the writhing mass of Howard and Liz.

The shots seemed to have no effect on the huge animal. It lowered its head and charged forward. Clamped its jaws around Liz's head.

I had my knife out somehow. A part of me instinctively leaned forward. Get that thing off Liz. But the bear was huge. Even on all fours it was as tall as me. Head the size of a lawnmower. I reached down and cut the cord around my waist, cut the straps holding me to Lilly while I kept my eyes on the beast.

It sniffled, its head down, its jaws around Liz's head. I pushed Lilly back behind me as I slowly edged away.

Screaming pierced the wind.

Except it wasn't Liz. Her body was limp. A rag doll in the animal's grip.

The screaming was coming from Howard, high pitched and terrified just inches from the bear's snout.

It growled and threw its head back.

Liz's body whipped into the air. For a grisly instant I thought she'd been decapitated, her head literally ripped off. Her body cartwheeled into the air.

No blood.

The bear had only the orange hood of her survival suit clasped between its teeth.

She landed awkwardly beside the animal, one arm out to break her fall, but she thudded into the ice and snow hard. The bear turned and roared, its body corkscrewing around to attack.

Two more shots. This time I saw the bullets impact with tiny sprays of red in its side.

That made it more angry.

It roared again, ignored the bullets, and turned on Liz who gamely tried to get to her feet and limp away.

Another noise. A yipping. The little puppy appeared from the darkness and ran right up to the bear and barked furiously at it.

The huge animal was perplexed for an instant and backed up. The puppy advanced.

The polar bear grunted and lunged forward to swipe at it, but Irene dodged and weaved.

After two seconds the bear had had enough and turned back to something with more meat on its bones. Liz had only managed to stagger two steps away.

Another roar.

But this one not from the bear. A shape rushed toward us from the darkness, the only light now from my headlamp. Whatever it was roared once more. Another predator?

It threw itself at the bear.

Roman.

Shirtless, naked from the waist up.

The Russian jumped onto the brute's back and wrapped one of his huge arms around its neck and stabbed furiously at its throat.

This surprised the animal enough that it reversed in confusion and tossed its head a few times before almost rolling right over. Dark patches of blood streamed from its head and neck. Roman did his best to stay on top but tumbled to the ground.

Shaking its head, the bear unleashed a gurgling snarl and reared up, then stamped down on Roman and clamped its jaws.

I realized why Roman was almost naked.

He'd taken off his shirts and wrapped them around his left forearm. He stuck this straight into the maw of the giant animal as it snapped at him. He screamed but still hacked at it with the knife in his right hand.

Otto moved cautiously past me, his gun out.

I glanced behind.

Bjorn was transfixed. Standing still and staring. Jang's little eyes shone bright from behind Bjorn's head in the back of the suit, the child's eyes reflected in the light of my headlamp.

Without thinking, I leaped straight at Bjorn and reached in and grabbed Jang by the scruff of his shirt and pulled. An instinct to keep the kid safe. He slithered out through the open neck of Bjorn's suit.

The Norwegian didn't act surprised.

He grabbed my hand, but not to stop me. He took my knife. I let him have it and stepped away, corralling Lilly before me as I went.

"Mitch, hey, Mitch!" someone yelled.

I turned.

It was Otto. "Keep the light on the bear."

It was true. I had the only light left.

The animal shook its head like a dog with a toy, ripping Roman's arm and body back and forth. I backed away another two steps but kept my headlamp focused on the animal.

The bear let go of Roman's arm as it realized it had a mouthful of something distasteful. The second it let go, Roman scrambled back, his left arm limp like a wet noodle, shredded bits of clothing left behind. His survival suit was tattered.

Two more quick shots.

Otto was to the right of the bear now. Two more shots.

This time the polar bear felt the bullets' sting. It growled and put its head down and charged at Otto.

Another scream filled the air. This yell smaller and barely audible over the wind. Bjorn sprinted at the animal, one hand high that gripped the knife. The bear bowled into Otto but the Norwegian arrived at the same instant and swung his blade down and then up to jam it into the underneath of the bear's neck.

The animal reared its head back and caught Bjorn square in the face with its skull. A hollow smack and our compatriot dropped to the ground like a sack of wet cement, a dark splotch left behind on top of the bear's head.

Irene scrambled behind the bear and continued yapping. The animal looked confused now with so many attackers. It turned to Bjorn's immobile body, but then turned back to the barking puppy.

Two more shots, muffled. Otto was right underneath the bear.

It sagged as if someone had punched it in the gut.

The animal growled again, tried to rear up away from whatever was stinging it from beneath, but the roar was muted. Sounded more like a roar of agony than anger.

His left arm dangling, Roman ran forward and jammed his knife into the underside of the bear's throat, like Bjorn had done. The animal snapped at him, then swiped with a huge paw that hit Bjorn and tossed him five feet away into the air.

Roman stabbed again.

One of the beast's swinging paws caught him broadside and

knocked him to the snow. It was struggling now, its fur and the snow under it black with blood. The wind screamed over the grunting.

Roman was on his knees and sagged over. The bear turned, its jaws wide.

One more shot rang out.

Otto stood beside the bear, the muzzle of his gun point blank at the base of the animal's skull. It dropped flat onto the ground, its legs splayed out.

Roman fell forward against the bear. He had his knife and reached back and stabbed the creature in the neck again and again.

I realized I had Jang in my arms, the child exposed to the howling wind. I looked back to see Lilly holding onto my leg and staring at the bloody scene. I unzipped my suit and let Jang crawl inside, his arms wrapped around my neck.

The animal twitched but its battle was lost.

I walked toward them cautiously. They had to be injured, I knew they needed help. Roman was half-naked, his flesh exposed to the tearing wind. At least fifty below, maybe colder. Bjorn had said exposed flesh became frostbitten in seconds at this temperature. We needed to get Roman covered with something.

Bjorn was inert on the ground. Otto stood over the beast. Liz limped in from the darkness. Her suit was ripped open. No hood. Her head exposed.

Irene barked and barked, the tiny noise almost lost in the gale sweeping snow and tumbling chunks of ice around us and the bear. The puppy advanced right up to the nose of the polar bear and yapped furiously.

The bear opened its eyes and grunted, then made a whining noise. Like a dog who wanted to go out and pee. I suddenly felt empathy for this poor creature, this beautiful wild animal.

It looked at Irene. The dog quieted down. The great animal sighed a last breath and went still, its eyes open but unseeing.

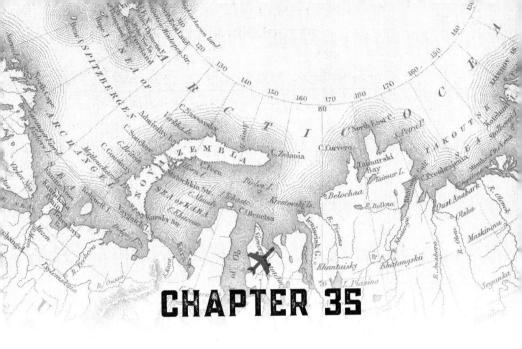

CHAPTER 35

Roman groaned. The Russian lay on the side of the bear, blood pooling and congealing in a frozen puddle beneath them both. The puppy, Irene, shivered beside him and licked the Russian's hand.

The wind howled in a buffeting roar of its own and almost knocked me from my feet. I had to lean into it to stay upright. I felt Jang's little hands gripping my inner layers. The wind penetrated even the wind-and-waterproof shell of the survival suit.

The immediate danger gone, the cold tore its claws back into me.

Liz reached the polar bear and dropped to her knees, then grabbed the dog and stuffed it in through the top zip of her suit. She dragged Roman down so he sat in the lee of the bear's huge carcass, away from the whipping gale. I bent over and grunted to haul Bjorn's body to the same spot. The Norwegian's eyes fluttered awake as I dragged him.

Otto was laid out on top of the bear and seemed to be hacking away at it with Roman's knife. I didn't bother telling him it was already dead.

"Lilly, honey, get in here." I pointed to a nook between the bear's forelegs.

It had dropped to the ground halfway on its side. Already the blood from its neck had frozen solid, but between there and its front legs, was a little furry blood-spattered cave big enough for Lilly to hide inside.

I pushed her in despite her protests and then did my best to huddle in behind her.

She sucked air in and out in desperate gulps, her eyes wide as she looked at me. Were her lips blue? Her whole face looked dark.

Jang reached out from inside my suit with a socked hand and held her mitts. "Calm," he said over the wind. "Remember, Lilly? Remember what we did? Breathe deep through your nose, close your eyes."

I had my face right in the polar bear's under-fur. It was gloriously warm and I luxuriated in it for a second before I turned to Liz.

"Are you okay?" I asked.

"I'm not sure," she yelled back.

The wind screamed around us in a burst of fury. I waited for it to subside a little before I asked, "How does Roman look?"

"He's lost a lot of blood."

She tried to close his suit up after tying rags around his wounds. Howard stumbled in from the darkness and sleeting snow with a light in his hand. He'd found Roman's headlamp and handed it to Liz. She used it to inspect Roman's body again.

I took off the synthetic cap I'd gotten back at the boat and gave it to her. I could already see hard white patches on her exposed ears and forehead.

Bjorn had regained consciousness. His suit was ripped as well. If he was bleeding, he seemed in better shape than Roman whose eyes, unfocused, rolled around in their sockets. Howard slumped against Bjorn and the bear.

Somehow the wind blew even more fiercely. Any stronger and we'd be ripped from the slippery ground if we tried to walk.

We couldn't stay here for much longer. Even using the bear's carcass as a windbreak, we'd freeze to death in this wind inside of an hour, and before that Bjorn and Roman and maybe Liz and Howard would die without proper protection.

Leaning against the bear, I ducked my head inside my suit and felt for the phone. I had to feel around Jang who held tight around my neck. In one pocket I had my journal, the vials of adrenaline and already-filled syringe.

In the inside pocket of my suit was Howard's disk and the bottle of water I'd filled with snow. I'd almost forgotten about the disk. There beside it was the phone. I jammed it into my groin and held my legs tight together.

Something thudded against the back of my head. I pushed my head back up through the opening of my suit.

Fur in my face. I turned. Hairy pelt behind me, too. I was in a fur cave. I used a mitt to feel around. It was a hunk of the polar bear's skin. A swath at least six feet wide and as many long. A polar bear blanket.

Otto stood in front of us and faced the blasting wind, a bloody knife tucked at his waist.

I returned inside my suit and pulled the phone out. Said a small prayer and pressed the button with a finger I couldn't feel.

It blinked on after a second. I pressed the map app with the knuckle of my forefinger.

The phone blinked off.

Out of power.

But it had been enough.

▼▲▼

"We need to go!" I screamed at Otto so he could hear me over the wind.

"Where?" he yelled back.

I pointed into the wind, up the slope.

"We are in Alert," I said. "Literally *inside* the dot of Alert."

When the map app opened, I had time to zoom in for a split second and the dot of "us" was right inside the pinpoint of the town of Alert. We were *here,* if the GPS signal beaming down from space into this tiny phone was true and accurate.

Otherwise we were dead. They would find us next summer, with yellow-glass skin, next to this bear.

"We go up the slope a few hundred yards," I yelled. "Then follow the contour. That's where the town is."

"Left or right?"

"Right."

"You're sure."

I nodded yes, then leaned down and lifted the already-stiff bear skin.

I said to Liz, "We're going to get help."

She nodded. The bear skin covering provided some warmth and she was doing her best to staunch Roman and Bjorn's wounds. Otto left her one of the knives, told her to slice open the bear carcass if she needed to, said that there was a thousand pounds of heat trapped inside the fur.

"I'll stay here with them and the kids," she replied. "Leave me this headlamp. You take the other one."

"And take one of the flare guns," Bjorn said. He had them in his pockets and handed one over with three cartridges. "We'll keep the other. The storm should pass soon. We'll fire it off if we don't hear from you."

The storm had lasted almost two days last time. No way they would survive two days out here if we didn't make it, but I said nothing and handed Liz my bottle of water. The packed snow had melted into a few mouthfuls of liquid at the bottom.

"Drink it right away before it freezes. And I have some adrenaline in my pocket, would that help?"

She shook her head. "Go as fast as you can."

Lilly was curled into a ball against the bear carcass. Her face obscured. She didn't move. I took hold and pulled her into me.

"Baby, Lillypad, are you okay? Can you hear me?"

Her body was limp, her eyes closed. Unresponsive. In a panic I was about to try and check her pulse when I felt a tickling on my neck. She was writing a skin sign. Down and across. Down and across. An "L".

"I love you, too." I squeezed her and held back tears.

I said to Liz, "I'm taking the kids with me."

She gave me a look and reached into her suit. "Take this, too?"

It was her small backpack with the canister. The precious biohazard container she'd been guarding. "If I don't get out of here, make sure this gets to Dr. McNamara, at the Columbia School of Medicine in New York."

"You give it to him yourself," I said, but took the pack anyway. The canister inside was about twice the size of a whiskey bottle. I put the pack inside my suit. Jang took hold.

"Come back for me, Mitch."

She held onto my mitt and squeezed. I nodded.

"You promise?"

She clutched my mitt with her bare hand and held my gaze. Her pretty face now blistered and scarred with streaks and patches of frostbite, her hazel eyes bloodshot and watery. The tip of her nose black, three of her fingers stiff and blotchy gray.

"I promise," I said as I pulled away. "I'll be back soon."

▼▲▼

One foot after the other.

Plant one foot and make sure to have a good grip against the gravel and ice and lean into the wind. Get my balance before lifting the other foot. *Don't think about anything else, Mitch.* Don't think about Emma.

Don't think about anything…

But that next foot.

Blinking and blinking and wiping my eyes with the back of my mitt to keep the riming ice from sealing them shut. Tearing away shreds of flaking skin with each swipe.

My world reduced to a speck of light six feet ahead.

Otto and I tied the rope to each other, with Howard trailing. He refused to be left behind, but he had no survival suit. I didn't think he would make it more than a few hundred yards in this wind before he froze to death.

Nothing I could say to convince him to stay.

Otto had Lilly on his back. She seemed unconscious, her arms and legs sagged at her sides, and strapped to him. Right in front of me so I could lean against her as I pushed him forward to keep balance. He was the stronger one so brought up the front.

Jang clung tight around my neck but didn't utter a word.

Life was all about expectations. My father had taught me that. How far did we have to go? A mile? I set that as my expectation. How far had we come so far?

Maybe fifty feet.

I can take it, I told myself, *I'm coming home.* One step at a time. You can take it. *You can't give up so close.* But it wasn't about me. If it was for only me, I would have curled up into a ball already, succumbed to the urge to get some sleep and drift off. What drove me forward was the little package right in front of me, on Otto's back.

Lilly. My Lillypad.

Otto stopped.

"What's wrong?" I yelled and shoved him to continue.

We couldn't lose momentum. I might never get going again. He stepped to one side and pointed, then shone the headlamp back and forth.

We stood in front of a huge sign. Not one sign, but a collection of signs. In big, hand painted letters in the middle placard it read, *Alert, Nunavut. World's Most Northern Station.*

A blast of wind rocked us sideways.

Otto reached for the nearest sign, one that read, *Coaticook, 4315 km*, with an arrow pointed to our left. I grabbed it as well for balance. I read other signs, *Angsta, Sweden. 2047 MI, Salem, NS. 4197 km.*

I looked left and right.

No lights.

Not as far as I could see, which wasn't far, but there were no distant lights in windows. No shadows of buildings. No floodlights piercing the darkness.

Had the town been abandoned?

A piercing bolt shot down my spine from my neck into the pit of my stomach. Did they even keep this outpost manned all year? It was pitch black. The sun gone down for six months. Did a NATO listening post even need people anymore? Didn't they only need equipment? Why would they send humans into this infernal hell?

Dozens of signs pointed in all directions, but none for the direction of the town itself.

"What now?" Otto yelled.

Calm. Calm down. I felt Jang's hands around my neck. The kid's presence seemed to calm the inside of my mind.

A sign.

Where would you put the sign to a town?

On the road in.

But if there was no road in…?

"We're on the runway," I said.

"What?"

I couldn't tell if he couldn't hear me or didn't understand. I closed my eyes and visualized the map I'd seen a half dozen times on the phone. The runway was near the water, off to one side. Otto said they landed Hercules transports here, almost as big as the 777 we'd crashed in. It was listed as an emergency diversion airport, he said.

"That way." I pointed right. "The town is about a mile and a half straight along the runway, then follow the road up."

"A mile and a half? Jesus Christ, Mitch—"

"There are some outer buildings at the end of the runway," I said.

That's right. A small cluster of buildings. Even if nobody was there, we could get into one, get out of the cold. Find some warmth. Call someone.

Otto was already leading the way.

We followed the edge of the runway, the markings of it visible now we knew what it was. Going this direction was sideways to the blasting wind—it threatened to sweep our feet out, but it made it much faster to travel.

We were almost there.

A few minutes later and a dark shape loomed from the cocoon of blackness around us. Another few steps and it became clear. A building.

Howard shrieked and stumbled past us, but fell heavily onto Otto who cursed and got tangled. The kid clawed at Otto as he tried to get up, and as soon as he was back to his feet he literally ran forward at the structure.

It looked like a small barn.

He made straight for the door on the side. For a second I worried it would be locked, but he opened it right away. I shrugged and picked up my pace. Who in the hell would be worried about locking stuff up here? Not like anyone would be breaking in. I managed a tiny laugh.

Nothing would be locked up here.

No lights. Only Otto had the headlamp and he played it off the interior and searched for any switches. Nothing. It looked like a storage shed. Empty.

Sweet relief to be out of the wind. It felt a hundred degrees warmer in here, even though it was probably twenty below.

"I'd say we should warm up," Otto said, "but I don't think we will."

"There's gotta be more buildings," I said. "There *are* more buildings."

"Does…does…anyone…have a…a…" Howard was a mess. I didn't know how he'd even made it this far.

"Match. Lighter," he finally managed to say. "There's…I think it's hay…"

"We could light this entire building on fire, if it came to that," Otto said. "But I got no light."

"Flare gun?" I took it out. "Would this light up something?"

"Maybe. I mean, yeah, it makes fire."

We considered it for a second. The wind pounded and drummed the structure. I checked Lilly. She was straining to breathe. Looked like she was asleep but wouldn't wake up.

"Let's go to the next building," I said. "There are more. I'm sure of it. Maybe they have lights and power."

Otto nodded in agreement. "Let's go."

"I...I can't..." Howard fell to the ground and curled into a ball.

"We can't wait for you. We'll come back."

Otto made his way back outside first. I paused at the doorway, reached into my suit and took out the biohazard container from Jang's hands.

"Howard," I said into the darkness, "you hang onto this? You stay still and we'll be back in a minute."

I tossed it to where I thought he was. A second later, I tossed him his disk as well.

▼▲▼

The wind blasted against us with howling fury. I had to lean almost parallel to the ground and hold onto Otto to keep from flying away. We slipped once and lost thirty feet in a terrifying tumble before we scrabbled upright in a mess.

One...more...

Another shape loomed out of the darkness. Not just an outline. One with a bright light shining from the inside.

In five grinding steps we managed to move downwind of the building where the wind curled in buffeting bursts that almost sucked us forward. We reached the edge of the structure and walked to the square of warm yellow.

There was someone inside, beyond the window's glass. Short-cropped blond hair. A man. He sat immobile at a wooden table as if he was waiting for something. I was about to rap on the window but hesitated. He had on a dark blue wool sweater with shoulder patches. Looked military.

My fist hovered over the glass.

Otto's fist banged against it, once and then twice and then harder.

Finally the man turned. Young. Not more than twenty or twenty-five with pale skin. He frowned and got up and took a step closer to the window. His nose inches from us as we pressed against the glass and yelled over the roaring wind. He motioned to the left—at a door—and nodded.

I tried to read his expression. If anything, he seemed afraid.

CHAPTER 36

I'm sorry I was—"

"Get out of the way!" Otto yelled. He shoved the door fully open.

The kid stumbled back. The wind howled in and brought with it whorls of snow. Papers scattered.

I entered on Otto's heels, one hand on Lilly on his back, the other gripping the knife—thick with congealed polar bear blood—in my right exterior pocket. The kid's face was slack-blank and slick with sudden sweat. His expression seesawed from fear to confusion and then back to fear.

"Wait, you guys aren't the compliance team?" he said.

The second he opened his mouth, I let go of my knife. Definite mid-Western Canadian drawl. He'd have to be a Broadway-trained actor to fake that. My attention refocused laser-like straight onto Lilly.

"Baby, sweetheart, can you hear me?"

Her arms sagged at her sides; her head lolled back and forth against Otto's back. He dropped to his knees and I scratched at the ropes holding her, but my fingertips were frozen. Jang unzipped the front of my suit and spilled out as I leaned forward.

"Help me!" I screamed in sheer desperation.

"Wait, who…where did…" The kid had closed the door but hadn't moved.

Otto unzipped and wriggled his arms from his suit. I lowered Lilly to the floor.

The sudden heat of the room felt like a blast furnace against my face. The smell of floor cleaner almost overpowering. And…was that pot? Was the kid smoking a joint when we came in?

It didn't matter.

My little baby's face was ice-white, her lips blue. She laid flat on her back. I struggled to pull down the zip on the front of her suit—Otto did it for me—then cradled her tiny body in my claw-like-frozen hands and knelt over her, my face in hers. She was tiny for her age to begin with, and had always been thin, but now her ribs stuck out like twigs in a plastic bag.

She was limp, her eyes wide but unseeing.

"Baby, please, no—breathe, please—"

"What the hell is wrong with you?" Otto roared at the kid. "Get a medical kit. Anything you got. Right now!"

"Breathe, Lillypad, it's okay—"

Her body convulsed. Her eyes swiveled to look at me. She sucked in a tiny wheezing gasp.

Still alive.

She was still alive.

Jang knelt beside her in front of me. "Be calm," he whispered into her ear, "remember what we talked about." Her eyes moved to him.

I gently rocked her back and forth. "Just breathe," I repeated over and over.

The warm air in here had to help, didn't it?

Jang's faced was riddled with patches of frost, his fingertips as white as mine. He stroked Lilly's hair and put one hand to hers.

Clattering noises from the next room.

Otto was on his feet, his survival suit unzipped from the top, the arms of it wrapped around his waist but feet and legs remained in.

"Come on, come on," he urged to the kid.

Another racket of things falling from tables and hitting the floor.

I focused on my daughter. Her body shook and convulsed, her lips now purple.

"Here, here, here." Otto dropped to his knees and handed me something with a shaking hand.

Blue. Plastic. An inhaler.

I showed it to Lilly and put it to her lips. She wheezed in with everything her little body had in it. The effect was immediate. A second later she nodded and I clicked the device again. She took a deeper breath.

My abject terror eased, the tensed every-muscle-in-my-body relaxed a little, the painful knot in the pit of my stomach shifting into something more resembling nausea. And then pain. Sixty seconds inside this furnace of a room and parts of me began to thaw out.

I ignored it.

Some color returned to Lilly's cheeks.

"Who are you guys?" The kid finally managed a full sentence.

"We've got four more people trapped outside, not far," Otto said. He got back to his feet.

"Out there?" The kid pointed to the door in disbelief. "Wait… trapped…?"

"My name is Otto Garcia. I was the Air Marshal on Allied Flight 695."

"Allied Flight…" Gears and circuits went into motion in the kid's head. He was obviously stoned, but a light finally went on in his eyes. "Are you serious?"

Otto didn't dignify this with a response.

"I got to get on the radio." The kid looked left and right. "In the other room."

"What's your name?" Otto asked.

"Jimmy Craig. I mean, call me Jimbo."

"Jimbo," Otto said in a calm and measured voice and reached to shake his hand, "what we have here is an emergency situation. When you fly a plane, aviate and navigate come first, communicate comes last once the situation is under control. Are you the only person here?"

Jimbo nodded in short quick bobs of his head.

"So then you're the only person who can help us. We need to stabilize, make sure these children and my friend here aren't in immediate danger of death, then help the ones outside as best we can."

"That's all the medical—"

"We have people outside. Right now I need you to find any and all parkas, blankets, any heat sources like chemical packs and butane. Anything warm. And water. We need water."

The kid had his hands up with a finger out for each item. "Okay, okay..."

"Do you have any weapons?"

"What...why?"

"We ran into a polar bear out there that almost killed us. Might be more."

"Oh, my—"

"Kid. Jimbo. Focus."

"Right. Yeah, we've got a shotgun in the lockbox, some shells." He stared open-mouthed at Otto for a second before he nodded again and then disappeared around the corner into the next room.

"And in sixty seconds," Otto called out, "once you get all that for me, we'll make that call together. Get on the radio. You're going to be famous, kid."

Otto turned his attention back to us. Lilly sucked in short quick breaths. Her lips weren't as blue anymore but now pinkish.

"You okay?" he said to her.

She nodded but didn't say anything. She sat up to demonstrate. I involuntarily squealed in pain.

"Everything okay?" Jimbo asked from the next room.

"Fine," Otto called back and moved toward me.

By sitting up, Lilly sat on my left hand cradling her. The sudden heat and pressure cracked my fingers from the claw-position they'd been frozen into. I pulled my hands out from under her and inspected them. It was the first time I'd seen them in proper light in days.

The tips of my index and forefingers of both hands were blue-black and all the fingers were splotchy blue and white. They shook as I attempted to get a better look. With the palm of one hand I tried to feel my face. Hard and lumpy.

"Don't," Otto said gently. He knelt. "Let's get a look at you."

"We need to get outside and get Howard, and Liz and the others."

"I don't think *you* are going anywhere. Come on, let's have a look."

I had my suit unzipped already, and he pulled it down from my shoulder, had me sit on a chair, and with my permission, tugged on the feet of it to slide off my body. A rancid stench immediately filled the air—like feces and sewage and rot but worse.

Otto didn't flinch. He tenderly unwrapped my left foot, peeled away each layer of sodden sock and wrapping to reveal toes, black and brown and bulbous. Flaps of skin sloughed off my legs and feet as he removed more clothing.

"I saw you drop off Liz's canister," he said as he unwrapped the right foot.

"I figured walking into a foreign military base with a weapon of mass destruction under my arm wasn't a good idea."

We both managed a small laugh. "You're right."

"It's in the shed. I'll let whoever goes down there from the base figure it out."

"And you gave Howard his disk?"

"I figured if he was going to die, he'd appreciate having his '*precious*' with him."

"He won't die. I'm going out to get him."

"He might already be."

How long had it been? Five minutes? Ten? How much longer could someone survive out there? The wind buffeted the building like some giant was outside hitting it with a bat.

"I'm not sure it was a good idea to leave Roman and Bjorn together," Otto said.

"What? Why?" They seemed barely alive.

"Not sure. Roman wasn't as badly injured as he was making out. He could have come with us."

"You think so?"

"I have a bad feeling leaving those two together with Liz."

The wind hammered the building again. I glanced up. Strong construction. Interior metal I-beams with oversized bolts and lots of concrete. Looked like it could withstand being hit by a bomb, but it shuddered in the onslaught.

"It will take it," Jimbo said as he returned with piles of gear over each arm. He saw me inspecting the walls. "This is like a once-in-a-century polar low. Twenty-four more hours of this. Wind going to hit maybe two hundred kilometers an hour out there."

He dropped the blankets and gear on the floor between me and Lilly. She had the inhaler in hand and took another puff.

"Hey, don't do too much." I groaned.

Bolts of pain shot like lightning from my fingers and feet up my spine and into my brain. Already my face felt like it was on fire.

Jimbo had one hand over his nose. "What in the hell is…" He looked down at my feet and grimaced. "Sorry, eh?"

Otto finished stripping off my socks and took my dirty survival suit. "Let's get you something clean."

"Yeah, there're some socks there. Some woolen mitts and such." Jimbo pointed at the pile. He ripped open a plastic package. "These are chemical heaters. Open 'em up."

He had a whole box and dropped them on the floor.

"And I got a bunch of parkas and boots and so on in the storage back there. Heavy stuff. Tell me what we need." He handed me a bottle of water and dropped a few more onto the floor.

I unscrewed the cap with the palm of my hand and held it pinned between my wrists and tried to sip it. My lip lanced in pain. Some drops dribbled into my parched mouth.

"Take it slow with the water." Otto stood with my suit. "What we need now is to make that call on the radio. Get some help on the way here. Once we do that, you and me, Jimbo, we're going to go rescue some people."

"Oh, yah, eh?"

The kid was stoned, but he looked up for about anything.

"So why are you out here by yourself?" Otto asked.

"This is the hydrogen production facility. We keep it separate, like, from the rest of the base. Big hydrogen containers up top."

"Hydrogen?"

"For the balloons, eh? That's what this building is. We launch weather balloons twice a day, all year, no matter what. Usually we're two, but Environment Canada has cuts, eh? So now it's only me. I came down earlier in the day from the base to send one off, and then the winds came up, so I decided to stay, right? Don't want to do that mile and a half walk back up in this. Golly, no."

Their voices echoed as they walked around the corner away from us into the next room.

I heard Otto ask, "How many people are at the base?"

"Seventy-five. Give or take. The Frozen Chosen they call us."

"And the transport?"

"The Hercules comes on Tuesdays—today—but probably later tomorrow when the wind calms down. Flies up from Trenton, Ontario."

"That's right on the American border?"

"Oh, yah."

They kept chatting as Jimbo explained the radio.

Lilly had one hand over her nose. I gingerly took some of the socks from the pile of new clothes, removed the packaging and tried to slip them over my feet.

"You guys okay?" I whispered.

"I'm okay, Mr. Mitch," Jang said. His face was scarlet around the patches of frostbite, but he didn't flinch or react in any way.

"Lilly?"

She was in her bright orange suit. The color in her face had returned with a vengeance, her cheeks now scarlet, her lips full and pink. She breathed easily. No signs of frostbite. I'd packed her oversized suit with every scrap of dry fabric and clothing I could spare in the past week, made sure to keep her high and dry.

"Yes, Commander?" Otto's voice on the radio in the next room was loud enough to hear over the wind. "This is Air Marshal Garcia from Allied Flight 695."

Not long now, Emma, I said to myself. I imagined her face at the news. I couldn't believe we made it.

"Yes." Otto's voice boomed. "Allied 695. We need immediate help."

The pain blossomed and lanced through my entire body, but something else as well. An itch I'd never been able to scratch. One deep in the back of my mind.

Howard insisted that he hadn't sabotaged the radio, yet someone had wrecked the "*transmit*" button on it. Rasheed. What had happened to him? He was the only one who really knew how to work that radio.

Otto's voice echoed loud.

After the crash, Adrian the cabin manager had honestly looked like he'd never seen Otto before. Otto claimed it was all part of the act, that Adrian knew who he was but had to pretend he didn't. Howard had said that Otto's gun wasn't standard issue for the TSA. The Glock 19, like my dad used to have. Wasn't standard for police, either. Was more of a hunting handgun.

Why would he suggest that we shouldn't have left Roman and Bjorn together outside?

And…

I didn't remember seeing Otto in First Class before the accident. Not in one of the pod beds. I'd looked around. He was in the regular class line up in front of me when we checked in. Did Air Marshals need to check in? Where did he come from before the accident?

Too many coincidences…

Otto said loudly, "We have four survivors here and four more outside. No other survivors have been picked up."

How in the hell would he know no other survivors were picked up?

A tingling dread eclipsed my pain.

I patted my pockets for my knife, but Otto had taken it with the suit. The flare gun, too. I had my journal and the adrenaline syringe in the jacket pocket from my inside-suit clothes.

"How long till you will be here?" Otto said loudly from the next room.

And why was Otto the only one doing the talking? Why hadn't I heard Jimbo?

"Kids," I whispered. "I need you to do something for me."

"Yes, Mr. Mitch?" Jang whispered back.

"I need you to go back outside. Very fast and very quiet?"

Lilly's eyes went wide but I put a finger to her mouth.

"Shhhh," I said. "Take as many blankets and warmers and socks as you can. Go right outside the door against the wall away from the wind."

Jang said, "Now?"

"Right now. Go, go, go." I gave Lilly a hug and squeeze.

She got up and waddled away in her suit. Jang dragged a pile of blankets. The little kid was in his sneakers and layers of clothes we'd wrapped him in since the plane. They looked at me as they reached the door. Otto was talking loud. I nodded at them as Jang reached for the door latch and I coughed as loud as I could.

Wind ruffled and scattered papers again. I smelled something more than the rot of my own feet. Something burning.

"Mitch? You okay?" Otto said from the next room.

I gritted my teeth and searched for something—anything—to use as a weapon. A laptop? A half-full garbage can? I settled on a heavy stapler and unhinged it and stuck it under my leg. I struggled to grip it with the palm of my hand.

Otto appeared around the corner and frowned. "Hey, where are the kids?"

"Where's Jimbo?" I asked.

"He's…ah…" Otto sighed and scratched the back of his head with his Glock in his right hand.

"Don't hurt my daughter, please."

"I really like you." Otto advanced toward me. "And Lilly is beautiful, just amazing. It really breaks my heart."

The weird smell became stronger. At first I thought maybe I was having a stroke—smelling toast, right?—but now there was definitely something burning.

"The thing is, Mitch." Otto leveled the muzzle of his gun at my head. "There can't be any survivors from Allied 695."

CHAPTER 37

O tto stood five feet from me, the muzzle of the gun not more than two. His arm steady. Finger on the trigger.

I counted in my head—two shots by Howard, and then two more in that chase to the boat?

Black smoke billowed into the corrugated metal ceiling twenty feet up.

"Where are the kids?" Otto said.

I gritted my teeth, the palm of my right hand squeezed around the heavy stapler. Otto had fired twice at the seals, right? And then three more shots at that bear when it first appeared...

"You got them in a cupboard?" Otto glanced left and right. The tabletops ringing the room each had storage doors underneath. "You know what's up there, right?"

When I didn't reply he said, "Hydrogen. There's like a thousand pounds of liquid hydrogen in a tank on the roof."

"Why are you doing this?"

He laughed. "You want the whole villain confession? I'm not a bad guy, Mitch—"

"You're an asshole."

He shrugged. "This whole mission went sideways. None of it was supposed to happen like this."

"Are you actually an Air Marshal?" I played for time and counted: two shots and two more and then two more and one to finish the bear...

"Does it matter? You're the wrong guy at the wrong time caught up in something way bigger than you. Where are the kids?" He pressed the muzzle directly against my forehead.

Licking flames now joined the smoke overhead.

"I don't have to shoot you," Otto said. "We can play a game with one of your feet, see how long you can take that. Although"—he looked over his left shoulder at the thickening smoke and flames—"it had better be a quick game. So I'm going to ask—"

A bang at the door.

My heart jumped into my throat. One of the kids? But the shape at the window was too large. Roman? Bjorn? A glimmer of hope surged in my chest. Maybe someone from the base?

Had he really called them?

Then another fear. Was he actually the Air Marshal? Was this a government plot? The CIA or something? Was Howard right?

Speak of the Devil.

The door swung open.

A snow-encrusted Howard stepped through. He feebly held a knife at his side and groaned what he must have hoped was a roar as he stumbled forward.

Otto stepped away from me. Swung the gun around. Howard hadn't covered half the distance before the shot cracked out. The poor bastard crumpled to the ground.

Otto pointed the firearm back at me.

"I really didn't want to use bullets," he said. "Then again, by the time this thing overhead explodes and burns I'm not sure that they'll—"

Without making a sound I ducked and charged straight at him. Did he have a plus-one in the clip when he started? Was he that kind of guy? Did he reload the mag? Did I count right?

He pulled the trigger.

Click.

His face expressed the beginnings of puzzlement. With one arm down to his left side, he fumbled at his suit pocket as my right-arm-swinging-haymaker with the open stapler slammed into his temple.

Surprise, asshole.

The stapler wasn't one of those little ten-page clippers you'd usually find on your desk. Someone here had been writing *very* big reports. This must have weighed five pounds in forged steel with over-sized staples, one of which wedged itself halfway into Otto's left temple.

I'd never gotten into a fight in my life—something my dad had never forgiven me for. With flailing fury my momentum carried me into Otto.

The stapler bounced off his head and knocked him to my left. He slipped and stumbled back, and had almost recovered when I hammered into him. I tried to lunge and set my foot down—but a lancing pain sent an electric bolt upward through my body leaving me screaming in pain as I tumbled to the ground in a mess over Otto.

The Navy SEAL was surprised by the attack—*if he was even a SEAL, the lying bastard*—but he recovered fast. With his left hand he grabbed my throat and dug his thumb and fingers into the soft part under the neck and gripped my larynx. Squeezed.

I gasped and writhed. Felt chunks of my skin sliding off in the struggle.

I wasn't even an armchair athlete. I laughed at my friends who made fun of me for not hitting the gym more. This guy was ten years my junior and trained to kill anything on two or more feet.

But I had something he didn't.

A daughter freezing to death outside.

I let him choke me while I waited for an opening. In that moment I didn't fear dying; I needed to hurt him as badly as I could. I struggled but he pinned me with his legs.

He yelped in pain. His legs holding me slipped free, but it wasn't me that hurt him somehow.

Howard loomed to one side, propped up on an elbow, blood

pooling around him. He hacked at Otto's side and arm with the knife.

Otto punched Howard straight in the throat with his right hand holding the gun. Howard managed to hack at the arm as he choked and Otto dropped the weapon. It clattered to the floor.

Empty—but maybe useful.

With everything I had, I hauled myself upward and jammed the stapler into his face again—this time straight into his left eye as he looked at Howard.

The reaction was powerful and immediate. His right arm came down around my right, his body spun and he snapped my arm back at the elbow.

A loud crack and another explosion of pain. He kicked down and this time crushed my left foot.

For a few seconds I couldn't even see beyond the bursting pain and my tearing eyes. I gasped for air.

"Goddamn mother…" Otto was on his feet and holding the left side of his face.

I curled into a ball on the floor.

Howard was flat on the ground, his head upside down to me but inches away. He gargled and struggled for air. "I...I knew...knew it," he gasped. "Otto…ass…hole…"

Calm. Calm. I heard my wife's words. Don't let anything happen to her.

The flames roared overhead and spread across the entire ceiling. The heat blossomed and burned my just-frozen face. Through watery eyes I tried to keep track of our attacker.

"I think we're going to need to make this self-defense," Otto said. He groaned as blood smeared down his face from his socket, the eye mangled. "I think Jimbo is going to have to finish you guys off with the shotgun."

The structure reverberated with the howling wind, the flames roaring down the walls. He must have lit some fuel or something. How much longer before the hydrogen tank ignited?

Otto disappeared around the corner into the next room.

I rolled to my left, struggled to one knee and felt in my pockets for anything I could use. Just the vials of adrenaline and the needle. My journal fell onto the floor and I ignored it.

Only one thing I could do. I had to rush him, push Otto back into the flames. I would die, but I could stop him, and maybe the explosion would bring help.

For Lilly.

CHAPTER 38

I steadied myself with my left hand on one knee. The smoke curled down to ground level and gagged me. I coughed and wiped my eyes.

My left foot a searing mass of pure pain, the sock covering it soaked in brown pus that oozed from within. The putrid stench of it gagged me even in the lung-burning smoke. My right side wasn't much better, and my arm dangled uselessly. I'd only have one chance at this—keep my head down and don't stop no matter what.

Another thought…

Where had I told the kids to hide? Against the wall? Damn it. How big was this explosion going to be? A thousand pounds of hydrogen? That had to be like a bomb. A big one.

I looked at the door. Maybe I should run. Where? All I had was one pair of jeans and a few layers of sodden shirts and wool socks.

A tug on my jeans.

"Hey, hey." Howard pulled at me again.

"Not now."

I readied myself.

Shove the asshole into the flames. Even if he shot me, he couldn't stop my momentum. Could he? What was it like to get hit by a shotgun?

"No, look." Howard tugged once more.

I glanced down.

He had a rectangular metal object in his right hand. A magazine. A spare magazine for the Glock. With ammunition in it.

"Hurry," he said as he spat up a mouthful of blood.

The flames in the next room cast a shadow from Otto. The outline moved and expanded.

I flopped onto the floor and grabbed the discarded Glock. With only one hand to operate it, I jammed it between my knees, hit the magazine release button on its left side, then reached for the new one from Howard. I spun the gun around with my hand with it squeezed between legs and pressed the magazine in.

"Look on the bright side," Otto said as he cleared the corner. "At least you won't burn to death."

I rolled onto my side and pushed the slide back with the gun still between my knees.

Otto hesitated at the corner, pulled back an instant, seemed to guess I'd try to rush him.

Thick sooty smoke curled around me. I gasped. Heard the shotgun pump.

A second later the bright flash and blast of sucking air right over me. He fired blind the first time. He pumped again.

I lifted my shaking left hand with the gun and had to wrap my index finger almost to the knuckle around the trigger. Couldn't trust my fingertips for anything.

Waited.

A blurry image separated from the flames.

The gun kicked back and almost spun out of my hand. Another bolt of pain shot up my arm.

I heard Otto curse, "Goddamn it," followed by a string of more explicit curses.

Spittle flew from my mouth as I gasped with the effort to stay focused. I repositioned the gun in my hand as quick as I could, held on tighter and aimed and squeezed off two more rounds.

Needed to keep him back in those flames.

From my side I rolled onto my knees, doing my best to hold the gun out. Flaming debris fell from the walls and drifted in black cinders in the roiling air. Beyond the flames the walls of the structure pounded from the winds outside.

I hobbled forward.

The heat intensified.

A screeching cacophony as part of the roof structure collapsed. Metal beams swung down from the ceiling and crashed into the cement floor halfway into the other room. Otto cursed again. A flash in the dark. Another booming concussion that sucked air past me.

"Take whatever you goddamn want," I yelled. "That container is in the shed. That's what you want, right? Go, call your friends, leave us the hell alone."

Metal groaned as the flames engulfed the walls. The awful stench of burning hair as my skin singed and hair curled.

I cleared the wall and swung my weapon around. A blast of merciful cold air sucked between the flames.

The door at the opposite end was open, bent back and flapping in the raging gale outside. The brief blast of cool cleared the air for a split second, but then…

The flames seemed to explode in renewed fury with the new source of oxygen. I had to shield my face from the searing heat. Jimbo was laid out over some radio equipment ten feet from me and almost black from the soot. Beside him an open locker door near a metal stairway to a second floor.

A pile of parkas and outdoor gear spouted orange flames on the floor. That had to be where Otto started the fire.

I pocketed the gun and stuffed my destroyed fingers into the Canadian kid's wool top and hauled. I backed away as fast as I could. My skin burning. Eyes streaming tears in the black smoke. Not just smoke, but some toxic concoction of burning plastics and fuel and insulation.

I started dry retching as I reached the door. Fumbled for the latch and threw it open.

A blast of air fanned the flames almost straight into me.

On the ground at my feet my journal's pages flapped. I hesitated an instant but knelt to pocket it, took hold of the kid again and managed to take two steps when a whomping concussion first flattened me and then flung my body into the air.

The wind captured and tossed me end over end into the frigid blackness.

CHAPTER 39

"A man who can't take care of himself will have a hard time taking care of a family," my dad said.

He stood on the deck of his sailboat in Jones Inlet Marina. Purple clouds heaved in the screaming winds over the flat green wetlands of Long Island.

"I'm not coming with you."

"One way or the other you are."

"I'm eight years old now. I don't have to listen to you. Anyway, what does a boat have to do with family?"

My old man bobbed up and down with the waves. "Your family is your boat, and sailing isn't about water. It's about self-sufficiency."

"Like you've taken care of your family?"

Only eight, but already I saw the vista of adulthood before me enough to hurt with words. He had just split up with my mother—a separation they called it, but I knew better, even at eight.

He looked away. "I have taken care of my family."

The lines in my dad's face seemed so deep I could crawl into them. Into their warmth.

"No, you haven't taken care!" I yelled, spat his own words back at him. "You're going to die alone, an old man, you know that?"

The purple maelstrom circled and descended behind my father.

He looked at me with my own eyes.

"We all die alone, son," he said.

▼▲▼

"Dad?"

The waves carried my father away, the purple fury raging behind him fading into black. The waves buffeted and pushed me back from him until he was gone. Away. Forever.

Something tugged at me.

Pushed at me.

I opened my eyes. Tried to open them. They were stuck closed. I tried to move my right hand to rub them, but cried out as a bolt of agony shot up my arm.

The pain jolted me awake. I heaved in a lungful of frigid air and ice crystals, then coughed it all back out.

My left eye opened.

But saw nothing.

Pitch black nothingness. I lifted my head and felt it shoved back.

The wind. That was the noise. The wind clawed and ripped at me.

The mind-fog of the dream faded with a surge of terror. The ice. The storm. The burning building and dragging that kid and…

Lilly.

I'd told her to go outside.

I struggled to what I thought was my knees and leaned into the buffeting squall and whipping snow. With the back of my left arm I wiped my eyes.

Couldn't see anything. Couldn't *feel* anything.

My forearm swiping at my eyes as numb as my face. I only knew it was there because I felt the interior pain of it, the sinews and bones, but maybe it wasn't even there. Maybe I was imagining it. Except for hearing the roaring wind I had no senses at all.

My thoughts an infinitesimal dot of nothingness in the void.

Was I…

Am I dead?

Is this it? How would I know?

Was this hell?

Please. God. Please help me.

If I could have cried I would have. For someone who didn't go to church much and imagined himself as an absent atheist, I'd been invoking God's name and praying a lot.

We all die alone, son.

Please. I can't.

Lilly.

CHAPTER 40

I blinked again and stared into the screaming void. Turned my head. There.

Not darkness. A wavering red smudge reflected. I rubbed my eyes again and perceived my arm blocking out the light.

You're not dead. Get up. I leaned into the wind and staggered to my feet. I noticed the snow was deeper now and provided some traction.

The flickering red had to be the building. The fire. The explosion. My mind reassembled the details. The hydrogen tank. Must have gone off like a bomb and thrown me away. Where was Jimbo? I'd been holding the kid. And where was…

I'd told Lilly to hide outside the building.

I forced my legs forward, my left arm attempting to shield my eyes.

Another thought: Otto. He'd exited the back door. He had a survival suit. And a shotgun. Had he gotten what he wanted? Or did he need to finish…?

I staggered into the wind.

The flames roared over the snow like a blowtorch in the gale. I advanced into the trailing edge of the inferno, my arm up now, guarding from the raging heat as much as the driving snow.

"Lilly," I yelled with a new found voice, and then screamed, "Lilly!"

I had to angle my head down away from the inferno. My body was clearly visible in the rippling light of the flames. Jeans. I had on jeans. One foot came out of the snow and dropped back in knee deep a few inches closer. Socks on my feet. Flapping fabric of a shirt on my arm.

Where was the edge of the building?

I couldn't make out much more than the flames. Even with the conflagration, visibility was limited to a few dozen feet in the blizzard conditions.

"Lilly!"

I edged closer.

"Mr. Mitch…"

At first I didn't hear the words, or maybe I thought my mind was playing tricks.

"Lilly, are you—"

"Mr. Mitch. Mr. Mitch."

This time it was unmistakable. I tried to lift my leg again but it was stuck.

Not stuck.

Jang had his arms around my calf. "Mr. Mitch," he yelled as loud as he could.

I dropped to my knees in the snow and did my best to wrap him into my arms, but couldn't manage more than to crouch over him.

"Where's Lilly?"

He took my right hand and pulled. I ignored the shooting pain. Already I felt so much better, my body lighter. I felt sleepy. Warmer.

Jang pulled me along with the wind. Away from the flames and into the darkness.

A small dot of color against the gray. "Daddy!" the dot squeaked.

My daughter.

I followed Jang around a ridge of black that stuck out from the white. A waist-high wall protected Lilly from the wind. A part of my mind registered that this was about where the shed had been.

I slumped into the snow beside her. Was she even real? It was hard to stay awake.

"Are you...you okay?" I stuttered.

"Daddy, Daddy..."

I couldn't understand her words. She had her inhaler. Good. Her face was so close to mine. So close.

"Let's rest," I said. "Rest a little while. Then we'll go."

So warm and comfortable here. I closed my eyes and let my mind drift.

We all die alone, son.

My father walked over the top of the snow. His hair unruffled by the vortex. "I told you that you'd come with me."

"I'm not coming," I replied. And then more forcefully. "I'm not going!"

My dad smiled and slicked back his gray hair. "That's good, son. That's all I wanted. For you to be your own man. To be tough."

He turned and cast off the ropes and faded away.

"Lilly?" I opened my eyes. The dim red glow from the flames was already going out.

"Daddy, we can't stay here." My daughter's face was inches from mine.

Jang was almost as close. "Which way, Mr. Mitch?"

I tried to shift my arms. I could barely move. The kids couldn't make it up that hill. Not in this. Even with that explosion, I doubted the people in the base would see it a mile and a half away in this raging storm and white-out-black-out conditions.

So weak. So warm.

I was dying.

No uncertainty about it. No fear anymore. So tired. No fear, except...

I'd leave my daughter here to die. Alone. In the darkness.

I remembered her room in the first house Emma and I owned. A few years ago, my little monster Lillypad, in her terrible twos making sure that I'd leave the light on when we had finished the bedtime story. Afraid of the dark.

She was afraid of the dark.

The light from the flames faded. Either that or my eyes were icing over. Some lucidity in my mind, enough to think…maybe all…of…

Come on, Mitch. Stay here. Awake.

I tried to blink but couldn't. Did I have the gun in my pocket? Could I do *that*? End all of our suffering? I put the thought away, but felt *myself* slipping away. My hands and feet felt hot now. Like steaming in a bath.

"Jang, go in my pocket," I said as loud as I could.

A second later he produced something. He held it close. "This, Mr. Mitch?"

The syringe.

Had enough to kill a grown man. Certainly enough for…

The two children. I couldn't leave them here. I didn't have long. Already the world dimmed away from my mind.

It wasn't just…the snow…the cold…

My mind slowed to a crawl. Stuttered a beat.

But where…the hell…was…

Otto?

CHAPTER 41

Alert
Canadian Forces Station
Nunavut

"Fuzani, you want some more coffee?"

"Call me Fuzz, everyone does."

It was a line Fuzani Curtis used a lot. All his life. It usually earned him a sly grin, the rhyme as cool as its owner's name.

Not here.

"Corporal Curtis, would you like some coffee or not?" Major Kumar's expression betrayed zero degrees of humor.

Fuzz stopped twizzling his pen around his finger and sat upright. "No, thank you, Major. Not at this time."

It had been a month-long struggle to get Major Sanjay Kumar onto a first name basis, but nicknames were obviously a bridge too far. Fuzz couldn't afford to burn any more bridges. He arranged his study notes into a neat pile.

The Major picked up a phone receiver and pressed the exterior line. "Could we please have a pot of tea in the Secure Operations?"

That Indian accent was something Fuzz's dad would have made fun of, but Fuzz really liked the Major, even with all his reprimands.

Sanjay Kumar was from northern India, or something like that. That was wrong. Bhutan maybe? Somewhere up in the Himalayas. He was born there.

Then again, Fuzz was an immigrant to Canada as well.

He had heard guys whispering in the locker room, making fun of his own Southern-fried accent. With a name like Fuzani Curtis he didn't have much of a leg to stand on to make fun of anyone else's name. He was born in South Carolina, but had lived almost all his life in Southern Ontario. When he dropped out of his second year of college, his dad had decided that the military was the best option for his errant son.

That was how The Fuzz from South Carolina had ended up at the North Pole.

Not quite the North Pole.

The Alert base was the most northern inhabited place on the planet, but still five-hundred miles from latitude zero.

He had managed to squeak onto the bottom rung of the Canadian military ranks as the most junior of non-commissioned officers. Corporal. On the desk in front of him were study notes for the Junior Officer of CSIS exam, the Canadian equivalent to the CIA.

His single year of programming courses at college had been enough to get him into a non-commissioned role at the cyber operations group in Trenton last year. He'd volunteered to come up to Alert, an assignment nobody else wanted.

The "Frozen Chosen" was what they called the thirty-or-so military staff here, plus the forty-odd private contractors that kept them fed and the dozen buildings running. All for basically babysitting a bunch of computers.

Fuzz stretched his neck and looked around the Secure Operations Centers. The SOC. Equivalent to the American SCIF—the Secure Compartmentalized Information Facilities. A secure room to guard against electronic surveillance and suppress data leakage of classified and military information and intelligence.

That line was right from his study notes.

The room was thirty-feet long and twenty wide, with metal walls connected together with rough welds and painted an uninspiring shade of blue-gray. Fabric panels hung every three feet. Reminiscent of a submarine more than anything else.

And that smell—a dull, sweet stink like his grandfather's house. Somehow greasy and gassy under the lingering odor of daily carpet freshener tonics.

Chipped Formica tables and basic black plastic-and-metal chairs. Cables snaked across the desks. Boxy old-school computers attached to monitors older than the *old* one he used at home to play World of Warcraft.

No windows.

Not that it mattered.

Six months of nighttime on his rotation made windows less than useless and more usually just depressing. He had a window in his eight-by-eight bunk room and kept the blinds closed at all times. He supposed it was better than an assignment in Afghanistan. That's what his mother had said. Less chance of getting shot.

The only thing you could die of out here was boredom.

That said, there had been some excitement. The past weeks, the Americans had been conducting war game exercises over the Beaufort Sea, and the Russians responded with their own mobilization of bomber squadrons and fighter overflights deep into international territory, and sometimes into national territories of NATO members.

And then that airliner went down right in the middle of it.

Gone.

Just like that.

He shook his head. They'd seen an initial blip as it crossed the North Pole, but nothing more than that had appeared on the data sheets, nothing more than a few ghosts he hadn't been able to verify. Some cryoseismic tremors—ice quakes—but then, that was normal as the glaciers calved and ice sheets buckled under the changing temperatures.

The media whipped into a frenzy over the airliner story. It covered the news cycle from top to bottom the last two weeks.

Another commercial jet that had vanished into thin air. No transponder data. No cries for help. They were searching over the Beaufort Sea right now. Dozens of ships and airplanes, but all of them waylaid by this huge string of low pressure systems. Polar hurricanes the media called them.

The conspiracy theorists had run rampant, and not only in the fringes but straight into the mainstream: Roman Kolchak, the Russian billionaire and arch-nemesis of the Russian Politburo; hundreds of millions in diamonds aboard; five-hundred pounds of lithium batteries in the hold that the NTSB had ruled as dangerous but somehow got on anyway; even a report of an illegally smuggled biohazard container with smallpox virus in it.

Terrorist attacks? Government cover-up? What had happened? That this was another unlikely accident was a story the public wouldn't stomach.

Already China and Russia and the Europeans and America were pointing fingers. The war exercises up here had taken on a more dramatic and deadly tone.

This installation was the tip of the spear for the entire joint American-Canadian-NATO Alliance intel operation for detecting any incoming aircraft or missiles where they weren't supposed to be in the Far North. It was part of the original DEW Line, the Distant Early Warning Line, or what they now called the North Warning System.

Things were heating up in the Arctic, and not from climate change.

The past month they had had a dozen alerts of Russian aircraft encroaching on Western airspace, and twice of perilously close flybys of American and Russian equipment. It was as if the Ruskies were testing the limits of what they could get away with.

The Fuzz was ready.

Major Kumar went back to his command computer in the far corner while Fuzz waited for support staff to bring in the tea. Fuzz suspected the Major spent most of his time surfing Facebook, but he didn't dare go near.

Instead, he began his round of the monitoring equipment, verifying cables and connections for the millionth time, running the same diagnostics to make sure all the sensors pinged back.

Fuzz mused aloud, "Do you think we'll sustain any structural damage?" He glanced at the exterior weather monitor; hundred-thirty kph winds, minus seventy-eight—and that was Celsius.

The Major replied, "This is a good test of our systems. We are somewhat blinded in a storm like this."

Already some of the VHF antennas were down.

And this wasn't only a listening post. The Defense Research group—together with the American DARPA—used Alert as the base for launching a fleet of covert submersible drones that spread out under the Arctic ice pack. A lot of stuff happened here that nobody else was supposed to know about, not even Fuzz.

A lot of spy stuff.

He checked a set of monitors looking at high altitude radar. Something blipped on it, a flagged anomaly from half an hour ago. He checked the false-positive analysis. Were the meteorological guys launching balloons from down at the runway in this? Not possible. Was it? Anything was possible in this crazy place.

He frowned and took a closer look.

The remoteness of it did weigh on your mind. Two hundred and fifty miles from the nearest other humans. Not just open water. Ice. Cold. Polar bears. Like being on the opposite side of the moon, and a constant nightmare to operate.

The running joke was that if the Russians invaded, the Base Commander would be at the door waiting for them with the keys and say, "All yours. Hell to resupply. Good luck with it."

A high-pitched siren jolted Fuzz almost enough to knock him sideways.

"Curtis, what is it?" The Major was on his feet.

Fuzz scrambled around a set of tables to the local radar feed. A large red bloom moved fast and low. "It's almost on top of the base."

"What is it?"

"It's…" Fuzz tried to decipher what he saw. The bloom faded as it moved toward the base. A flock of birds? There weren't any birds this far north. And in a hundred-thirty-plus gale? "I don't know, sir."

Whatever it was had disappeared, or gone under the radar, but even Russians weren't crazy enough to fly in this weather.

Were they?

"Keep checking," Major Kumar said.

Fuzz worked on crunching data from eighteen other sensors and tried to cross-correlate in a big data tool called Splunk that he was sure the Major had no idea how to use. Growing up playing video games had finally reaped some rewards. Whatever that contact was, it was so low, he wasn't even sure it was an aircraft.

The Russians were the kings of the Arctic, there was no contest.

They had huge tracked-transports, Arctic-modified hovercraft, and even the strange half-aircraft-half-ship vehicles like the massive ekranoplans. With heightening tensions, the neo-Soviets running Russia now had been rumored to be considering building a fleet of missile-armed *Lun*-class winged-ground-effect ekranoplans.

That was the only thing Fuzz could imagine might be capable of withstanding the conditions outside. Those were terrifying pieces of equipment.

Was this the first shot in an unraveling global conflict? Was that what was happening?

The Major had just sent a "Code Red" to NATO command. That was one signal level down from the one used for the threat of imminent nuclear war.

Were the Russians *invading*?

One thing that wasn't a joke about Alert, something they told you when you got here: there was no help coming to this place. You were on your own.

Fuzz crunched more data, tried to get a track on the huge thing that swept close by for a few kilometers before going away. Maybe they were testing using a massive storm as cover for sending in attack ships?

He was deep into a spreadsheet when another alarm went off.

This one not from his bank of computers.

It was the exterior alarm, the yellow light spinning and whining over the entrance. The Major ran for the door to make sure it was locked. They never locked stuff up here. Who the hell would try to break in? There was nobody out there for thousands of miles.

But something *was* trying to get in.

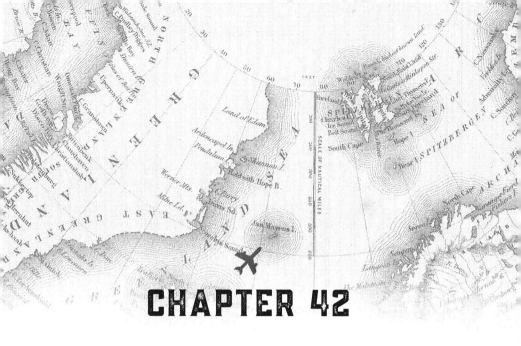

CHAPTER 42

Major Kumar and Fuzz gawked up at the grainy image on the six-by-six inch CRT monitor connected to the outside camera.

"Is that a polar bear?"

The big animals did sometimes set off the exterior alarms. Maybe they wanted a warm place to sleep, maybe curious, maybe attracted to the smell of Kumar's curries. Or maybe they wanted to eat the nice juicy humans so thoughtfully packaged inside. Fuzz couldn't blame them for dreaming beary dreams.

"It is most certainly not," the Major replied. "Go and unlock the sidearms cabinet. Bring me mine, and get yours as well."

Fuzz paused a beat.

It was someone—some *man* by the size of him—in what looked like an orange survival suit, with something in his arms. A container? The motion-sensing exterior lights had come on and lit him in a cone of gritty light.

Was there someone else behind him?

Impossible to tell.

Visibility was a few feet, but strange shadows seemed to lurk in the depths of the buffeting winds that thrummed even from inside the concrete-reinforced bunker.

"Should we open the door?" Fuzz asked.

"If we do not, whoever that is will die."

"This is a secure facility. We're not supposed to—"

"Are you in fact telling me my job, Corporal Curtis?"

Fuzz straightened his back. "No, sir." Except he had read that he should never let anyone unknown into a Secure Operations Center. Not without prior and verified orders.

"Then get to the sidearm cabinet, and check again the doors and trackers."

"Coats?"

"Use your God-given intelligence, young—"

But Fuzz was already off at a run. He slammed open the interior set of metal double doors and scattered his study notes to one side and brought up a keyboard.

"Log...exterior...doors..." he muttered to himself as he typed. He hit the enter key. A full string of negatives. "No exterior doors opened or closed in the past six hours."

So nobody had gone in or out.

Except one sensor. One sensor was out. Didn't mean it had been opened or not. Just no readings.

"Log…chip…staff…" A graphical image popped up that graphically displayed the positioning of all the location chips of everyone on base. All accounted for. So whoever that was, they were not from here.

Did this have something to do with the object that passed by outside?

Had it crashed?

His heart raced. He felt it skip a beat. That palpitation thing he hated that he'd inherited from his mother. *At least you won't get shot,* her words echoed in his head.

"Damn it."

He ran for the sidearm cabinet and shakily put the keys in from the lanyard around his neck. Swung it open. Grabbed two of the Browning 9mm in their holsters with belts.

Another alarm rang.

What the heck was that one? He scanned the monitors.

"Do you guys want this tea or not?" came a voice over the intercom.

Fuzz ran to the interior door and hit the buzzer. "Not now."

He ran back and slammed open the double doors. Handed one of the Brownings to Major Kumar and strapped the other around his waist. The Major already had his weapon out and nodded at Fuzz to do the same. He remembered he'd forgotten to get the coats. Too late now.

"Shouldn't we...ah..." Fuzz stuttered, his weapon now forward. Hands steady, he noticed.

"No time, Corporal Curtis. Get ready."

Major Kumar keyed in the exterior emergency door's code. It buzzed. The figure had slumped against the outside. Was pinned against it by the wind.

With his left hand, the Major released the door handle. It opened inward so it could be opened when snow piled outside. The pressure of the wind behind it slammed it open.

The man fell to the ground and the container spilled out of his grip.

Both Kumar and Fuzz trained their weapons on him, their eyes wide. The object that fell from the man's hands began to move. To writhe. To *uncoil*.

Fuzz's hands shook. He couldn't believe what he was seeing. He glanced at Kumar to find out what to do.

But the Major was on his knees, the wind roaring in and scattering snow and papers. His weapon down. He laid down face-first, flat against the ground as if he was praying.

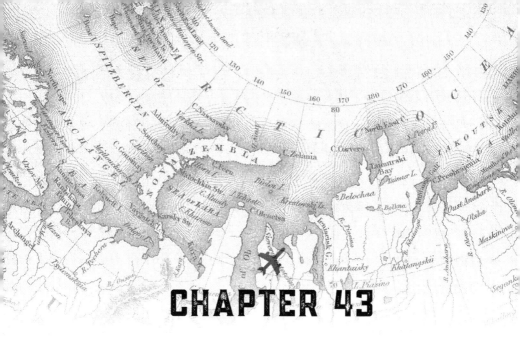

CHAPTER 43

Brigadier-General Jacques Allard bent his face away from the prop blast of the quad-engine Hercules. The aircraft rumbled down the runway, its engines whining high as they struggled to pull the squat gray slab of its body forward through the snow with enough speed for the airfoils to lift its massive bulk. It roared away past him and faded into the gloom, leaving behind wingtip-spilling vortices of snow.

For a heart-jarring instant he didn't think the beast would make it as it disappeared down the hill and slid toward the Arctic Ocean, but just when he feared the worst, it lumbered into the night sky. Its warning lights blinked over the icepack and faded.

"Goddamn ancient piece of..." the General muttered under his breath, not loud enough for anyone to hear.

The Hercules that dropped him here was almost fifty years in service. A jack-of-all-trades for the Far North and tough as hell, but fifty years was fifty years. About the same age as he was, and *he* was beat up as hell.

A few years back, a Herc like that one had crashed on a routine re-supply mission to Alert. Everyone survived the initial accident, but four people froze to death before the rescuers managed to get to them two days later.

The General hadn't wanted to make the four-thousand-kilometer trek from Trenton CFB to this frozen wasteland. He had to literally risk his life to get here, but these were his men.

His command.

"Was that the last of the survivors?" the General asked his PA, a young kid from Medicine Hat who had been terrified to find out he had to come up here.

For two days they hadn't been able to make it up. The massive storm had made it impossible. This was the first Herc. The General liked to be the first one in, no matter what.

The kid looked longingly at the part of the sky where the aircraft had receded into the blackness. "General, that's what I was told."

"Let's get on with it, then."

"Can I interview everyone?" asked Richard Marks.

The NTSB investigator had disembarked from the Hercules with him. He didn't have to be here. He'd volunteered when he heard. Right away. These NTSB guys were dedicated.

"You can talk to anyone you like," the General replied. "As long as I get a report."

"You got my word on that, sir."

The General trudged across the calf-deep snow, crunching through the crystallized top layer. He'd been told snowfall was unusual for this area. A polar desert they called it. A polar vortex was what they called the storm. Once-in-a-century events now seemed to happen once a year.

The rescue team had set up floodlights in the lower section of the Alert base near the runway, around the buildings—if these could be called that anymore. The structures were completely flattened as if they'd been hit by a bomb. All of them, razed right down to the foundation, what was left of them scraped away as if by a giant's hand. It was hard to even see what remained.

The darkness up here seemed to eat the light.

"General, Mr. Marks, I think we've got something."

A young Lieutenant—the General could tell by the shoulder patches on the parka—motioned to him from a low rise in the icy snow. The General tightened the cinch on the hood of his parka, reducing his vision to a tight circle straight in front. Already the cold seeped in and he'd only been onsite for ten minutes.

His breath came out in billowing white clouds of vapor.

He walked over, one careful step at a time. The Lieutenant grabbed a powerful handheld light and shone it on the discovery while he wiped away the snow with his other hand.

It was a man. Frozen into hard pack beside a part of a foundation.

His head down, but skin exposed. The flesh yellow and glassy. He was hunched over something. Was he one of theirs? Couldn't be. Everyone had been accounted for.

So who was this?

The Lieutenant dug into the snow around the hapless man. After a second he pulled something out. He peered at it. Held it close. Opened it and leafed through it.

"Looks like a journal, sir," the Lieutenant said.

"Any names?"

The young officer took a second and squinted. "Mitch Matthews, sir."

"*Mitch* Matthews?"

"That's right, sir." He handed over the ice-encrusted book.

"Can I take that?" Richard Marks asked.

The General nodded yes, and the Lieutenant handed the notebook to the NTSB investigator.

Richard took the journal, and the General looked over his shoulder, back at the spot where the Hercules had vanished. "Dig out whatever is under him," he said.

He walked away, stepped through more of the scoured wreckage before he stopped and looked at the pinpoints of stars in the dark vault above.

"What in the hell happened in this godforsaken place?"

CHAPTER 44

October 19th
Washington, D.C.

Emma Matthews fished out two prenatal vitamin pills from her jean jacket pocket. One blue pill, one red. With her other hand she picked up the glass of water the admin assistant had brought her. She picked the red pill first, put it in her mouth and tried to raise the glass, but her hand trembled so much that she spilled onto her dress. She managed to get a mouthful and swallowed, but replaced the glass on the table instead of trying the second pill.

Two weeks she hadn't slept. Not really.

Two weeks since she'd said goodbye to her daughter and husband. Her Lillypad and Mitch. Every word and image from those last minutes now burned into her memory, etched into the fabric of the waking nightmare that had become her life.

They flew her to Washington from New York this morning. Said they needed to see her. She had checked all the cable channels in the predawn darkness, but nothing new beyond the churning frenzy of conspiracy theorists.

They told her to not talk to anyone. She hadn't. Why would she? She had expected to be herded into a room of a hundred other grieving families, to see awful pictures of wreckage, but she was totally alone.

Shepherded into this room by herself.

She sat on a soft beige leather seat. Four of the same seats set in the middle of the carpeted room. Two each facing the others across a polished cherry wood table. Soft recessed lighting over wood-paneled walls. Straight in front of her the logo of the NTSB—an eagle and shield—in frosted white etched into glass. No other furniture. No other people. Not even any sounds except the rustling of her smoothing and smoothing down her dress.

Two weeks.

Two weeks since she'd seen the flight tracker app freeze. She'd checked the flight every ten minutes, was being silly, she'd said to herself. Then it froze. The plane. Stopped moving on the map. She laughed and told herself to stop it, but then went to a different website. Nothing. Before the flight was even supposed to land in New York, the story had already broken in the media.

Allied 695 disappeared in the Arctic.

Frantic calls to lines forever busy. It was all a blur. Tearful demands for information. A desperate trip into the Hong Kong airport to join a melee of other nervous people, all screaming for answers, mobbing the Allied Airlines desk. At first the officials said their networks were down, that there was some kind of system malfunction.

The third day she decided to make the flight back to New York. She was terrified to fly alone, but she hadn't told anyone else yet she was pregnant, and her mother was too sick to travel. She needed to be home.

She got back to their apartment in Brooklyn, and half-expected Mitch and Lilly to be there.

They weren't.

Only silence. Absolutely terrifying silence.

She stayed with friends. Everyone tried to get her to take sleeping pills, anti-anxiety pills, but she refused, either that or took them and tossed into garbage. She had a life to protect, the one inside of her.

She forced herself to try and sleep, but anytime she did, she dreamed. Of Lilly and Mitch, of the airplane going down…

The media had whipped into an absolute frenzy. When she'd gone back to the house to get some clothes, she'd been mobbed by them and Mitch's family had to step in and almost got into a fist fight. They'd volunteered to come with her today, but they—whoever they were—said she had to come alone.

Alone.

Why hadn't she told them not to go? Mitch had seemed to want her to ask him to stay. Why hadn't she said, yes, I need you. I need you to stay. Why didn't she—

A door opened beside the NTSB logo, a recessed door built into the wood paneling. A man entered. Kind eyes, but tired with deep circles under them. A shock of white hair neatly parted to one side. Rumpled suit, open-necked white shirt.

"Mrs. Matthews?" the man said and held out his hand.

Emma nodded, yes, but had to keep her shaking hands together in her lap—not because she didn't want to be polite, but she felt like she might fall apart if she didn't keep her arms tight at her sides.

"I'm Richard Marks, the lead investigator for the NTSB." He withdrew his hand. "Did you bring the items we asked about?"

She nodded again, this time tilting her head to one side where the envelope with pictures of Mitch and Lilly with some samples of her husband's handwriting.

"Mrs. Matthews, I need to ask—"

"Why is nobody else—" she blurted out but stopped herself. "What did you find? Did you—" Again she didn't finish her sentence and brought up one hand to her mouth to stop the word coming out.

Tears clouded her vision. She wiped them away with the shaking hand.

Richard looked over his shoulder—at a camera?—and nodded. The door opened again, but nobody appeared.

Emma wanted to scream, wanted to tell them to stop torturing her and tell her…

Something bobbed up and down through the doorway. Something

blond. Another man appeared behind it.

"Momma?"

That voice. Emma burst into tears and dropped to her knees.

"Momma!" Lilly ran around the opposite chair and Richard and straight into Emma.

She opened her arms and wrapped them tight around her child, the tears flowing, her body wracked with sobs of disbelief. "Lilly, baby, my baby."

She squeezed so tight that she had to consciously let go for fear of crushing her.

"I'm okay, Momma, I'm okay."

Emma released her and wiped away the tears and began laughing. Her little girl looked so perfect, it seemed unreal. Was she dreaming?

Richard and the other man stood back at a respectful distance.

Emma looked past them at the door. Nobody else. She wiped another tear from her cheek. "What about—" She couldn't form a sentence, but they understood.

Richard's smile faded. "I'm very sorry, Mrs. Matthews…"

CHAPTER 45

Three years later...

From fourteen thousand feet of altitude, the Himalayan peaks glistened in the mid-morning sunshine, the sky a brilliant blue. In the near distance, a foothill lay enveloped in a cushion of white, a gorge of brown and gray rocks and pebbles leading down and then up its ravined side.

Further in the distance was the real peak; muscular, stratified with brown ridges under the distant snow. Jumbled icefields, a giant checkerboard of hundred-foot cubes, spilled out from the glaciers that slumped down its sides. The scale almost impossible to comprehend.

Everywhere the frosty white mountains were covered in ice. A dark cloud scudded across the peak ahead, casting it into darkness.

▼▲▼

"You want to try and walk?" Emma Matthews said to her daughter.

The two-year-old shook her head. "Too tire."

"We won't go much further. Look, you can play with the rocks. Nanni want to play with some rocks?"

The invitation was enough to encourage the tyke to disembark from the carrier on Emma's back. She grunted with relief as she extracted the little monster and leaned against the rock wall of the trail leading up.

Emma put one hand over her eyes to block the sunshine and squinted to get a better look. That dark cloud looked threatening, but it was far away.

"This is why they call the Himalayas the Third Pole," Emma said to her daughter. "You see all that ice. The glaciers?"

Nanni was more interested in the promised rocks on the trail.

Lilly appeared around the bend in the trail. "That's right, Mom. These glaciers are the biggest freshwater reservoir in the world."

Emma waited for her eight-year-old daughter to get within reach and threw one arm around her and kissed her cheek with a big wet one. "Who made you so smart?"

Lilly laughed and pushed her mother away.

"He did," she said, and pointed back down the trail.

CHAPTER 46

Water.

It was always all about the water.

I stopped on the trail and unscrewed my bottle—it took me a little while—and drank a deep sip. I drank water at every opportunity I could now. Nobody called me a camel anymore. I gulped down as much as I could and took a moment to admire the Himalayan peaks glowing white against the brilliant sky.

The Third Pole.

That's what they called this place. So much ice up here. So much *water*.

"Dad, you coming, slowpoke?" Lilly danced around the corner up ahead and made a funny face and stuck out her tongue.

I wiped the sweat from my brow. "Oh, I'm coming, and I'm going to beat all of you to the top."

Pretty good on these new feet, but I was a bit wobbly when it came to hiking up steep gradients on the prosthetics. The doctors had fitted me with new outdoor hikers for the trip, and I wasn't used to them yet.

I concentrated to screw the top back on my bottle. These robotic hands I was more used to. It was amazing what technology could do these days. No wooden stumps like old-time pirates. I could squeeze and hold things. I wasn't able to feel anything with these fingers, but who knew? Maybe one day.

Emma came bounding down the trail and grabbed and squeezed me. "I love you, Mitch. Did I tell you that today?"

Only three or four times so far. "I love you, too."

We said that a lot to each other these days.

She kissed my cheek, wet and sloppy on purpose, before she laughed and let go. A lot of kissing and hugging these past years, often between the tears and frustrations, but more laughing lately. More celebrations of the simple things in life. And being together always. Never letting ourselves be apart.

She bounded back up the trail ahead of me.

One step after the other, I followed my family up the trail. My mind went back. It kept retreating into time and reliving the events. My doctor said it was part of the process.

One step.

And then another.

I didn't remember much of the end of the ordeal at Alert after the explosion. Not really. I could recall being crouched in the snow with Lilly and Jang huddled around me. Flashes of Otto. The gun. The fire. The syringe. Jang told me that I instructed him to jam it into my chest. To squeeze out whatever he could deep into me.

The memories are fuzzy.

Somehow, I got up. I sort of remember that. Gripped Jang and Lilly in my arms despite the pain. They wrapped themselves in the blankets from Jimbo, held onto me as best they could.

And I walked.

One step in front of the other.

My only impression was that it felt like the hand of God had lifted me up that trail. Like I was going to Heaven. I felt warm. They said that the center of the low had passed us, the wind changed direction, helped push me in the right way.

Maybe my prayers had been answered.

A mile and a half up the incline, up the road to the base. A raging hundred-mile-per-hour wind as the temperatures dropped to a hundred below, and me in nothing but a pair of jeans and socks and a shirt. But nothing was going to stop me.

Nothing.

I was not going to leave my little girl to die alone in the dark.

One step. And then another.

That mile-and-a-half walk had become a hotly debated subject among doctors and the public about what the limits of human endurance were. I'd paid the price. My body had been ninety percent crusted in deep frostbite, my arms literally frozen solid in place around the children, my legs chunks of flesh-ice.

I'd collapsed into that building when they opened the door.

Corporal Fuzani Curtis had saved my life. Done what CPR he could until the emergency techs got there. The "Frozen Chosen" did an unbelievable job keeping me alive, in an induced coma, until we were flown on that first Hercules, back to the world.

The men and women in the base had gone straight down the hill, in the middle of that storm, to save the others. Lilly had told them everything they needed to know. Where to find Liz and Roman and Bjorn entombed in the warmth of the newly-deceased polar bear.

Howard survived.

He had crawled out the door beside me when the hydrogen tank had exploded. Been thrown clear. He'd burrowed under the snow, the know-it-all knew a few Inuit tricks. Enough to keep him alive till the cavalry of Frozen Chosen had charged down the trail. He'd even burrowed the unconscious Jimbo under the snow, too. Amazing.

Howard had been in the hospital recovering almost as long as me. An agony I wouldn't wish on my worst enemy.

Two years of skin grafts and facial reconstruction, and it wasn't over. Frostbite had the same effect on the skin as a third-degree burn, and the skin was the largest organ of the body. They'd had to amputate both legs below the knees, both hands, my ears, my nose. Even my corneas had frozen solid, but even those they'd been able to replace.

When I got my new feet, when I was cleared to leave the ICU, they wanted me to start to learn to walk. I refused, but not because I didn't want to learn to walk.

I insisted that I learned to swim before anything else.

"Come on," Lilly urged and grabbed my plastic hand. "Let's go."

I surged forward on my prosthetics and bounded past her. "Last one to the top is a rotten egg."

She giggled and ran behind me.

Her asthma was gone. Doctors said it sometimes happened.

My decision to head for Canada had been the right one. At the time, I went on my gut, but in retrospect it should have been obvious— when I changed my watch, I switched it twelve hours to match the brightest part of the day.

That was the same time zone as New York. East Coast time.

It was only after I'd appeared like magic from the frozen wasteland that the truth had started to unravel from the clutches of the lies. It was only after we'd appeared, miraculously alive, that two days later a Russian icebreaker announced that it had found the other half of the plane.

The other half of the plane didn't sink.

It was blown away in the storm, just as we had hoped, the massive wing propped up in the sky acting as a sail. The Russians said they suddenly found it because once we were discovered alive, they knew where they had to look.

Everyone had been looking in the wrong place, including the Americans.

Was it a lie?

Who knows?

I personally doubt the Russians would have even "found" the other survivors if we hadn't appeared, alive, from nowhere. I had a feeling the other half of the plane might have just disappeared—been *made* to disappear. Otto's words still echoed in my mind, "There can be no survivors from Allied 695."

Even the identity of the supposed rescuers in the Zodiac boats was initially muddied. The Finns categorically denied any knowledge, and after days of changing accounts, a Russian GRU outfit finally said it was one of theirs, but the botched rescue attempt had been a misunderstanding. A problem with using military troops for a civilian mission.

They didn't explain why their men lied and said they were Finnish Marines.

The Russians kept repeating that it was all a mistake, that some of the men had trained with the Finnish Marines, but they weren't on active duty with them. We had misunderstood.

The GRU said that they knew of the terrorist, Pemba Ldong—who we called Shu—on the plane reported by the Chinese, and when we started shooting, the GRU soldiers shot back. They weren't trained for it, they repeated, not for rescue operations.

They said after we left with all their communication gear they were stranded. The group was out of radio contact for over a week.

Maybe.

Maybe not.

The Russians even had the balls to claim we'd enacted piracy on the high seas when we stole one of their boats. Two of their men died. That wasn't a joke. I was sorry about that—I was sorry about everyone who had lost their lives in this—but there weren't any radios in that boat we'd stolen, not that I'd seen.

Where was the black box, and what happened to the flight deck voice recorder?

They were never recovered.

The Russians said they managed to save the passengers from the rear section of the plane, those that had survived on the ice, but before they could recover the plane the second storm hit and the wreckage disappeared under the waves.

Then there was Josh.

I'd told enough of my tale to make him the real hero. Told his kids how he had overpowered the hijackers and took back control of the aircraft and saved over two hundred lives. He received a Presidential

Medal of Freedom posthumously, and he deserved it.

▼▲▼

My journal had become the only written record of the event. Still officially "classified," but that didn't stop an avalanche of seven- and even eight-figure publishing offers. I hadn't accepted anything yet. I already had everything I ever needed.

"You know what that peak is called?" I said to Lilly.

We'd become closer than I could have ever imagined possible, forged a deep bond through this tragedy. I'd never been as close to my own father as I'd wanted, but that perceived gap had disappeared when my father walked away over that snow in my waking dream on the ice. Was it his ghost? It didn't matter. How I felt was what mattered.

"What's that mountain called, Daddy?" Lilly put an arm around me and squeezed.

"Gosainthan is its name in Sanskrit, the most ancient of all languages," I explained. "It means 'Place of Saints', and the Tibetans call it Shisha Pungma."

We were in Tibet.

Where it had all *really* started.

It was all about the water, like I said. I squinted into the distance and marveled at the endless frozen fields high in the peaks.

There were never any diamonds aboard the airplane. That turned out to be an accounting error, or more likely, purposely falsified information.

And it was never about Roman's billions or the vendetta against him from the Russian Politburo, but maybe that had played a minor part. He'd given up his claim to ownership of his oil empire, Rosomakha. Of course, he'd salted away a billion and change, but he was using the money to fund Liz's genetics work on the cure for rare diseases in Africa. She'd made it out with her canister after the Alert staff had recovered it from the wreckage, and she made it down to Columbia University. With the help of Roman.

They were getting married next month. We were on our way there after this visit to Tibet.

Bjorn was back to plying the seas to make them safe for cetaceans. With his newfound celebrity, he'd raised all the money he needed.

Howard had revealed his disk of dirty digital secrets to a world waiting on his every word. Nobody was really surprised, but he'd become the most famous black hacker in the world. No, that wasn't right. He was now the most famous *hacker* in the world. Period.

He was still a bit crazy, but kept on his meds—and I think in his circles, a bit crazy was an advantage. He had come to visit me in the hospital even while he convalesced, and I think he was happier having robotic hands than his original ones.

The whole disaster was only possible because of the destabilized world we'd come to live in. Where countries—America included—believed that they could get away with anything.

The event had shone some uncomfortable light onto China.

The two replacement pilots allegedly had a background in its own secret service—even though they were Allied employees and 777 pilots—but their bodies were never recovered, and neither were many of the deceased passengers whose bodies were blown away in the storm. There was no official record of the mechanics that came onto the plane before we took off, either, even though there were dozens of witnesses who saw them.

The Chinese government was having a hard time explaining it away, making noise about rogue elements, but even America was to blame.

The US Government had been the one that had told the Russians that Roman was aboard the flight, even after the Russian oligarch had begged for amnesty. The Russians were pointing fingers back at the Americans.

None of that mattered.

Because it was never about any of that.

The real reason was on the trail behind me.

FINAL TRANSCRIPT AUDIO
National Transportation Safety Board.
Mid-Flight Disappearance Allied 695,
Boeing 777, NTSB/AIR.
Washington, DC

R ichard Marks put the last recording tape into the machine. After three long years, this was it.

"This will be the end transcript for the investigation into Allied 695. We have interviewed all the survivors, all the ground crew. This discussion will be free form with final analysis and recommendations."

Richard Marks indicated to Peter that the floor was his. This was the last time he'd have to feel this asshole shadowing him everywhere.

Peter said, "Let's start with what we know. The plane was diverted—"

"Hijacked," Richard said.

"—onto a new flight path. We have that from radar and satellite images. It lost altitude."

"And due to decompression, the passengers blacked out."

"So it diverted from its flight path a thousand miles, low and off radar, and then doubled back at what must have been barely a thousand feet of altitude to further evade radar. They had to be heading somewhere to land that plane. The plan wasn't to crash into the ice."

Richard said, "If they flew that low, passengers should have regained consciousness. Which they didn't. Did they keep the cabin depressurized? Is that possible? I think someone put a chemical into the ventilation system."

By the time they had survivors into hospitals and tried to test them, it had already been too long. Nothing—the people, the clothes, blood samples—had a trace of anything identifiable. It was conjecture, and Richard hated guessing, but a chemical agent made the most sense.

Peter said, "Whoever was flying could have been going for a diversion airport. The survivors said Captain Josh Martin took back control of the aircraft."

Richard sighed loud enough that it would be heard on the recording. This guy was still trying to point a finger back at Captain Martin, still trying to do everything to muddy the water.

"The plane came down at approximately 2:50 p.m. GMT on October fourth," Richard said, "which was 10:50 p.m. Hong Kong time. After the plane crashed, it split into two parts on drifting ice, which then moved apart at an unknown distance due to high winds."

"And that's about all we know," Peter said, "with what's left of that plane now fifteen thousand feet down with a layer of ice over the top. It might be decades before we recover any physical evidence."

After the survivors were recovered, the official governmental enthusiasm for spending money on recovering the sunken plane parts was decidedly muted. Budget restrictions, all the countries involved had somehow declared. Like nobody wanted to know.

"If the CVR and black boxes are even down there," Richard said. He suspected they might not be, that the Russians had stolen or destroyed them. "Three hundred seventy-eight people got onto that plane, and over two hundred survived."

A miracle given the events, but a terrible loss of life.

And one dog. The puppy made it out, too.

Peter said, "The object that Corporal Curtis saw on the radar was later confirmed to be the shockwave signature from the hydrogen tank explosion at the meteorological station. The heat bloom moved quickly down the coast in the high wind, giving the radar impression of a large vehicle tracking at high speed."

"It wasn't a Russian attack as NATO first feared."

"That alert—"

"From Alert."

"Almost set off World War III before the Pentagon de-escalated."

"And the only recorded version of the event is this." Richard held up the now faded and dog-eared journal. "The next point of contact was at the Alert Canadian Forces base, when Mr. Mitch Matthews appeared from the polar night and knocked on the door. So what don't we know?"

"Who was Otto Garcia?" Peter said. "That's my main unanswered question."

Richard gave him a long look. "He said he was an Air Marshal."

"There was no Air Marshal listed by the TSA on Allied 695. None at all."

It wasn't that unusual, Richard had to admit. Unlucky, but not unusual. Most flights inside the US had Air Marshals, but due to government cutbacks, they had to reduce staff. Long haul international routes were the hardest to staff. Nobody admitted it, but there were often flights with no Air Marshals these days.

But somehow this Otto Garcia—and he doubted that was his real name—had smuggled a weapon onto the flight. Perhaps several weapons. He couldn't have acted alone. The third body in the flight deck had never been resolved, either.

Richard said, "Mr. Matthews said that Otto Garcia used the word 'mission.' He said that he said, 'This whole mission went sideways.' This would imply some military training, at a minimum."

"He boarded the flight using a United States passport, which was later determined to be forged," Peter said. "Obtained illegally under a false name."

Roman and Liz, and eventually Mitch himself, had done their best to identify the frozen remains of the body recovered next to the journal. They were quite sure it was the man who called himself Otto.

The corpse had been somewhat mangled—maybe by the explosion? Who he was, his real name, all of this was still a mystery.

Richard said, "What about Garcia claiming to be a Navy SEAL?"

"The US military has denied any knowledge of this person, and no facial recognition or DNA samples match any known person on record, living or deceased."

Peter's comment sounded like a replaying of a recorded statement from somewhere in his mind.

"I will say this," Richard said. "Whoever staged the hijacking, they overplayed their hand."

"How so?"

"It was no accident that Roman ended up on that plane at the same time as those five hundred pounds of lithium batteries. That Isabelle Tremblay obtained questionable permission to carry the biohazard container into First Class. All scheduled for different routes the day before, yet were funneled onto this flight at the last moment. Even Mitch Matthews and Captain Martin were last minute additions. Everything to fuel conspiracy theories after the fact."

"Now you're the one wandering into conjecture," Peter said. "Coincidence is not causation."

Richard continued, "I think it was designed to divert attention from the real target."

"Which was?"

Richard said nothing for a few seconds. "You're right. I am speculating."

"So what's the *final* theory?" Peter asked. "Officially and for the record?"

Richard knew the real reason, but first he had to wrap this up.

"The primary goal of the NTSB is to advocate actions to improve global transportation security. In this case, the only corroborated information we have is that it was a hijacking. If Mitch Matthews hadn't survived, I doubt we would have even known that much."

"You're hypothesizing again."

Silence for a few seconds.

"There is one recommendation I'm going to make," Richard said.

Peter sat up straight. He obviously hadn't expected anything. "And that is?"

"That we harden the transponders, on all commercial flights. They're built to withstand hijackers and impacts, but they're not up to spec to stop a full nation-state from using its resources to mess with them, hack into electronically or modify them." Richard took another long look at Peter. "Nations including our own."

"That's it?"

"That's it."

It was over. The NTSB investigation finished.

Peter paused to look at Richard before clicking the *stop* button on the recording device.

But Richard wasn't finished.

There was one thing he hadn't shared. Someone had anonymously mailed him a newspaper clipping, faded and grainy, of a group of men in front of a *bodego* in Colombia. One of the men looked a lot like the man who called himself Otto Garcia. The caption under the photo was in Spanish, and complained about ongoing operations of the CIA in South America.

Peter smiled and collected his suitcase and got up to leave.

"There is a second thing I'm going to do," Richard said.

"And what's that?" Peter stopped halfway to the door.

"Publishing."

Richard held up the journal one last time.

"I'm going to personally encourage Mitch to publish this. *He* can speculate all he wants."

"You're sure that's a good idea?"

The way Peter said it, he meant, was it good for Richard? He didn't care though. He was up for retirement, and being retired from the NTSB meant he might take up investigating things on his own. Like investigating who the hell Peter really worked for, and who Otto Garcia was. The Russian GRU, the Chinese MSS, the American CIA, the dirty underworld of dark ops all seemed to have a hand in this somehow.

Richard intended to find the truth. The people who lost their lives deserved that much, but all he said was, "Better than nothing."

"And since we're off the record"—Peter glanced at the tape recorder, now off—"what's your final theory?"

CHAPTER 47

The Himalayan mountaintops glowed around us as we crested the ridge and stopped. I sucked the thin air in and out in heaving gasps. I needed *bionic* legs, not just prosthetics.

Jang stood on the trail behind me, the sunshine bright in his eyes. He was the real reason.

He waved at me and then ran giggling up the pathway, a Tibetan prayer wheel spinning in his hand, an orange *kashaya* robe worn by the Theravada monks—unchanged in over twenty-five centuries—wrapped around his small but growing body.

For this wasn't any boy. This was Jangchup Gyatso.

Fifteenth Dalai Lama of Tibet.

Jangchup was the literal reincarnation, according to the Tibetans, of the fourteenth Dalai Lama who had died several years before. He had to be the reason that they—whoever *they* were—had risked bringing down a commercial airliner. It wasn't that he was so valuable in himself, but all the water he controlled was.

Water.

It was all about water. It was the thing I'd been terrified of all my life, but no more.

The Russians, and everyone else, wanted control of the north as the ice melted and the newly-opened passageways became highways for goods in the twenty-first century. As the glaciers melted, they were going to flood the cities of the world at the same time as changing weather patterns caused massive droughts.

Always about the water.

One thing that wouldn't change was that the soon-to-be ten billion people of planet Earth would need fresh water, and the biggest source of it was here—trillions upon trillions of dollars worth of it—in the glaciers of the Tibetan plateau.

Up to the 1950's, the Qing Dynasty of China had recognized the sovereignty of Tibet, which was later rejected by the People's Republic of China. They'd begun a slow but steady campaign of damming up the rivers high in the Tibetan plateau, potentially blocking off rivers that supplied fresh water to two billion people in Southeast Asia.

The Dalai Lama was the heart and soul of the Tibetan people, and the Chinese needed to control the hearts and minds to be able to control the water.

The twentieth century had been about oil, but the twenty-first was going to be all about water. Fresh water to drink, rising waters flooding cities and forcing migration, and new lands and resources opening up in the Far North as the planet warmed.

One positive from the whole ordeal was that the Chinese government, under intense global public scrutiny after the event, had decided to abandon much of its plans to impose its will on Tibet. It had taken some steps to grant the Himalayan province semi-autonomy, and guaranteed the safety of Jangchup to return.

"Hey, hey, take it easy!"

Jang and Lilly laughed as they chased each other around me. I wobbled on my new feet.

Around the corner came Mr. Fuzani Curtis, the young man who'd saved my life. He'd passed his exams and was a freshly minted Junior Officer of CSIS. Barking and yapping around his feet came our dog Irene, the little white bulldog we'd rescued from the ice, now all grown up.

With them came our escort, a pack of monks—a special order called the *tulku*—wearing the same robes as Jang. The *tulku* were Tibetan Buddhist Lamas, spiritual teachers, who had taken a vow to help all other sentient beings escape suffering in this world.

Pemba Ldong, the "terrorist" on the flight, was a *tulku*, sworn to protect his Dalai Lama. The Chinese government had been trying to impose their own imposter version of the Dalai Lama onto the Tibetan people. The monks judged that the new Dalai Lama's life was at risk. So they tried to smuggle him out on the flight from Hong Kong under a false name.

That's what I kept hearing over Howard's phone when we'd escaped the attackers.

Not "telco," but "*tulku*."

The Russian GRU unit who claimed to be our rescuers knew who they were looking for, even the terminology. Roman and myself had heard the word "telco", but they were saying, "*tulku*."

Pemba was never a terrorist. He hadn't been involved in any bombings, but he had condoned some of the struggles, so became branded. In the end, he had lived—and given his life—exactly how he would have wanted.

It was true that Pemba had taken Jang from his parents. That was true. But they gave him to the monks willingly. He'd already had a few years of monk training even at five when I first met him. It was a great honor.

Anyway, that was *my* theory.

Someone had hijacked the plane to get to Jang.

They didn't want to just kill him.

That would have been easy, but it wouldn't have been enough. Why? Because the Dalai Lama could reincarnate himself.

Whoever hijacked the plane, they needed Jang to mysteriously vanish and to be able to hold on to him in secret for as long as they wished.

If the Tibetan monks ever declared a new Dalai Lama, their opponents could then parade out Jang any time they wanted and declare the whole process—the Tibetan religion—a farce. It was the only way they could win this argument.

Like I said, just a theory. But a trillion-dollar theory.

▼▲▼

Otto was a ghost that no country had claimed. He was my own blind spot. I'd suspected everyone else, but not the strong American.

They found him frozen in the same spot where I'd crouched with the children, clutching the blankets we'd left behind. I had dropped my notebook from my pocket there. He must have found it as he searched for us.

He was physically much younger and stronger than me, but ultimately it was not our bodies but our minds—our will to survive—that enabled me to go on while he perished in that storm. The power of the mind over physical reality. Whatever reason he was there for, it was no match for my love of Lilly that made me go on.

Jang was ahead of me. "Come on, Mr. Mitch. You are rotten egg, yes?"

He stood smiling and seemed to glow in the midday sun.

Pure unadulterated love and tenderness radiated from his smile. I had saved this boy, and he gave me meaning in my life in return, but maybe, just maybe…this boy could grow into the man who could save us all. Help save humanity from itself.

On the ice, Bjorn had said that the only thing possible for the human race to correct itself from destroying the planet was a massive viral pandemic, or turning our weapons of mass destruction upon each other, or some other apocalyptic event.

Jang had replied to him quietly and said, no, there was another option.

Wisdom.

THE END

FROM THE AUTHOR

A sincere *thank you* for reading. In the next section is an in-depth personal discussion of the background and themes and ideas from *Polar Vortex*.

AND PLEASE

If you'd like more fiction like this, please leave a review on Amazon. As a self-published author, the number of reviews a book gains on a daily basis has a direct impact on sales and new readers, so leaving a review—no matter how short—helps make it possible for me to continue to do what I do and support my family.

I read and appreciate each and every review.

IF YOU WANT MORE RIGHT NOW

My closest similar book is *CyberStorm*, a novel about a family struggling to survive a disaster in New York City. It's being made into a film, and has been translated into over twenty-five languages. Search for CyberStorm on Amazon.

JOIN MY COMMUNITY

Every month I give away book-themed t-shirts, mugs, posters and free books, and I also tell you about my writing life, upcoming books, and deals and discounts.

Please visit – **MatthewMather.com** – to join me.

UPCOMING BOOKS

My next release is *The Dreaming Tree*, the first novel in a near-future detective series that I'm really excited about. Search Amazon for "matthew mather dreaming tree".

"INSIDE READER" PRIVATE GROUP ON FACEBOOK

Visit the URL below to request to join:
facebook.com/groups/matthewmather/
Or search for "Matthew Mather Reader Group" on Facebook

SOME OF MY OTHER BOOKS

All part of Kindle Unlimited

CYBERSTORM

Award-winning million-copy bestseller *CyberStorm* depicts, in realistic and terrifying detail, what a full scale cyberattack against present-day New York City might look like from the perspective of one family trying to survive it. Search for *CyberStorm* on Amazon.

DARKNET

A prophetic novel set in present-day New York, *Darknet* is the story of one man's odyssey to overcome a frightening new technological terror, and his incredible gamble to risk everything to save his family. Search for *Darknet* on Amazon.

NOMAD (4 book series)

Earth has only days until annihilation.

A story of family, redemption, love and hope set amid a brand new category of cataclysm—all the more plausible and terrifying as the science behind was developed by a team of world-class astrophysicists. Search for for *Nomad* on Amazon.

THE DREAMING TREE

Everybody wants to live forever, but some people shouldn't live at all.

After a near-fatal car crash, Royce Vandeweghe wakes up to find he's one of the first patients to undergo a radical new procedure: a full-body transplant. Convalescing years later and suffering from waking nightmares, he answers the door at his Long Island home and meets Delta Devlin, a New York detective who sees things nobody else can— visions created by a mutation to her eyes. Search for *The Dreaming Tree Matthew Mather* on Amazon.

ATOPIA CHRONICLES (3 book series)

In the near future, to escape the crush and clutter of a packed and polluted Earth, the world's elite flock to Atopia, an enormous corporate-owned artificial island in the Pacific Ocean. It is there that Dr. Patricia Killiam rushes to perfect the ultimate in virtual reality: a program to save the ravaged Earth from mankind's insatiable appetite for natural resources. Search for *Atopia* on Amazon.

AUTHOR DISCUSSION ON POLAR VORTEX
From the author, Matthew Mather
Themes and Background

Hello Reader,

First off, thanks so much for reading my work. This is a self-published title, so a sincere *thank you* again from myself and my family for supporting us.

My father, David Alan Mather, passed away while I was writing this book, so this will forever be a special novel for me. When he became ill, I wanted to write a book about the power of the love between a father and child, and this is the story that came out of that—so thanks again for coming on this journey with me.

Deep breath.

The other big theme in this book is water, and I'd like to finish with a talk about that in depth—pun intended.

Before we do, a few side notes.

One mind-blowing thing that happened while I was finishing this book was that the world's geologists had to convene an emergency meeting to update the World Magnetic Model, which is the basis for all modern navigation, from ocean-going tankers to Google Maps.

The magnetic pole has been moving so fast the past few years that they realized inaccuracies in the navigation models being used had exceeded acceptable limits for navigation errors, so they had to fix it before ships started getting lost. Not just that, but there was a massive geomagnetic pulse under South America in 2016 that shifted the field as well. We might actually be in the middle of a magnetic field reversal—and without fear-mongering, if it flipped very quickly or the field died down fast during the reversal, it could wreak havoc with our modern global networks.

So that's something to watch out for, and I invite you to look it up (a great article on this in Nature, search for "Nature earth's magnetic field acting up" or "what if earth's magnetic poles flip").

Next, commercial flights over the Arctic, and even directly over the North Pole, are common now as planes have become more reliable and longer in range. Inevitably, some of these have had to execute emergency landings in remote places. While I was writing this, a plane on its way from Beijing to Seattle had to come down on a remote Alaskan island—and there are many more cases of this I invite you to look up.

I'd also like to take a second to discuss how realistic Mitch's last stagger up the slope to the Alert base was. I'm basing this off the very real story of Mr. Seaborn "Beck" Weathers, who survived the 1996 Everest disaster where eight people died on the mountain.

Beck became separated from his fellow climbers at 27,000 feet (on 29,000+ foot Everest), and was blinded by the altitude and a ferocious blizzard. Disoriented, he wandered off and lost his gloves and head coverings. He ended up alone, laying on the ice with his face and hands naked and exposed, and fell into a hypothermic sleep while the wind raged at over a hundred mph and the temperature dropped to a hundred below.

Abandoned for dead, after a whole night out like this, he managed to get up the next day and wander into camp. Both his hands and face were frozen solid. His fellow climbers say they looked and felt like porcelain. His feet were frozen as well. Yet he managed to walk out on these frozen feet, with frozen hands and even blinded. And the guy is still alive today, twenty years later—and back to flying airplanes, if you can believe it.

So I think Mitch's final journey is well within the realm of possible.

And, I admit I'm skating on thin ice (yes, the puns continue) when it comes to Tibet and China and the Dalai Lama. I'm not particularly knowledgeable about the political situation or what people who live there really think. I see these "Free Tibet" bumper stickers, but a few early readers pointed out that some Tibetans actually like being part of

China, and that historically the rule of the Dalai Lamas was not always omnibenevolent (by which I mean, they weren't always nice). The real situation is far more complex than I have time to explore in this book.

I'm also, perhaps, turning China into a "bad guy" by making the motivation behind the plot revolve around controlling water in the Himalayas. Diverting of these rivers is a real thing, and I invite you to look up dams and China and India and the fight over water in that area. The rivers coming out of the Himalayas actually do provide fresh water to about a third of the world's population. But, humans everywhere in the world have been damming rivers and fighting over it for thousands of years—China isn't doing anything any different.

My point was more that all that frozen water in the Himalayas is worth a lot of money if it was looked at that way, and it made for a big payoff in a fictional novel.

Moving on.

I'll mention that I've personally been into the Arctic. Last time I was there, it was in the summer in northern Norway and Sweden and I walked under the midnight sun with herds of reindeer. I have been far enough north in Canada during the winter to experience perpetual darkness, and I have experienced temperatures down to -60F and snowshoed across vast frozen lakes in midwinter. I've gotten frostbite on my cheeks, which was a weird experience—exactly like getting third-degree burns once it starts to heal.

I invite anyone who's been in the Arctic to leave their own comments in reviews as I'm sure everyone would be interested to read them.

I even tried to convince the Canadian military to let me go up to the Alert base while I was writing this novel. They have a weekly supply flight—the Hercules aircraft I describe in the book—that goes from Trenton, Ontario, all the way up there and back. To their credit they actually considered my request to hitch a ride, but Major Sandra Andrusiak, the current commanding officer, had to deny my request. She said there were sensitive military operations right now and it would be impossible to get me clearance.

Which may have been lucky for me, as going up there is literally risking one's life. That story about the supply flight crashing and passengers freezing to death is true. You can look that up if interested. One of the previous base managers, Mr. Bill Stafford, was generous enough to lend me a few hours of his time to talk about the Alert base, their mission, and all the buildings and outbuildings and so on—enough to make this realistic.

All that being said, I would like to finally wade into the deep underlying themes of *Polar Vortex*: water and the Arctic. I don't want to over-agendize the story, and I definitely don't want to get into a discussion of whether it's caused by humans or not.

The thing is, either way, things are changing, and *fast*.

Just as I was finishing writing this book, a news story appeared about the very first commercial container ship, from the Maersk company in Denmark, navigating the Arctic sea route from Asia to Europe past Russia, loaded down with Korean electronics. That's not hyperbole. That's simply a ship navigating a sea route that has been frozen and impassible before (side note: over a hundred thousand people died building the Suez Canal, which maybe isn't needed as much anymore as the new route is much shorter).

Same goes for the famed "Northwest Passage" through Canada's frosty reaches. Polar explorers a hundred years ago died in futility trying to find a way through something that didn't exist then because it was frozen solid, but now, the ice has melted. Ships are starting to pass this route now as well, instead of using the Panama Canal.

This isn't up for argument—it's reality. It's happening.

All of this melting ice and permafrost has opened up vast new areas accessible for resource and mining and oil companies—and wherever there are resources to be had, there are countries ready to assert their claims and find ways to get at it. These reasons and more are why the Far North is becoming increasingly inhabited and even militarized.

That was part of what I wanted to highlight in this book.

One way or the other, the planet is heating up, and this coming hot spell might be the start of an extinction-level event (and I'm infinitely sad for the loss of our biodiversity, but this is another topic). The Earth, however, has been through this before—there have been at least five previous mass extinction-level events in Earth's history. Our planet will be just fine in the longer run.

Humans, on the other hand, might not.

The changes to the Earth in the 21st century will (in my opinion) force hundreds of millions of people into migrations, from one country and area to the next, away from rising waters and heat, and the key to all this is water.

"Whiskey is for drinking, water is for fighting," as Mark Twain famously penned.

My personal fear is that the coming waves of migrations and shortages of water might drive some very unpleasant conflicts—wars—in the near future. Where a lot of the struggle for power in the last hundred years was over oil, in the next hundred I think it will be about water.

Which was what this book was ultimately about.

You don't need to agree with me and my opinions, and I invite you to email me if you'd like to discuss—but I hope this book might help stimulate talks with your own friends and family and children and mothers and fathers about your own opinions on these topics.

When Bjorn, the exasperated and jaded environmentalist in *Polar Vortex*, says that for the Earth to heal itself, humanity needs to be cleansed by some apocalyptic event—Jang replies, no, there is another solution.

Wisdom.

And that's what talking helps to create.

Thank you so much for reading and sharing your time with me.

Matthew Mather
December 17, 2018

ABOUT MATTHEW MATHER

In just five years, Matthew Mather's books have sold a million and a half copies, been translated and published in over 24 countries, and optioned for multiple movie and television contracts. He began his career as a researcher at the McGill Center for Intelligent Machines before starting and working in high-tech ventures ranging from nanotechnology to cyber security. He now works as a full-time author of speculative fiction.

AUTHOR CONTACT
Matthew Mather
author.matthew.mather@gmail.com

Made in the USA
Middletown, DE
06 March 2019